The Emancipation of Mary Sweeney

by Dani Larsen

The

Emancipation

of

Mary Sweeney

ISBN 978-0-692-32207-9

Dedication

I dedicate this book first to my dad, Bert Hempe, whose grandparents this book is about, and my brother, Michael, who passed away at age nineteen. I wish they were here to read this story as I know they would have loved reading about the adventures of Mary Sweeney. Secondly, to my descendants, who are also descendants of Mary and John Troy: My children; Michael, Michele, Nicolas, Anthony and Danielle. My grandchildren; Benjamin, Catrinna (who also calls me "mom" as I raised her from the age of three), Brandy, Andrew, Joseph, Ryan, Brenden, Joshua, Delilah, Zachary, Jimmie, and my great-granddaughter, Dora. As well as my sister, Juli.

There are many people who have helped me with this book, and I want to thank all of you and tell you how much I appreciate each and every one of you. Many thanks to my friends: Dianne Meyer, Sandi Cleveland, and Louise Solis. Also, many thanks to my family readers; my granddaughter, Catrinna Crase, my son-in-law, Scott Teem, my mom, Vivian Hempe, who left this world in 2009, Gary and Rachael Larsen, and my dear husband, Darris Larsen, who helped me with a lot of the historical information. The comments, criticisms, and suggestions, each of you gave me added to the fabric of this exciting story about my great-grandmother. Also, thanks to Xel Moore, for designing the cover, Cameron Barry and Jon

Schuller, for assisting with the HTML format, and last, but not least, thanks to my son, Nicolas Crase, who not only read the book, but is my Chief Editor. He also formatted it and published it for me, as his computer skills far exceed mine. Without the help of each one of you, this book would not have been published. Much love and thanks to all of you.

Prologue

"May you be in Heaven a half an hour before the devil knows yer dead."

I'll never forget the spring of 1954. I was nine, and a very shy, timid girl, with a vivid imagination. For some reason, I worried about everything. My mother was a worrier, and passed that trait on to me. Her stories of being an orphan by the age of six; losing her mother when she was three to consumption, and her father in the logging camps when she was six, haunted me. Whatever the reason "death" was a word that petrified me.

The old ranch house in Pleasant Valley, Oregon, was filled with strange, musty odors and eerie, creaking sounds. Questions like, 'Is this the smell of death?' filled my overactive mind. I was too shy to ask such questions as I would surely be laughed at. While my cousins and brother were outside playing, I sat in the big over-stuffed chair in the living room looking at the old family albums.

My grandmother and grandfather looked so young in their wedding photo that I almost didn't recognize them. I loved the photo of my dad, and his brothers and sisters, when they were very young. However, the photo reminded me of death, as I knew that my dad's older brother, Joseph, died at the age of twelve from diphtheria. I didn't recognize many of the people in the old pictures. Someone had neatly labeled all of them with names and dates, but I wasn't familiar with most of them. Then I came upon two smaller photos that were the same as the two large oval framed pictures that hung on the living room wall. I had been attracted to those portraits when I first arrived. One was of a handsome dark eyed man with a large mustache that curled up on both ends. He looked like "Wild Bill Hickock" in the movies my brother and I went to on Saturday afternoons. The other portrait was of a pretty young woman with long hair pulled back from her face. The labels in the albums identified them as John Troy and Mary Sweeney Troy.

Just then, my father came in from the kitchen where several of the adults were quietly talking. "What are you doing, Dani Sue?" I loved it when he called me his nickname.

"Daddy, your brown eyes are just like the man's in this picture. Who is he?"

"That's my grandfather, John Stephen Troy. He died in 1934. This is my grandmother, Mary Sweeney Troy, when she was young. Your grandmother is their daughter."

"She was very pretty. Is that who is sick upstairs?"

The noise of the screen door slamming interrupted our conversation, when several of my cousins came in the house. Daddy took the photo album and put it back in the middle of the coffee table. Then he took my hand and led me outside to the swing on the front porch. I was suddenly overwhelmed by the unfamiliar sounds of the ranch, with the magnified noises of the animals in the barn and fields, and the insects echoing through the valley.

"What's the matter, honey?"

"It's louder here than I thought it would be."

"It's just the normal sounds of a ranch, nothing to be afraid of."

"Daddy, what does Great-Grandma Troy look like now? I've never seen anybody who is almost 100 years old. Why is she dying, Daddy?"

"She is very old, and her body has been working for a long time. I guess you could say she's just plain worn out. Ninety-six years is a long time to live. Did you know she came from Ireland as a young girl all by herself to San Francisco? Would you like to talk to her before she leaves this world? Her mind is fine, but she's very weak and can't talk for long."

"I would like to talk to her very much, Daddy, if I can talk to her alone. I don't like to talk much in front of a lot of people."

"I think that could be arranged. You stay here, and I'll see if she's awake and feels like talking."

A few minutes later he returned and led me up the stairs, down the long hallway to the closed door at the far end. Aunt Fan was dabbing her eyes as she left the room. She patted me on the head as she passed us by. I was really scared as I stood next to her bed. My hands were tightly rolled into fists and my fingernails pinched my palms.

"Dani, I would like you to meet your great-grandmother, Mary Sweeney Troy. She hasn't seen you since you were a baby. Grandmother, this is my daughter, your great-granddaughter, Deanna, better known as "Dani".

"Dani, Deanna," she repeated slowly. "Both are good Irish names, me girl. How nice that ye wanted to see me. Most of the wee ones are scared of the likes of a wrinkled, old lady like me."

Although she spoke slowly and softly, her voice still held a kind of strength and excitement. Her sweet voice, which still had a prominent Irish brogue, was almost spellbinding.

Finally, I found the nerve to speak. "You are not as wrinkled as I thought you might be for being the oldest person I've ever seen. Were you here when there were covered wagons and Indians?"

She chuckled softly, "Oh yes, me girl, on this very land. Yer great-grandfather knew Chief Joseph and Chief White Bird personally. He used to tell some mighty good stories about the Nez Perce Indian wars."

She smiled and closed her eyes for a minute as if remembering those days. Finally, she opened them and spoke again. "We had no electricity, or running water, in our first little cabin, but everything changed when your great-grandfather built this place right over that wonderful spring."

She paused and took a deep breath between each sentence. "Those were the good old days, but they were also times of great hardship. Ye might be a little too young to appreciate the memories of me life. Nobody has wanted to listen to me stories for a long time."

"I'm not so young. I'll be ten in September."

A smile came across her face, and she laughed softly before responding. "Yer right, me girl, yer not so young after all."

She spoke slowly, breathing heavily in between her well-chosen words.

"I was only fifteen when I left me parents' home in Ireland, and came to this land. I remember well the words me brother, Jerry, graced me with just before I left me beautiful homeland; *'May you have the hindsight to know where you have been, the foresight to know where you are going, and the insight to know when you have gone too far.'*"

"In the last ninety-six years, I've had some good foresight, and some good insight, but I wish I'd had more hindsight."

"I don't think I understand what you are saying, great-grandmother."

"I'm not expectin' ye to understand me now, me girl. Someday, ye'll remember what I said, and ye will understand. I've witnessed a lot of history in me lifetime. I've reflected a lot on those events these last few years."

She coughed several times, and it was a few minutes before she resumed speaking.

"I wrote down everything I could remember from as far back as about 1873. That was the year I left me parents, and brothers and sisters, back home in Ireland, and ran off to make me fortune in America. Oh, what an adventure that was! It was ten years later that John Troy and I were married, at Saint Mary's Cathedral, in San

Francisco. That church was destroyed by a big fire in the 1906 earthquake. Yes, me girl, those were the days."

She closed her eyes again, and a warm nostalgic look appeared on her face.

"I lived in San Francisco during its young wild days. Then there was the 'evil one'," she shivered as she spoke that name, "the Chinese massacre, the gold rush in Eastern Oregon, and the deaths of so many friends and loved ones over these many years. Oh, it's been a most adventuresome life, me dear. I'd love to tell ye about it, but I'm afraid I don't have much time left. Are ye interested?"

"Oh yes! I would love to hear all about it."

"Dani, me girl!" Her laugh seemed a little weaker now. "I'd love to stay and tell ye all about it, but ninety-six years is a lot of tellin', and I'm real tired. Me poor old body is worn out and ready to quit working. I tell ye what. If ye really are interested, and ye will promise to take care of it, I will give ye me diary for safekeeping. When yer older, read it, and then read it again ten years later, and then pass on the history to yer children. No one else in the family has asked much about their Irish roots. If ye lose the history from me, yer ancestors will be robbed of their heritage." Her breathing seemed to be getting shallower as she spoke.

"Remember this, me girl, there are some things, beside the Lord who is always number one, that should always be most important to ye. Family, friends and yer land! Everything else doesn't mean too much when it comes right down to it. This land here has provided the ground for our family's nurturing. John and I worked hard for many years to get this land. Our good friend died to keep it from those who would have stolen it from us. This land should be owned by those who care for it, by those who realize its value, by those who will use it to help take care of family."

She spoke slowly, but with a kind of pleasure I could hear in her voice and see on her face. I was thinking they must be wrong, that she couldn't be dying.

"The book is in my drawer here, underneath me old bible. You take it and put it away for safekeeping. Then read it when ye are much older. Okay?"

"Oh yes, Grandmother! Thank you. Thank you! I'll take good care of it."

I carefully opened the top drawer in the stand next to the bed, and saw all of my great-grandmother's treasures. There was a stack of beautiful, hand embroidered handkerchiefs. I glanced through the small white folded cloths, which were all edged in different colors with lovely tiny matching flowers embroidered on each one. I knew they were done by my great-grandmother, as my grandmother had shown me some one time when I visited her house. There were three rosaries in the drawer. Two looked fairly new, but the one on top of the old bible was made of tiny wooden beads, with tiny strands of rope in between each bead, which were well worn, and a bit frazzled. The plain wooden cross and the beads looked well used. Several much read and faded holy cards were stacked in the drawer between the handkerchiefs and the bible. On the other side of the bible was an old leather pouch with what looked like a faded family crest, which looked like it had been hand painted, but was now cracked by time. A pretty old comb with a couple of broken teeth lay on top of the bag, but the tiny stones that decorated the top still sparkled. The bible was black and looked very old. I picked up the fragile book and found a small leather journal underneath it. The printing on the front had been gone over many times with a fountain pen in shaky writing, but it clearly said, "Mary's Story". I leafed through the pages, saw a mixture of penciled pages and fountain penned writings, and I knew that I had to take care of this book with my life. I took out the book along with the much used rosary. Then I asked my great-grandmother if she wanted her rosary and she nodded.

I took her hand and weaved the rosary between her fingers. I folded her hands together giving them a gentle squeeze. It was then that I realized how fragile she was. It felt as if her hand might break if I squeezed too hard.

"Would it be okay if I told your story some day?"

"Oh yes, that would be lovely, me dear. Now that I've given ye that book, I feel like me work on this good earth is finished. I'm ready to meet me maker and to see John, and me mum and pop. Don't ye be a cryin' when I'm gone. Ye hear me, girl? I'm lookin' forward to seein' the next world. Always remember this, Dani, me girl. *May you be in Heaven a half an hour before the devil knows yer dead.* That is just one of the many sayings me mum taught me as I was growing up, and I never forgot any of them. If I've got a chance to get to heaven, I don't want that devil pullin' on me coattails."

I reached over, kissed her forehead, and smelled a musty odor of death on her breath as I repeated the saying for her, word for word.

"Thank you."

She took another deep breath before continuing.

"One thing more, when yer stumped on makin' those important decisions in life, jest remember to follow the signs to yer own destiny. Wherever the Lord leads ye, follow right along. He'll lead ye right every time if ye follow his ways. He's always been there fer me, and he'll be there fer ye too.

"Ye go now and remember me in yer prayers. I'll pray for ye if'n I'm able, too. Now give yer old great-grandmother a sweet goodbye kiss, and let me take me final rest." She sighed, closed her eyes, and smiled peacefully.

I kissed her forehead again and was suddenly overwhelmed by the sweet sickening smell of decay. I left, and no one was outside her room, so I put the diary in my book bag, which was hanging on the coat rack by the front door. Then, I went outside to play with my cousins, and my brother, without any fear of the ranch and its two thousand acres. A couple of hours later, my dad came outside.

"The angels came for Great-Grandma Troy a little while ago. They took her to heaven to join her husband and son, and many of her friends who were waiting for her."

I couldn't believe she was gone already. I was speechless. Then I remembered her words, and I knew that she had been waiting for death to come and take her, and that the devil wouldn't have a chance with her. I knew she was where she wanted to be, and I was happy for her. She did not fear death, and even seemed to welcome it.

We stayed in the old ranch house for three days until the funeral. None of my cousins were my age, so I stayed by myself most of the time. I sat in the living room, looked at the old photos and magazines, and listened to my parents, grandparents, aunts, and uncles talk about the old days and Mary Sweeney Troy's long life. I thought about mentioning her diary, but I felt she wanted only me to read it. Unless she told someone she gave it to me, my instincts told me I would not have been allowed to keep it, so I left it in my bag and packed it away in a box for many years.

When I finally read her diary, I found a story rich with history and sprinkled with old Irish sayings, blessings, and proverbs. It was a tale about a brave young woman who came half way around the world all by herself. As her diary was written in many short stories, with many of the details missing, my story of her life is woven with the fabric of fiction. I knew, if I spiced up her life a little, she wouldn't mind.

I'm sure that anyone, who reads about this courageous, young Irish immigrant, will find her as unforgettable as I have.

Part I

Chapter One

"Macroom, County Cork, Ireland"

September, 1873

"Things are not always what we believe them to be."

Tears filled her eyes as Mary Sweeney lifted her long gray skirt and leapt over the O'Brien's broken down fence. Usually, the late summer sun felt good beating warmly on her face, but today it burned the despair into her heart. Mary closed her eyes and turned her face directly toward the glowing ball that peeked through the clouds. Taking a deep breath, she tried to ease her pain and enjoy the luscious green land that she loved. Generations of her family had tilled the earth, raised livestock and anything that they could get to grow in the fertile, but rocky soil. Her nostrils were filled with the smells of the rich loam beneath her feet, and the sweet aroma emanating from the flowers sprinkled across the meadow. The soft cool breeze washed her face and pressed her shabby patched skirt against her bare legs. Birds called to each other cheerfully, bees went about their business as they went from flower to flower, and she could hear horses whinnying from the farm she was leaving. She tried to keep her senses filled with the things she loved, but the sun disappeared behind the clouds, leaving her shivering as the moment faded away.

An ominous feeling came back to her. Having been ingrained with religion, and superstition, she blessed herself and said aloud one of the Irish blessings her mother spouted often. *"May the sun shine warm upon your face, and the rain fall soft upon your fields."*

She considered the sun's disappearance behind the clouds as the second bad omen of the day. Sure that they always came in threes, Mary wondered what the third would bring. An old tree stump disrupted her thoughts as she stumbled over it, falling to her left and tumbled down the embankment, landing on her backside at the foot of the craggy hill she had been walking atop.

Surprised and embarrassed at her foolishness for not paying attention, she quickly got up, brushed off her tender bottom, and found herself staring at a carved sign at the crossroads.

Confused at which way the sign was pointing for a minute, she came to her senses and realized that some pranksters had turned the sign the wrong way. 'Perhaps it was a leprechaun,' she thought, 'As the locals would surely know the right way to Macroom, and the harbor city of Queenstown, formerly known as Cobh.'

As she dusted off her long skirt she noticed the ragged hem. Her bosoms ached inside the bodice that had become too tight. She struggled to pull the signpost out of the hard ground. She saw the loose dirt at the bottom of the sign, so she picked up a large boulder from the hill, using it to bang the post from side to side, until she was able to turn it in the right direction. When it looked right, she pushed the loose dirt back up against the post with her feet until it was feeling sturdy. Then she piled rocks around the base to secure it. Although tired from the work, she felt strangely exhilarated. This was surely the third omen, a sign that she should follow. If she had followed the sign without thought to where she was going, she would have headed to the port city instead of the little village of Macroom. She felt a strange compulsion to follow the path that the sign had beckoned her to go. This must be where she would find the solution to her problem.

"God must be leading me this way. If I can find a position in the city, I can change me life and help me family, instead of being the burden of another mouth to feed." Mary wiped away the tears and spoke aloud.

Instead of heading to her parents' cottage on the outskirts of the village of Macroom, she turned toward the port city and began to walk, reflecting on the day. If she found a new position in the city, the news about the loss of her job on the O'Brien's farm wouldn't be so hard to tell her mum. Margaret Sweeney's lined and weathered face didn't need any more stress. Liam O'Brien's return from Wales, with his wife and new baby, meant that he would be taking over her job at their farm. The family needed everyone's wages to pay the rent and put food on the table in these trying times. They were so afraid they'd lose their little cottage and have to go to the work houses, where they would all be split up. After her father had injured his foot, he needed help on the small farm to cultivate the meager potato crops, as well as to tend to the few sheep. Catherine and Margaret had lost their jobs and were helping him run the small acreage. Her two younger brothers, Jim and Jerry, had to work in the bogs gathering peat to sell for fuel and they were earning very little. Johanna was too young to work, and her mother tried to take in laundry, but most people were doing their own these days. Her Uncle Sean worked on another neighboring farm, but often drank his wages, which was a sore point for his sister's husband. She had gathered the peat with her brothers, and she couldn't stand the backbreaking work, for the pittance it brought in.

Her Da had said, "There'd been plenty enough potatoes before the famine to feed the entire nation". The crops hadn't yet come back to the plentiful bounty they once were. "The Great Famine" was supposed to have ended eight years before she was born. Mary knew that if she didn't find a job in the city her dreams for the future were bleak. She envisioned herself in the bogs forever, and later leading a harsh life like her mum.

Determined to get a job in the city, she wiped her tears with the edge of her dress and hoped that someday her dreams would come true. She wanted so badly to become a teacher, but after watching her mum's dreary existence flash before her eyes, she was scared, as her face often replaced her mum's in her recurring dreams. Mary prayed that she wouldn't be doomed to the same hard life.

'I'm going to change me life. I don't have to live like me mum does!' It was too far to walk to the city, but if she could hitch a ride on one of the many carts heading to town, she could be back before dark. She had been paid for the day, but was told she could leave before lunch. Mary wondered again about the sign, and she thought about what her father had often said; "Things are not always what we believe them to be," and he had always said that "faith will move mountains." Her faith pulled her like a magnet toward the County Cork port city.

A man driving a cart full of tomatoes to the city came along, and he let her ride with his young son on the back of the cart. The cart bumped along on the rocky road, while she chatted with the boy who reminded her of her youngest brother. The father and son both wore dark blue faded caps, were shoeless, and their hands were stained red. They stopped by the docks of the port city, and as Mary climbed out, she thanked them for the ride.

The salt sea air filled her lungs as she inhaled deeply to relieve the anxiety that filled her head. She dusted off her skirt again noticing how time had faded the once brightly colored dress. This had been her confirmation dress. Her mother had stayed up late sewing lace around the edges of the sleeves and the top of the bodice. It had once been a lovely dress, but now it was faded and worn.

'Tis too small,' she thought. 'Still, tis the best I've got, so it'll just have to do.' She pulled the old piece of yarn out of her thick hair and smoothed back the dark red curls. Combing her hair with her fingers, she pulled it all back to the nape of her neck, and tied the yarn around the mass of overflowing ringlets, trying to make herself appear a few years older than her fifteen years.

Shops lined the main thoroughfare leading into the city. She decided to start on one end of the street and work her way to the other. 'Surely, I will find someone to hire me.'

The first shop was a bakery, and the fresh bread, which was left from the morning bake, still smelled wonderful. Mary licked her dry parched lips, and she tried to quiet her growling stomach's reaction to the lingering appetizing aroma. Before she could say anything, the old man sweeping behind the counter said; "Sorry, lass, no handouts. I have four sons and twelve grandchildren, and they get the day old bread."

"So, then I suppose, sir, that ye have no positions available as well?" Mary asked in a voice that she tried to make sound strong, even though she was shaking.

"No lass, I'm sorry, but yer wastin' your time lookin' for work around here. All the shops are barely stayin' in business these days. Everyone is tryin' to keep their own family workin', and we seem to have trouble doing that. The only work I've seen available is on the ships that come into port, and I don't think a young lady, like yerself, would be very suitable to that kind of work."

"Thank ye anyway, sir." Mary replied with disappointment in her voice, holding her tongue from telling him that she was just as strong as any boy. She was proud that among her ancestors were some great Irish women warriors, as well as the famous Scottish warriors, "the Gallowglachs". The MacSweeney clan had settled in the Cork area around 1300.

"Aw, just a minute now," he said as he pulled an end off of one of the loaves he had in a large round basket on the counter. Handing it to her he said, "It's not good to be lookin' for work on an empty stomach."

Mary wanted to turn down the bread, but she had only eaten a piece of cheese hours ago for breakfast, and her stomach was growling loudly. Red with embarrassment, she thanked him and went outside, heavy with disappointment. As she nibbled slowly on the piece of bread, savoring each bite, she watched the men unloading the ships in the harbor. She knew she should go into other shops and ask about work, but the baker's words had made her think that it would be futile. She sat down on the hard bench on the wooden walk that lined the front of the small row of shops, feeling very let down. Watching the unloading made her wistful, and she started daydreaming about her family being able to afford the luxury items she knew came on the ships from America, and the Orient. She fervently wished they could all go to the United States. Contemplating where her destiny was headed now, she ate the bread, feeling guilty for not saving it to share with her family.

The thought of America kept returning to her mind. Finally, she decided that if she were to change her life, she was going to have to be strong and go after what she wanted. Another deep breath of air gave her the courage she needed to walk down to the pier. There were two big ships in port, and lots of loading and unloading being done by big strong men. She strolled along the docks reading the signs, listening to the sounds of male conversation that echoed everywhere. The Captain of the biggest ship was talking to one of his men as they stood facing the inlet. Mary strolled slowly and quietly behind them.

"I believe we have enough crew members for this voyage, but I haven't found a decent cook or cabin boy for the trip. The cook on the last voyage just about killed us all with his poor culinary efforts. Passengers bring their own food aboard ship and share with each other, but my crew needs someone to cook for them. It shouldn't be hard to find some bloke, who wants free passage to America and a few extra coins for his trouble. I'm going over to the Inn. Join me, Mate, and we'll discuss the coming journey over a pint of ale."

As he turned around, he ran into Mary, who had been intently listening to their conversation. "Oh, excuse me, Miss," the tall bearded man said, "I didn't realize ye were standing there. Is there something I can do for ye, ma'am?" he said, bowing as he doffed his hat to her.

"Oh, sir, no sir, I mean, yes sir. I was wondering about passage on yer ship. What do ye charge, sir? Ye are going to the United States, aren't ye, sir?"

"Yes, Miss. We will be checking in at Boston Harbor, where many will be stayin'. I believe a few of the passengers will be signin' their naturalization papers in Philadelphia, then takin' the train to San Francisco, or catchin' another ship heading round the horn bound fer the Barbary Coast."

"San Francisco! Oh, how I'd love to go there!" Mary exclaimed, sure that her destiny had been revealed to her.

"The fare, Ma'am, is thirteen pounds to Boston, which includes all of your baggage, and another eight pounds if ye go on to San Francisco and want to book yer passage around the horn. Are ye interested in going, ma'am? The ship's list is getting quite full, so if ye are planning on the trip ye need to pay yer fare right away, or there will be no space left. We leave on Monday next, before the Irish winds kick up and hold us back." As he said these last few words, he looked her over slowly. Arrogance took over his face, as if he was making sure she understood that he came from a higher class, and his voice took on a sort of pitying tone, when he looked at her shabby dress and saw her wistful look.

"Oh sir, I'd love to go, but I don't have thirteen pounds," she felt her face turn red with the shame of it all. "I'm sorry, I wasn't eavesdroppin' really, but I just overheard ye say that ye needed a cook for the journey. Sir, I'm a good cook. Could I cook for ye and yer crew for me passage to America?"

The big man looked at her and laughed, a big boisterous laugh, throwing back his head. The other man joined him, and Mary felt the eyes of everyone on the docks staring at her. Finally, realizing her embarrassment, he stopped laughing. "I'm sorry, Miss, but the thought of hiring a girl to cook for this rowdy crew I've got sounds pretty humorous."

"But, sir, I cook for me family of nine, several times every week."

"Nine, ye cook for nine?"

"Yes, sir. There's me mum and da, two brothers, three sisters, and me Uncle Sean. I make really good bread and biscuits, and I can cook potatoes lots of different ways. My brothers say I cook better than mum does, course they say that when mum can't hear them."

"Well, I'm sorry, Missy, I just don't think that would work. We need a strong lad for the job, one who can lift heavy pans. This is just not a job for a woman, or a mere girl. Why don't ye see if ye can raise the passage, little lady," he said, patting her on the head. Before she could speak again, he turned quickly, brushed her aside, and scurried off with his first mate, as if he couldn't stand to be bothered with her poverty any longer.

She could hear them laughing as they headed up the hill toward the Inn. Blushing profusely, she folded her arms, walking quickly toward Macroom, and the safety of her family. Luckily, she caught a ride on the back of a neighbor's wagon. He had just taken a load of wool to Cork, so she only had to walk a short distance. It was getting dark as she crossed the meadow headed towards the cottage. Jerry, her brother, was hurrying toward her.

"Giorraionn Beirt Bothar." He greeted her with the familiar Gaelic saying.

"Two shorten the road." Mary greeted him back like she always did.

"Mary, where have ye been? Mummy is worryin' herself sick about ye." He joined her, putting the shawl he had brought with him around her shoulders.

"Oh, Jerry, I'm okay except for being very down hearted. I've lost me position at the O'Brien's, and now I don't know what I will do."

"I'm sorry, Mary. I know how ye hate the fields and working in the bogs. If I were a few years older, I'm sure I could get a better position. I look as old as ye do, but just because I'm only fourteen, mum won't let me work on the ships until I'm fifteen."

"Yer right, ye do look as old as I do. Maybe mum will change her mind when she hears I've lost the position at the dairy and let ye go down and apply on the docks."

"I hope so, Mary, I hope so. With Da and his bad leg and all, if we don't bring in some money we might all be skin and bones by spring, or living in a work house." Jerry looked worried.

Mary suddenly saw her brother in a new light, recognizing her own frown in his face. They did look alike. Most folks thought they were twins. They had the same turned up noses with a sprinkle of freckles, and their laughing green eyes with long lashes framed their almond shape. Her mother said she thought she was dreaming when they had placed Jeremiah in her arms. She immediately said, "No, this is Mary when she was first born." After checking beneath the blankets, she believed that this was indeed a different child. The last couple of years Jerry caught up with Mary in height, and their resemblance was almost uncanny. He had a thick mop of curly dark red hair, the same color as hers, only his came to just below his ears. An idea began to creep into Mary's thoughts, which became increasingly exciting and more feasible, as she began to work out the plan in her mind.

"Jerry, I want to talk to ye after dinner. It's important." Her eyes twinkled, and she laughed as her mood lifted. She now knew how her plans could come to fruition. They reached the old thatched roofed cottage as the swiftly increasing winds whistled at their backs.

Chapter Two

"The Sweeney Clan"

September, 1873

"It is easier to beg forgiveness, than to seek permission."

"Mary, me girl! Where in the world have ye been? I've been worryin' meself sick, just thinkin' bout what might 'a happened to ye!"

"I'm sorry, Mummy. I was tryin' to find work. Mrs. O'Brien said Liam is comin' home and needs work with the new baby and all. They are given him me position."

"Lord a' mercy, what'll happen next? I guess ye'll just have to go back to work in the bogs, or the fields, Mary. If things get any worse, we'll all be forced to go to the workhouse in Macroom."

"I've got a better idea, Mum," Jerry piped in, "I could get work on the docks. I look old enough." The boy put his arm around his mother's shoulder and gave her a little squeeze.

"I won't have it. The work is dangerous, me boy, and ye are not old enough. Ye'd have to lie about yer age. You two wash up now and hurry before the young'uns eat yers too. Mrs. McCoy gave me a small piece of a freshly slaughtered lamb. There's a few bits of meat in the pot this time. She is worried about us, as she said that the O'Learys came by on their way to the workhouse. The family was in a terrible state as all of the children were cryin'. It seems their landlord evicted them, and they have nowhere else to go. No one is able to help them out, as they can hardly feed their own families."

Mary felt sick as she thought of her friend, Kathleen O'Leary, headed to that horrible place. Everyone knew what living there was like for a family. Fathers were harshly questioned about their ability to feed their families when they arrived, and then the family was immediately and permanently separated. The only time the family could see each other was on Sunday. It was like a prison, as they couldn't leave the building, had to wear uniforms, and silence was a rule, as well as no card playing, or disobeying orders. The ten-hour day for men was spent breaking stones, the women knitted, and older children had industrial training. The food was mainly a weak oatmeal porridge called Stirabout. Many people died of typhus, cholera, or dysentery.

The thought of the workhouse, was what made Mary make up her mind about the idea that had been prancing around in her brain since her brother met her outside the cottage. She knew she must talk to Jerry after they ate dinner, in order to convince him to go along with her, so they could avoid the workhouse.

She had been very hungry until she heard about the O'Learys, and the memory of her lost lamb added to her angst. The tiny lamb she had raised from birth had disappeared at too young an age, and Mary was sure it had ended up on someone else's dinner table. If her family had eaten the lamb because they were starving, she knew she would have felt differently about its loss. Not knowing what happened left her with only her imagination. In her mind, her pet had become a martyr. She saw her mother as a martyr as well, when she went without to feed her family. Mary had made a vow not to become a martyr too.

When she dished up the stew, she didn't take any meat. There was only a little flavor of lamb and not a lot of potatoes left anyway, but the savory liquid vanquished any hunger pangs that might arise that evening. The herbs and spices her mother grew in their small garden, and collected in the meadow, always made her meals better. Mary thanked the Lord for the meal she was eating, knowing it was better than what a lot of Irish folks ate these days.

When her mother went outside with little Jim to help him bring in more peat bricks for the fire, Jeremiah Sweeney limped in with Sean Foley staggering behind.

"I can't believe ye came home like this again, Sean. I suppose ye spent yer pay drinkin' the afternoon away again."

Her father's angry tone with his wife's stepbrother was a sign to the rest of the family that it was time to finish their chores, but Mary was expected to serve the men their meals while her mother was outside, so she quietly prepared and served their bowls of stew.

"No, Jeremiah, I have some money left. Me friends were buying me ale for me birthday, so I only bought a few."

"Lord almighty, Sean, when are ye goin' to grow up? Don't let yer sister know that ye've had too many again. Eat yer supper, and get yerself off to bed, so ye won't have trouble gettin' up in the morning. We're struggling to survive here! Don't be spendin' money on spirits, or ye might be findin' another place to live!" Jeremiah's face was red with anger.

Sean's drunkenness made his lips run freely. "Now, now, Jeremiah, remember one of me dear sister's favorite sayings: *May those that love us, love us, and those that don't love us, may God turn their hearts, and if he doesn't turn their hearts, may he turn their ankles, so we'll know them by their limping."*

"Ye think it's funny to make fun of the man who took ye in as a small babe? If ye don't face yer drinking problem now, ye'll be facin' it someday, and someday might be too late to save yer hide. Yer poor father and mother would be turnin' in their graves to see their boy actin' like this, and yer dear sister doesn't need to see it either."

"Margaret's like a mother to me!"

"Aye that she is, so why don't ye quit disgracin' her family name?"

Only Mary heard the conversation between her father and his wife's stepbrother, as she cleared the children's dishes and set bowls full of the steaming thin liquid in front of the two men. They always ate in shifts. The younger children ate first, then the older ones. The men ate next, and Margaret Sweeney ate last, if there was any left.

Margaret Foley was only sixteen when she married Jeremiah Sweeney. An Irish beauty, she had auburn hair and eyes as blue as the sky. Although a tiny lass who stood only a few inches over five feet, she had a large personality, full of spirit. A turned up nose and dimpled chin helped Jeremiah Sweeney fall in love with her at first sight. Many men pursued her, but she only had eyes for him. Jeremiah was a tall, broad shouldered man with muscular arms, due to his hard work on his father's farm. Black curly hair and hazel eyes accentuated his strong square jaw and winning smile.

They were married in the spring of 1845. Patrick was born a year later, and Timothy arrived in 1847, the year "The Potato Famine" hit Ireland. The two babies died in her arms in 1849. Their tiny, frail bodies suffered from scurvy and malnutrition. They both finally succumbed, two weeks before an influenza outbreak took many lives in the village. Margaret was devastated, and she wanted to die herself, until little Sean gave her a reason for living.

Margaret and Jeremiah took in her stepbrother, Sean Foley, after her father and his new young wife died of that same influenza, leaving the tiny boy an orphan. Sean's real father died without marrying his mother, and Margaret's father married the young girl to save her shame. Margaret's own mother had passed of the coughing sickness when her daughter was twelve. The Sweeneys' strong faith in God helped get them through those years. Taking care of the little orphaned boy helped heal her broken heart.

Mary's sisters and brothers began arriving two years later. The end of the famine in 1851 brought Catherine. Margaret arrived in 1855 and Mary in 1858. Jerry was born in 1859 and Jim in 1860. The youngest, Johanna, joined the family in 1861.

Their home was a small simple cottage built out of stone, with a thatched roof made of straw and clay. The main living area was a large room with a cooking hearth and eating area. Jeremiah, a self-taught carpenter, had crafted the few pieces of furniture including; a wood table with four benches, and a bench seat with a back that was next to the hearth. The tenants before them had built a stone half wall that divided the house, which provided some privacy for the family when they filled the tub on Saturday nights with water they heated on the hearth. Nine people lived in the small cottage.

Margaret Foley Sweeney filled her bowl with the little bit that was left in the pot, as her children did their nightly chores. Her beauty had turned into a more matronly look, as worry lines now accentuated her features, and her smile was rarely seen. Her clothes hung on her thin body, her hands were calloused, and her nails bore dirt that wouldn't wash off from her work in the fields. She sat down wearily at the table to eat.

Mary went outside to find Jerry, who was helping his little brother bring in the last of the bricks of peat. She motioned to him to speak privately, and he approached her quickly.

"What's up, Mary? Why do I think ye are planning something mum might not approve of?"

"Jerry, ye have to swear ye will not tell anybody about me plans. I know this will work, and it will be best for everyone. The way things are here in Ireland, we could all end up in the workhouse in Macroom just like the O'Learys. Don't ye think it would be best for the whole family to go to America?"

"Mary, ye know they would never leave this land."

"I know, Jerry. That's the point. They should consider it before the family starves, or we are forced to go to the workhouse, and the whole family will be separated anyway. Me plan is to go to America first, and to make enough money to bring ye all over."

"Mary, ye can't go over there by yerself, besides ye have no way or money to get there."

"Oh, but I do. I've got it all figured out. They're looking for a cook for the crew of the "Harmony", which is sailing for America on Monday next. They won't hire a girl, but they'd hire a strong boy like ye. We look just alike and are about the same size. We can go down to the docks tomorrow, and ye can get the job. Then I'll cut me hair like yers, wear yer clothes and go in yer place. I can pass for ye easy. Please, Jerry, for the good of the family."

"All by yerself? I would never forgive meself if something happened to ye."

"Nothing is going to happen to me. Then Mum would have to let ye get a job on the docks, and there would be one less mouth to feed. Jerry, I just have to do this. I can feel it in me bones... this is what I'm supposed to do."

"Mum and Da will be so mad and so worried about ye... and I'll be worried meself!"

"Remember Murphy's saying? *'It is easier to beg forgiveness, than to seek permission.'* Come on, Jerry, please? I don't want us to end up at the workhouse. I want us all to have a chance at a good life! Please, Jerry, if ye love this family, this will be the best for everyone." Mary pleaded with a look she knew her brother couldn't resist. Since they were children, she could get him to do anything for her.

"Oh, all right, but I'm not feeling good about this."

"Ye won't be sorry, Jerry, I promise!" Mary squealed and kissed him. "I'll meet ye at the crossroads at quittin' time, and then we'll hitch a ride and go down to apply tomorrow, okay?"

"Mary, promise me ye'll be careful. Maybe I should go with ye on this trip."

"No, Jerry, mummy needs ye. What with Da's bad leg now, she needs ye here till he's better. I'm planning on ye all joinin' me in America."

"Well, maybe, but I love this land, Mary. I'm not sure I want to leave it, except to see ye."

"I know, I love me Ireland too, and ye, me dear brother, but I feel like me destiny is elsewhere."

"Ye always did have an adventuresome spirit, Mary."

A storm came in with a roar of thunder, followed by a flash that lit up the sky just as the family finished their chores. Water poured down from the dark clouds immediately drenching their thin clothes. The two siblings began shivering with cold as they covered their heads with their arms and ran into the small cottage to dry their clothes, and to warm their bodies by the fire.

When the wind whistled through the old thatched roof, and put the flame of the oil lamp out for the last time, they went to bed. Their hay filled mattresses felt warm after they put the stones they heated by the fire under their blankets. Mary was concerned about the now raging storm, as balls of ice the size of large pebbles, pelted menacingly against the stone walls and threatened the fragile roof. What if the storm went on for days? It wasn't even winter yet. They needed the sunshine to return for a few weeks, so they could get in a few more supplies before winter arrived.

Mary prayed for the good weather to return for her own reasons, but the wind continued to howl keeping her awake. The wool nightgown and long stockings weren't keeping her warm. She kept pulling the quilt her grandmother had made for her up to her chin, but her sisters kept pulling it, along with the other bedding, back to their side of the bed. She tossed and turned, and her eyes wouldn't close as she dreamed of a new life in America. The storm worried her. If it continued, the ship might not even sail.

Restless, Mary got up to get a cup of water from the pail in the kitchen. The family took turns bringing water from the pump well with a wooden shoulder yoke that spread the weight evenly across their bodies. They were lucky the well was close. Many of their neighbors had much greater distances to go for the water necessary to run a household.

When she started to return to her room, she heard Sean gurgling. Thinking he was choking, she went over to him. When she was a small child, she adored Sean, but as she grew older she had become afraid of his angry temper and controlling ways. He had grown into a handsome man with an Irish grin and a thick mop of brown hair. He had a charming personality, except when he was drinking. As she leaned over him, she could smell the stale liquor on his breath. Suddenly, his hands grabbed her arms and pulled her on top of him. She struggled to get away from him, but his strong arms and hands held her tight.

"Let go of me, or I'll scream for Da," she hissed fervently.

"Oh, Mary, sweet Mary, just give yer uncle a little kiss. C'mon, show yer dear uncle a little appreciation fer all he's done fer ye." His strong arms held her tightly. His hot stinking breath made her stomach queasy. The drunken grin on his face made her so angry that she opened her mouth and bit through the wool shirt that came between her and his shoulder. She bit down as hard as she could on the small bit of his flesh she caught between her teeth. When he didn't budge, she pulled her head back violently feeling his skin and the wool tightly in her teeth. A scream rolled forth from his lips as he threw her off of him, and she landed on the cold hard cottage floor.

Jerry came from nowhere, "Did he hurt ye, Mary?"

"Hurt her? She hurt me! Took a piece out of me shoulder, she did, the little vixen."

"The truth comes out when the spirit goes in!" Mary seethed at him.

"If ye ever touch her, or any of me brothers or sisters again, Sean, I swear I'll kill ye with me bare hands." Jerry's face was red with anger as he started to reach for his uncle with clenched fists. Just then, his father entered the room.

"What's going on out here? What is all this noise?"

"Sean was just having a bad dream. That's all, and Mary and I came to wake him up from his nightmare. Are ye awake now, Sean?" Jerry said, controlling the anger in his voice, but showing his uncle an angry grimace that his father couldn't see.

"Yes, I'm okay. I'm sorry I woke ye," he said, still slurring his words and rubbing his shoulder, but sober enough to know Jeremiah

Sweeney would have thrown him out if he'd known. "Go back to sleep. It must have been the storm that give me the nightmares."

As Mary and Jerry parted at the doorway to their rooms, Mary whispered, "Do ye see why I must get away, Jerry? This is not the first time he has tried to grab me."

"Aye, Mary, I'll help ye all I can." He took her hand in his for a moment and said tenderly, "I'll miss ye, Sis."

"I'll miss ye too, little brother."

Chapter Three

"Planning the Journey"

September, 1873

"If you're lucky enough to be Irish, you're lucky enough."

Mary woke up early and realized the storm was over. After dressing quietly, so she wouldn't disturb her sisters, she went through the cottage and out the front door. The sun was just coming up behind the few left over clouds, and a vivid rainbow could be seen in the distance through the mist that still lay over the green land. Mary saw another sign in the rainbow; surely this was a confirmation that she should seek her 'pot of gold' in America. She hurried through her chores and told her mother she would go into the village to seek a new position this afternoon. She didn't like lying, but felt that it was necessary this one time.

She crossed the bridge into the little village of Macroom, crossing the beautiful Sullane River that ran by the old Macroom Castle. Jerry met her at the crossroads as he had promised, and they walked briskly down the road toward Queenstown. They caught a ride with a merchant from Macroom, reaching the docks in mid-afternoon. Jerry was hardly listening to his sister as she chatted excitedly all the way to the city about her coming adventure. He was so worried about what she was planning, and he kept pointing out the things that could go wrong, but Mary's mind was made up, and he could see there was no stopping her, short of telling his parents, and he knew Mary would never forgive him for that. It seemed like they were standing on the docks for an hour before they saw the Captain coming down the gangplank of the "Harmony."

"Excuse me, sir, remember me? I spoke to ye yesterday about the cook's position on yer vessel?"

"Listen, little lady, I told ye yesterday I'm not hiring on any woman."

"Oh yes, sir, I understand. I've brought me brother with me who wants to take the job. This is Jerry. He's older than I am, and he's almost as good a cook. He wants to go to America too. We figure if he goes over there first, he can bring the rest of us over later."

"Now that's a much better idea, lass. The crew won't be quite so rowdy with a strappin' young lad, the likes of him, as they would be with the likes of a young lady such as yerself. Ye look like a strong lad. Are ye?"

"Yes, sir, I'm very strong. I've been choppin' wood fer the fire since I was a small boy and carryin' water from the well. I'm working in the bogs now where I haul loads of peat into town to sell, but I hate the work."

"Well, I do need a cook, and we're leavin' with the high tides Monday next. Have ye any problems with that, me boy?" The big man looked Jerry straight in the eye and held out his hand.

Words seem to be stuck in Jerry's throat as he shook the man's hand. Finally, he said, "No, sir, none at all, sir. I'll be here early Monday morning."

"No, laddie, ye'll need to be on board the ship by four bells if yer sailin' with me."

Jerry looked at Mary and saw her firmly nodding her head up and down. "Yes, sir. I'll be there." His voice was stronger now.

"Seems we've struck a bargain, laddie. I'm Captain James Stallings. What's yer name again, son?"

"Jerry Sweeney, sir, of Macroom, County Cork."

"Okay, Jerry Sweeney. Ye report to me First Mate when ye come aboard. His name is Johnson. He'll be the one givin' orders. Ye'll know him right off."

"Thank ye, sir." Jerry reached out to shake the large man's hand again, but he had already turned away, abruptly dismissing them. The captain climbed the hill, and he headed for the lively sounding pub that sat on the hill above the docks.

"That leaves me two days to get ready. Ye'll have to cut me hair jest before we leave for the docks." Mary was elated now that Jerry got the job. All her plans were falling into place.

"Cut yer hair! Can't ye jest tie it up?"

"What if it comes down, Jerry? I must fool them all the way over, or I could be in danger. Some of those men on the docks looked like they could be trouble."

"Mary, I really wish ye wouldn't do this. I'll be so worried about ye, 'til I hear yer okay, and so will mum. Please write as soon as ye get there, or whenever ye can post a letter. I have a few pence saved that I was going to buy mum a couple more chickens with, but I'll give it to ye. I should be makin' more now, since she'll have to let me work on the docks. Ye'll need some money, so ye can find a place to stay till ye find work."

"Thanks, Jerry. I kept a few pence from my last pay. Mum never counts it. She just takes the money and puts it in the tin in the cupboard. I figure I'll be savin' them money for not having to feed me anyway. We'd better hurry, Jerry, before mum starts wonderin' why we're late."

The merchant, who had given them a ride, left them off a short distance from home. They jumped over old man Bailey's fence, took off the shoes they wore only to church on Sundays, and ran through the luscious grassy meadow feeling the soft blades tickle the soles of their feet. The people of Macroom had laughed at Tom Bailey for his inventions, but they had changed their minds when the aqueduct system he invented helped him make it through the "famine years", while many of his neighbors had starved. He was a friendly man, but he didn't socialize a lot. It wasn't that he wasn't well liked, nobody really knew him. Villagers considered him a stranger, so children were told to "stay away from him".

Because of his undeserved reputation, Jerry and Mary always warily crossed the pasture. By cutting through his land, they got home in half the time it took using the main road. The siblings loved to spend time together. Mary had mothered him since they were very small. Jerry loved her almost more than his mother, but not in the same way. They had formed a unique bond, which neither of them felt with their other siblings. They confided in each other, knowing they could express their innermost feelings without criticism, and they could trust each other to keep those things private. They never laughed at each other, no matter what the other said.

It was a lovely day, and the brilliant colored wild flowers that sprinkled the green meadow were beckoning Mary to pick them.

"Jerry, let's pick some flowers fer mum. I only have a few days left to spend with her, so let's bring her a big bouquet to brighten her dreary day."

Mary picked several of the large late blooming sunflowers. Then added buttercup, larkspur, and some fragrant purple flowers that grew among the others. The beauty of the field added to her high spirits. The colors of the flowers reminded her of the pattern in her beloved quilt. Grandmother Sweeney had given it to her before she died, along with some colorful stories of the history of the Sweeneys, going back to the 1300's when their name was MacSweeney.

She had been enthralled with her grandmother's storytelling, and she loved to hear about how the MacSweeneys had saved some of the Spanish from the English, when the Armada had shipwrecked on the Irish Coast, and how they had built some of the castles in the Cork area. The castles of Mashanaglass, Castlemore, and Clodogh, were all lived in by the clan and probably built by them. They had fought to keep them alongside the MacCarthys, but lost the castles to the English. Then she told her about their "Gallowglach" warrior ancestors, who originated in what is now southeastern Scotland, which was once an Irish kingdom called Dal Riata. She told Mary that was where her sister Catherine's coloring had come from. The dark hair, green eyes, and fair skin came from the Spanish soldier who had married a lass in the MacSweeney clan in the mid 1500's. This is now known as the "Black Irish".

Mary stood still, momentarily enjoying the soft breeze blowing against her back, as she watched the wind pick up the earth's small seedlings from the hearts of its offspring, and carry them off to another meadow, or garden, to bloom anew in the spring. As she inhaled her beloved Irish air, she saw herself as a wildflower seed about to be transplanted to a new and prosperous land, destined to bring her ancestry there, just like the new flowers would bloom where they never had before. Mary arranged the flowers into a lovely bouquet, and she stood there in a state of bliss, daydreaming, as the aroma of the blossoms filled her senses. Lost in thoughts of a better life across the ocean, enjoying the sweet fragrances of the bouquet in her hand, Jerry's voice suddenly brought her to the present.

"Mary, look out!" Heavy footsteps pounded behind her as she turned around. She knew it was a large animal even before she saw it. The huge bull was closing in on her fast. Jerry was already straddling a heavy oak tree limb. Mary froze, knowing there wasn't time to do anything. As if in a trance, she slowly stepped backwards praying fervently: 'Dear Jesus, Mary and Joseph, please save me from this beast. Don't let me die like this!' She pleaded, unable to breathe. The back of her leg touched the fencepost just as the huge snorting bull pranced in front of her. As if a statue, she stood perfectly still, unable to move from fear. With flaring nostrils, the big beast stared into her eyes as he bent his head and gently ate the wildflowers, which were still clasped tightly in her fist. When he finished, he snorted as if in thanks, turned abruptly and pranced off leaving Mary almost catatonic.

"Young lady, are ye all right?" The voice from behind her seemed to bring her back to life. "Miss, are ye hurt?" The voice asked again as Jerry came bounding toward her.

"Mary! Mary, me God, Mary, I thought ye were a goner for sure." He kissed her on the forehead saying, "Bless your little Irish heart and every other Irish part."

"I'm okay," she said weakly, turning to see the source of the other voice. She was surprised to see the mysterious, Mr. Bailey, standing with his cane behind the fence.

"Oh, sir, I'm sorry we trespassed across yer field. I'm really sorry, sir. I'm Mary Sweeney, sir, and this is me brother, Jerry. We were a little late getting home, and if we go through yer field, we get home much faster. I was just pickin' me mum some flowers, so she wouldn't be mad at us fer being late when we get home. I'm really sorry!" Mary was speaking so fast that Mr. Bailey burst out laughing when she was finished.

"It's okay, me dear. I'm just happy that yer not hurt. I saw ye in the field and was coming to warn ye that I'd just begun putting the bull in this pasture. I know ye think I'm a bad fellow, but I'm really a right nice person, if I do say so meself. Ye jest don't know me. Are ye sure yer okay, young lady?" He was an older man with spectacles resting on his nose. His face held a merry smile amidst the mustache and neatly trimmed gray beard. He had a little tan wool cap on top of his head and eyes that crinkled when he smiled.

"Oh yes, I'm quite fine now and very happy to be alive, sir, thanks to the kindness of yer bull." Mary laughed as she plopped down on the ground, her legs suddenly feeling weak. "I'll be fine. I just need to sit down for a few minutes until me heart stops beating so fast."

Jerry sat down beside her, as the older man bent over and slipped through the wooden fence slats joining them on the grass. They could see the bull far off at the other end of the pasture, and they all kept an eye on him ready to move quickly if necessary.

"Well, ye must have the luck of the Irish today. *If you're lucky enough to be Irish, you're lucky enough.*" The old man laughed. "I see ye ripped yer pants climbin' that tree, son. This will help ye pay fer another pair." The old man said as he handed Jerry some coins.

"Oh no, sir, I can't take yer money. These pants were already torn, sir, it wasn't yer fault. And besides, we shouldn't have been in yer fields." Jerry was still feeling guilty.

"Never ye mind. I will get mad if ye don't take me generous offer. Here, buy ye each something new. It will make this old man happy. I'm happy to have met some of me neighbors before I leave the country. I'm going to be taking a trip soon, and I won't be around for a while, so don't be surprised if ye see some children around here. My family from Glenbeg is coming up to stay here and tend the farm while I'm gone. They live in the Peafield area of County Cork. My brother-in-law, John Troy, owns a small farm there. He's sending me sister, Anna, and half of their brood over here to help me out. So, ye take this now, young man, while I'm in a generous mood, and be off with ye before yer mum starts lookin' fer ye."

Mary took the money, thanked him profusely, and kissed the old gentleman on his whiskered cheek. Jerry shook his hand, and they both ran across the field toward the white cottage in the trees on the far side of the huge pasture.

Chapter Four

"Silent Goodbyes"

September, 1873

"May you have the hindsight to know where you have been, the foresight to know where you are going, and the insight to know when you have gone too far."

The weekend was nostalgic for Mary. She spent it reminiscing about the good times with her family, saying goodbye, and I love you to each one, without them realizing her meaning.

The two siblings had spent Saturday afternoon at the little market in Macroom. With the money the old man had given them, Jerry bought a very used seaman's jacket and hat. Mary's purchase was a pair of used boots and a cheap yard of cloth, to repair Jerry's old clothes, so she could wear them.

Luckily, it had been Mary's turn on Saturday night to take a bath. When she slipped into the old tub, she knew it would be the last bath she would get for a long time. Languishing in the wonderfully warm water, she pondered when and where her next bath would be. She asked herself why she wasn't afraid. Maybe she would be tomorrow. Excitement was her only emotion. She told herself it was due to her strong faith.

"He will lead me and I will follow." She whispered to herself. Whenever she contemplated not going, the melancholy returned. Praying always took away that feeling. She crossed herself and quickly spoke to him in her own words.

"Lord, please guide me safely to the new land. I will follow whatever path ye choose for me. Please help me to control me temper and let it not intrude on yer plans for me and please, Lord, send along my guardian angel to help me get safely to America, and also to help me bring me family over later."

Sunday would be her last day with her family for a long time. Everyone did their morning chores, and then they enjoyed their biggest breakfast of the week. If the chickens laid enough, everybody got one egg with their biscuits, butter, and homemade jam, with milk or tea. During the rest of the week, they only got biscuits and tea. A skinny cow, and a couple of chickens, provided milk, butter and eggs for the family. Sometimes, there was extra to sell. They were trying to save up for a rooster, but were having trouble buying enough feed for the animals. After breakfast, they walked to the parish church, Saint Colman's, on the other side of the Bridge in the Village to attend Sunday mass.

When they returned home from church, the neighbor came to fetch her parents. One of their children was sick, and her mother knew all about medicinal herbs, so she was called upon by many people in the area. While they were gone, Mary and Jerry spent most of the afternoon getting Mary ready for her journey. Mary gathered everything she had put on her mental list, including the few dresses she owned and other female articles she would need later. She patched the clothes that Jerry had given her late Saturday night after her sisters had fallen asleep. The female clothes went in the bottom of the old sea bag that she retrieved from the barn. It had belonged to Grandfather Sweeney. Then she neatly folded the boy clothes, including the ones she planned to wear in the morning. She just couldn't leave the small quilt, so it had been packed in between the two different genders of attire, along with the small leather pouch that held her bible and rosary. She had received the beads, and bible, for her confirmation two years ago, and Jerry had hand tooled the pouch. When no one was looking, they hid everything in the smokehouse.

Mary took time to spend a few special moments with each of her siblings and also to say her silent goodbyes. Mary convinced herself that her family would understand after she was gone. Her sisters were dear to her. Margaret was a tall young woman; strawberry blonde with a porcelain complexion. She was named after her mother and maternal grandmother as was the custom for the second daughter. Young men had just started noticing her fresh innocent face. Catherine was just as lovely in a completely different way. She had the Black Irish coloring; fair skin, dark hair, and eyes. Catherine, as the firstborn daughter, was named after her paternal grandmother.

Mary and Jerry's features were a unique combination of both of their parents, but one wouldn't say they resembled either of them. Jerry, as the first born son, was named after his father and paternal grandfather, Jeremiah. Jim was named after James Foley, his maternal grandfather. Mary and Johanna were named after two of their aunts.

The Sweeneys were all blessed with good looks. Mary was happy with her face. She thought it was pleasant, but she felt like a wallflower compared to her older sisters. 'They are like roses, just beginning to bloom.' She thought she was more like a sunflower. Johanna, eleven, was tiny in stature with long fair hair. Her face still had a cherubic charm that highlighted her large blue eyes. Mary compared her to a daisy, as she was sturdier than she looked, with a strong, determined personality.

"Catherine, I jest want ye to know that I'm really proud that ye are my sister. I know mum and da are proud of ye too. I want ye to know that I love, and appreciate, how ye always help everyone and do extra chores when necessary, without ever complaining."

"Mary, I know how hard ye work as well. I love ye too."

She talked to her older sisters as they washed the dishes and cleaned up after another meal of potato stew. She talked to little Jim and read to Johanna for the last time, but Mary didn't say anything to her uncle. The awful feelings she harbored in her heart toward him surprised her. Mary couldn't remember feeling like this before, particularly toward a family member. When she looked at him, she was sure she should follow her dream.

'I must get away from him and his lecherous hands.' She said a prayer: 'Forgive me for me heart full of hate, and please protect me sisters from his dirty hands.'

Mary spoke to her parents together. As usual, they were the last ones to eat supper that Sunday night. Mary chose her words carefully that she used to say goodbye, hoping that when Jerry told them she had gone to America, they would remember her words and understand their meaning.

"Mummy, do ye think that God has a plan for our lives?" She had waited to eat with them.

"Yes, Mary, I believe that he does. We must have faith in God. Faith in his knowledge of what is best for us, and we must let him lead us in the right direction. I knew that I'd be your father's wife from the day I first met him. The Lord just seemed to bring us together. Our time together has often been for the poorer, rather than the richer, as far as that goes, but we have always been rich with love. We have God, our children, and each other, which is all one really needs for happiness. Someday, Mary, ye will meet an Irish lad who'll sweep ye right off yer feet to yer own little cottage, and ye'll have a nice brood of yer own. I like to think of me favorite Irish blessing. It helps me accept whatever the Lord has in store for me. *'May the road rise to meet you, may the wind be always at your back, may the sun shine warm upon your face, the rains fall soft upon your fields, and until we meet again, may God hold you in the palm of his hand'.*"

"Yes, Mummy. That's one of me favorites too. I don't know. Somehow, I feel God has a different callin' for me."

"And what do ye fancy that might be, Mary?" Her usually quiet father inquired.

"Oh, I don't know, Da. I just feel that me destiny might lead me down a different path. I feel like I was meant for something special." Mary spoke with a wistful look on her face.

Her father laughed a big booming laugh. "Darling daughter, ye are a lovely lass. Don't ye realize that everyone feels they are meant for something special? It's only when ye get to me age that ye realize each of us is just a small pebble in a large river. In the end, it comes down to this: We're born, and then we marry, have children, grow old, and die. Get yer head out of the clouds, girl, and accept yer destiny."

"Yes Da." Mary gently kissed her father on the forehead and kissed her mother on the cheek. "Thanks for being such lovely parents. No matter what me future holds, I'll always love ye both very much."

Two hours after the cottage was silent for the night, Mary and Jerry met by the smokehouse. Quickly, Mary put on two layers of shirts, trousers, and stockings. Then she donned a wool sweater, the pea jacket and black boots. When she was completely dressed, she pulled out a knife and handed it to Jerry. "Cut me hair."

"Oh, Mary, I can't cut yer beautiful hair."

"If ye don't cut it, the Captain will recognize me and, I will be in trouble. Besides, it will grow back. Yer hair is pretty long. I only need it as short as yers." She tied a piece of yarn around the back of her hair.

"Just cut on this side of the yarn." She closed her eyes as her brother cut her hair off with one swipe. He stood there holding her hair in his hand, feeling as if he'd just severed ties with his sister forever. Finally, he put the clump of hair in his pocket, unable to throw it away.

"There is no turning back now, is there?" Mary lifted the heavy bag over her shoulder.

"Here, let me carry that till we get there. I don't want ye tired out before ye leave. Save yer strength for chores on board ship. Ye better practice lowering yer voice, so ye sound more like me." They climbed the fence and walked through Mr. Bailey's pasture again. Mary noticed a light in the big house and wondered what his family was doing up in the middle of the night.

It was a long way to walk, but they took many shortcuts and arrived in a couple of hours. No one was around when they reached Queenstown, so Jerry walked her down to the bottom of the hill where they said their last goodbyes. They had said so much in the last couple of days that there was nothing left to say when they got there. Jerry held her gently for a moment, then blessed her with the saying their father would utter most often.

"May you have the hindsight to know where you have been, the foresight to know where you are going, and the insight to know when you have gone too far."

They were both close to tears as she smiled bravely and waved at him. Lifting the heavy bag to her shoulder, she blew him one last smiling kiss through her tears and walked up the gangplank to begin her adventure. As she started her new life, she uttered the blessing she knew her mother would have said to her if she had been given the chance to say goodbye.

"May there always be work for your hands to do. May your purse always hold a coin or two. May the sun always shine on your windowpane. May a rainbow be certain to follow the rain. May the hand of a friend always be near you. May God fill your heart with gladness to cheer you."

Jerry's eyes hurt from trying to hold back the flood of tears he felt at the loss of his sister. Life wouldn't be the same without his beloved Mary. He climbed to the top of the hill, and he sat there at the edge of town under a big tree. The view of the harbor was good, and he wanted to watch the ship sail just in case she changed her mind at the last minute. The sailors were preparing the ship to sail with his sister aboard. He wanted desperately to go down there, drag her off of the ship, throw her over his shoulder and carry her home but, Jerry knew she would be furious, and he couldn't stand the thought of her being angry at him, so he fought off the temptation.

The wind was beginning to blow, and the "Harmony" rocked gently in the breeze. Jerry sat twenty yards from the road, where he could also see the passengers as they boarded the vessel. He was surprised to see Mr. Bailey's horse and buggy come slowly down the road. There were three people in the buggy. An old man was driving the team. A strong young man sat in the back with the trunks while Mr. Bailey leaned over his cane talking to the older man. Then he happened to glance toward Jerry sitting by the tree. Recognizing him, he gave him a curious nod, surely wondering what he was doing there at that time of the morning. When Jerry saw the trunks in the back of the buggy, he realized that Mr. Bailey was going on the "Harmony." He began to worry that he might have endangered his sister's trip by letting Mr. Bailey see him.

Jerry sat there for what seemed like hours, until all the passengers and cargo were on board and settled. He wiped tears from his face as the seamen finally pulled up the anchor, and the ship set sail for the other side of the Atlantic. He waited until after the glorious Irish sun rose, and the ship disappeared, before he got up and walked toward Macroom to break the news to the family, of his sister's departure.

Chapter Five

"Life on the Harmony"

September & October, 1873

"Drink to the health of your enemies' enemies."

As the big ship moved beneath her and out into the harbor, Mary's homeland tugged at her heart. She was faced with the truth about how far away San Francisco was and how alone she would be from now on. Her fear of what that path may hold for her was suddenly a frightening reality. As she watched her beautiful Ireland disappear out of the galley porthole, she wondered whether this was a dream come true, or the beginning of a nightmare. Butterflies of excitement and worms of fear were rumbling through her body as she felt a little sick to her stomach. She prayed that she wouldn't be seasick as she tried to settle her stomach by concentrating on her new job.

Random thoughts filled her head as she checked out the galley. 'A strange new beginning... disguised as a boy... aboard a big ship... headed for a new land... on the other side of the Atlantic... her family still in Ireland.' She etched the view of her homeland in her mind, wanting to never forget what it meant to her. The cool ocean air made her shiver, as the rising sun came up brightly shining through the small porthole. Mary took one last look, and she saw only the dark blue shimmering ocean leading her to her new life in the west. Looking around the galley, she started opening cupboards and bins to see what she had to work with.

No one had paid much attention to her when she boarded the ship. The seamen were busy getting the ship ready to sail. The first mate muttered a greeting and then brushed her off as if he didn't have time for her. He told her to report to the galley below and to stow her things under the bunk behind the galley. There were two other bunks there, but they didn't look like they were being used. She hoped she wasn't sharing sleeping quarters with anyone else. That was something she hadn't thought about. 'It would be much easier to keep me femaleness a secret,' she thought, not knowing that whoever slept in those beds might also be her protection.

Mary chose the farthest bunk that had a ledge above the coarse lumpy mattress, stowed her bag, and went back into the galley. She began by locating all the cooking utensils, so she wouldn't look like a fool when she needed things. Then she checked the food supplies. She found plenty of flour, sugar, salt, lard, coffee, tea, and potatoes. There were two kegs of apples, a small slab of smoked pork, a barrel of green beans, eight scrawny onions, and several barrels of fresh water in the small room that was used to keep the goods cool and fresh. Mary had already seen chickens being loaded in cages as she boarded. 'Eggs for now, supper for later,' she thought. These were meager supplies, to say the least, to feed a crew of fifteen for a month or more. "Thank God for the potatoes," she murmured, as the first mate entered the galley.

"Hey, where's the tea and coffee? Come on, lad. Get a move on! The crew will want biscuits and a hot drink to warm their bones after the chill of the morn' and workin' on a wet deck. They'll be down in shifts once we are fully out to sea, so get yer arse busy."

"Yes, sir." Mary said, in her new deeper pitched voice. She put kindling and wood in the stove and lit it by lifting the glass on the oil lantern, which hung close by, catching the flame on a twig and holding it in the stove until the fire caught. The large urn, which sat on top of the stove, must be for coffee she surmised, so she quickly filled it with water from the keg in the corner. Then she threw a measure full of beans on the counter and began crushing them with a mallet. After she got the coffee started, she heated water for tea. Biscuits were next on her agenda, so she scooped out flour into a large tin bowl that she found hanging on the wall with other pots and pans. Then she added water and a small amount of yeast. She mixed the doughy mass until it looked and felt just the way it should. She dropped the dough in small masses, a few inches apart, on the big cast iron skillet that she found hanging on the galley wall. She added some small pieces of wood to the stove to make sure it was hot enough to cook the biscuits. Just as she slid the first batch onto the shelf above the open flame in the big oven, the crew began arriving, looking to fill their empty stomachs. Mary poured the men coffee or tea into tin mugs that were stacked inside an open basket next to a row of tin plates.

"Biscuits will be out of the oven in a moment." Mary tried to sound manly as she spoke.

"A young lad who knows how to cook?" One of the men started teasing her upon entering the galley. "The biscuits will probably fall to the bottom of our stomachs like lead!"

However, when he tasted her biscuits, he changed his words. "Hey, laddie, yer all right. These here buns taste good even without anything on em." The man with the earring in his ear shoved another biscuit in his mouth as he talked.

They ate in shifts with the captain and the first mate last. Later, she learned this was the only meal served this way. The first day was different because the officers were needed on deck until the ship was well out of the harbor and into the open sea. After that, the officers ate first. Mary was their waiter as well as their cook. The captain gave her a written list of duties, after confirming the boy knew how to read.

She was to feed the rest of the crew in shifts of five each, meaning she would serve three shifts of meals, three times a day. Rising at the crack of dawn, Mary spent the major portion of her day in the galley leaving her little time to worry about her plight. The little free time she had she spent practicing how to act like a man. She constantly worried that she would respond in her natural voice, rather than the deeper voice she now used.

Many of the passengers were seasick. She could hear their retching and moaning as they leaned over the railing above. Whenever she heard them, she said a little prayer of thanksgiving that her stomach wasn't acting up. Although the work was strenuous, and she was tired all of the time, Mary began to feel more confident that she would be able to maintain her brother's identity until she reached her destination. Worry dominated the first few days of her journey. She knew that discovery was possible at any moment. After a few days she started to let her guard down, as she soon realized the men were too busy to pay any attention to the young cook.

The crew usually acknowledged her with a grunt, or a demand for more food. Mary organized the galley the way she wanted it and planned her time accordingly. Everything seemed to be running smoothly, which gave her a false sense of security. She began to relax her alertness and was caught off guard when one of the seamen suddenly noticed her.

"Hey, boy, bring me some more tea," the large bald headed sailor hollered in his deep rasping voice. His sudden anger surprised her, and her hands began to shake. Mary grabbed the pot off the hot stove and rushed to refill the mug in the man's hand. He didn't see her come up behind him, and just as she poured the boiling water he moved his cup. The hot steaming liquid poured down the man's arm instead of into his cup before she could respond to his quick movement.

"Hey, ya burned me, ya little poofter! Why doncha watch what yer doin'! Drat! Now, don't jest stan' there lookin' stupid, clean up this mess and GET ME SOME TEA!" he bellowed, with a red, angry face. Mary was so flustered, and embarrassed, she wanted to run somewhere, hide her face, and cry, but she knew her brother would never act that way, so she mustered up her courage and stood up to him.

"I'm sorry, sir," she said in her new deep voice trying to control the trembling she felt inside. "Ye moved yer cup just as I was pourin'. I didn't mean to do it." Thinking quickly she added, "Here, sir, have some more, and we can all *drink to the health of your enemies' enemies.*"

The other seamen burst out laughing at her boldness of quoting the Irish toast. The tall skinny one with the beard decided to give his mate a bad time.

"Hey Jack, give the lad a break. A big bruiser like yerself is enough to scare the wits out of a big man like me. Quit bullyin' the little man. Besides, I think he's a real good lookin' young bloke, meself."

They all laughed again, and the big man said, "Yeah, I suppose ye would be lookin' at one such as him. Well now, let me get a look at the lad. I've always been partial to young fellows, meself."

Mary felt suddenly naked, and very vulnerable, as the big man grabbed her arm and held her while he looked her over hungrily. He held her face so close to his that she could see the deep scars and lines embedded in his face. His stinking breath smothered her with its rank odor. She wrenched herself out of his hold as her Irish temper exploded. She screamed in a deep bellowing voice, "Keep yer damn hands off me, sir! I don't have a likin' for ugly old men such as ye."

She rushed to the galley stove breathing heavily. After pulling the tray of biscuits out of the oven, she slammed it down in anger. They looked at her in surprise. The tall thin one smiled and winked at her when she looked his way, but the big man's lecherous grin sent a shiver down her spine.

Both men paid more attention to her after that. Mick was the tall thin man's name. He was always nice and friendly, but she caught him smiling at her backside several times when she was bending over the stove. The big man did more than just look at her, he tried to pinch her bottom every time he got the chance. If he succeeded, he would laugh like a crazy man as she hollered at him to leave her alone. Mary soon realized why the Captain had not made her sleep in the regular crew's quarters. One afternoon, when "Big Jack Bane" grabbed at her, the Captain happened to walk in and see what was going on.

"Bane, I'm tellin' ye right now, leave the boy alone. I gave the lad separate quarters because of the likes of ye, and I don't want him bothered in the galley either. Leave 'em alone, or I'll leave ye off at the next port! Is that clear, matey?"

"Aye, aye, sir," Bane said as he hurried out of the room, but he still leered, and he continued to reach for her every chance he got. Now, her every waking moment was full of worry, and she slept fitfully as she was racked with apprehension and nightmares. Fear of him made her long for the safety of her homeland and the bosom of her family.

It wasn't until the tenth day that she saw any of the passengers. When she finally did, she felt she wasn't quite so alone. She might not have seen the old man if he hadn't come into the galley. Her back was to him when he entered the room and asked her, "if the captain were about." His voice brought Ireland fully to her mind, and she turned around to see her neighbor, Mr. Bailey. He was so surprised to see her that he just stood there with his mouth open. Mary almost spoke with her natural voice as she was so happy to see him. Just as the words started to flow from her mouth, she remembered to lower her voice. "Mr. Bailey, are ye going to America, too?"

"Why yes, me boy, I am. I am really surprised to find ye here. Do yer mum and pop know yer here?"

"Well, I'm sure they do by now, sir. Me sister will have told them by now. It's all for the better, sir. I'll be sendin' them some money as soon as I can."

"I'm not so sure they would see it that way, lad. Jerry, isn't it? Ye know, lad, for some reason ye look a bit different to me, then ye did when I saw ye in the meadow that day with yer sister. In fact, maybe it's that ye sound different than ye did that day."

Sweat began to roll down Mary's back from the sudden knowledge that her disguise might soon be discovered. Mary's brain worked quickly.

"Well, sir, I was just getting over an illness when I saw ye last, sir. So, ye didn't really hear me normal voice then."

"Oh, that was it, was it? Well anyway, lad, I'm glad to see ye. Come topside when ye can. I'd like ye to meet me nephew, John Troy, who is traveling to America with me. He's a few years older than ye are and a fine upstanding young man. I'm sure ye two will get along just fine. I'm happy to know that ye both will have an acquaintance in America, because I'll be goin' back to Ireland in a few months. John has come to start a new life for himself. Me, I'm too old and too much in love with me beautiful, Erin, to leave that lovely land for any length of time. *The land of Ireland is one place that heaven has kissed with melody, mirth, meadow, and mist.*'" He quoted the old saying. "If yer lookin' fer work there, I might be able to help ye. I'm helpin' me nephew get a job with the railroad."

Mary was afraid that Mr. Bailey would discover that she was Mary, instead of Jerry, so she avoided him after that. She planned to find him when the ship docked in Boston, and to reveal to him her identity then. Maybe he could help her find a job. The knowledge that he was close made her feel much better. Just knowing that she now knew someone else in America helped that homesick feeling, which crept up often. Mary's spirits lifted drastically after she ran into Mr. Bailey. The apprehension she felt for the evil, Mr. Bane, was the only thing that put fear in her heart.

Chapter Six

"Bane Attacks"

October, 1873

"The clouds parted fully, and the moon shone briefly on his diabolical face."

A good night's sleep came rarely to Mary after Bane entered her life. When she did sleep, the seaman entered her dreams, turning them into nightmares. Her sleeping visions usually were of Jack Bane entering her quarters during the night. She could feel his lecherous hands on her, then hear his raspy voice yelling to the captain, 'Jerry is a girl!' Most nights she woke up with dread in her heart and covered in sweat, not sure whether the burly sailor had really been there. Whenever he entered the galley, fear would overcome her, and she would have to work hard to stop herself from shaking uncontrollably. She just felt a sense of evil coming from him. Intuition told her this man was led by the devil. Nightly she prayed, 'Keep me from the 'Evil One's' reach.'

If she walked by him while he was eating, or would have to pour him tea or coffee, he would grab for her leg or behind. She always had to be on guard. One morning, he waited for his mates to leave and came back when she was alone. He grabbed her tightly by the arm, pulled her close to him, and whispered suggestions of lewd and filthy acts he wanted to perform with her, the likes of which she could never imagine. Turning quickly, she jabbed her knee between his legs as hard as she could, and she twisted his finger backwards until he let go of her arm. Crying out in pain, he let go to console the aching between his legs.

"Don't ye ever bother me again, ye filthy pig!" Mary cried out, in her almost natural tone of voice. Realizing her error, she returned immediately to her lower voice and seething with anger hissed: "Mr. Bane, don't ye ever bother me again, or I'll tell the captain, and he'll have ye off this ship at the next port".

"Is that so?" He grabbed both of her arms, pulling her up to his face. "Well ye better remember this, laddie! If'n ye tell on me, by the time we reach port yer neck'll be slit from ear to ear, and ye won't be able to tell anyone nothin'. Ye understand me?" His dark eyes penetrated right through her, and his breath burned her face. Never had she felt so vulnerable, or so afraid, as she did at that moment. Two other seamen entered the galley just then, and he let go of her. Seeing her fear, the anger in his face morphed into a satanic grin as he left, still rubbing his crotch.

Mary's nightmares had begun that night. There was a lock on the galley door, and it seemed secure so far, but she knew it was so flimsy it could easily be broken. Someone had already tried the lock on several occasions. One morning, when she had slept soundly the night before, she found the galley door unlocked even though she was sure she had locked it the night before. Since no one bothered her, she wanted to believe it had been Captain Stallings, but Mary thought Jack Bane was more likely the one trying to get in.

As she got in her bunk one night, the ship began to roll more heavily. The sailors had said that they were on the edge of the squall that was seen earlier in the day, and that it would be difficult to miss completely. She hoped they would not suffer through too much rain, wind, and swells. She prayed the experienced crew could get them past the storm safely. She took the small bible from the leather pouch, with the MacSweeney crest etched into the bag, and read by the light of the oil lamp she had hung on a hook above her bunk. When it started swinging back and forth violently, she put out the flame. The wind whistled through the boards that separated her from the stormy deck above. She laid the bible on the ledge above her bunk on top of its leather case, intending to put it away in the morning. Pulling her grandmother's quilt up over her head, trying to keep out the noise of the storm, she tried to sleep.

The wind died down for a time, and Mary drifted into a deep sleep, when from far away she heard a click. Suddenly wide awake, she realized the sound was not the lock turning, but the door opening. Fear filled her, and her heart began to race. She didn't know what to do. As if by instinct, she slipped quietly out of the bunk standing flush against the short wall to the right of her bunk, which hid the sleeping quarters from the galley on the other side. There was no moon because of the passing storm. Darkness swallowed the galley. Silently, Mary felt her way around each familiar object in the dark. Everything had its proper place in the galley to keep it neat and clutter free, and to keep the items stationary in rough weather.

Listening carefully, she prayed that she had been dreaming. Then she heard another click as the door shut. Someone was in the galley. The storm had subsided a little. The clouds began to clear away, and the moon spilled its light through the galley porthole. When its dim glow momentarily lit the galley, she saw a large figure standing by the water kegs.

'Dear Lord, please let the captain be here for a drink of water.'

The clouds parted fully for a moment, and the moon shone briefly on his diabolical face. She was frozen with fear, and panic, at the sight of Jack Bane. She knew he was here to hurt her, to have his way with her, even thinking she was a boy. The moon disappeared as he felt his way down the wall toward her bunk and the bulkhead behind where she stood. Getting control of herself, she swiftly dropped to her knees, quietly crawled around the bulkhead, and hid in the small space between the large kegs of flour and sugar. There was no way she could avoid his path. Not finding her, he would surely come this way. The small aisle in the back of the galley led only to her bunk and the food storage. She had two choices; she could stay where she was and hope he didn't discover her, or she could run out of the galley and topside to face the weather, hoping to find someone to help her if she made it that far.

Before she could think, he was there. She could feel his evil presence and smell his body odor. The stink of his sweat was so powerful, she wanted to vomit. She covered her mouth to ward off his smell, and to cover the sound of her own breathing that grew louder with each breath. He slunk past her and then she saw his shadow lean over her bunk. When he stood up straight, Mary made her decision.

Quickly, she crawled out of her hiding place. Knocking into the sugar barrel on her right side, she caused it to rock back and forth noisily. The man turned around reaching for her in the dark, and he got a hold of the nightshirt she always wore to bed over her trousers. She reached out and grabbed the heavy skillet from the wall with her right hand. He grabbed the front of her nightshirt and yanked her back towards him. At the same time, she swung the skillet towards him as hard as she could. He let go of her when the huge wrought iron pan slammed into his arm as he swore with pain. Seeing her chance, she made a break for the galley door. Angry now, he pursued her as the pan clambered heavily to the floor. He reached for her as she pushed the door open and wrestled her to the ground.

"No ye don't, ye little bastard, ye aren't going to tell on me. I'm going to get what I want, and if ye cross me, little man, I promise ye, I'll get even with ye if it's the last thing I do."

His strong arms held her close to him, so she couldn't move her arms, and his stinking breath permeated her lungs. Holding her with one hand, he began groping toward her pants. Struggling frantically, she began to bite, kick, and scratch the evil man who held her. Finally, she slammed her head into his chin. When he lowered his face, she bit down on his nose as hard as she could. He screamed as he let go of her, and his nose ripped in her teeth. She jumped up and rushed out the door, tripping as she climbed the stairwell to the upper deck. After falling on her knees twice, she finally got topside and slammed the wooden hatch behind her. The stinging rain pelted her face, and the wind made it difficult for her to stand. She knew she wouldn't survive a struggle with him above deck in this weather. An image of Bane cutting her throat before throwing her overboard flashed in her mind.

The clank of the hatch door opening sounded behind her. Crawling now, she scampered quickly across the ship towards the passenger deck, but her stocking feet slipped on the wet deck. She could hear his terrorizing laugh as he closed in on her. His sea legs would make it easy for him to catch her. When she reached the passenger deck hatch, she lifted the heavy door with amazing ease and dove in headfirst. Bane grabbed her leg as she fell. Trying to kick him away, she tried to catch hold of the wooden ladder to the lower deck, but he wouldn't let go of her leg and held her dangling below the hatch. She could see many passengers bent over receptacles as the storm turned the contents of their stomachs to vomit, while the rest moaned, wept or slept. She finally grabbed hold of the edge of the wooden stair, trying to hold tight, as he tried to pull her back up above deck. Small splinters impaled themselves under her fingernails as she dug in.

He laughed with glee as she screamed in pain. No one heard her above the noise of the creaking ship and violent storm that pounded the deck. Her fingers felt like they were ripping apart, and she knew she couldn't hold on much longer. He was twisting her leg mercilessly. The pain was overpowering as blood rushed to her head. The pain in her fingers was unbearable, and she let go against her will. As he pulled her back above deck, he suddenly let go. She screamed as she fell into unconsciousness.

Chapter Seven

"Discovery"

Late October, 1873

"May the saddest day of your future be no worse than the happiest day of your past."

When she opened her eyes, strange faces surrounded her. Dark brown eyes stared at her from an unknown handsome face sitting next to the bed. A pensive worried look met her eyes. Beside him, an older, vaguely familiar man smiled, and she realized that he was holding her hand. When she saw Captain Stallings, she was reminded of where she was and her struggle with Bane.

"Well Missy, ye sure put one over on me." The captain spoke first. "I really thought ye were yer brother, Jerry. Ye know ye were right, ye are a darned fine cook. I should have known no boy could cook that good. How are ye feelin'?"

"I think I'm okay. What happened?"

"Mr. Bailey and his nephew have been right worried about ye. Don't be concerned about Mr. Bane. He is in the brig, and we'll be puttin' him ashore first thing when we reach Boston harbor. Mr. Bailey rewarded the Chinaman who saved ye, and he has also offered to pay yer passage, but ye did a fine job of cookin', and we don't have another cook, so if ye will just teach one of me crew to cook like that, we'll forget the price of yer passage."

"Thank ye, sir, but I signed on to do the cookin', and I'll be happy to finish me job for the wages we agreed upon, sir. If it be all right with ye?"

"Very good me girl, Mary, is it? I'll fix the lock on the galley door, or ye can sleep down here with the other lassies if ye prefer. We've about ten days left before we reach port. One of the passengers is a doctor, and he checked ye out and said that other than a few bruises, probably a headache, and some other aches and pains, he thought ye would be 'fit as a fiddle'. He said that yer injuries are minor, and that ye were mostly taken by fright. Course, we all understood the faintin' spell once we realized ye were a young lady instead of a young man."

Mary flushed with embarrassment, wondering who saw what that told them she was a girl. She had many questions: 'What had happened? Who was this Chinese man? And what did he do?' She was too exhausted to ask. Mr. Bailey gently wiped her forehead with a wet cloth.

"Mary, me girl, I knew there was something different about yer brother, Jerry, when I saw him this time. I want ye to meet me nephew, John Troy. He's from the Peafield area in Glenbeg, which is about 30 miles east of Macroom. He's on his way to America to start a new life there."

"It's very nice to meet ye, Mister Troy."

"It's a pleasure to meet ye as well. I am so impressed by yer gumption in undertaking such a journey all by yerself and in disguise too."

His voice was strong and vibrant, his smile; warm and inviting. She looked at his kind dark eyes and was suddenly tongue tied. Was she dreaming, or was he really as handsome as she thought? When he smiled at her, she felt like a little girl who was shown a big red lollipop and told she couldn't have it. Shyly, she smiled back, closed her eyes and fell back to sleep hoping the young man would still be there when she woke up.

Several hours later, when she was wide awake, she felt relief for the first time since she was first accosted by the big sailor, knowing that the evil, Mr. Bane, was actually gone from her life. She smiled, remembering the dream she had just before waking. Her mother was again spouting one of her everyday sayings, *'May the saddest day of your future be no worse than the happiest day of your past.'*

Mary was up and about the next afternoon, feeling strong enough to cook the evening meal for the crew. Immediately, she missed the freedom of being a man. The men acted so differently around her now that they knew she was a woman. Again, she felt the oppression that comes with being a woman, considered only chattel by men. But they were so polite, and they no longer used foul language in front of her, so it was hard to be angry with them for their treatment of her as a female. She realized, they were showing respect for her in the only way they knew. After she talked with Mr. Bailey, the excitement she felt before she left Ireland had returned, and she again began to daydream of a future in America.

Mr. Bailey told her he was sure he could find her lodging and work in San Francisco, and that he would lend her the money to get there from Boston. He had many emigrant friends who lived in that city. The captain told her that Mr. Bane would go back to London to answer to an earlier charge of murder that he had just learned about from one of the other crewmen. He also told her not to worry about testifying against him since they will not be pressing charges. The courts in England would surely convict him of his previous crimes and send him to the gallows. It seems, "during one drunken' shore leave, Bane bragged about rapin' and killin' a couple of no-good women and a few young Chinese boys in London." He had signed on the "Harmony" to make his escape because the authorities were looking for him.

Mr. Bailey also promised to find a job for the young Chinese man who had left his lower deck to rescue her from Bane. Mary was disappointed she had not met the man, and she did not understand why he was not allowed on their deck. She complained to Mr. Bailey and his nephew, so they presented her case to the captain who listened politely, but declined by saying that "no one else wanted 'yellow men' on this deck." Although she was angry about the treatment of the man who rescued her, as a woman she felt powerless to help him. She tried to go to the lower deck to see him, but was stopped by a seaman with an angry scowl.

A shiver of fear had momentarily gripped Mary upon hearing about Bane's murderous past, but Mr. Bailey convinced her that the courts of London would try him justly, and she would have nothing more to fear. The cloud that dampened her spirit, during most of the trip lifted, and her usual radiant smile returned. Once again, she felt exhilarated about her destiny. It was more than just the worry of Jack Bane being lifted from her spirits. It was the company of John Troy, which brought the most sunshine into her life. Never before had she felt the stirring inside that she felt when that handsome young man was nearby. Always confident, and talkative before, she now found herself almost speechless when he was present, which confused and angered her. These feelings were definitely not part of her plans for her "destiny". It bothered her because she constantly found herself making excuses to find him and talk to him.

Mary kept asking herself, 'Am I making a fool of myself over him? Am I chasing him?' She was not experienced in the way girls were expected to act in the presence of a young man, and besides, Mary had never been around a young man who interested her before. Leastwise, not one for whom she had such overpowering feelings. Those feelings were very confusing to her, and she found herself praying constantly for direction. When she boarded the ship in Ireland, she had thought life would be much simpler when she got to America. Mistakenly, she had assumed she would at least be treated as an equal. Her plans were to find a good paying position and to bring her family over from Ireland. Someday, she wanted to find a nice young man and some acreage, but a man had not been part of her present plans. She tried to fight her strong feelings as she was very afraid of ending up just like her mother. Her journey had certainly been an unforgettable adventure for a young girl, but it wasn't over yet. She still longed to see San Francisco.

'Maybe we could see it together,' she thought. 'I must go talk to him about his plans, but is that proper?' She debated with herself while she dried the pots and pans and put them away. Finally, she decided to find out what his plans were. When the galley was clean to her satisfaction, she went to her bunk and pulled out the pretty comb her mother had given her. When she pulled it out of the sea bag, the small leather pouch with her family's crest on it fell out and dropped on the deck. She picked up the pouch and rubbed her fingers fondly over the MacSweeney Coat of Arms that held her spiritual beliefs. 'How did it get back in my bag?' The last time she had her bible was when she had laid it on the ledge the night of Bane's attack. Someone must have put it back in her bag. The colors in the crest were beginning to fade, and the paint was beginning to chip. The shield that Jerry etched and hand painted held the old crest of a lizard in the center on a green colored strip between two larger panels with three black boars on yellow backgrounds. Two boars were above the lizard and one below. Above the small crest was an arm covered in blue armor, bent at the elbow and holding a battle axe. The bag held her rosary and her tiny bible. The ship suddenly lurched to the left, and she remembered what she was doing and put the leather pouch back in the deepest part of her sea bag.

She ran the small comb through her short hair, wishing it were long again. Whenever she combed her hair, she thought of her father who loved her long hair, especially when she piled it on top on her head with the glittery comb holding it there. She felt a surge of homesickness remembering her father's face. Her hair had grown a lot since they sailed, but it would take it a long time to reach the middle of her back again. She pulled the thick curls back and set the beautiful comb to hold them at the nape of her neck, although it was so short that the curls on the side stayed loosely by her ears. Then she put on the old, worn bonnet to protect her face and hair from the sun and the ocean air. It felt strange putting it on. She had become used to her male role. 'I surely don't need any more freckles though', she thought looking in the tin cup she shined up nightly, so she could see her reflection in it. Pinching her cheeks and lips a little, she took off her apron and brushed off the well-worn gray skirt that she had worn almost every day while at home in Ireland.

The two men were standing together by the railing at the back of the ship when she approached. Both gave her a warm smile and were genuinely happy to see her.

"Well Mary, ye are a pretty sight for an old man's eyes. I must say the doctor was right, ye are lookin' fit as a fiddle, me girl."

"Thank ye, sir, for everything ye have done fer me. Ye have taken the burden from me shoulders, and for that I am very grateful. I promise to repay ye, sir, for all yer kindness."

"No need to repay me for anything. I'm jest happy that ye are all right. Let a poor old man do a good deed. That's how we old folks can earn our way to Heaven."

"Mary, me Uncle Thomas is the most generous man I have ever met. I always say, 'He has the ability to tell a man to go to hell, so that he will look forward to making the trip.' He is accompanying me on this long trip because he has recommended me for a good position with the railroad in Eastern Oregon. A man who works for Henry Villard, of the newly formed Oregon Railroad and Navigation Company, is an old friend of his. He wrote Uncle Thomas that they need men to be crew bosses on the line that will go through the Blue Mountains in the Eastern Oregon territory. It will take a few years, I guess. I hear that Oregon is very beautiful. I was hopin' to make enough money to buy me a piece of land there in a few years, if it turns out to be as nice a place to live as I've heard it is from others," the young man said enthusiastically.

"Well now, lad," his uncle began, "don't ye be misunderstanding me now. I came over to see if San Francisco was all that I've heard it is, but I'm a selfish old man. Yer plans just gave me an excuse to come see if the land is as bountiful as they say, but then I'm goin' home," he said with a chuckle as he strolled down the deck. "I'll leave the two of ye alone for a while."

"He's givin' ye the blarney now, lass, because he's one of the kindest men I've ever known. It's well known that during the famine he saved many a poor folk from starvin' to death. He shared the stores he had with everyone!" The young man spoke with a smile that she felt clear to her soul. Mary knew that Mr. Bailey's warmth and generosity must have been inherited by his nephew. His eyes were a deep warm brown that sparkled when he smiled, and combined with his beautiful white teeth, dark brown hair, and handsome Irish features she found it hard to take her eyes from his face. Mary stared so long that time seemed to stand still. Pulling her thoughts together, she finally spoke.

"So yer goin' up to Oregon, Mr. Troy? I thought it was just wilderness up there. Will ye be doin' the hard labor of buildin' the railroad yerself, sir?" She wanted to know all she could about the plans of this soft-spoken man who stirred her emotions so easily.

"Yes Ma'am, certainly I will. A man can't expect the men who work for him to respect him, or to even listen to him, if they don't see that he knows exactly what he's doing. How else can he tell others to do it right? Puttin' through a railroad is a dangerous job too, what with dynamitin' and all."

"Dynamitin'? Oh no, sir, I'm hopin' nothin' will happen to ye. Will ye please be careful, Mr. John Troy?" She was suddenly concerned that she might never see him again.

"It sounds like ye might care a wee bit for me, Mary." His eyes twinkled as he spoke. "If there's an inkling of a chance that ye might take a likin' to me in the future, I'll be careful just thinkin' a lovely lass, like yerself, might be worryin' about me."

His dark brown hair kept blowing in his face, with the strong winds above board, and she suddenly reached up and gently pushed the hair back from his eyes. He smiled warmly. She blushed and again became tongue tied. "I don't know what to say, sir."

"I don't want ye to say anything Mary, me girl. Just promise to give me a chance when I'm worthy of askin' ye, when I've got somethin' to offer a lovely young lady like yerself."

He leaned over and got so close to her that she thought he was going to kiss her, when suddenly the magic moment was broken by loud voices from the other side of the ship. They heard a splash as gunfire rang out. He took her by the arm as they rushed to the source of the commotion, and they were shocked when they saw what the seamen were shooting at. Far off now, in a small lifeboat, they could see the unmistakable Mr. Bane and a companion. They were rowing as fast as they could, toward the south, away from them. Mary's jaw tightened as she felt a gripping fear wrenching her stomach. She knew he would get away, and she put her hand to her throat as she remembered his threat. They'll dock in Boston Harbor tomorrow. He would make it. She could feel it in her bones, and he would look for her.

Chapter Eight

"Boston, Massachusetts, USA"

Early November, 1873

"May the dust of your carriage wheels blind the eyes of your foes."

The steamship's passengers disembarked in Boston Harbor at midday. It took most of the morning for the big ship to dock and anchor in the busy harbor. Then the passengers had to stand in line to be checked before they entered the country. They needed to be free of illness and sign their name next to their name on the ship's passenger list. Mary wrote her name next to Jerry's, but his name had been crossed through and hers scribbled above it. They were lucky to pass through quickly, as it was a cold foggy day in the harbor. The three passengers' breath took cloudy form in the crisp autumn air.

"Winter is coming early this year," they heard a vendor say as they passed the open fish, fruit and, vegetable waterfront markets. They checked into a small but clean Inn close to the docks. A distant relative of Mr. Bailey's was the Inn's owner. They needed lodging while they waited the arrival of the "Lexington". It would take them around the horn and on to San Francisco. The ship was due in Boston sometime within the next couple of weeks, depending on the weather.

The morning after their arrival, John knocked on Mary's door and was surprised to find her fully dressed, putting on her shawl, and ready to go out.

"Top of the mornin' to ye, Mr. Troy," she said with a thrill of excitement in her voice. "Isn't it lovely out? I thought I would walk down to the docks and enjoy the salt sea air. It reminds me so much of me homeland. I want to see if I can find someone who can post a letter for me, so I can let me family know I have arrived safely."

"Oh, but Miss Sweeney, please don't be goin' anywhere by yerself! Ye know we really don't know where Mr. Bane is right now, and he did threaten yer life. I don't want to scare ye, but I don't want ye takin' any chances. Besides, there are a lot of muggin's and harmin' of men and women in this city, especially on the waterfront. It is jest not a safe place for any lady, or gentleman, to be about alone."

"Well thank ye, sir, for being concerned about me. Please call me Mary, sir. Surely, yer right. I was thinkin' of County Cork's harbors, I guess, and I was tryin' to forget Mr. Bane. Ye have been so kind to me already. I hate to rely on ye and yer uncle all of the time."

"Please call me John. It is me pleasure to look after a lass as lovely as yerself. There is no where I'd rather be."

Mary felt a flush of delight at his words.

"The truth of it is, I would never forgive meself if anythin' happened to ye. I feel badly now because I've got to leave ye alone with me uncle for a few days. I must go to Philadelphia to apply for my naturalization of citizenship papers. It's a simple thing, just signin' a paper and swearing an oath of citizenship, but there'll be a few days goin', a day there, and a few days comin' back, and I'll be worryin' about ye the whole time."

"That is nice of ye to say, John. What about me, John, shouldn't I apply for citizenship papers too?"

"No Mary, I asked about that. It seems women don't have much of a say over here. Only men can apply because only men vote, and that's what being a citizen allows ye to do, so I guess they figure there's no reason." His face got red as he spoke. He was embarrassed remembering the man's harsh laugh: 'Women? Citizens? Hey boy, you better learn what it's all about. Women ain't nothin' but chattel just waitin' to service a man, so she can take care of his needs and bear his offspring. We sure don't want women votin', now do we, Sonny? So, watch what you say!'

With that, the tough talking man in the old union army jacket waved John out of the line, dismissing him while he continued to laugh contemptuously. John still felt his face burning red with anger and embarrassment.

"Well, citizen or not, I've got to find me a job, so I can pay me own way. I don't like it that yer uncle is payin' me way. That is not what I intended when I left Ireland. I didn't want to get meself obligated to anyone, even folks as nice as ye and yer uncle. I'm goin' to see if I can work in the kitchen of this Inn until the ship leaves, so I can start paying yer uncle back."

Grinning at her appreciatively, John said, "I do admire yer spunk Mary, me girl, but please try to stay out of sight, so ye won't be seen, just in case one of Bane's swarthy mates stops in for some vittles and recognizes ye."

"Sure, and yer right, John. Thank ye so much for all that yer doin' fer me. I can't tell ye how much I appreciate it."

They were both smiling, awkwardly, when they were interrupted by a quiet knock on the door. John turned around and answered the door letting in the short Chinese man. He introduced the man who had saved her from Mr. Bane. John told her that Ah Kim had heard her screaming from his deck, which was right below the galley. He arrived just in time to tackle Mr. Bane as he was pulling her out of the hatch just before she fell. If the little Chinese man hadn't tripped him at that time, Mr. Bane surely would have pulled Mary back up by her leg and done God knows what else to her before he killed her. The Captain had arrived as Ah Kim was fighting Bane off with some self-defense techniques he had learned in his homeland. She had only seen Ah Kim from a distance, but she recognized him now as he took off his little cap and bowed, first to her and then to John.

"Vely nice to see you are okay, Missy. Also, vely nice to see you again, Meester John," The man spoke politely and with surprisingly good English. He was dressed in a dark blue silk tunic with loose silk pants of the same color. He had on little black shoes, and his black hair was pulled back into long braid in the back. He wore spectacles, had a little mustache, and a neatly trimmed beard that came to a point below his chin.

"How are ye, Ah Kim? I don't think ye have formally met the young lady whose life ye saved. This is Miss Mary Sweeney. Mary, this is Ah Kim. His name means "gentleman" in Chinese.

"How do ye do, Mr. Kim? *'Long may you live and may smoke always rise from your roof.'* Thank ye so much for helping me. It seems ye are well named, as it certainly was gentlemanly of ye to risk the wrath of the captain to come above deck to rescue me."

"Eet was my pleasure, Missy Mary." The man was about her height, and he politely bowed when he spoke to her with a pleasant smile on his face. "Thank you for your kind words. I do not like Meester Bane vely much, for many reasons. One reason I do not like him is the insulting words and names he uses, when speaking of people from my country. Most of my relatives do not understand his words of cruelty, but I studied the English language with my great-grandfather, who was a great scholar in my province. He said a boy with my name must have a proper education and know how to be a gentleman in all countries, so people of all nations will see the Chinese people are not all poor peasants. He wanted the world to know we are wealthy in knowledge. We are merely sons and daughters of Confucius, trying to follow our wise ancestors' teachings."

"I am very impressed, sir, with yer intelligence, yer bravery, and yer kindness. Yer great-grandfather was right, for ye represent yer country well. I am very happy to meet ye." Mary said, with genuine pleasure in her voice.

"Mary, Ah Kim is going to watch over ye while I am gone. He is going to Oregon to work on the railroad with me. I have asked him to wait and travel with us when I return. He has graciously agreed. I have found a ride with a couple of other men who are going to Philadelphia, for the same reasons. We have rented a buckboard and will share the costs. I am to meet them as soon as I pack a few things. Ah Kim will accompany ye wherever ye wish to go. Please be careful, and keep yer eyes open, Mary Sweeney." John bent over and kissed her gently on the forehead.

Mary flushed with genuine pleasure and stammered, "I will, John Troy, and ye take care, so no harm comes to ye. Are ye ready to take a walk to the waterfront, Ah Kim?"

"Yes, Missy, I'm ready. Please let me take thee on a less crowded path to that destination, for your safety. We can avoid where the European sailors hang out, and our journey will be less worrisome."

She went out with Ah Kim several times during the next few days. Although she sometimes felt she was being watched, she never saw Mr. Bane, or anyone else she recognized. They spent much of their time in the Chinese area of the city.

The food was so bad at the Inn, she had no problem talking the owner into giving her the Assistant Cook's position, which included serving customers, cleaning the dishes, and sweeping out the eating areas. When the regular cook got drunk and didn't show up for work again, she was promoted to his position. When she baked a batch of biscuits for Mrs. O'Grady, the older woman was glad to have her cooking for her customers.

It took John Stephen Troy only seven days to get all of his business done in Philadelphia and to return to Boston, but the "Lexington" had been detained and would be another two weeks before it arrived in port. In the meantime, John worked at the docks unloading cargo ships, while Mary cooked the Inn's daily meals. Mr. Bailey hired a carriage and driver and drove around the countryside seeing the New England coast. Ah Kim checked with Mary every morning to see if he could get her anything, and if she didn't need him that day, he worked for his cousins at a laundry a few blocks away.

Mary was amazed at how many relatives Ah Kim had. He explained that ancestry is very important to the Chinese people, so they keep track of the whereabouts of all of their relatives. It seemed as though everyone was a cousin, aunt, or uncle to Ah Kim.

On the day before their scheduled departure, Mr. Bailey talked John and Mary into quitting their jobs a day early. He wanted to give them a tour of the Massachusetts coast, which he had been exploring. Mary put on the dress she wore the day she went to Queenstown, seeking her destiny, and added a blue bonnet she just finished sewing. Mrs. O'Grady gave her a basket full of food and two jugs. One was filled with sweet tea, and one was full of whiskey. At the last minute, she grabbed her grandmother's quilt to make the grass and buggy ride more comfortable.

Mr. Bailey knew where he was going, so he rented the buggy and drove the team himself. He told them he was going to take them to see the Plymouth area and tell them about their new country's heritage, but after he learned it was thirty-four miles from Boston, he decided to stop instead at a high point overlooking the rugged coastline. Mary spread out the quilt, and they sat down to enjoy the biscuits and jam, fried chicken and hard-boiled eggs. Mary drank tea while the two men passed the other jug between them. When they asked Mary if she wanted a drink, she responded quickly, "No, thank ye, I don't touch the spirits, especially since I've seen the effects it can have on a man. I used to think the world of me Uncle Sean, but after seein' the changes in him brought on by the drink, I don't care if I ever have a drop of it."

John turned the jug down when his uncle passed it to him the next time. He smiled at her as he asked for a cup of tea, but Thomas Bailey took a swig from the jug and toasted himself.

"I drink to meself and one other, and may that one other be he who drinks to himself and one other, and may that one other be me." He then wiped his face with his sleeve and decided to go for a walk. "I think I'll stroll down this path a ways before we head back to Boston."

Mr. Bailey was carrying his jacket over his right shoulder, and the jug was swinging freely in his left hand, as he walked down the path with his fancy black bowler tilted on the side of his head.

John laughed and yelled loudly to his Uncle, *"May you live all the days of your life."* To Mary he said, "Me uncle likes a drink now and then, but he just becomes a more likeable fellow when he's drinking. If he acted like yer uncle, I'm sure I'd feel the same way ye do about the spirits."

"I'm sorry, John. I had no right to say anything to ye about yer drinking. I'm not yer mother nor yer wife." Mary said shyly, embarrassed about her earlier words.

"Would ye think about becoming me wife, Mary, when I come back from Oregon and have somethin' to offer ye?" John gently took her hand and looked deep into her green eyes. "I'd ask ye to marry me right now and take ye with me, but I don't know much about the land, or the Indians, and don't want ye to be in any danger."

"I'm very flattered by yer proposal, Mr. Troy, and I'm truly happy that ye did ask me to just think about it, because I'm not sure

I'm ready to become a wife." Mary chose her words carefully as she was filled with a flush of pleasure and excitement at his words. "Though if I was ready, ye'd surely be the one I'd pick, sir. And by the time ye return, John, I'll surely have made up me mind whether or not I want to marry ye, or whether or not I want to get married at all," She spoke in a teasing tone.

"Oh girl, don't ye be breakin' me heart now by tellin' me ye won't marry me when I return, cuz I'm countin' on that hope and some letters from ye to keep me spirits up while I'm away."

She smiled at him. He leaned over as she closed her eyes and waited with baited breath, for his soft lips to meet hers, when they heard a sharp cry off in the distance. They jumped up, simultaneously, and ran to the hill overlooking the path that John's uncle had taken. They saw him, at the same time, lying in the middle of the road several lengths away. They probably would have thought he was just drunk, if they hadn't also seen a dark figure, on horseback, lean over and use his horsewhip on Mr. Bailey once more before he raced down the path in the opposite direction.

John and Mary ran down the road and found his uncle bleeding from whip marks on his face and hands. His clothes were torn and hanging from his limbs. His bowler was smashed and covered in dirt. His jug lay overturned by the side of the road. Mary picked it up, pulled out the cork, and handed the jug to Mr. Bailey, who gratefully took a few drinks as he gasped for air and tried to tell them what happened.

"Who was that? Did ye recognize him? Did he steal yer wallet?" John kept battering him with questions.

"I didn't really see him. He had a hat on and a bandanna over his face, and he came at me from behind. I was tryin' to cover me face from his whip and never got a good look at him or his horse. I think he was a goin' to rob me and ran when ye two showed up," the old man said, looking pretty ragged.

"It was Bane, wasn't it?" Mary felt it in her bones.

"Oh no, girl, I don't think so. If he were smart, he'd be long gone from this area by now."

"I don't know, Mr. Bailey, he threatened to kill me if I told on him. I remember well, the evil way he looked at me when he promised revenge."

"Don't ye worry about it, lass. That fella was much bigger than Bane and not quite as ugly." Mr. Bailey tried to reassure her.

"I thought ye didn't get a good look at him, Mr. Bailey? Ye wouldn't be sayin' that just to appease me cuz yer thinkin' I'm a weak little woman, would ye?"

"Now Mary, me girl, I wouldn't do such a thing. I'm sure he was just a local scoundrel lookin' fer me wallet. Now, help me up and let's get back before he steals the buggy, and I have to pay for that. Besides, we got to get a packin', that ship leaves tomorrow."

Mary was quiet on the way back, while tending to Mr. Bailey's cuts with the old tablecloth, as John drove the buggy. Quietly, she said to him, *"May the dust of your carriage wheels blind the eyes of your foes."* He smiled up at her as the whiskey erased his pain.

When they reached the Inn, they helped Mr. Bailey to his room, and Mary returned to hers. She locked her door and put the chair under the knob while she packed her things. She tried to calm down by telling herself Mr. Bailey was probably right. Bane probably had left the area since the police were looking for him. When John came to take her down to dinner, she told him that she wasn't hungry, she had a headache, and was going to bed early. John brought her some biscuits, tea, and apples and told her to knock on the wall if she needed anything.

Mary thanked him, put the chair back under the doorknob, got in bed, and stared at the ceiling. She tried to think of those special moments that day with John, but when she did her memories were interrupted, just as they had been earlier in the day by the memory of Mr. Bailey's scream.

'Maybe I should marry John now. He would take care of me.' Then she chastised herself for being so weak. 'I came here to find me destiny, wherever it leads.' Praying for strength, freedom from fear, and for Bane to receive his final reward eventually brought her a restless sleep.

Chapter Nine

"Leaving Boston"

November, 1873

"Nothing is as easy as it looks, everything takes longer than you expect, and if anything can go wrong, it will at the worst possible moment."

Mary slept very little that night. Feelings of doom kept her mind alert and worried. She could feel that something was wrong, but she didn't know what she could do about it. The next morning, she felt even worse as the lack of sleep added to her stress. The water she poured from the ewer on the nightstand was tepid, and it didn't help much when she splashed it on her face. Her thoughts were elsewhere as she tried to concentrate on dressing and packing. When someone knocked on the door, she jumped from fright, even though she was expecting John and his Uncle. Her hands shook as she opened the door.

Both Irishmen seemed nervous too. John's eyes cautiously searched the hallway, and Thomas Bailey was leaning on his cane. His bruises and scratches were more noticeable than yesterday.

"Are ye ready, Mary? We need to be hurryin' this mornin'." John was not in his usual, easy going, frame of mind.

"What's wrong? Ye are making me really nervous." Mary's terror was growing.

"Just do as I tell ye, please Mary." John lowered his voice to an urgent whisper and looked deep into her eyes as he spoke. "We have a plan. We're leaving now with no goodbyes to anybody, including the Innkeeper. We'll be goin' out the rear of the Inn. Just be as quiet as possible and don't be askin' any questions. Ye need to trust me!"

John took Mary by the arm, picked up her bag, and led her swiftly down the stairs and out the back door. Ah Kim and two of his cousins were waiting in the alleyway. One took her bag, the other two carried two large trunks, which she assumed were John and Mr. Bailey's. There wasn't a buggy waiting to take them to the ship, which surprised Mary, especially when the two men seemed to be in such a hurry. Then she noticed that only Ah Kim and one of his cousins followed them to the ship. She didn't see the young man who was carrying her bag. Concerned that her things were being stolen, she turned around to ask Ah Kim, who just raised his finger to his lips before she could say anything. Mary prayed the man would be at the ship with her possessions.

The long walk to the pier was tiring. By the time they reached the boarding plank, her feet were aching miserably. She was not used to the high button shoes she was wearing. They had been one of her few purchases when she arrived, as she had only brought the pair of men's boots, and a pair of very old worn shoes with her. Her feet felt raw where the narrow shoes constantly pressed on her feet. The old stockings were worn too thin, and they were not giving her any protection from the abrasiveness of the new leather. As she walked up the boarding plank, she looked forward to resting her feet, but when she reached the deck, she was surprised that John rushed her below deck to their cabin. John led her down to the second deck and rushed her into a small private room, which Mr. Bailey had paid extra for. Thankful to finally be able to sit down, Mary rested on the old trunk that Ah Kim and his cousin had set down in the middle of the room, and she noticed immediately that her bag was nowhere in sight. Before she could raise a complaint, John spoke to Ah Kim in a loud voice.

"Ah Kim, I would like to ask another favor of ye. As this trunk is getting very shabby, I have purchased this new one, which I had delivered to the ship early this morning. I will quickly transfer my belongings to the new one and ask that ye will dispose of the old one for me. Perhaps ye have a cousin who would like to have it. I will gladly pay ye to take it and to do whatever ye want with it. Here are two bits, for yer trouble."

"Thank you, Mr. Troy. You are very generous. I'm sure one of my cousins will be able to find a use for this trunk. A little airing out will take the dampness out and make it smell like new again." Ah Kim bowed as he spoke.

"Mary, me dear, please make yerself comfortable." John resumed speaking in an unusually loud voice. "I know ye have been feeling poorly, so perhaps ye would enjoy a nap before we sail."

Mary started to speak, but John put his fingers to her lips and handed Mary a note with some money in an envelope.

Dear Mary,

Please don't speak. I have changed your traveling plans because I am worried about your safety! Mr. Bane has booked passage on this ship under a different name. Neither the Captain of this ship, nor the Constable of Boston would listen to my plea to have him arrested. There is no arrest warrant for him here, so there is nothing we could do. The captain of this ship did not want to bother with what he considers an immigration problem, and the "Harmony" has already sailed. I feel your life is in danger here! Ah Kim is going to accompany you to San Francisco by other means. He assures me that you will arrive safely. Mr. Bane will think you are on the ship, for some time. Please follow Ah Kim's advice and do as he says. I am leaving you in his care. Have a safe trip! We will see each other soon. Please think of the one who cares about you often, as he is missing you already.

I remain devoted to you,

John S. Troy

Mary looked so surprised, when she finished reading the note that John took her face in his hands, kissed her gently on both cheeks, and then softly on her lips. Then he opened the empty trunk and motioned for her to get inside. She was shivering with fear as she put the note in the envelope, and she put it in the bodice of her dress close to her heart. She climbed in and curled up on top of the blanket that lined the bottom of the trunk. Pulling her knees close to her chest, she laid on her side. Ah Kim deftly covered her with a lightweight muslin cloth. A panicky closed in feeling came over her as he closed the trunk, but when she noticed a few small holes in the lid, she realized that she would be able to breathe. She heard the trunk latch firmly and then was jostled around as they lifted the trunk and put it between the two Chinese men's shoulders. Ah Kim and his cousin carried her out of the cabin. This couldn't be happening to her! Murphy's Law kept running through her head. *'Nothing is as easy as it looks. Everything takes longer than you expect, and if anything can go wrong it will at the worst possible moment!'*

The two men were laughing and talking in Chinese, as they carried the heavy trunk down the gangplank through the alleyways. Mary tried to breathe calmly, but a memory kept flashing through her mind, of the time the Doherty boys had locked her in their smoke house when she was nine. She had been there for four hours before her father found her crying hysterically. They had been playing a game of hide-and-seek, and the brothers had assured her that this was a perfect place to hide. When she hadn't come in for dinner, the family started looking for her. That instance had left her with a fear of small places.

When they finally opened the trunk, Mary found herself in a small two room flat where her bag was waiting for her. Ah Kim introduced her to Ming, another cousin, then left her there with the young woman, for several hours. When he returned, he told her that the ship had sailed, and that Mr. Bane had boarded just before it left. Unfortunately, he had also seen several of Bane's friends on the dock after the ship had departed.

Mary had many unanswered questions: Would she ever get to San Francisco, and how? Would she ever see John Troy or Thomas Bailey again? What did Bane want with her? Why wouldn't he leave her alone? Mary sensed that he was so evil that he would kill her for revenge. She knew she had damaged his nose when she bit him that night, as her teeth had felt bone. Ah Kim said he would explain everything that evening and left her in anticipation. Exhausted, she finally fell asleep on the small hard sofa and dozed fitfully, wishing for the first time that she were back home in the old bed with her sisters, safe and sound. Bane's face kept invading her dreams, keeping her from a sound sleep. Mary said the rosary prayers on her fingers, and she worried what tomorrow would bring, as she waited for her new best friend to come and rescue her again.

Chapter Ten

"A New Disguise"

November, 1873

"May the ten toes of your feet always steer you clear of misfortune."

Mary woke up on a mat in a corner of the room, and tried to remember the events of the night before. Ming was sleeping peacefully on a mat of her own nearby. Mary thought Ming was the most beautiful girl she had ever seen. Ming's shiny ebony hair was pulled into a bun at the nape of her neck. Her dark hair, porcelain skin, and tiny features were so perfect that Mary couldn't stop staring at her. Mary was embarrassed when the almond shaped black eyes opened, and the Chinese doll smiled at her. Mary closed her eyes and went back to the night before. She was amazed that she had slept at all, considering her state of mind.

When Ah Kim had returned, Mary was dozing on the small sofa while the young Chinese beauty was brewing tea on the little wood stove in the corner. The cousins were with Ah Kim, and they brought steaming rice balls, dumplings, and strips of pork with snow peas. Mary had not eaten since early morning, and although she'd never before eaten anything like what they offered, she ate voraciously. She was surprised at how good the food tasted and how much she liked the flavors. It took her a while to figure out how to eat with the two wooden sticks they gave her instead of a fork. Ming showed her how to use the foreign eating utensils, and after a little practice she succeeded and wolfed down her share of the menu. The hot tea tasted so good that she drank three of the tiny cups full. Ming took her hand and led her into the second room, where the hand-woven colored mats were rolled up and stacked in the corner. Ah Kim followed them, bowed politely, and asked if he could speak with Mary privately. Ming bowed and left the room.

"Missy Mary, you must get a good night's sleep now. My esteemed relatives are helping me form a plan to get you out of this city without any of Bane's friends seeing you. We must leave right away if we are to meet Meester John, and Meester Bailey, in San Francisco. The harshness of winter will settle upon this land soon, so haste is required. If we do not leave first thing in the morning, our trip across the country will certainly be perilous. We could also be forced to stay in Boston until the blossoms return in the spring. I promised those esteemed men that I would get you to San Francisco safely, and I believe if we leave tomorrow, I will be able to do that. We will finalize our plans tonight and rise early in the morning. Is there anything you need, Missy Mary?"

"I put all me trust in ye, Ah Kim, and thank ye for all yer trouble. Mister Bane would have killed me if ye had not saved me on the ship. I am honored ye are with me."

Mary tried to hide the fear, which still hung heavily on her heart. Ah Kim bowed again and left the room. She felt like a newborn lamb at the mercy of the shepherd who was the only one who could save her from the wolf. The Chinese people, and their customs, were very foreign to her, and communication with his relatives was difficult. She hoped that Ah Kim would always be close. Her only knowledge of the Chinese people came from the rude remarks, and jokes, she had overheard from the sailors on the ship. Most of those conversations consisted of slurs, like "slant-eyes" and "yellow-skins". She thought Ming's eyes were beautiful, and she didn't see much difference in the color of their skin and hers. The only remark she remembered Bane saying was something about their love of opium and gambling.

"Ye can always bait a Chinaman with a game of poker, or some of the white powder, and then ye've got em at yer mercy. Confucius couldn't even save 'em then."

When the sailors had finished laughing, one of them told a hair-raising story about Bane keeping a young Chinese captive while on shore leave. The story began with Bane promising him opium, for helping him do some evil deed, but before the sailor could continue the story, Bane shut him up with a knife to his throat, as he whispered angry words in his ear. Mary remembered the sweat on the man's brow and the look of sheer terror on his face, when Bane had finally released him.

'Was that opium she had smelled the night before?' She wondered. After Ming had extinguished the lamp, and they had settled down on their mats, a sweet smelling odor had seeped under the door from the other room where the men were meeting. If the odor was opium, she wondered if she was feeling the effects of the drug. She hadn't slept that soundly since leaving Ireland. Her head hurt a little too. Uncle Sean always had headaches after a bout with the bottle. 'Did she have a headache from worry, or was there another reason?'

Ming opened her eyes again, and the two women rose, rolled up their mats, dressed, and combed their hair. They went down the hall where they relieved themselves in a hole in the middle of the floor. Ming made sure no one else was around when Mary went in and stood outside until Mary came out, then led her back to the flat. Mary was almost sick from holding her breath because of the rank odors in that room. Ming opened the window and brought Mary a cup of tea and a rice ball, and she soon started feeling better.

Ah Kim came in with a brocade jacket, silk pants, as well as some black slippers, and he told Mary to please put them on. When she was dressed, Ming motioned to her to sit down on the floor, then she placed a muslin cloth around Mary's shoulders and opened a tin with some kind of black dye in it. Starting at the roots, Ming combed the wet substance carefully through Mary's hair, effectively turning her dark red locks to black, but the dye did not take out her natural curl, so Ah Kim told her they needed to cut her hair again.

"The curl in your hair will give you away, Missy Mary, we must cut it."

This time the tears flowed as Ming parted her hair down the middle and cut her hair to just below her chin, all the way around and just above her eyebrows in front. Ah Kim heated a flat stone on the stove, and Ming used it to flatten the little bit of curl that remained, as she combed all of her hair out straight and under, all the way around. Ming used a piece of charcoal to outline Mary's eyes trying, to make them look more like the shape of Ming's eyes. The finishing touch was to apply a yellow-beige powder to her face, hands, and arms to cover her numerous freckles. When she looked in the small cracked hand mirror that Ming handed her when she finished, Mary did not recognize the face that looked back at her. Except for her large eyes, she looked remarkably Chinese.

Ming showed her how to walk humbly, like Chinese women are expected to walk, and how to properly bow. Then Ah Kim revealed his plans to get her safely out of Boston. A prominent Chinatown resident had died, and there was a funeral procession that afternoon, leading out of town to the Chinese cemetery, where all Chinese people were buried until their bodies would eventually be returned to their homeland. According to Chinese belief, the soul would not rest until the body reached home for a proper Chinese burial. When the procession passed their flat, they would casually mingle with the mourners as they headed to the burial grounds.

"Missy Mary, we must use every precaution, as Mister Bane's friends might be looking for me too. I believe there might be a price on my head for helping you on board the ship. I must stay away from you until we are out of the city. You and Ming will join the crowd of wailing women and hide in the burial grounds after the service. I will bring a wagon with supplies to pick you both up in the woods. I will bring your bag with me. Just do what Ming does and try to remain calm. I promised Mister John, I would take good care of you, and I will do that, Missy Mary." He smiled, reassuringly.

"I put my faith in ye, Ah Kim. *'May the ten toes of your feet always steer you clear of misfortune.'*"

"Ah, Confucius would like that proverb. Are you ready?"

"I'm ready." Mary took a deep breath and prayed to be strong. The men left just before the procession arrived. Mary and Ming joined the throng of people, and they ended up in the middle of the crowd. She kept taking deep breaths, trying to dispel the tightness in her chest, which she knew was due to the fear that threatened to overwhelm her. Walking and wailing with the other women, she soon realized that no one was paying any attention to her, and she started to relax. Looking down, as she had been told to do, she followed Ming's actions. The procession was like a parade and many Americans, of other cultures, were lining the streets to watch the spectacle.

Everything was going smoothly until she took a quick look at the crowd watching the funeral procession. As they approached the corner that turned onto the main road out of town, she saw the familiar faces of two sailors from the "Harmony". They were two who always hung around with Bane and were just about as mean. Mary felt panicked. Time stood still as fear paralyzed her. Ming saw her fear and grabbed her hand, shaking her back to the present. The rest of the crowd closed around them, and in unison the women shut their eyes and wailed. When she closed her eyes, real tears welled up in them. A yell from the spectators caught her attention, and she opened them in time to see the two sailors yelling and chasing a small Chinese boy down the street.

"That filthy, little 'yellow eyes' stole my money. Grab the heathen!" The shorter man hollered as he ran up the narrow alley after the quickly fleeing child. The larger man ran clumsily after him, pushing another man out of his way, taking a swig out of a liquor bottle at the same time.

Mary sighed in relief, as the women continued down the street to the outskirts of town. As the mourners spread out around the enshrouded body, Ming led Mary to the edge of the crowd. The two girls moved quietly into the large bushes behind the proceedings and hid inside. Ming sat on the ground without moving for the longest time. Mary admired Ming's concentration as she was having trouble sitting still. No matter how she sat, some part of her body began to ache or became numb. She kept quietly trying to change positions as the branches kept poking her. They sat there for so long that Mary had nothing to do but think. She missed her family dreadfully and would have given anything to be in the little cottage, sitting by the hearth, instead of cramped up and hidden inside a bush in Massachusetts. *'There is no fireside like your own fireside,'* she kept saying to herself.

It seemed like just yesterday that she had gone through her divine awakening at the crossroads. Now she wondered if she had misread the omens that day. Then she decided it didn't matter, because she couldn't change what had happened since then. Here she was, in America, furthering her adventures by trekking across this vast land with two young people with whom she could barely communicate, even though she now resembled them. For the moment, she was also one of the Chinese immigrants that were treated poorly because of their skin color, by the other immigrants who had come to America. The journey ahead now frightened her more than she had ever imagined it would. Mary had felt the prejudice against the Irish Immigrants while she was working at the Inn, having to endure Irish "Mick" jokes and other bigoted remarks. She was now disguised as Chinese; the people who were not treated much better than black people, who had been captured against their will and brought here as slaves. She was beginning to realize that America was not the haven for equality and freedom that the world thought it to be.

It seemed like they were there for hours before the crowd left, and dusk began to settle over the countryside. Still, Ming did not move or speak, and every time Mary started to speak Ming would quietly put her finger to her lips and shake her head "no" to her. When Ah Kim finally arrived, Mary was cramped with pain.

"Missy Mary, Ming, you may come out now. We are the only ones here."

Mary was so stiff she could hardly stand up when she climbed out of the bushes. Amazingly, Ming stood right up and appeared to have no ill effects from hours of sitting in the same position.

"I am so glad you have gotten to know my dear cousin, Ming, as she will be traveling with us to San Francisco. My Uncle has arranged a wedding for her there with a fine young man from the same province in China. Ming will marry Quan as soon as the wedding can be arranged in San Francisco's "Chinatown.""

"I thought she was married to the man who lived in that flat back there."

"No, she was just staying with another cousin, but we told the owner of the building that she was his wife, so there would be no questions."

"Congratulations, Ming, I hope ye will be very happy!" Mary spoke directly to the fragile Chinese beauty whose pleasant smile beamed back at her.

"Thank you for your kind wishes."

Mary was surprised at her almost perfect English as she had only heard her speak broken English before.

"Quan is from a strong and handsome family. I know my father will have chosen a kind man who will be a good husband to me and a loving father to our children."

"I am happy for ye." Then she turned to Ah Kim, "Are we going to stay here tonight?"

"No, Missy Mary, we are going to travel for an hour and then stay with some of our cousins who live deep in the forest. I am confident they will welcome our arrival. Their leader is a good friend of my uncle's. He was kind enough to help my uncle when his wagon broke a wheel on his way west many years ago. Their campsite is a secret as many Americans would run them off if they knew they were here. The clan keeps to themselves. Only a few of their members go to town for supplies on rare occasions. They grow their own food and trade for whatever they need. We must go now if we want to find their camp before it becomes too dark."

"I am very tired. Would it be all right if I lay down in the back of the wagon?"

"Certainly, Missy Mary. My carpetbag will make a fine pillow. We will be there soon. Have a good rest."

Mary nestled in among the bags, bedding, and supplies, and promptly fell asleep, even though the rough road made the wagon ride bumpy beyond belief.

Chapter Eleven

"The Mysterious Society in the Forest"

November, 1873

"Gently he kissed her eyes and cheeks, and ended by kissing her lips so softly, and sweetly, that she thought she would melt from the heat."

It was a rough ride, and Mary's bones ached. She was so exhausted she could hardly keep her eyes open, but the bumpy road made it difficult to sleep. The wooden wheels often bounced heavily, as they hit the large rocks, and ruts, in the road. She woke up when the wagon finally came to a stop. When the wagon didn't start moving again, she sat up. Although it was dark, it was a clear night, the moon was almost full, and the stars twinkled in the sky. They sat on the edge of a vast meadow in the forest. It was so quiet it was eerie. So she was relieved when the crickets resumed their noisy banter.

Ah Kim and Ming sat silently on the wooden seat in the front of the buckboard. The horses started acting as if they were disturbed about something. Ah Kim was having trouble holding them back. On the other side of the glade, three young Chinese men dressed in bright colored silk tunics entered the clearing on magnificent horses. Mary's eyes were drawn to the rider in the middle. The man sat proudly in his saddle, as if he were royalty. His elegant silk garments were brighter than the others, and he appeared to be the leader. All three men wore their hair in the traditional long braid that Ah Kim had told her was called a queue, but these men's heads were shaved, except for the braid. There was something about the baldness that made them look powerful and strong. Mary couldn't take her eyes away from the rider in the middle. As they neared the wagon, she could see that his piercing eyes were not brown like the other two men. Each man wore a gold pendant, adorned with some Chinese symbols. The two outside riders wore dark blue silk tunics, with black silk pants and leather boots that fit snugly to their knees. The man in the middle wore a tunic of bright red silk, with a black sash at his waist. His tunic was open down the front, and his bare chest displayed the brilliant pendant in the moonlight. Mary felt herself blushing, as she mentally admired his muscular body.

As he came closer, she forced her eyes back to his face, when his deep blue eyes, the color of the sky, met hers. He smiled at her, and she suddenly felt safe and warm. Then she remembered her disguise, and she remembered what she had been told a Chinese girl should act like, so she lowered her eyes. When the leader spoke, it was with almost perfect English.

"Good evening, travelers. May I ask your names, and what you seek in these woods?"

"My name is Chong Ah Kim. I am the nephew of Chong Hong Chang of Shanghai. I am seeking the esteemed and honorable Chow Jin of the Tong. May I ask who I am speaking with?"

"My name is Chow Lien. I am the son of Chow Jin. What business do you have with my father?"

"My uncle and your father became friends many years ago, when they were young men. I have a message for your esteemed father from my uncle. I am also here to return property your father was kind enough to loan to my uncle, long ago. If you are his honored son, then I have also come to ask you and your father for help. The young lady riding in the back is in grave danger, and my cousin and I are escorting her to San Francisco. The young maiden has traveled a long way, and there is an evil man after her who is seeking revenge, for a minor infraction. The 'Evil One' has vowed to take her young life, and has sent other men, of similar nature, to pursue her. Is it in your power to help us?"

Mary had never heard Ah Kim speak such perfect English before, and it surprised her.

"If your words ring true, my father and I will help you. Please follow me."

The young man flashed another brilliant smile, as he turned the reins and led the black stallion snorting and prancing into the woods. Ah Kim followed him closely, and the two other men followed the wagon. Mary sat in the back of the wagon with her beloved quilt wrapped around her, to keep her warm. She was glad the two men were following them, as the blackness behind them and Ah Kim's words made her again wonder, if someone was following them, and what she had done to make them so angry. The light from the moon shining through the trees made their travel easier, on the narrow path through the forest.

A dim light ahead grew brighter when they entered a much larger clearing, where six small cabins surrounded a larger one. The cabins were lit and well protected, as sentries were posted all around the outer edge of the clearing. Smoke rose from the larger cabin, and a campfire was burning in a circle of rocks, where several women were cooking over the open fire.

The small caravan stopped in front of the large cabin. Chow Lien went inside and returned with an older man. Both men towered over all of the other men. The older man had a tiny thin beard and mustache, which were neatly trimmed. He wore a red silk cap on his head that matched his red tunic. Chow Lien and his father wore the only red tunics. The older man was a little shorter and stouter than his son, but he too was handsome. Chow Jin put his hands together, as if in prayer, and bowed to them. Ah Kim stood up in the wagon and bowed back.

"My esteemed father, this man's name is Chong Ah Kim. He says his uncle is Chong Hong Chang, who is an old friend of yours. His uncle has sent him to you with an important message. Ah Kim is also asking for protection, from those who would hurt the young woman who is traveling with him. He appears to be an honorable man, and as my esteemed mother foretold, 'an interesting stranger would arrive when the full moon rose,' so I brought him to you as he requested."

"I am honored to meet you." Ah Kim bowed. "My uncle speaks very highly of you. You saved my father, and his two brothers, when they went west to seek their fortune. I was told that they were attacked and robbed between Massachusetts and Pennsylvania, and that you, Chow Jin, and some of your men, kindly saved them from the murderers. I bring you my uncle's apology for taking so long to return your kindness. I am here in their name, to give you reparation, but perhaps we should speak of this privately. As my uncle's nephew, I also ask for protection for the young woman that my cousin, Ming, and I are traveling with."

"Please come inside where we may discuss in comfort, my honored friend, Hong Chang, and his words. Hong Chang's nephew will always be welcome in my home."

Chow Jin smiled broadly, bowed, and welcomed them with an exaggerated sweep of his arm. His handsome son was there in an instant to help Mary down from the wagon. Taking her hands in his as she stood up, he pulled her toward him, and she fell directly into his arms. Laughing boldly, he put his hands around her waist and effortlessly lifted her to the ground. "I am intrigued by your disguise, but your beauty is far from hidden beneath your unusual appearance." He whispered the words as he set her down.

Mary pulled away from him, feeling young and vulnerable.

"Sir, I'd ask ye to keep ye hands to yerself!"

She tried to act angrier than she really was, but she didn't know how to react to the feelings that had flooded through her when she was in his arms. His eyes sparkled as he laughed, took her by the arm, and led her into the large cabin. Minutes later, she found herself sitting on a beautiful carpet by the warm hearth, next to an older woman, whose beauty even in middle age was overpowering. The young man introduced her as his mother, Lily. The woman had blue eyes like her son's, so Mary realized that his mother probably had a European mother or father.

An hour later, Mary was eating a large bowl of rice and fish heads and drinking hot tea. The rice was steaming, and the fish heads even tasted good. Ah Kim suggested to Chow Jin that he dismiss everyone that he did not fully trust. The head of the tong cleared the room, except for his wife and son and the three newcomers.

"I trust all of the members of our secret society with my life, and my wife and son's lives, but some things are better only spoken of between a few. My wife is also my astrologer, and she accurately reads my tea leaves. I take her advice on everything."

"I do not want to endanger my traveling companions, or anyone else, with the story I will be telling." Ah Kim bowed to all. "I trust that all here understand that this story will not be repeated outside of this room." Then he began to relate the story of long ago.

"When my father was young and newly married, he and his two brothers came to America to seek their fortune. They worked for many months in New York City, at their cousin's laundries, until they earned enough money to buy supplies for their planned adventure. They were headed west when they came upon the band of murdering thieves. The bandits destroyed their wagon, stole their supplies, and beat the men. They were getting ready to hang my father and my uncles, when Chow Jin and his men arrived. Their skills saved them from the men who wanted to kill them because of the color of their skin. Chow Jin slew three of them single handedly. The leader, and two others, got away. My father and uncles owed Chow Jin their lives. He not only rescued them, and restored them to good health, he also gave them money to replace their lost goods, and he helped to finance their search for the gold mine."

"Did you know your uncle also saved my life, Ah Kim?" Chow Jin interrupted Ah Kim's story. "There was one in our society, who was not the good man he pretended to be. Although he took the oath of our society, he was a man who spoke with two tongues. Hong Chang caught him sneaking up behind me, with his long knife raised against me. Your uncle repaid his debt."

"My uncle did not yet repay your generosity. If you will permit me, I have a bag for you." After searching through his carpetbag, Ah Kim brought out a small leather pouch and handed it to Chow Lien. "This bag of gold repays the money you gave to my uncle, and it also gives you one-quarter share of the fortune that has so far been discovered. My father, and his brothers, did find a gold mine in Eastern Oregon. They filed the claim under an assumed name, because our people are treated poorly in the area, and brought out only as much gold as they could safely bring with them. My father drew a map to the mine, which contained no words or names, so that no one could identify the area, but the three brothers. Each brother put into their own memory the way to the mine, but each carried only one third of the map, and for their safety, they each took a separate route home. My uncle, and one brother, made it home to China. The third brother, who was my father, Chong Hop Kee, was murdered. His gold and map were stolen in San Francisco aboard the ship that was going to leave that day to take him home. My cousins, at whose home my father was staying before he departed, wrote to my uncles, describing the man who was known to have killed him. I believe that man is Jack Bane."

Mary let out a gasp at his words.

"He is the same 'Evil One' that is after this young girl, who is traveling under my protection. I have not only been sent to repay your debt, but also to find my father's portion of the map, so that the mine can be found without my two uncles having to return to America. They are elderly and not in good health. They asked me to represent their claim, and to see what I can do to finalize the deed. I have seen the other two parts of the map, and have memorized them, but my father's map was the most important part, as the mine is located on it. I need it to find the mine. Bane will have difficulty finding it, as he needs those two parts to tell how to get there."

Mary surprised herself by interrupting. "Ye mean ye were watching Bane, and that is how ye came to save me?"

"Yes, Mary. It has taken me several years, and much traveling, to find the man who killed my father. When I have taken back my inheritance, I plan to avenge my father's death, and to return his honor. I believe it was his gang of men who accosted the three brothers in the first place. As a result, he is aware of your secret society, and he fears them. But, he does not know that I am the one he should be afraid of. Bane has hidden the map somewhere, but I don't know where. I searched his quarters thoroughly on the ship. I was interrupted the first time and barely got away, leaving evidence of my search. I believe he moved the location of the map after that. I am afraid he has become suspicious of me, and I hope that he does not know who my father was. I will be going to Oregon to try to find the mine, from the memory of my uncles, and hope that Bane will not be following me. First, I am escorting my friend, Miss Mary Sweeney, to San Francisco."

"If he is headed west, why do you think this girl is in danger from him?"

"My cousins have heard his friends asking about Miss Sweeney. When he tried to accost her on board the ship, she was able to maim his face, before I tripped him on deck during the storm, and she was able to get away. As it was dark and stormy, I don't think he knows which one of the Chinese men stopped him, and was responsible for his arrest. Fortunately, the captain and first mate arrived at that moment. After I told them what happened, they took him away. I am sure that he was very angry when he found out that she was not on the other ship, on her way to San Francisco as planned, which he also booked passage on. My cousins overheard a conversation in a Boston tavern, of which two men said that they had jumped ship and made it back to shore with orders to find her. He will certainly suspect me, when he finds out that I am traveling with her, so they will also be looking for me. I am not sure of his motives, as I do not understand why he should be so angry with her, except for the scar on his face. You must have made him very mad, Miss Mary."

"Mr. Bane is a very evil man. I just tried to get away from his lecherous clutches when he entered me room that night." Mary's voice broke as she spoke. The news that Bane killed Ah Kim's father made her fear him even more.

Lily and Ming took her to one of the smaller cabins, gave her a tea they said would help calm her down, and washed the powder and charcoal off her face and arms. The tears she had shed left splotches on her cheeks and smudges around her eyes. Lily had men heat water to fill a big tub for Mary. She poured in some oils that smelled like jasmine and made the water soft and silky. The bath helped her to relax. Ming brushed her clean hair when she got out of the tub, and the curl came back.

"We must do a better job on your disguise this time." Lily brought in a comb and some black dye in a small bowl. Ming parted her hair in the middle and combed the mixture through her thick hair, pulling and straightening it as it dried. Then she took a tiny piece of charcoal and lightly lined her eyes, making them look more Oriental. A yellowish powder was dusted all over her body, with a final dusting of a translucent powder to keep it on for a longer time.

"Let me find you some clean clothes." Lily came back with a red silk tunic that was lined in white, a pair of white pants, and tiny white shoes. "Chow Lien just told me what they are planning, and I believe these clothes will be appropriate. After you are dressed, we will join the others, and they will tell you what they propose."

"You are even more beautiful now, little one." Chow Lien said to her as she entered the room. "Your eyes are blue and not brown, but my eyes are blue, so you could be a distant cousin."

"We are all listening, my son. What is the plan you wish to propose?

"I have an idea, Father. Let me escort our guests as far as the railroad station in Albany, New York. When they arrive, they can purchase tickets to Chicago. From there, they can travel all the way to San Francisco by rail. The danger will be in getting from here to Albany. The train should take seven to ten days to reach Sacramento, California, and will arrive in San Francisco soon after. I believe it would be safer, for everyone, if we do not tell the other members of our society, the young lady's identity, so that no one else will be in danger for having that knowledge. I suggest a false marriage ceremony, so that our people will only identify Miss Sweeney as my bride, or perhaps my concubine, who arrived from China as a special gift for Chow Lien from his grandfather. We can travel as man and wife, and Ah Kim and Ming can pretend to be our servants. If they have followed you, Ah Kim, they should be confused by the marriage, and believe that you just escorted my bride here from China. We will be your protectors until we reach the train station. Three days of traveling should get us there. If everything seems safe, we will part company. If you wish us to escort you further, you will only need to ask. I will take our two best swordsmen with us. What do you think, Father?"

"I think that is a good plan, Chow Lien. What is your opinion, Ah Kim?"

"I too believe it is a good plan. I cannot think of a better one. Thank you very much, my honored friend, for your help and your trust, and for your previous kindness to my family."

"Thank you, my friend, for bringing us this rich bounty, with kind words from your uncle. We will begin preparing immediately for a marriage feast and false ceremony in the morning. The wedding couple should be able to leave by early afternoon. I will tell the people that their marriage was arranged in China. Miss Sweeney, do these plans also meet your satisfaction?"

"If this will get me out of the reach of Mr. Bane, I leave me life in yer hands. I do prefer to be known as a wife, rather than a concubine." Mary had been contemplating the plan while they spoke. She just wanted to get to San Francisco, so this dangerous adventure would be over.

"Lily, please prepare the bride for an early morning ceremony. If we have the marriage and wedding feast early, the couple could travel quite a distance before dark."

"What will people say when ye return without me?"

"They will not ask. Many men in our society have families who live in China, and they often do not see their families for many years.

They will assume we were married, and you returned home to live with your family, or that you ran away, as some brides do."

Lily laughed, as she put her arm around Mary, and took her back to the smaller cabin and her sleeping quarters. Then Lily set about giving orders for the preparation of food, flowers and fireworks, for the morning ceremony. The bustle of the late night activity kept Mary awake, so she decided to read from her bible. She hadn't opened it since that awful night on the ship. Her mind was still fuzzy about that night. She was still confused as to how the bible got back into the case, since she didn't remember putting it away. 'I must have though, because that's where I found it, back in its little leather bag.' She took out the bible and began reading. When she felt tired enough to sleep, she reached for the candle to blow it out, and as she did, she dropped the bible on the floor. A brown folded piece of parchment fell out of one of the pages. When Mary picked it up, she realized why Bane was really following her.

The map was very detailed, but there was no writing. Bane must have hidden it in her bible, sometime before that night, and was coming to get the map back before they arrived in Boston. Whoever had found the bible after that night, must have just returned it to its bag, without knowing the map was there. No wonder he was sending men to track her down. It wasn't she he was after, it was the map!

Pulling her mother's quilt around her shoulders, she stepped outside and called Ah Kim quietly. He came immediately.

"What is it, Miss Mary? What's wrong?"

"Come in here, Ah Kim. I have something important to show ye."

He looked carefully around to make sure everything was okay, before he went inside. Ming was awake now too.

"I know why Mr. Bane is after me, Ah Kim. I think this belongs to ye. It fell out of me bible as I was reading. He must have hidden it there, sometime during the trip, and he was looking for it that night. I was in the way, so he wanted to silence me too."

"Yes! That would be the perfect place to hide it, as I searched all of the crew's quarters after I searched his, except for yours! Thank you, Mary. You have proven to me that my intuition is again right, that you are a fine honest young woman. I must plan a way to get them to stop following us. Let us go through with the plans for tomorrow. Get some sleep, Missy Mary, and do not tell anyone about our secret. This map puts us all in extreme danger."

"Thank ye, Ah Kim. Goodnight."

Mary couldn't believe how smoothly the wedding ceremony, and feast, went the next day. Ming and Lily began early, to get her ready for the pretend marriage ceremony. They told her she wouldn't have to say a word. She could smell the Oriental cooking odors, from the moment she woke up. There was a huge feast planned after the ceremony. Some girls brought fresh wildflowers they had picked in the meadow. They made a lovely floral wreath for her head, and turned two trees into an archway with the fragrant blossoms. Then they put flowers on the table in the large cabin, where the wedding party would eat. Suddenly, she found herself meeting the handsome Chow Lien underneath the flowers, with Chow Jin standing in front of them. Although she knew they were using a Chinese name for her, and that the ceremony was not real, she almost wished it were.

Today was like a dream, instead of the nightmare her life had become.

The ceremony and feast were over before she knew it. A man was playing music on a type of guitar she had never seen before, and entertaining the people, when Chow Lien told her to get prepared for travel.

Ah Kim drove the little decorated covered wagon, with Mary in the back. They left the buckboard there, and Chow Lien followed on his horse, with two of his men by his side. They all had long swords hanging from their waists. The wagon was covered with bright colored flowers, ribbons and silks, and Mary felt like a princess. They made camp that night, and she and Ming were told they would sleep in the wagon. Ah Kim was folding a piece of heavy parchment paper, when he came to the wagon to talk to her.

"I have formulated a plan that I think will work, Miss Mary. I am going to copy this map exactly, changing only a couple of small things, which I hope will not be noticed, but will change the entire location of the mine, if one is following the map. Then we will put it back exactly where it was, to let them steal it back. They will think we did not find it and never knew it was there. They will take the map to Bane and leave us alone."

"Ye are very wise, Ah Kim. How long will it take ye to copy the map?"

"I will work tonight by candlelight until it is finished. I think we should let them catch up to us on the train. We will be safer there with many people around us."

Mary rode one of the horses the next day, as she had a lot of experience riding in Ireland. The three day trip was quiet, except for the wonderful conversations she had with Chow Lien. He was very intelligent, and he had traveled far and wide. He also spoke five languages. Although Mary was very attracted to him, she knew their lives were too different, and being married to him was only pretend. She could never be his wife or his concubine. They talked about many things and became close friends. When time came for them to part, she found it difficult to say goodbye.

When they reached the outskirts of Albany, they camped far away from the road. Chow Lien and Mary sat by the fire and he held her hand as he spoke to her. His hands were warm and made her feel safe. It was a strange evening. She felt so comfortable with him that she laid her head on his shoulder, and she didn't want to leave. They did not have to speak, they knew each other's thoughts. Finally, he walked her to the wagon to say goodnight. When she turned to him to say something he put his finger to his lips, kissed them, and then put his fingers to her lips. Gently, he kissed her eyes and her cheeks. When he ended by kissing her lips so softly and sweetly, she thought she would melt from the heat it produced in her body. As she climbed into the wagon, she was dizzy with emotions. She slept fitfully, dreaming of the handsome adventurer and what might have been.

The next morning, the cold light of reality woke her as she packed her things and took off her disguise. She went to the nearby creek and washed her hair, face, arms and neck, with the soap Lily had given her. Then she looked at her reflection in the little tin cup. Her hair was still very dark, with only touches of red, and the water brought back her natural curl. There was a darker cast to her skin and the darkness around her eyes was still there, but lighter. When she returned to the wagon, she folded the beautiful silk garments Lily had given her to keep, as a remembrance of their friendship, and she put them in the bottom of the trunk that had carried her off the ship. She put on the dress she had worn to the port city in Cork, that fateful day, and added the light blue bonnet to her hair. Short dark curls peeked out from under the bonnet. Mary laced up the black shoes and put the shawl around her shoulders. Ah Kim gave her the new map. She carefully put it in the bible, hoping that Bane did not know exactly which page he had placed it. Then she put the bible in the leather pouch and laid it in the top of the trunk.

Chow Lien gave her a gentle squeeze and hug, with one last kiss on her forehead, as he said goodbye. Mary couldn't hold back the tears, as she walked in with Ah Kim and Ming to the train station. She carried her old sea bag over her shoulder, and they carried the trunk between them. Ah Kim also carried his carpetbag. Mary said a quick prayer to Saint Christopher, to guide them carefully, while wondering if she would ever make it to San Francisco at all.

Chapter Twelve

"The Map"

Late November, 1873

"May the flowers of love never be nipped by the frost of disappointment, nor a shadow of grief fall among your friends or family."

Chow Lien had been right about his estimation of the time it would take them to travel to the outskirts of Albany, New York. The walk to the train station the next day took the three travelers a little over two hours. They would have to change trains in Chicago, and again when they reached Ogden, Utah, but Ah Kim said they should arrive in San Francisco in about a week, if there weren't too many unforeseen delays. He explained that trains often break down, or rails became covered with debris from rock slides, along the way. Mary hoped she wouldn't get there too late to see John before he left for Oregon. The ship had sailed about five days ago, and it could easily arrive in the port city before they did. She knew that John planned to leave almost immediately, as the delay of the "Lexington" had already made him late for his appointment with Henry Villard, and it was important for him to get that job.

When they arrived at the train station, Ah Kim gave Mary the money John had given him for their travel across the country. He told her to buy three tickets to Chicago. The man behind the ticket counter looked at them strangely as she put the cash in front of him for the tickets.

"Who are you traveling with, ma'am?"

"I'm traveling with me two friends."

"I think you would all be more comfortable in the last car."

"And why is that, sir?" Mary asked indignantly.

"Ma'am, need I remind you that your friends are of the Oriental persuasion? And with your darker skin I assume you are a half breed of some type. I believe you would all be more comfortable in the last car."

"What? What!" Mary felt her face turn red, as she was suddenly hot with anger. "I cannot believe what ye just said. I thought this was a free country, a place where all people are treated equally. If a person is charged the same price for their ticket as a white person, then he should be able to sit where he wants. I happen to be a white woman. Me name is Mary Sweeney, and I come from County Cork, Ireland."

Ah Kim calmly and politely interrupted her, and he bowed to the ticket master, saying in the broken English she had first heard him speak.

"Vely solly, sir. Missy Mary Sweeney is our honored employer. Missy Mary vely upset, sir, as her grandmother just die. Missy Mary needs our help and company during this sad time."

Understanding Ah Kim's motives, Mary calmed down and took over. "I insist that me servants travel with me in the main compartment. If there is a problem with that, then I will be filing a complaint with this company when we reach our destination. Will I need to do that?"

"No ma'am! That will not be necessary. I'm sorry for my mistake."

"I dare say, ye should be!" She took the tickets and walked off, mumbling under her breath with anger.

"Miss Mary, you told him your name! Bane's men will have no trouble finding us now."

"I'm sorry. That made me so angry, I wasn't thinking clearly. Ye did want them to find us, didn't ye?"

"Yes, but we don't want to be too obvious about it and make them suspicious of the map. I want them to believe that it is the original one."

"I am sorry."

"I'm probably worrying too much. We need to hurry, Miss Mary, as the train is due to leave in ten minutes."

Ah Kim and Ming sat across from her in the main passenger compartment on the train. They were in the second to last car. Ming had made rice balls and brewed some tea, which she carried in an old jar, before they left the camp. Ah Kim bought three loaves of bread, beef jerky, two blocks of cheese, and apples from a cart at the station. The last few days had been tiring for all of them. Mary tried to keep her eyes open as she wanted to see the beautiful New York countryside, but she kept drifting into slumber. The seat was hard, and the ride was rough, but she curled up hoping to sleep soundly.

Ah Kim tried to stay awake too, but the train movement made sleep easy after the long walk to the station. He tried sitting straight up in his seat, but his head kept nodding, as he dozed in between the bumps. Ming laid her head back and slept. Mary tried to get Ming to trade places with her, so she could have her turn stretching out on the bench, but Ming just smiled, shook her head and sat by the window.

The train moved very slowly through the large cities and the small towns, and it sped up when they traveled in the open terrain. It made half hour stops in Schenectady, Utica, and Syracuse, and they had a two hour layover in Buffalo. At each stop, passengers either left the train or boarded it. Ah Kim estimated they were traveling about 16 or 17 miles per hour, on the average. When they stopped in Buffalo, Mary was surprised at how large Lake Erie was, she thought it looked like an ocean. The train traveled along the shores of the beautiful blue water until they reached Cleveland. There was a map of their train route posted on the front wall of their car, and Mary saw that the border between the United States and Canada ran down the middle of the lake. Ah Kim had studied the geography of the states and told her a lot about her new country. He said the big city of Toronto was not far on the other side of the deep shimmering water, and that they had been very close to the famous Niagara Falls when they were in Buffalo.

Mary decided she should stay awake as much as possible, as she might never get this way again. Since Ah Kim seemed to be a wealth of knowledge about the country, she wanted to take advantage of that and learn all she could about the land where she had chosen to live. Their next long stop was at the west end of the lake in Toledo, Ohio. Although it was cold and windy, they got off the train for a few minutes to stretch their legs. Then the route would take the train through rural Indiana. It was getting dark as they left the Ohio station, but Mary could still see the brilliant oranges and reds of the autumn leaves that sprinkled the rolling hills, as the train rumbled past. When it got so dark that she couldn't see anymore, Mary finally slept soundly until the next morning. When she woke up, she saw the sun shining on the shimmering waters of another beautiful lake, Michigan. In the distance, she saw the western shore of the lake was littered with houses and two story buildings. She realized that they were almost to the famous city of Chicago, where they would be changing trains.

Although the sun was shining, the wind was blowing and the temperature was freezing. Mary didn't know how cold it was, until she got off the train. Chicago's weather was much worse than Toledo's. The wind swirling off the lake was bitterly cold, and the bones in her face ached for almost an hour after they went inside the station to buy their tickets to Ogden, Utah. The line of passengers entering the station was long, and it took a while to get inside. They were carrying the trunk and bags, which also slowed them down. Their train wasn't due to arrive for another four hours, so they purchased their tickets, bought more food supplies and some hot tea at a little stand inside the station. Mary went into the washroom to better clean the powder and charcoal from her face, and when she wet her hair the curl came back, although the color was still dark. Ah Kim and Ming waited for her on a bench in the station while she purchased the tickets, so they wouldn't have the same problem they had encountered in Albany.

When she returned to the bench, a lady and man dressed in finery were making rude comments about her Chinese friends. Mary was infuriated and about to say something, when Ah Kim took her by the arm and led both ladies to another side of the station to wait for their train.

"It is better not to draw attention to ourselves, Miss Mary. Those people are not aware that people of all colors and customs inhabit this world, and if they were to travel to China, they might be the subject of ridicule, just as the Chinese people are in this country."

"I am sorry, me friends, and ashamed that people here treat ye in such a manner. I just wanted to give them me opinion. I will try to control me Irish temper from now on."

"Thank you for your concern, Mary. Not everyone feels as you do."

When they finally boarded the train, they found the new passenger cabin to be a little more comfortable than the last train. Hard cushions lined the backs of the seats and padded the benches. The train from Albany to Chicago had taken 55 hours to get there, even though it was supposed to only take 48. They had to wait four hours for the train, as they had missed the one that left an hour before their arrival. They felt good about their progress when they realized they were at least a third of the way to San Francisco.

When they left Illinois and entered Iowa, the land was quite brown and barren, as fall was quickly turning to winter in this part of the country. The corn fields had been picked, and the cut wheat fields were the color of dry ochre. There were ominous looking clouds in the sky and rain was already beginning to beat against the train windows. The train was packed with people, making it hot and humid, but when they opened the windows, torrents of water sloshed into the car, as the wind swirled the rain around the countryside. The train rocked on its wheels, as it headed west and fought with the raging storm. Thunder and lightning were booming and hitting close by, when they reached Des Moines, and nobody in the car was sleeping. The conductor came through the car trying to calm the frightened passengers.

"It's just a little Iowa storm. Everyone, please try to keep calm. We'll be past the storm in an hour or so. We're only stopping here to pick up a few more passengers and some freight. Then, we'll be on our way."

Ah Kim estimated that they had traveled about 330 miles from Chicago to Des Moines. Because of the weather, it had taken them about 20 hours. He told her they were very lucky that the next part of the trip would be a lot easier than it had been, when he had traveled through there several years before. There was a new bridge, the United Pacific Missouri River Bridge, in Council Bluff that had just opened at the end of March. Before that, the trains had to cross the Missouri by ferry, to continue westward across America, which took a long time as only a few cars could fit on the special made ferries with the added rails. The bridge was about 120 miles past Des Moines and they easily went across it. Omaha was only about 15 miles further. The storm had raged all the way across Iowa, and Mary tried to imagine how dangerous the trip would have been by ferry.

The rain and wind began to subside when they reached North Platte, Nebraska. After a short stop, they headed on to the Wyoming territory. Everything quieted down that night, and the passengers finally slept. When they woke, they were surprised to see bright sunlight and a completely different terrain. Chicago had been a pretty modern city with tall buildings and fancy carriages. However, Cheyenne was just the opposite, with sprawling wooden plank sidewalks, a general store, post office, and saloon. A marshal's office on the main street close to the train station made them realize this was the new frontier, the "wild west". They had traveled about 250 miles from North Platte to Cheyenne.

They got off the train and took a walk to stretch their legs, as they had an hour before the train was supposed to leave. They knew that their departure could easily be delayed for any number of reasons. Cheyenne was where they began to think that they were being followed again. After Mary and her friends got back on the train and settled in, two men got on the train and started acting suspicious. They looked like cowboys, but their clothes looked new and their boots weren't too well worn. When they spoke, their voices sounded more European than American. They sat two rows behind Mary, and she felt as if they were watching her. Ah Kim quietly observed them from his seat. They only rode the train a short distance and got off in Laramie. Ah Kim told the women to stay there and quietly followed the two men. They went to the telegraph office and sent a telegram. Ah Kim tried to listen at the window, but he couldn't hear what was being said. He watched from around the corner, as three other men came out of the saloon and met with the two from the train. After a long conversation, the five men unleashed five horses from the front of the saloon and rode off.

Ah Kim told Mary, he was sure they were up to something, but he didn't know what. The 26 hour trip seemed to go smoothly from there to Ogden, Utah, where they changed trains again. Mary was beginning to feel good, as she knew they were now two-thirds of the way to San Francisco. She hoped Ah Kim was wrong, and she prayed those men were just cowboys from a ranch outside of Laramie, and that their friends had just come to meet them to bring their horses. It was around 30 hours later, as they were about an hour outside of Reno, when everything went wrong.

After the two men left the train in Laramie, Ah Kim had taken his money bag out of his carpet bag, took out enough for the tickets they would need to purchase in Utah, and gave the smaller pouch to Ming. He left only a few coins in his carpet bag. Ming hid his money bag in her mat, which she had rolled up under the bench, where it couldn't be seen. She made sure that no one else saw her hide the bag. She pulled the bag with the bread, jerky, cheese, and apples out at the same time, so anyone would think she was just getting the food out from under the bench.

They decided to eat their lunch before they got to Reno. When they had finished, Mary stated she would like to make a toast to Ming's upcoming marriage, and to assure their successful future in America. Mary lifted her cup of tea and toasted her friends, with another of her favorite Irish blessings: *"Here's to health, peace and prosperity; May the flower of love never be nipped by the frost of disappointment, nor a shadow of grief fall among your family or friends."*

They all drank their tea and Ming refilled the tiny Chinese cups she had brought with her. With their stomachs sated, the three travelers were trying to rest, when two men entered the train from the back and suddenly appeared next to their seats, with pistols in their hands and bandanas covering their nose and mouth.

"Nobody moves, and nobody gets hurt!" The taller man's loud voice woke up everybody in the car. A woman squealed as the shorter man held a gun on the other passengers, while his friend continued barking orders.

"Put your purses, money, watches, jewelry, gold, and anything you have with you that's valuable in this bag when we come to you. I want everything. If you try to hide anything, I will not hesitate to shoot. Is that understood?"

Another young woman with a child began weeping. A huge bang frightened them all, as the little man fired his gun, shooting a hole through the train window by the little girls head.

"Shut up, Lady! There ain't nothin' to cry about, lessen you don't shut your mouth and give me all your valuables."

It was quiet, except for the sounds of the passengers taking off their jewelry, while they put them in the bag along with their pocketbooks. His pistol still smoking, the man went from passenger to passenger, holding out the empty burlap sugar sack in front of them. He made a couple of the men stand up, to make sure they weren't hiding money. The bigger man watched them all. When he came to the three immigrants, he made them all stand up. He spoke gruffly to Mary, as he pointed his gun directly at her head and cocked it.

"Open that trunk!"

Mary could hardly breathe, and her hands were shaking, as she unlatched the lock. The man reached in, rifled through her belongings, and picked up the little leather bag. He laughed heartily, when he looked at her family crest, as if he'd found gold. Opening the bag he looked inside.

"Ah yes, just what I need, a bible to save me soul!"

He removed the book and slipped it into his pocket. Ah Kim emptied his carpet bag of the few coins it held, into the sack, and Ming added her ear rings. As they didn't find anything else of value in Mary's trunk, the bible was all they took. Taking their bag of loot, the two men jumped from the moving passenger car as the train moved slowly up a hill. Another cowboy on a black and white Pinto came out of the trees, at the top of the knoll, leading two saddled horses. Swiftly, the train robbers leapt on the moving horses and took off in the other direction.

The woman with the child began crying again, and one man pulled the emergency brake. As the train came to a screeching halt, the passengers were thrown to the floor. It was at least two hours before the train moved again.

The conductor and the engineer came through the cabin, demanding to know why the emergency brake had been pulled. Most of the women passengers were hysterical. Everyone began talking at once. The engineer told the conductor to get something to write on, and to talk to everyone while he went to check the rest of the train to see if they had stolen anything else, or done any other damage.

Mary couldn't seem to talk, so Ah Kim answered the conductor's questions. He wrote down all of their names, and addresses where they could be reached. Ah Kim gave them one of his cousin's addresses in San Francisco for all of them. By each person's name, the conductor wrote down what the robbers had taken from them, their version of what happened with the robbers, and any description they could give of the two men, or their accomplice who had met them outside the train.

When the train finally began rolling down the tracks again, Mary was still shaking and hadn't spoken a word. She still saw the gun aimed at her head, and she just sat there staring straight ahead. After the train had stopped in Reno, Ah Kim sat down by her.

"Miss Mary, are you all right? They are gone now. We can stop worrying and hiding now. I am sure those men were after the map. Let us hope that when Bane gets it, he accepts it as the real one. It is over for now, Miss Mary. We should reach the East Bay by tomorrow morning, then we'll take the ferry across the bay and be in San Francisco. The trip has taken us a little longer than I expected, as it has been about nine days already."

Her mouth was so dry, she could hardly speak. Ming poured her some tea, and she sipped it slowly for several minutes before she began to feel better.

"I'm okay." She whispered finally, and promptly fell sound asleep for several hours. When she woke up, they were only about six hours outside Sacramento. In a few more hours they would arrive at their final destination. Her dream of life in America was becoming a reality. Feeling much better, she searched in her trunk for the few sheets of paper and the pen and ink she had bought in Boston. It was time to write a letter to her family. She had only sent a short note from Boston, saying she had arrived in America. Her parents would certainly be worried. Concern for them was what kept her from feeling good about her arrival in California. The dream would only come true if she could bring them all to America.

Dear Mum and Da, Jerry, Margaret, Catherine, Jim and Johanna,

I love you and miss you all very much. America is wonderful! The trip has been uneventful, and I am doing fine. I am on a train and will be arriving in San Francisco in a few hours. I will be mailing this from there. Please think about coming over to join me, as I will be sending you money for that reason. It is beautiful here, just like Ireland, and jobs are plentiful. Please, please, please prepare to join me! I will write again, as soon as I am settled. God bless you all and keep you safe. Please forgive me for leaving as I did, and for causing you so much worry.

With love from your daughter and sister,

Mary Sweeney

November, 1873

Chapter Thirteen

"San Francisco"

December, 1873

"It is with a heavy heart that I write this. I very much wish that I was there to welcome you. Please be careful, and think of me often, as you are never out of my mind."

The last few hours on the train were the longest. All of the passengers were full of conversation about the train robbery. Most were complaining about what they had lost to the thieves. Mary and Ah Kim spent a lot of time talking to the three men who sat across the aisle from them. They had traveled all the way from Chicago on the same trains and had been in the same compartment, since they left Ogden. They were businessmen who had teamed up to seek their fortunes in Virginia City. One of them had left a wife and child in Chicago, and he planned to go back and get them as soon as he got settled.

Nevada had become a territory in 1861. The discovery of gold and silver had brought many easterners to the Virginia City area. As a result of the "Big Bonanza", thousands were swarming to the area in search of the valuable ores. The married man chided the other two, saying he "hoped that they would not be led astray by the many saloons and brothels" that were said to line the Virginia City streets. Luckily, the men had hid most of their money in the bags they had stowed in the baggage car. According to the conductor, those bags had not been touched. Many of the passengers had lost everything. The men got off the train in Reno, where they planned to purchase a buckboard, horses, and other necessities, to travel on to Virginia City. Mary and her friends enjoyed the men's conversation, and they appreciated their equal treatment of the immigrants. They were sorry to have to say "goodbye".

Several people boarded the train in Reno. Mary wondered if they had searched for the shiny treasure and given up, or whether they were some of the lucky ones who had struck it rich. The newcomers were much more aloof than the ones who had just left the train. The last stop before they reached the San Francisco Bay was Sacramento. Many people boarded the train at that depot making their compartment full again, as it headed through the valley toward the famous city across the bay. When the train stopped on the east side of the bay, Mary and her companions got off the train and walked to the docks to wait for the ferry that would take them to their final destination across the bay. The sky was filled with pinks and purples, as the sun set over the beautiful city. Mary's eyes filled with tears at the sight, with relief that she had finally reached San Francisco. She realized that much of her excitement was from the anticipation of seeing John Troy again, and her feelings surprised her. Dusk was falling as they reached the docks. There were many thriving businesses on the wharf, and she could see the brand new cable cars, filled with people, going up Nob Hill to elegant tall homes that awaited them.

The Clay Street Hill Railroad had just finished building the first horseless cable car line, which opened for public service a few months before that. She had heard people on the train talking about it, and how it was going to replace the horse drawn carriages that struggled up the wet cobblestone streets. When they said that the horses had been whipped to pull the heavy cars up the hills, and that many of them had slipped and been dragged to their deaths, tears came to her eyes, as horses were always respected and treated well in Ireland.

Ah Kim had been here before, so he knew the city well. It was dark when they finally reached the street where one of his cousins lived above the laundry business that his family owned. The family had received Ah Kim's letter and welcomed them all graciously to their home. The women in the house quickly prepared them a delicious meal, after they poured them tea to drink while they waited. When their stomachs were full, the cousin went to a small cubicle in the corner and retrieved two packets that he gave to Ah Kim.

"Two men came by the laundry last week and asked me to deliver these letters to you. The one named John Troy said they were good friends of yours, and that it was important that you received these as soon as you arrived. He said they were sorry that they could not wait for you, but that it was very important for them to leave immediately. They were going to travel as far as Portland with a group of men they had met. People told them that it would be safer than traveling alone. The group was leaving the next morning."

Mary's joy at arriving at her destination suddenly turned to disappointment and depression. Ah Kim saw the look on her face and tried his best to calm her fears once again.

"Don't worry, Miss Mary, I'm sure you will see them soon. Let us look at what they have left for us. One of these is addressed to me, and one has your name on it."

He handed her the packet with her name printed in bold letters on the front, and she held it close to her heart, waiting patiently while Ah Kim opened the other one. Ah Kim's letter explained what his cousin had just told them about the importance of their immediate departure. They were afraid that John would miss his appointment with Henry Villard, if they did not leave for Portland as soon as possible. Enclosed in the packet was $100, which he asked Ah Kim to give to Mary as a gift from Thomas Bailey. It was for any emergencies that she might have, and to tide her over until she was gainfully employed. Also in the packet were directions on where Ah Kim should go to find John Troy, when he was able to come to Oregon, and a letter of recommendation and introduction addressed to Henry Villard from Thomas Bailey.

Mary opened her packet carefully and tearfully read the letter from John Troy.

My dear Mary,

I had so hoped you would arrive before I had to leave. It is with a heavy heart that I write this. I'm sure that Ah Kim has brought you safely to San Francisco, as he is an honorable man. Unless I go to work immediately for Mr. Villard, which may very well be the case, I will try to return soon. My uncle decided to come with me, as we are already late for the appointment to meet with Mr. Villard. He wants to make sure I am settled before he leaves.

I am enclosing a letter of recommendation and introduction that my uncle has written for you. I am also enclosing the address of an acquaintance of his from Ireland. This lady should be able to find a position for you with the aid of his letter. Although he does not know her very well, he has heard only good things about her.

We both hope that you are well, and that your new life in San Francisco will be as you had hoped. I very much wish that I was there to welcome you. I will write to you as soon as I am settled, and I hope that I will see you very soon.

Please be careful, and think of me often, as you are never out of my mind. I am already missing you greatly.

Your ardent admirer,

John S. Troy

Mary tried to smile after she read the letter, but she was filled with disappointment, as she realized that it would probably be a long time before she saw him again. After spending the night at Ah Kim's cousins, Mary got dressed in her best dress, and Ah Kim took her to the address that Mr. Bailey had left for her. Mrs. McConnell was very nice, but said she already had a full staff at her house. Mary and Ah Kim sat in her parlor while she checked with her neighbors, to see if they knew of anyone who was looking for help. One of her neighbors gave her the name and address of a woman who always seemed to be hiring.

Ah Kim escorted her to the address, and told her that if she hired her, he and his cousin would bring the rest of her belongings over that afternoon. A heavyset lady, with a German accent, answered the door. After Mary introduced herself, and asked her if she could speak to Mrs. Gordon, the woman took her into the hallway and called her mistress. She did not invite Ah Kim in, so he just bowed and waited on the porch. Mary curtsied politely to the large woman, when she finally came to speak to her.

"Me name is Mary Sweeney, and I am looking for a housekeeping position. Here is a letter of recommendation and introduction from Mr. Thomas Bailey. I am a hard worker, and very honest and trustworthy, ma'am."

"Hmm. Are you Irish? I thought I caught an accent." The gruff woman had a distinct English accent. The woman seemed to be looking down her nose at Mary. She peered through her little spectacles, with a prim and haughty look.

"Yes ma'am. I arrived from Ireland a short time ago."

"I don't usually hire 'micks', but I am without an upstairs maid right now, so I guess I'll give you a try. Greta will show you where the servants sleep. I expect you to be on duty from 7:00 a.m. until 6:00 p.m. Monday through Saturday. If I need you on Sunday, I will let you know on Saturday afternoon. You will receive $1 a day and get your wages every Saturday. Greta will inform you of your duties, and you will report to her every morning at 7:00. You will leave and enter through the back servant's entrance, and cause no problems. You will not talk to me, nor to my guests. When my son comes home from college, you will stay away from him. Is that understood?"

"Yes ma'am. When do ye want me to start?"

"Right now! I have a dinner party tonight, and Greta needs help immediately."

"Certainly ma'am. I just need to let my escort know that he is not needed anymore."

"The servant's entrance is through the kitchen. Report to Greta through there. You are dismissed!"

Mary hurried through the dining area and entered the kitchen. She told Greta that Mrs. Gordon had hired her, and asked where the servant's entrance was, so she could tell her friend that he could leave. She said goodbye to Ah Kim, and he told her that he would return with her belongings in a couple of hours.

"Thank ye, Ah Kim, for all ye have done for me. Please thank Ming and yer cousins too. I hope to repay ye someday."

"It has been my pleasure, Miss Mary. Ming is to be married Sunday. I know she would like you to be there. I will pick you up at 1:00 p.m., if that is all right?"

"I would love to come. I hope I am not needed here. Be sure to come to the back entrance, as I am only to go in and out of that door."

"Yes, Miss Mary." He bowed to her before he left.

Mary was dressed in a maid's uniform, when Ah Kim and his cousin returned with her trunk. She was helping in the kitchen, as there was a dinner party for twelve people scheduled for 4:30 p.m. Mary was to help serve the guests, and she would not get off until all the dishes were done.

Greta did not seem very happy, but she was very efficient. There were two other girls that were hired for this evening only, and everyone was busy preparing for the feast. Mary thought everything went well, but after all the guests left, Mrs. Gordon chastised Greta and Mary about what Mary considered small matters. She thought the soup had not been hot enough, and the coffee was bitter. After Mrs. Gordon left the kitchen, Greta made a face and began to complain about her boss.

"I don't know why I continue to work for her. I have never seen such a difficult woman! I hope you last longer than the last girl. She was only here for a week. One word of warning, Mary, stay as far away from Geoffrey Gordon as you can. That young man has gotten more girls fired than I can count on one hand. He is nothing but a lecher, and his mother can't see it. She adores the rascal. I guess I'm too old, because he doesn't bother me. However, I'm sure if he sees a pretty young thing like you, he'll be all over you."

"Thanks for the warning Greta, I'll try to stay away from him. How often is he here?"

"He comes home every weekend. You can retire now. I'll check to make sure everything is perfect before I go to bed. I don't need her yelling at me when I get up in the morning."

Sunday came, and Mary wasn't needed, so she was waiting when Ah Kim knocked on the servant's entrance door. Ming looked radiant at her marriage ceremony, which was very much like Mary's false ceremony in the forest. Quan was a very handsome man, and Ming looked very pleased with her father's selection. After the wedding and feast that followed, Ah Kim walked Mary back to the Gordon's mansion.

"I'm not sure when we will see each other again, Mary. I may leave in a few days. There is a group called 'The Workingman's Party' that is protesting the Chinese people as laborers. There was a warning in the Chinese San Francisco newspaper yesterday that riots may break out at any moment. If they do, I will be heading to Oregon. I hope that you will be okay without my assistance."

"I am so sorry, Ah Kim. I read the article in the "Examiner" which said that an Irishman, Denis Kearney, is a leader of that party. I am so ashamed of a countryman acting like that."

"There are men with prejudices in all countries, Mary. It is not your fault. Will you be okay if I leave?"

"Yes, Ah Kim, I will be fine. Do what ye have to do."

"Mary, I have a very important envelope that I would like to leave in your care. You are the only person that I trust. Can I leave it with you?"

"Of course. That will mean that I will see ye again to return it."

"Perhaps. However, I would like you to safeguard it for me." He pulled an envelope out of the inside pocket of his outer coat. "Please do not open it unless you receive word of my death. One of my relatives will find you if that event happens. Only open the seal with a trusted attorney and my close relatives present. This must be our secret, my dear friend. I will let you know if I ever want it back, but you will probably have it for many years, if that meets with your satisfaction."

"I would be happy to take care of this for ye. It is the least I can do to repay ye, for all ye have done for me. I will hide it in a safe place."

"Thank you, Mary. I may not have time to say goodbye, if I leave, so let us say goodbye now." He bowed deeply, then took her hand and kissed it with friendship, before he left.

Mary went to her room, took out her quilt and her sewing kit. She opened one of the patches, put the envelope securely inside it, and then sewed the patch back into the quilt.

The job at the Gordon's ended two months later. Geoffrey Gordon had returned home in the middle of the week after Mary started working there. Greta and Mary overheard the loud voices upstairs, shortly after his return. It was clear from the loud conversation that Geoffrey had been expelled from Berkeley, but they couldn't tell from their words what had prompted his expulsion. He had been accepted at the new college that had opened in 1868, in September, and was asked to leave only a few short months later. Mrs. Gordon's loud voice seemed to imply that she was angrier with the school, than she was with her son.

The next day, Mary ran into Geoffrey when she was cleaning the upstairs parlor. The first thing he did was try to kiss her.

"What are ye doing, sir? Leave me alone!" She pulled away from him.

"So you are the new maid. A pretty one, you are. Don't you want to have a little fun? I can assure you of many pleasurable days working here, my dear."

"No thank ye. I have heard that ye are the reason that many a girl has lost her job here."

"Just rumors, my sweet. Those girls were just not good maids. If you don't like my attention, I can make sure you don't have a job either."

"Please sir, just leave me alone! I just want to do me job." Mary quickly ran out of the room, and from then on she tried to stay as far away from him as she could, but two months after she began working there, he cornered her in Mrs. Gordon's room. She was polishing the furniture and didn't hear him come up behind her. Suddenly, his hands were under her apron and squeezing her breasts. When she realized what was happening she reacted with anger. She was holding a crystal vase that she had just cleaned, and she quickly swung around and hit him with it. The vase slipped out of her hands as it hit his left shoulder and slammed to the hard floor, splintering into a thousand pieces.

He was laughing as his mother entered the room.

"What is going on here?"

"Yer lecherous son just grabbed me breasts!" Mary was furious.

"You lying little 'mick' whore! I've been watching you throw yourself at my son ever since you met him. Now you've broken the vase I bought from Paris, and you've hurt my son. You're fired! Get your things and get out immediately. I will take the cost of that vase out of your pay. Be out of here within the hour!"

Mary was so shocked, the only thing she could think to say was, "It'll be me pleasure!" She ripped off the apron as she flew down the stairs, her face red with anger. Greta met her at the kitchen door.

"I'm sorry, Mary. I knew it wouldn't be long. Stop at Mrs. Andrew's house across the street on your way out. She knows a lot of people, and she might be able to find you another job. I'll give you a recommendation, if you need one. Good luck to you!"

Mary was out of the house in twenty minutes, dragging her trunk behind her. She had started to calm down and wondered where she would go now. Greta handed her a note on her way out. She decided to take her advice and went across the street. When Mrs. Andrews answered the door, Mary just handed her Greta's note.

"That woman is impossible to work for. Her son has always been a problem. I heard of a woman that is looking for a housekeeper and governess for her daughter. I don't know her personally, but I've heard she's a lovely lady. I think her name is Hannah Goldstein, and she lives three blocks over. It's the big gray house on the corner, you can't miss it. Good luck, my dear!"

Hannah Goldstein opened the door after about five minutes. She was quite elderly and walked with a cane.

"Can I help you, my dear?"

"Me name is Mary Sweeney. I was told that ye needed a housekeeper and a governess, and I came to apply for the position."

Hannah liked the young girl immediately. "Come in, my dear. Let's have a cup of tea and talk about it."

An hour later, Mary was putting her things away in an upstairs bedroom. She was so relieved to be there. This was going to be a lovely place to live. Mary couldn't wait for Rachel Goldstein to come home from boarding school this weekend, as she couldn't wait to meet the girl she would be overseeing. After she was done unpacking, she went downstairs to prepare dinner for her new employer.

Part II

Chapter Fourteen

"The Reunion"

March, 1877 ~ Four Years Later

"May the roof above you never fall in, and your friends gathered below never fall out."

Mary Sweeney opened the door on the oak hutch that her father had made for Mrs. Goldstein as a thank you gift, and she ran her hands over the ornate hand carving that trimmed the massive piece. She carefully removed the fragile plates and began preparing the dining room for Mrs. Goldstein's next meal. Mary spread the clean linen tablecloth on the large oak table and placed the lace trimmed napkins that she had hand embroidered to match. Although the tablecloth only had a border trimmed with lilac colored lace, Mary had embroidered the beautiful tiny flowers on each napkin, as well as trimmed them to match the table cloth. When the table looked perfect to Mary's eyes, she added the centerpiece that she had filled with pink and white roses from Hannah's garden that morning. Small fragrant limbs from the lilac tree that was in full bloom, mingled with the roses in the bouquet, permeating the room with a fragrant aroma that was almost intoxicating. The arrangement was the crowning glory to the table, as it cast a pastel glow on the otherwise stark white China. She removed two sterling silver candleholders from the cupboard and placed long pink tapers in them, then added small rosebuds at the base of each, to make delicate flower rings surrounding the candleholders. Then she took the other arrangement she had made, in a fine crystal vase, into the parlor where Mrs. Goldstein usually entertained guests, and placed it on the table in the middle of the room. Tonight's supper was waiting in the oven, and several already prepared meals were waiting for her employer in the ice box in the pantry. After putting the final touches on the dining room, she took off her apron, hung it on the nail in the pantry, and took her coat out of the closet in the front hallway.

Mrs. Goldstein sat reading in the big chair in the library, by the warm fireplace, with her cane by her side. The elderly woman smiled when Mary entered the room. Hannah was fond of the young Irish girl. Mary had all the qualities she wanted in a governess and a servant. In fact, she had all the qualities any mother would want in a daughter. Witty, truthful and compassionate, Mary was more like a sister than a governess to her daughter. Hannah Goldstein had born her only child late in life, and there had been a great distance between the mother and daughter, until Mary arrived. Hannah adored Mary's kind ways, and the thought provoking proverbs and blessings that she delightfully spouted. The old woman felt very protective toward the young Irish immigrant, who had lived with her ever since her employment began four years ago.

Until recently, Mary had spent all of her time at the Goldstein's. Since her family arrived from Ireland several months ago, she had spent at least one weekend a month with her family. Hannah played an important part in helping Mary bring her family to America. A nice bonus, and an advance for some of her pay, had made all the difference. Mary's father had repaid her kindness with a gift of the hand carved oak hutch.

"Mary, dear girl, please give your mother and father my love. I'm sorry I don't feel up to attending their anniversary party, but I'm sure it will be a lovely affair. I'm looking forward to hearing all about it on Monday. Here's your envelope, Mary, and one for your parents, now go and enjoy yourself."

"Mrs. Goldstein, ye are so kind. Rachel will be there to represent yer family. I will send the girls over with some food from the party, and to check on ye. If ye need me for anything, me sister lives on Polk Street, and everyone knows Robert and Margaret Sweeney, so they will be easy to find. Margaret's marrying a man with the same last name sure made things easier for everybody."

"That is unusual, isn't it?"

"Not really, Sweeney is a pretty common name in Ireland. There are lots of Sweeneys. They are all related, and ancestors of the four Clans of MacSweeneys who settled in Ireland centuries ago. They originated in Scotland. The original Clans were highly paid and valued fighting men."

"That is fascinating, my girl. It's good that you know a lot about your ancestry."

"I would like to know more. Me grandmother told me that the clan we descend from hid many of the Spaniards from the English when they shipwrecked on the Irish coast in the 1500's. I've been told that is why we are often called Black Irish. Catherine is the best example of that in our family. Those with fair skin, dark hair and green or brown eyes are considered to be the mix of Spanish and Irish descent. I don't know why all Irishmen didn't help the Spaniards, as they practiced the same religion."

"Don't feel too sorry for the Spaniards of that era, Mary. They drove my ancestors out of Spain around the same time, as well as the Moors, and then there was the Spanish Inquisition."

"Yes, I heard about the Inquisition, but I didn't know they drove the Jewish people out of Spain."

"Yes, King Ferdinand and Queen Isabella passed a decree that expelled all Jews out of Spain, whether they were native to that country or not. I have some books on the subject, if you are interested."

"I would love to read them. Are ye still angry with the Spanish people? Many of the Irish still hate the English because of our long feud, but I always try to remember the old saying, *"However long the road, there comes a turnin'."*

"No, my dear, I'm not angry. It only makes me sad. I find it strange how people tend to judge others by the color of their skin, or their religious beliefs, or because their customs are different than their own. I often wonder how God allows such hatred and bigotry to abide in this world."

"Yes, I often wonder that too. I must be going now. I'll see ye early on Monday morning. Although Rachel is staying with Kate Murphy this weekend, they will be checking with ye a couple of times each day. Get some peace and quiet, and enjoy yerself."

"All right, my dear. Have a good time."

Mary took her small bag out of the closet, buttoned her cape, and went out into the crisp March air. She began walking briskly the ten blocks to her sister's home, but she slowed down when she got close to the Chinese area of the city. Deciding to take a detour, she walked past the place where Ah Kim's cousins' laundry used to be, and she felt very sad. Several Chinese businesses and homes had been burned and looted in the riots that had ensued, during the "Workingman's Party" protests that occurred shortly after she went to work for Mrs. Goldstein. She had not seen Ah Kim since the day of Ming and Quan's wedding. After everything had calmed down, she went to the laundry to make sure everyone had survived the melee, and found the building burned to the ground, with no sign of its occupants. The people in the Chinese Cookie factory next door, either didn't speak English well, or pretended not to, as they acted as if they didn't know what she was talking about. She tried to converse with several Chinese people in the area with no success. No one seemed to recognize the names of Ah Kim, Ming or Quan. For four years she had searched for their faces whenever coming to this area, to no avail. They had been her only means of contact with John Troy and Thomas Bailey. She had gone back to Mrs. McConnell's home to see if she had heard anything of Mr. Bailey, but the woman's daughter-in-law had answered the door. She said that Mrs. McConnell had gone to her final reward six months before, and they were in the process of selling her house. The young woman said she had not received any mail addressed to a Mary Sweeney. Mary lost track of all of her friends. Were they dead? Would she ever see any of them again?

She stopped for a minute to look in the window of the shop, and she watched a man make fortune cookies. His swift moving hands reminded her of Ming making rice balls, and she began to reflect on her life since arriving in America. When her family had arrived, she couldn't have been happier, but her destiny had not brought her the happiness she had hoped for. True, the trip from Ireland had been exciting and dangerous, and she loved the beautiful city by the bay, but something was missing. She found herself envying Catherine and Margaret, who were obviously happy with their new husbands. Mary was beginning to realize that her mother's life wasn't as dismal as she had once thought it to be. Her parents were happy in America, and they loved each other deeply. They were now living in a small cottage north of San Francisco. Life was much easier for them here, and they saw all of their children often. Her parents' love for each other had never faltered, they still treated each other with love and respect.

Jeremiah Sweeney was a proud man who would never accept charity. He always repaid his debts with cash, or with his carpentry skills. Margaret Foley Sweeney had always understood her husband and children. She calmed Irish tempers during lively family discussions, and she always brought a cheery attitude into any conversation. Jeremiah's broken leg had never healed properly, so he was not able to perform hard labor. A proud man, he didn't like his wife taking in other people's laundry, so he began collecting seashells and rocks from the beach, and then he polished and painted scenes on them. People flocked to the sandy beaches, so Jeremiah built a small wooden table, and bought an umbrella to keep out rain or sun, and spent most weekdays selling his collection.

Margaret just said, "God never shuts one door, but only opens another." Her husband's self-esteem returned, and on days he ran his little souvenir shop, Margaret would come along and practice her reading. One would often find her sitting on the shore with a blanket wrapped around her, a bonnet or scarf over her hair, and her nose in a book. The happy couple often exchanged glances and smiles during the day. After so many years together, they easily communicated without words. They both missed their beautiful homeland, but agreed that life for their family was much easier in America.

Mary stood at the window, watching the expert cookie maker, for at least five minutes. The bell in a church tower rang, jolting Mary back to the present. She turned and hurried toward her sister's house. It was important for Mary to get there in time to help her sister prepare the pies and cookies for the surprise "30th Anniversary Party" for their parents, which was planned for Sunday.

Margaret owned the only home large enough to accommodate the family. Jim and Jerry shared a small apartment down by the docks, close to where they both worked. Catherine's family was growing too fast for their small home. Married two years, Catherine and Tom Hurley were expecting their second child. Tom had been happy to emigrate with the Sweeney family. Johanna stayed with Catherine, so she could be close to school and help her sister with the baby. She attended the same private school Rachel went to, as Mrs. Goldstein had arranged a scholarship for her. Johanna spent much of her free time at the Goldstein's with Mary and her best friends, Rachel and Kate Murphy. Johanna, Rachel and Kate were inseparable and they all loved Mary.

Margaret and Mary had spent much time planning the coming celebration. They were to spend the evening and all of Saturday baking apple and rhubarb pies, making dressing, cranberry and applesauce, and polishing Margaret's new silver. The sisters enjoyed each other's much needed company. Although the day had begun with the usual fog hanging over the city, the sea breeze had swept away the haze, and the sky was now a glorious blue. The spring sunshine warmed Mary's face, reminding her of that fall day at the crossroads that had changed her family's destiny. They had forgiven her the pain that she had caused them by her sudden disappearance, but only after they were all safely in their new land. They still chastised her teasingly about that decision, but she knew they were all happy with where she had led them.

Everything was going well, except she missed the friends she had made on the way, and she often worried about running into Mr. Bane. His name still filled her with terror. Mary prayed often for him to meet his end, and would then pray for forgiveness for such evil desires. She kept a watchful eye out for him, wherever she went. Although her choice at the crossroads had brought happiness to the rest of her family, she felt that something important was missing from her own life. Everything about today reminded her of that destiny. That longing she felt four years ago welled up inside her, a longing that told her that her destiny was yet to be fulfilled.

Mary loved Hannah Goldstein, and she knew that the woman needed Mary, not as a servant, but as a companion, friend, and governess to her daughter. Her husband had died the year before Mary had arrived on her doorstep. Hannah was very sad at first, but Mary's companionship had helped both her and her daughter return to a more normal life. Their only other living relative was a niece who lived in New York City. Her late husband's money and holdings were in San Francisco. Hiram Goldstein had put their holdings in the hands of a trust officer at the bank, so that his wife would never have to worry about anything. However, Rachel's rebellious attitude toward her mother had put them at odds with each other. Hiram's death and Rachel's problems consumed Hannah. Mary's arrival had saved the older woman's sanity and her relationship with her daughter. Mary talked her into bringing Rachel home from the boarding school, to enroll her in a private school in the city. Rachel had been in the boarding school since she was eight years old, only coming home once a month. Laughter returned to the Goldstein home with Mary, who cheerfully spouted her now well-known sayings at the appropriate moment. Rachel loved her new life at home, especially after she, Johanna, and Kate Murphy became best friends. Lost in reminiscent thoughts of the last four years, Mary almost passed the house. When she looked up, she realized she was next to the white fence that surrounded her sister's beautiful new home.

"Hi Maggie, I'm here!" Mary called as she took off her cape and hung it on the oak coat rack in the hallway, another of their father's handiworks, and left her bag to the left of the front door. Maggie came down the stairs with an empty laundry basket in her hands.

"Hi Sis, how was yer day?"

"Very good, Maggie, and how was yers?"

"It went quite well, considering all the things I had to do today. I was very fortunate the fruit and vegetable markets were filled to the brim with luscious produce that I didn't grow this year. I think Mum and Da will be surprised, and pleased with the celebration we have planned. Jerry and Jim are taking them to mass early Sunday morning, and plan to arrive here around noon. If everything goes well, we'll be ready to surprise them when they arrive."

Maggie walked into the kitchen with Mary following. She had already prepared two plates with slices of roast beef, cheese, freshly baked bread, and two glasses of milk for their lunch. Suddenly famished from her walk, Mary sat down and ate every bite, licking her fingers and enjoying every morsel. When they were finished, they began making pie and cookie dough. The two sisters giggled while they baked, just like they used to back home in Ireland. The first time they had baked pies when they were young girls, they had made a big mess, and they were having as much fun this time too. Maggie had flour all over her blouse and apron, and Mary's clothes and face were smeared with flour and blueberries. Laughing loudly, they didn't hear Robert Sweeney and his friend come in the front door.

"Come on in the kitchen, John, I want ye to meet me wife." They heard Robert's voice only when he opened the swinging kitchen door. Mary was still laughing at Maggie's last cookie as she waved hello to Robert and glanced at the man standing behind him. Their eyes met, and recognition hit them both like a thunderbolt.

"John!"

"Mary!"

Ignoring Maggie and Robert they rushed into each other's arms, gushing with excitement.

"Where have ye been? I thought I lost ye forever. Mary Sweeney, I cannot believe it! I had no idea Robert was related to ye. He told me his last name was Sweeney, but that he had two brothers, so I didn't think ye were any relation."

"Robert is me brother-in-law! Maggie is me sister! She just happened to marry a man with the same last name. I've been working for a very nice family for the last four years. A different family than Ah Kim left me with. Have ye seen him? Is he okay?"

"Yes, Ah Kim is in Oregon, mining for gold. We were working on the railroad, but the money for supplies and workers ran out, so the project has been delayed. I took some time off, went back to Ireland to visit me family, and I just returned."

Ah Kim's trusted face came to Mary's mind. The concerned expression he wore at their last meeting had left her with concern about his welfare. She thought of the envelope that she had carefully sewn inside one of the panels of her quilt, and was relieved to hear that her dear friend was in good health. John's voice brought her back from the past.

"I'm heading that way again soon. In fact, I'm leaving Monday with the cavalry, to help put down the Indian rebellion that's brewing up there right now."

"So soon? John Troy, now don't ye be going off and getting yer scalp removed after I just found ye again. *'May the good Lord take a likin' to ye, but not too soon.'*" Mary remembered quoting the same blessing to Ah Kim as they had said goodbye that day.

John laughed and then tried to quell her fears. "Now don't ye be worrying! I'll not be losing ye again, little lady! Yer not obligated to anyone are ye now?"

"No, No! I haven't had time to be meeting with anybody!"

"Then Mary, I hope ye don't mind if I come a calling on ye." His brown eyes sparkled, and the new handlebar mustache gave him an older, more sophisticated look. Her heart began to thump furiously in her chest, and a passion arose inside her, stirring those same feelings he had brought out in her when they first met on the ship.

"I'd be delighted," she said, with the blueberry juice still smeared on her cheek.

"Well, Mary, are ye going to let us in on what's going on here?" Maggie asked, motioning to Mary to wipe her face, as she handed her a towel.

"Oh Maggie, I'm sorry. This is John Troy, the man, who with his uncle, helped me get to America and get settled, and helped save me from a man on the ship, who... well he wasn't a nice man."

"Mr. Troy, it is very nice to meet ye." Maggie said, "Would ye have a cup of tea?"

"I would love one, Mrs. Sweeney."

"Maggie, call me Maggie, and thanks so much for looking out for me sister, cuz she's a mighty special person."

"I can't tell ye how happy I am to have found her again. Robert, thank ye so much for inviting me over to yer family's celebration."

"Ye are welcome. I'm so glad we met, or ye wouldn't even be here."

"Yes, tell us how ye two met." Maggie asked.

"Well Maggie, I stopped after work at O'Shaughnessy's Pub, seein' as how they were celebrating Saint Paddy's Day, and John was sitting with some friends of mine and a Cavalry officer. We got to talking and found out we were both from County Cork; him from Glenbeg, and me from Midleton. When he asked me if I knew of a boarding house where he could stay for a couple of nights, I insisted he come home with me, and enjoy the festivities. Hope that is okay with ye, Maggie, me dear?"

"Of course, it is okay. If ye hadn't invited him here, Mary and John would never have found each other again. Now tell us more about what happened, Mary."

"I have a lot of questions, meself, Maggie. John, have ye seen or heard anything about Mr. Bane?" Mary asked, afraid to hear the answer.

"Now Mary, don't ye be worrying yer pretty little head over the likes of him. I'm sure the man will meet his maker soon, if he hasn't already." A chill ran down his spine, as he thought of the words he'd heard that Bane had spoken about Mary, only two years ago.

'I'll have my way with the little Irish vixen one way or another, someday. She ruined me life. My nose is so ugly, where she bit me, that no woman will look at me decent.'

John didn't tell Mary what he'd heard, or that Bane had been in Oregon when he'd left the country. He quickly changed the subject.

"I'm afraid me uncle, Thomas, died not too long after we parted company in Oregon, under rather suspicious circumstances. He died on the ship on his way back to Ireland. It seems his heart just failed him. However, the purser who found him on board the ship sent a letter home with his body, which said, "He died with a look of fright on his face that terrified those who found him."

"I'm so sorry! He was a lovely man." Mary's eyes filled with tears remembering the gentle, sweet man, who had done so much to help her. She remembered the day she had met him in the pasture, in Ireland. "He was a man who certainly has been lifted up to Heaven immediately. A man with a heart like his, most certainly, has gone directly there. I am sure that he arrived in heaven a full half hour before the devil knew he died."

John smiled, happy to hear her beloved blessings again. "Yes, I'm told they held a wake in Ireland that was as good as Saint Patrick's."

"Do ye think Bane had anything to do with his death?"

"I've wondered about that ever since, Mary. Guess I'll never know what really happened. They said there were no marks on him. His death certificate said 'probable heart attack'."

"I hope I didn't cause his death. He would never have gotten involved with Bane, if it wasn't for me!"

"Now Mary, we don't know if Bane had anything to do with it."

"Oh, yes we do! I can feel it in me bones. I know he was the one, or one of his friends. Satan has many friends." She choked back tears as her eyes filled with water. "When did ye last see Bane?"

John hesitated before answering, but decided he shouldn't withhold anything from her. "The truth is Mary, I saw him jest afore I left for Ireland, in Eastern Oregon. He was riding with several mean looking fellas heading east. He is still looking for some gold mine. He's after gold, not ye." John couldn't see what good it would do to tell her what he'd heard, not now anyway.

"Who is Bane, Mary?" Margaret interrupted. They had been so involved in their own conversation they had completely ignored Robert and Margaret's presence.

"I'm sorry Margaret. Bane, well, he sort of gave me a few problems on board the ship."

"I thought ye said your trip over here was uneventful?"

"I'm afraid I was not entirely truthful about that, Maggie. I didn't want to frighten anyone. I was afraid ye wouldn't join me if ye thought the trip might be dangerous, and I didn't want to worry Mum and Da."

Mary and John took turns relating the events of their trip on the "Harmony", as Maggie poured tea for the two men, and Mary made them plates of food.

When they were finished, Mary asked John, "I wrote ye and yer uncle several letters, but I didn't know where to send them, so I just addressed them in care of the Post Office in Portland.

Did ye get them?"

"No Mary, I did not receive yer letters. I wrote to ye in care of the Chinese laundry, where we left letters for ye and Ah Kim, but me letters were returned marked: "Not at this address - addressee unknown"."

"The laundry was burned to the ground during the riots, and I haven't been able to locate Ah Kim's relatives. Working for Mrs. Gordon didn't work out either. She is not a very nice person."

"I'm sorry. Did me Uncle get ye that position?"

"It wasn't his fault. His letter introduced me to an acquaintance of hers, who didn't know Mrs. Gordon well. When I left there, a nice neighbor lady got me in touch with Mrs. Goldstein. I'm sure if Mrs. Gordon received any letters from ye, she would have burned them. I see how we lost touch with each other."

"Let's not let that ever happen again, Mary. I'm so happy to have found ye again."

The four of them spent that evening and the next day laughing and talking as they hung decorations, set up chairs, and prepared for the surprise anniversary party. Mary smiled at John and said a silent prayer of thanks. Out loud she recited an Irish blessing: *"May the roof above you never fall in, and your friends gathered below never fall out."*

Chapter Fifteen

"The Anniversary Party"

March, 1877

"May you die in bed at ninety five, shot by a jealous spouse."

Everything was perfect for Jeremiah and Margaret Sweeney's anniversary, until the unexpected guest arrived. Most of the celebrants were thrilled to see him, but his arrival almost ruined the party for Mary. Her parents had been duly surprised when they walked in the door and saw the bright colored banners wishing them a "Happy 30th Anniversary". John and Robert had worked late the night before hanging the decorations that the four of them had spent much time making. When the Sweeneys' offspring, their husbands, and friends, yelled "surprise" and popped out of their hiding places, tears of joy welled up in Margaret's bright blue eyes. Jeremiah Sweeney broke into loud Irish laughter and kissed his wife's joyous tears. The happy couple beamed throughout the festivities. They spoke of how the last thirty years, the good and the bad, had only made their love stronger.

When the guests descended upon Jeremiah and Margaret with love and well wishes, Jerry handed them glasses of champagne. As the oldest son, he made the first toast to his Mother and Father to begin the celebration: *"Here's to health, peace, and prosperity; May the flower of love never be nipped by the frost of disappointment, nor shadow of grief fall among your family or friends."*

Everyone shouted in unison, "Slainte!" (slawn-cha) The Gaelic toast meaning: health.

One by one, the Sweeney children offered a different toast to their parents, with either an Irish blessing or proverb.

Margaret went next: *"May there be a generation of children on the children of your children."*

"Slainte!"

Jim raised his glass: *"May God grant you to be as happy as the flowers in May."*

"Slainte!"

Jerry refilled their glasses and Catherine took her turn: *"May the saddest day of the future be no worse than the happiest day of your past."*

"Slainte!"

Johanna was in line to take her turn, even though her glass held only lemonade: *"With the first light of sun ~ Bless you, When the long day is done ~ Bless you, In your smiles and your tears ~ Bless you, Through each day of your years ~ Bless you!"*

"Slainte!"

Finally, Mary took her turn: *"It is easy to be pleasant, when life flows by like a song, but the man worthwhile is the one who will smile, when everything goes dead wrong. For the test of the heart is trouble, it always comes with years, and the smile that is worth the praises of earth is the smile that shines through tears."*

"Slainte!"

Jerry filled the glasses once more and Jeremiah Sweeney raised his glass again: "I am so proud of me wonderful children and me beautiful wife. I want to toast ye all with a blessing that is a most appropriate blessing for this special day."

"How does one measure time? No, not in days, months or years; it is measured by the most precious of all things ~ Love. Without which, all beings and things, whether brave and or beautiful, would perish."

"Slainte!"

His wife spoke last, as tears of joy streamed down her face: *"May ye all live long, die happy, and rate a mansion in Heaven!"*

"Slainte!"

Jeremiah and Margaret entwined their arms, raised their glasses and together thanked their children in their native Gaelic; "Go raibh maith agat".

After the traditional Irish toasts, Mary introduced John Troy to her family. They liked him immediately. Mary beamed as she looked at his handsome face. She admired his dark eyes and hair, his fair skin and straight white teeth. He had become even better looking since she had seen him last. His shoulders had filled out, and the new mustache gave him more character.

Mary had grown into a woman and he thought her maturity had brought her even more beauty. At nineteen, she was no longer a girl, and John was now twenty-six. He loved her strong-minded personality, and found her laughter contagious. If staring at her hadn't been rude, he would have spent the party just watching her. Her parents saw the look in his eyes, when he spoke to her, and smiled at each other knowingly.

Johanna and her two friends were also impressed with Mary's new friend. They hung around him most of the day, charmed by his good looks and humorous remarks. The three teenagers just giggled and occupied themselves by teasing the family, especially Mary and her new beau, but when the unexpected guest arrived, the girls turned their attention to him.

When the champagne bottles were empty, the guests were served a fabulous feast of roast turkey, mashed potatoes and gravy, sweet potatoes, cranberries, fresh fruit, and vegetables, most of which Margaret had grown in her backyard garden. Margaret brought out her home-made Irish ale after dinner, and Jerry began playing the fiddle. The family only drank on rare occasions, unlike many of their friends and neighbors in Ireland, who often celebrated at the end of every week. When the Sweeneys drank, it was usually the ale made from a very old recipe that was handed down from their ancestors. No one knew how old the recipe was, but they all enjoyed it.

The music turned from toe tapping to a full-fledged Irish jig. They danced on the dining room floor, after the women cleared the large oak table, and the men moved it into the hallway. The girls took turns dancing with Jim, and each other. Even Jeremiah was dancing, in spite of his bad leg. John took Mary's hand and led her around the dance floor, with a wide grin on his face. He was as light on his feet as she was, and they danced almost every dance, until Jerry stopped playing so he could take a rest and imbibe some more spirits himself. When the music stopped, Mary fell laughing into John's arms, as if she'd done that all of her life. Her mother handed them full glasses of ale. Mary rarely drank, and the liquor made her feel euphoric and lightheaded.

The young couple sat on the bottom stair of the winding hall staircase and enjoyed the thirst quenching ale, laughing and trying to catch their breath. As she listened to him talk, she realized how comfortable she was with him. When she talked, he really seemed to listen to her and care about what she was saying. Mary liked everything about him.

"Promise to marry me when I come back?" He asked her suddenly.

"Marry ye? Why John I just met ye." She giggled.

"I've been thinking about ye for the last four years, lass. I feel like I've known ye all me life. I don't want to leave ye again, but I want to have something to offer ye, and right now I don't have anything. So will ye promise to wait for me, Mary, me darlin'?"

"Yes, John!" Mary looked in his eyes with love. "I'll be waiting for ye, so ye better come back or I'll really be mad at ye."

"The only reason I wouldn't come back is if I'm dead, me girl, cuz yer the girl I want to marry."

"Don't ye be talking like that, John Stephen Troy! Ye'll be back or I won't forgive ye, and ye won't want that a bothering yer soul forever, would ye? I'd never let ye rest."

"I'd love every minute of it, me girl. Don't ye worry none. I'll be back, and right soon too. Don't ye be worrying about me."

Mary was about to spew forth one of her Irish blessings when there came a knock at the door. When she opened the door, she was so surprised at the face that met hers that she stood there with her mouth open. Sean Foley hadn't changed a lot. He only looked a few years older. Her uncle greeted her with a hug and kiss, to which she responded coldly. She could smell the liquor on his breath. "Mary, me girl, how are ye? I ain't seen ye since ye took off in the middle of the night a few years back. Ye look mighty fine. Even better now since yer body's done a little more growing." He rushed past her into the living room to greet the rest of the family. She was so upset at the sight of him that she just stood there dumbfounded.

"Where's me dear sister and her fine husband? I wanted to be here for this special occasion. I didn't think I would make it on time. There was a storm at sea which delayed the ship. We just docked this morning, and I spent the rest of the day finding this place."

Margaret and Jeremiah came to greet him, followed by pleasantries from the rest of the family. Jerry was the only one, besides Mary, who didn't seem happy to see him.

"What's wrong, Mary? Who is that? Ye don't seem too happy to see him." John saw the sudden scowl Mary wore and Jerry's frown, as he joined them.

"He's me uncle, well sort of. Mum and Da raised him, after mum's da died in the famine. Sean never knew his real father. Me grandfather married Sean's mum before he was born to give him a name. Mum just told me that a few weeks back when I asked her about him. When me grandfather Foley and Sean's mother died, Sean was but a babe, so me parents took him in."

"Then why aren't ye and Jerry happy to see him."

"Let's just say we had a little falling out before I left Ireland, and leave it at that." Mary said. "Perhaps he's done some changing since then."

"I doubt it, Mary, I doubt it." Jerry murmured. "But Mum and Da are happy to see him, so let us try to make the best of it."

Sean had put on some muscle since Mary last saw him. He worked in the bogs for over a year, after she left, and was now a big strapping man who would most likely beat almost any man in an arm wrestling contest. Irish good looks, including curly auburn hair, freckles, straight white teeth, and dimples, made him a man that any lass would look at twice. But, Mary couldn't forget that night at the cottage, and she wondered if he still held those lecherous urges beneath his hearty good looks. She decided to give him a chance, but she planned on keeping an eye on him.

Margaret led him to the kitchen to fix him a plate of food, and Mary took a deep breath. Entirely sober now, she returned to her conversation with John.

"Do ye have to leave tomorrow? It doesn't seem right that ye have to leave so soon, now that I found ye again."

"I know. We always seem to be headed in the opposite direction. We are leaving tomorrow morning to catch up with the rest of the cavalry, which leaves Sacramento on Tuesday. It seems there is an uprising of one of the Indian tribes in Eastern Oregon. The cavalry is asking for volunteers to help them put the Indians down. General Howard is already there, and this bunch is headed there to meet up with him.

"It'll be safer riding up there with them. I'm hoping there won't be any fighting, and I'm not sure I will join them if there is. I don't feel too good about killing people who lived there before the white man ever got to this country. I figure they might feel like the Irish do about the English in Ireland."

"Yer right, John. It doesn't seem much different."

"Maybe I'll run into the famous "Buffalo Bill" or some such famous fella and hear some good stories." He tried to lighten the conversation. "But, don't ye be worrying none now. I'll be real careful, so I can come back to get me pretty little lassie."

"I'll be praying for yer safety every day that yer gone, John Troy. How long do ye think I'll be praying?"

"Long as it takes me to make enough money working on that railroad to get us a parcel of land to live on. I will write as often as I am able. The work on the railroad is supposed to start back up on the line going through to Huntington. Some sort of politics, and lack of supplies, put the project on hold for a while. They are ready to begin again, and asked me to run a crew of Chinese putting the rest of the rails down. Ah Kim and his cousins are mining while they're waiting to join me crew. I'll be back as soon as I can."

"I'll be saving some money too, so that we can have some nice things to start our home with. John, I'm happy to be betrothed to ye, and I'll be counting the days until ye return"

"Mary, Mary, I'll miss ye, and hearing all yer little sayings!"

"Here's another for ye to remember: *'May you die in bed at ninety-five, shot by a jealous spouse!'"*

John laughed, as he pulled Mary back out on the dance floor and Jerry started fiddling again.

"Maybe ye should be talking to me parents about yer proposal." She uttered, as he expertly guided her around the floor.

"I already did, and they said yes."

"Why John, how did ye know I'd say yes?"

"I know ye love me Mary. I can see it in yer eyes."

"Aye, John, yer right. I do love ye! I think ye are me destiny." Just then, they ran into Sean and Rachel who were dancing too. Mary was immediately concerned about her young charge's welfare, and couldn't help frowning at Sean. He just looked at her and laughed. Sean's smirk spoiled the rest of the day for Mary. Her intuition told her to watch him, which took a lot of her attention away from her last day with John.

Sean took turns dancing with the three young girls. They all seemed to be taken with him. Even Johanna seemed to adore him like a big brother, instead of an uncle. At least he didn't bother Johanna, or so she assumed, seeing the way she acted around him.

The other two girls couldn't take their eyes off of him. The three of them stood in a line waiting their turn to dance with him. Mary felt sick inside. How could she warn these girls without telling on him? What if he had changed? Maybe it was just the drink that had made him act that way that night in Macroom? If he had changed, she didn't want to ruin his new beginning. Her parents thought of him as a son, and they would be devastated if they knew about that night, but she knew it would hurt them more if he bothered one of the girls. Mary was torn and decided to talk to Sean herself. Jerry was keeping an eye on him too. He kept playing fast tunes to wear Sean out, so he couldn't get too close to the girls.

When Sean went into the kitchen with Rachel, Mary excused herself and followed them through the swinging door. Rachel was filling two plates with food, and Sean was filling two glasses with ale.

"Who's the second glass of ale fer, Sean?"

"I thought I'd bring one to Jerry since he's been fiddling so long. He looks like he could use something to quench his thirst."

"I thought maybe ye was planning on giving it to me Rachel here." Mary said protectively.

"Thanks, Sean. I could use a glass of ale." Jerry came from behind her and took the glass out of Sean's hand. "Rachel, why don't ye take those two plates to yer friends, and I'll fill up another one and bring it to ye?"

"Thank you, Jerry!" Rachel was unaware of the coolness in the air. "You are so lucky, Mary, to have such a big family that all takes care of one another like yours does. All I have is my mother, bless her soul, and she's not very young anymore."

"Yer a lucky girl, Rachel. Yer mum is a wonderful woman, and yer family history is something to be very proud of. By the way, when ye girls are ready to go to Catherine's, John Troy and I will be driving ye girls in his buckboard."

"I rented a rig, Mary." Sean spoke up. "I'll be glad to give the girls a ride home."

"No, thank ye, Sean. John and I will be taking the girls home."

"Yer new to the area, Sean. Ye'd probably get yerself lost and never find yer way back." Jerry added. "Go on now, Rachel. I'll bring yer plate right away." He picked up a plate off of the stack and put a slice of turkey on it.

As soon as Rachel had left the room, Mary turned to Sean. "Sean, ye better not lay a finger on any of those lasses, or I'll be damning yer soul to hell."

"Why Mary, me dear niece, what has come over ye? I am offended ye'd even think I'd be doing any such thing."

"I'll never forget what ye tried to do to me in the cottage that night in Macroom?"

"Dear girl, what are ye talking about? What night in the cottage?"

"Ye know darn good and well what happened that night. Ye were drunk and tried putting yer filthy hands all over me."

"Don't forget, Sean, I was there too." Jerry was getting angry also. "Yer darn lucky I didn't tell Mum and Da what ye was trying to do to Mary."

"I don't remember nothin' like that happening. It must have been the drink, because I would never knowingly put me hands on any young lasses."

"Well, I fer one find that hard to believe, seeing how ye got yerself quite a reputation with the ladies in Macroom. Is that why yer here? Did the villagers run ye out of town for yer gallavantin' ways?"

"I don't know how ye can say such a thing, nephew. I finally raised enough money fer me passage."

"Listen to me, Sean." Mary interrupted. "If I have to tell Mum and Da, I will, and they'll disown ye forever. Do ye understand me?"

"And I'll whip ye from here to kingdom come!" Jerry added.

John walked in the kitchen just then, and feeling the tension in the air he said, "Did I interrupt something?"

"No, nothing at all!" Sean took his glass of ale and left the room quickly.

"I told the girls we'd take them home in a while because they all have school tomorrow. If that's okay with ye, John?"

"All right, Mary, me girl. That will give me a few minutes alone with ye on the way back here, so I can say a private goodbye. I'm to meet the other men tonight, as we leave early in the morning."

"Well, maybe I should be going along to chaperon this goodbye?" Jerry said, kidding his sister.

"Now Jerry, I'm not a young girl, anymore!" Mary blushed, as she spoke.

John laughed, but reassured her brother anyway. "Don't worry, Jerry. I love and respect yer sister, and plan on marrying her as soon as I can. I'd never compromise her in any way."

"I know that John, or I wouldn't even let her leave with ye."

"As if I can't make up me own mind about who I'll go with."

"Awe, Mary. We didn't mean to offend ye. We both love ye. That's all."

Sean spent the rest of his time talking to Jeremiah and Margaret Sweeney. They offered him a room until he found a place of his own. He agreed, and he said he would take them home in his rented rig, so they could stay a little longer. Jerry and Jim were leaving as they had to work early the next morning.

Mary wasn't going back to the Goldstein's until morning, because she wanted to help Margaret clean up after the party, so John took her back to her sister's house, after dropping off the three giggling girls at Catherine's doorsteps.

The happy couple sat cuddling on the hard buckboard seat, neither wanting to say goodnight. When Mary's hands got too cold in the chilly San Francisco air, John finally insisted they say goodbye.

"Mary, just remember, I love ye very much, and I'll be back as soon as possible." He gave her a kiss that was so full of passion that she didn't want him to ever stop. His soft lips stirred feelings deep within her. She waved as he drove away, trying to catch her breath and slow down her heart, before climbing the steps to her sister's door. She touched her lips and closed her eyes, to capture the memory of that last kiss. That memory would keep him alive in her heart, until he returned.

Chapter Sixteen

"Mary's Aching Heart"

Spring, 1877

"Everything would have been perfect, except for the fact that she still hadn't heard from John."

The memory of John's last kiss, and words of love, kept Mary's spirits high for a while after he left for Oregon, but she soon realized that she missed him dreadfully, and wished he would have asked her to go with him. She felt conflicted, as she also knew that Hannah and Rachel still needed her, and that she wouldn't have gone with him without a wedding ring on her finger. Mary wasn't the type to feel sorry for herself, so she kept busy during the day trying to forget her aching heart. That wasn't so easy at night when her dreams were inundated with him, and a new life in Oregon.

Whatever she did seemed to remind her of John. When Catherine gave birth to her beautiful baby boy, Mary was by her side. Holding her nephew for the first time made her wonder what her own babies' tiny faces would look like. She was elated when a letter from John arrived three weeks after he left. Mary decided to write to him once a week, whether she received a letter in return or not, as his second letter didn't come for several more weeks. She had the address of the post office, in Baker City, and assumed he might get a lot of her letters at once. She thought he probably didn't get into town that often, especially if he was working far from there. Mary tried not to worry about him, but it was difficult. The reports of the Indian War brewing in the Oregon Territory constantly nagged at her. Also worrying her were John's words about Bane being in Oregon. 'What if he went after John?'

Rachel Goldstein's coming out party kept Mary busy for several weeks. She had so many preparations to take care of that by the time she went to bed she was too exhausted to worry. There was the house to clean, food preparations to plan, decorating to oversee, invitations to send, and Mrs. Goldstein and the three girls to outfit for the special evening. After weeks of preparation, the day arrived and Mary anticipated a perfect evening.

She spent the morning overseeing the kitchen preparations. The catering company she had hired arrived early with all of the items Mary had finally decided on. The quantities she had ordered should be enough for the amount of guests they were expecting. The food for the gala included five different canapés and champagne to be served first, then plates of assorted meats, cheeses, vegetables, breads, and cakes that were to be arranged buffet style on the large dining room table. Hannah didn't have enough room for that many people at a sit down dinner, and many parties that Rachel attended had been served similarly. The champagne and bottles of wine were for the adults, and a large punch bowl was in the center of the table, for those who didn't imbibe and for the younger people at the party. Four girls had been hired to serve the beverages and canapés, and to clean up when the party was over. After checking to make sure everything was going right in the kitchen, Mary did a final check throughout the downstairs where the guests would mingle. When she thought everything was perfect, she climbed the winding staircase to help the girls dress for the ball.

Rachel's gown was made of light blue silk and it looked lovely on her. It had a round neckline, dainty puffy sleeves, and a beautiful full skirt that enhanced her tiny waist. The dark blue velvet sash and matching trim on the sleeves were the same shade as Rachel's eyes. It was a simple but elegant dress, highlighted by Hannah's gift of a deep blue sapphire necklace. Her tiny dark blue velvet slippers, and the matching ribbon that held her thick black hair high on her head, accentuated her heart shaped face.

"Ye look like a beautiful porcelain doll." Mary told the beloved girl, when she was finished dressing.

The three best friends had spent the previous day helping Mary hang decorations, and doing the last minute cleaning and rearranging. Neither Kate nor Johanna belonged in the same social circle as Rachel, but they all attended the same school, and as her best friends, Rachel would not have a party without them.

The Sweeney family had pooled their resources to finance Johanna's apparel. Margaret purchased the pink taffeta, and Mary spent hours designing and hand sewing the gown that her little sister would wear for the special occasion. Catherine dyed the white satin shoes, she had worn at her own wedding, to match the pink in the fabric. Her two brothers paid for the delicate pink and white lace shawl she would wear around her shoulders. Hannah Goldstein loaned her a lovely amethyst necklace. When Mary pulled Johanna's curls high on the back of her head, with a white comb and a pink taffeta ribbon, she looked like a princess. Her golden hair accentuated her high cheekbones and large blue eyes. Mary told her little sister that she had become a beautiful young woman.

As lovely as Johanna and Rachel looked when Mary finished, neither of them could compare to Kate Murphy. Kate had a sensuous look, which the two other girls lacked. They still looked like schoolgirls next to her. The girl was blessed with a well-developed body that made her appear older than her two friends. Kate brought her dress and accessories to Rachel's early in the day, so they could all get ready together.

When she came out to show Mary how she looked, her beauty took Mary's breath away. Thick dark red hair fell to her shoulders and was held back with a dark green velvet ribbon that framed her oval face. The ribbon was made from a leftover piece of the stunning velvet gown she wore. The dress had long sleeves, a full skirt, and a plunging neckline. Her shoes matched her dress perfectly. A stunning emerald pendant lay provocatively on the flesh that overflowed from the top of her dress. Her almond shaped green eyes sparkled, when she showed her lovely white teeth, full red lips, and enchanting dimples. Kate was a happy girl who possessed a deep bubbly laugh that made her more endearing. Johanna and Rachel didn't care that Kate was always the center of attention, because they were her two biggest fans.

The much anticipated ball was a huge success. All three of the girls danced all evening. Handsome, rich, young men took turns twirling the lovely debutantes around the floor. The small group of musicians that Mary hired played beautiful music. Kate's dance card was filled first, and several young men crowded around her whenever she wasn't dancing. At one point, four young men brought her a cup of punch. Johanna and Rachel had a wonderful time, as well as everyone else in attendance.

It was late in the evening, when Sean Foley crashed the party. He looked very handsome in a rented tuxedo, so Hannah Goldstein welcomed him, after he introduced himself as Mary and Johanna's uncle. Mary was in the kitchen when he arrived, overseeing the clean-up by the caterers. The evening was almost over when she realized her uncle was there. Johanna told Mary later that she had invited her uncle to the ball.

Sean immediately set his sights on the gorgeous redhead. Irish charm made him very attractive to young ladies. After dancing with Johanna and Rachel, he took Kate by the hand and escorted her to the dance floor.

"Kate Murphy, yer certainly a lovely sight. A vision of loveliness ye are, me girl."

"Thank you, Mr. Foley. It's nice to see you again. I didn't get to talk to you very much at Mr. and Mrs. Sweeney's anniversary party."

"Well, ye know how it is, little darlin', ye've got to pay attention to yer family."

"Yes sir, I know. There are certain unwritten rules one has to follow."

"Yes, and ye know me little Mary Sweeney wouldn't be happy if she saw me dancing with ye this evening. In fact, she wouldn't be happy to see me at all."

"Why is that, Mr. Foley?"

"Call me Sean, darlin, call me Sean. Mary's never taken a likin' to me Kate. I don't know why. I've tried so hard to be a good uncle to her. She was always partial to her brother Jerry, and Jerry and I just never got along. Maybe Jerry poisoned her mind against me.

Anyway, I don't want to upset things here tonight, so I'll just be watchin' yer beauty from afar, if that's okay with ye."

Kate blushed. "You flatter me, Sean."

"I was wondering, pretty lady, if I could escort ye for an evening in San Francisco sometime soon?"

"Oh, Sean, I don't know. I'm not allowed to see men alone, especially men your age."

"I wouldn't want ye to get in trouble with yer folks, but ye know I'm only a few years older than Mary. I could send a carriage for ye, one of these evenings, and show ye some of the excitement on the Barbary Coast. Ye know I'm a respectable fellow, now don't ye? What else could I be, related to prim little Mary Sweeney?"

"I'm sure you are, Sean. I didn't mean anything. My parents are very strict though."

"I understand. If ye don't want to see me, it's okay."

"Oh no, I'd love to see you. I just know my parents wouldn't allow it."

"Well, maybe we should just keep it our little secret. It might not be a good idea to even tell Rachel or Johanna. I certainly don't want to harm yer reputation none."

"Well, I don't know."

"If ye were just a few years older, it would surely be all right. I tell ye what, I'll send a carriage to pick ye up one block from

Rachel's house, on the far corner next Friday around seven. If ye don't want to come, jest don't show up. If ye do, jest tell yer parents yer spending the evening with Rachel."

"If at all possible, I'll try to be there. I'd love to see the Barbary Coast."

"Okay, darlin', I'll come meself. Now, don't ye worry about a thing, it'll be a wonderful evening. We'll just go out for a cup of tea." He winked at her and smiled his most charming smile, kissed her hand, and left her breathless by the punch bowl, just as Mary came out of the kitchen.

Sean walked up to Mary first. "Hello Mary, how's me dear niece tonight?"

"What are ye doing here?" Mary spoke coldly, upset to see him. "Ye ruined the last party for me. Who invited ye to this one?"

"I just wanted to see Johanna on her big evening. I'll be leaving right away. She certainly has turned into a lovely young lady, hasn't she?"

"Yes, she has, and ye keep yer filthy hands to yerself. Do ye hear me, Sean Foley?"

"Now Mary, hang on to that temper of yers. I'd never touch that sweet young thing, jest like I'd have never bothered ye if I'd been in my right mind. I don't even remember the occasion, girl. That was another reason I came this evening. I wanted to apologize to ye for whatever I did that night. I'd never do anything to hurt ye, or me sister, ye know that don't ye, girl?"

"I hope not. And don't be calling me girl. Jest don't ever let anything like that happen again, Sean, or I swear I'll be telling Mum and Da."

"Don't ye be worrying none, little niece. I'll be leaving now, so I won't be disturbing yer party anymore."

"I think that's a good idea. Goodbye, Sean."

"Goodnight, Mary." He gave her that brilliant smile, and she got a cold chill down her spine as he left. She still didn't trust him.

After he left, Hannah said it was time to serve the cake, and she got busy and forgot all about Sean Foley. The party ended at ten. After Mary finished in the kitchen, and saw all the guests to the front door, she was exhausted. Hannah had said goodnight about an hour earlier, leaving Mary to oversee the final cleanup. It was an exciting evening for the older woman, but she was so tired when it was over that she could hardly climb the stairs. Hannah asked Mary to take her place at the door for the goodbyes, and excused herself, before retiring.

The girls were still giggling and laughing when Mr. and Mrs. Murphy, and Jerry Sweeney, picked up Kate and Johanna to take them home. Mary went to Rachel's room to help her take down her hair and hang up her gown.

"Ye certainly looked lovely, Rachel. Did ye have a good time?"

"Oh Mary, it was wonderful! I can't wait for the next party. I never expected it to be that much fun. I was dreading it, in fact. It wouldn't have been as much fun without Johanna and Kate. I think they had as good a time as I did. Victoria Hill's ball is next month, and I'm really looking forward to it. I wish Jo and Kate could come too, but Victoria will never invite them."

"Does Victoria attend your school?"

"Yes, but she thinks she's better than everybody else. To tell you the truth, Mary, she seems to have it in for the Irish. We got in an argument about it last week. And well, she really doesn't like Kate. I think she's jealous because Kate is the most popular girl at school. I know she won't invite either of them. She thinks they are beneath her on the social registry. Maybe I shouldn't go either." A flash of disappointment crossed Rachel's face.

"Rachel, ye'll be going to her party. My family is simply not wealthy like everyone else here tonight. We can't afford to buy her a new dress for a ball once a month. Johanna was very excited to attend tonight. The Murphys are very rich people, though, so I'm sure Kate will be feeling poorly about it. It's too bad there are people who think they're better than others. I know there's a lot of bad feelings toward the Irish, but it's not yer fault, and there isn't anything ye can do about it. I'm surprised that Victoria came this evening, knowing the girls were going to be here."

"I didn't tell her they were coming. I was afraid she'd make a fuss and stop all the other girls from attending. I didn't want Jo and Kate to be hurt in any way by her remarks. Victoria better not say anything at school, Monday, or I'll be ready to slap her face."

"Ye have been hanging around us Irish 'micks' too long now. Seems like ye have developed a temper, me girl. Don't ye be slapping anyone or ye'll be ousted from school. At least ye only have another week and school will be out. Don't worry about us, the Irish are tough. Yer party was wonderful! Yer a lovely young lady, and yer mum and I are very proud of ye, and that's all that matters. So don't ye worry none. Get yerself to bed now."

Mary kissed Rachel on top of her head, as the girl climbed into her big feather bed. Then she blew out the candle on the dresser and quietly left the room. The evening had been wonderful and Mary was as happy as Rachel was about its success. Everything would have been perfect, if it weren't for the fact that she hadn't heard from John.

Her prayers were answered when a letter arrived the next day.

My dearest Mary,

Words cannot tell you how much I miss seeing your sweet smile. I am so glad that I found you again. My heart soars, thinking of your soft lips and our last kiss. I cannot wait until we are together at last.

I must now speak of other things or I will become sad, because I miss you so much! Let me relate the happenings of the last six weeks: I didn't have the time in my last letter to tell you of our trip here, as the mail was going out shortly and I wanted to get that letter off.

It was a long rough trip getting here. I have never enjoyed sleeping on the hard ground, and find it even harder to sleep while listening to snoring noises from soldiers sleeping in nearby tents. I wonder how long it takes the soldiers to get used to those nightly sounds. It amazes me that they sleep at all. It would seem to me that any tribe of Indians could easily have found us by simply putting their ears to the wind.

There is a war brewing that could break out at any time. The Nez Perce nation is getting very restless, and things could explode over just about anything. I pray nightly that the government will relent and let the Nez Perce stay in the "Valley of the Winding Waters", as they call it. White men have named it the Wallowa Valley. I am torn between siding with my fellow countrymen or the gentle "dreamers" who were here long before the white man arrived. I cannot help to think the white man is wrong on this one, but I also feel I must protect the women and children if the Indians do decide to go on the warpath. Leaning too far toward the side of the Indians could make me very unpopular with the white settlers, and perhaps could cause me to lose me my position on the railroad. I am in a quandary.

This trouble has been brewing for many years. I've gotten to know one of the soldiers quite well, and he told me a little of the history of the area. It seems, it all started when President Grant issued a proclamation in 1875 that opened the Wallowa Valley to settlement. That automatically took the rights to the valley away from the Nez Perce, who have always lived in that valley. General Howard is in charge here, and he wrote to the Secretary of War, advising them that they might provoke war if they tried to force Chief Joseph and his tribes out of their beloved valley. General Howard was transferred to Fort Vancouver last year, and he spent much time talking to the Chief himself before writing that letter.

The general is a very interesting man who seems to be very well liked by his men. He is a man of average height and is missing an arm, which I heard was shot off during a cavalry charge in the Civil

War. His thick beard, mustache, and full head of hair are pure white. They say he is a deeply religious man, with a quiet, but friendly, manner. He is known to be honest, kind, fair, and willing to believe the best about anyone.

It seems Chief Joseph has many of the same qualities. He is very honored and respected by his people. I think he is probably in his late thirties and is very tall and handsome. My friend told me that many say his chin and mouth are very much like that of Napoleon the first. Alokut is his younger brother. He is taller than Chief Joseph and is also very handsome. They are both known to be happy, carefree leaders of the younger men, and seem to be well liked by both Indians and white people.

The white settlers in the Valley started the latest problems. They sent the governor of Oregon a telegram, in February, which was filled with lies. They said that the Indians were driving off, and killing, the settler's livestock and threatening the settlers. The governor sent General Howard here with two troops of cavalry. He found that the Nez Perce weren't anywhere near where the trouble was supposed to have started. That was when General Howard wrote his letter.

Everything really got fired up last summer between the two groups when two settlers, A B Findley and Wells McNall, thought their horses were stolen by some of the Nez Perce. They went to the Indian village with rifles, looking for their horses, and accused the Indians of stealing them. A young warrior, named We-Lot-Yah, tried to take the gun from McNall when he threatened the Indians. McNall yelled for help, Findley fired and killed the young unarmed warrior. The two white men escaped unharmed. The Indians like Findley, but *they do not like McNall. The Nez Perce were very angry when the settlers found their horses grazing quietly near the Findley ranch.*

Agent Monteith wrote to General Howard asking him to protect the Indians. He stated that the attack had been entirely unprovoked by the Indians, and that the settlers committed "willful, deliberate, murder." But, some of the settlers tried to provoke the Indians into fighting back, hoping to get the Indians removed from the land they wanted. The Indians held a council and the younger warriors wanted revenge. Chief Joseph sent an ultimatum to the settlers, demanding surrender of the guilty men.

If Chief Joseph hadn't withdrawn his threat, there would have been war. After much discussion between Joseph and the general, the chief agreed to keep his tribe on the south side of Hurricane Creek, if the whites would agree to stay on the north side. The white men promised to try the guilty men before civil authorities. When the trial was finally held in Union County, the Indians refused to testify against Findley, because they liked him, but they were very unhappy when the jury of local ranchers acquitted both men. Realizing the Nez Perce were still angry, Howard appointed a commission to settle the matter, hoping to stop a war before it started. Chiefs Joseph and Alokut seemed to be agreeable to the commission's first proposals, but the stubborn settlers refused to give up their claims to the land. The commission finally concluded that the Nez Perce tribe should move to the Lapwai reservation. Joseph refused to agree and quit the council, believing his people owned the land, (and rightly so). A military post was established, and the commission decided that unless Joseph agreed to leave within a reasonable amount of time that he and his people should be forced to reservation lands. Perhaps, you now understand why I feel the Indians have a right to be angry.

The Indian Bureau notified the Chief that he had until April 1, 1877, to come on the reservation peaceably. That is why there was the rumor of war when we headed up here. A council was called at Lapwai, but Joseph did not arrive on time. During several days of meetings and speeches given by both sides, which began in May, General Howard put another well respected chief into the guardhouse, when he became angry. He thought the chief would cool off, but he didn't, and then Chief White Bird, of the Lamtana tribe of the Nez Perce, wanted war with the white man. A final meeting was held on May 15th when Agent Monteith explained where each band was to relocate.

The General gave them thirty days to relocate to the reservation, but I fear there will be a rebellion, after what I heard today. When they finally released Tulhulhut, the prisoner "inflamed his heart to seek revenge on the whites," instead of causing him to repent, as General Howard hoped. With Chief White Bird wanting war also, I believe it to be only a matter of time.

As my work on the railroad continues, I guard my back and place some of Ah Kim's cousins as lookouts while we work. I pray that no hostile Indians will regard the color of our skin as simply the color of the enemy's skin. I pray that some miracle will happen to stop this war before blood is shed.

Please pray for us all, Mary, as I fear the coming months will be dangerous times for all abiding here. Do not worry too much, as I have made friends with many of the Nez Perce people. They know I do not agree with what is happening and would change it if I could.

They are a peaceful tribe, who only want to fish and hunt on the land they love! What is happening is not right, but I do not know what can be done to stop it.

I miss you and love you, Mary Sweeney, and hope everything is going well for you and all of your family. I will write soon, so that you will not worry. I'm sorry this letter is so long, I hope it is not too tiring to read. I needed to get my feelings on paper, and you are such a caring person, I hoped you wouldn't mind listening. My heart is yours, Mary. Please write soon, as I yearn to hear from you.

Yours faithfully,

John S. Troy

Mary read the letter twice, held it to her heart, and prayed for the safe return of the man she loved. She put the letter in her pocket, and when the day was done, she went to the little desk in the corner of her room and began writing a return letter by candlelight.

Chapter Seventeen

"Awakened Innocence"

June, 1877

"You can accomplish more with a kind word and a shillelagh, than you can with just a kind word."

Mary dipped the pen into the ink often, as she put her thoughts neatly on the brown linen stationery that Hannah had given to her for her birthday.

Dearest John,

I so enjoyed reading your letter, even though your words bring worry to my heart. Please take care to protect yourself, John Troy, as you mean everything to me.

I too feel pain in my heart for the Nez Perce people. I found the facts of their proposed resettlement very disheartening. Certainly, we Irish can understand their dismay. In our history, our lands were taken over by many countries and still the English rule our homeland.

I miss my dear Ireland, even though it was my choice to leave that beautiful land. If I would have been made to leave, I'd not have gone willingly. The Nez Perce predicament clarifies the reasons, in my mind, why our own Irishmen have been fighting to rule their own country. You and I can understand the Indian's love of his land. Why can't they all live together? Chief Joseph and his people were there first. Why does the American government feel they have the right to take it away from them? It sounds as if many of the white settlers only think of their own wants and needs. Are we not all newcomers to this land? And children of the same God?

There have been similar problems here, in San Francisco, only the Chinaman is the one being treated poorly. One of our own Irishmen stirred up hate toward them. Many people argue that the Chinese people are not even human. This upsets me greatly! As you and I know, there is no finer person than Ah Kim. I would never have made it here, if it were not for him and his family. Just knowing him has opened my eyes to many things. I guess most people are afraid of what they don't understand. I have to admit that I was full of fear when I left the ship in that trunk. When I arrived at Ah Kim's cousin's home, everyone was speaking a language I did not understand, and no one understood me very well, except Ah Kim. I'm sure they felt the same about me. To really know these gentle people is to love them. I do not understand why all men cannot live and work together without killing each other. If women were allowed to vote, perhaps the laws would be different.

I did not mean to go on and on. I am concerned about your welfare. I am praying that this will be over soon and that you will be safe. Please give my best to Ah Kim and his cousins. I am so lucky to have my family close again. Have you heard from your family? I am looking forward to meeting them someday. Tell me about your family. We have not spent much time talking of these things.

I am anxious to hear that you are safe, so please write soon, as your letters mean everything to me. I pray a rosary for you every night.

You have my heart and all of my Irish blessings.

Your betrothed,

Mary Sweeney

San Francisco, California

June, 1877

P.S. I thought I might add an appropriate blessing: "You can accomplish more with a kind word and a shillelagh, than you can with just a kind word."

When she finished writing and the ink was dry, she folded the paper carefully and sealed it with wax. Then she wrote the address on the front and set it on the stand by her bed. Kneeling by her bed, she said a rosary and begged Jesus to keep John and Ah Kim safe. Then she prayed for everyone she knew. As good as things were in America, life was hard!

The next morning she rose early, took her shawl out of the drawer, and put it around her shoulders. It was windy and foggy in June in San Francisco. She put on her bonnet and went to post her letter. It was damp outside from the morning fog and the front steps were slippery. When she went around the side of the house, she ran into Rachel who was just coming down the back stairs.

"Mornin' Rachel. Where are ye going so early?"

"Oh, Mary. I'm going over to Kate's for the day." Rachel was noticeably nervous and in a hurry. "I left a note on the table. Kate might spend the night tonight, if that's okay."

"Of course it's all right, but ye shouldn't leave without talking to yer mum or me."

"I know. I just didn't want to wake anyone, so I thought I'd just leave a note. I've got to hurry, Mary, or I'll miss the cable car." Mary was surprised at Rachel's curtness, as it wasn't like the girl at all.

As she walked down the hill, her thoughts were on the people she had prayed for. John and Ah Kim were foremost in her mind. Her family was having some problems too. Da's leg was bothering him again, and he hadn't been able to go to the beach lately, and Mum's eyesight was getting poorer and poorer. Her sister, Margaret, lost the baby she wanted so badly, while Catherine was pregnant with another child that they really couldn't afford. Her two brothers had been in jail a couple of weeks ago, after getting into a brawl with a gang of Chinese haters on the waterfront. Hannah graciously loaned Mary the money to bail them out. Mary didn't know what was going on with Rachel, but her intuition told her she was hiding something. It wasn't like her to leave the house without permission.

Rachel desperately wanted to confide in Mary, but she had given Kate her word that her secret would be safe with her. She couldn't tell Mary she was going to see Kate, to try to persuade her to change her plans. A note to Mary and her mother was in the kitchen, and she had left by the back door hoping not to be heard. It surprised her to run into Mary outside the house. She didn't want Mary to question her, as she didn't know how to answer without feeling like she was lying. Her note was short and simple:

I have gone to Kate's to spend the day with her. I'm sorry to leave without talking to either of you, and I hope you both forgive me for not asking for permission. I decided late last night to go, although Kate asked me to come earlier in the week. I will be home before dusk.

Do not worry.

Rachel

When she ran into Mary, she knew she had to say something, so she just avoided the reasons for going and hurried off. The cable car took her ten minutes to arrive a few blocks from Kate's. It took her five minutes more to walk to Kate's large two-story home. Her friend's family had money. Joseph Murphy was a smart man who had worked hard to get his education at Trinity College in Dublin. His father had been a professor at that prestigious University, where they both had to pretend they were protestant, as Catholics were not accepted at that time. Joseph came to America where he could freely practice his faith, shortly after obtaining his degree. The banking industry was happy to have a man with his credentials working with them. His smart head for finance helped him quickly earn great profits in the stock market. He soared to the top of his field quickly, and now owned two financial institutions.

Maureen O'Riley was a teller at the first bank where he was employed. She fell for the good looking Irishman the first time she saw him. They were married two years later. Maureen conceived Kate on their wedding night and her three younger brothers followed at yearly intervals. The beautiful Kathleen Mary Murphy had always enjoyed an independent personality. Maureen worried about the strong-minded girl from the beginning, but Joseph saw his own personality in his daughter, and he was happy that she was going to be a strong, independent, American woman. The headstrong girl grew up wanting for nothing, as Kate's doting father granted her every whim. Nothing was too good for his daughter, and as a result, she never learned to wait for anything. Her vivacious personality, and strong will, made Kate a natural leader and a favorite of her teachers. Rachel and Johanna adored her, and wished they were as strong and independent as Kate, but they also worried about her.

Rachel was worried now, as she climbed the tall staircase leading to the huge mansion. The butler answered the door and told Rachel to go up to Kate's room. Rachel knocked lightly before she entered, and found Kate lying on the bed eating breakfast from a tray.

"Kate, what are you doing still in bed? I thought you'd be up getting ready for your rendezvous by now."

"Hi, Rach! No, I thought I'd sleep late, so I would look rested this evening. I've been awake for some time though, daydreaming, until Louis brought me some food. I'm glad you came over. I wanted your opinion on what to wear."

Rachel was amazed at how beautiful Kate looked, even first thing in the morning. Her red hair lay in curls surrounding her delicate face on the green satin pillowcase. She looked like an oil painting, framed by the pillow. Her emerald eyes sparkled with excitement, and her delightful dimples lit up with every word she spoke.

"I was hoping I could talk you out of going, Kate. I have a really bad feeling about this. I'm very worried that this man is not as nice as you think he is. Do you know him? I mean, really know him? After all, he is older, and he's encouraging you to lie to your parents."

"Rachel, Rachel, do not worry. I really like him, and I'm sure he likes me. He is just protecting me and our good names. You know my father would never let me go out with him. This is the only way we can see each other, until I'm older. He's from a good family, so I'm sure he's a gentleman. I trust him. If I tell you who he is, it will just give you another secret to keep. Since you don't know who he is, you don't have to lie. I'm protecting you, my dear friend."

"What if your mother should talk to mine and mention that you spent the night with me tonight? What if my mother tells your mother that you didn't come over till very late? What then?"

"Don't worry, Rachel. Our mothers don't know each other that well. They don't go to the same church, and we're out of school now, so they won't run into each other there. You can just say you don't know where I was. That will leave it on me. I'm the one that will get in trouble, not you."

"What about Mary? She goes to the same church as you do, and she looked worried when I ran into her this morning. You know Mary, she can read me like a book."

"Rachel, Rachel, quit worrying. I'll take care of it. Now, you can help me get dressed and spend the day with me. My parents won't question me, when I leave with you to spend the night. I can't wait for tonight. He is so romantic!"

"Please, Kate, don't tell me anymore. I just can't help worrying."

Kate laughed, as she hopped out of bed gleefully. "Let's run down and get some more orange juice, before I decide what to wear tonight. I'm thirsty."

She pulled on the green satin robe that was lying on the end of her bed, then slipped into matching slippers. The green, of which, matched everything else in the room. Taking Rachel by the arm, Kate opened the door and led her down the staircase.

"I wonder what Johanna is doing today." Kate bounced down the stairs.

"She came by on Tuesday and said she was going to stay at Catherine's, to help with the children this week. Her sister hasn't been feeling well. I haven't seen her since then."

"That's probably best. If she knew, I'm afraid she'd slip and tell Mary anyway."

The girls spent the day together, laughing and talking. Late in the afternoon, Kate told the butler to tell her parents that she was spending the night at Rachel's, as the two girls walked out the door. Kate was dressed in a dark blue velvet gown with a bustle in the back, her breasts bursting in the low necked bodice. Over her shoulders, she wore a simple navy blue cape that hid her outfit completely. Her matching blue shoes, necklace, earrings, and rouge were in the carpetbag she carried. They walked to the cable car where the two friends boarded and stood, holding tightly to the overhead straps, until they reached the stop closest to Rachel's house. When they got off, Rachel said goodbye to Kate before she headed home.

"Please take care, Kate!" Rachel hugged her friend.

"Aren't you going to tell me to have fun?"

"Of course, have fun! You are coming over later tonight, aren't you? Just come up the back way. I'll tell Mary your father's carriage dropped you at the corner, if she sees you, but I think she might stay at Margaret's tonight. Anyway, I'll see you later and please take care."

"I'll tell you all about my wonderful evening, when I get there, my dear friend."

Kate hugged her again, and then happily skipped down the street to the corner where the carriage was to pick her up. Rachel watched her and felt fear for her friend. She had a bad feeling about this and wanted, desperately, to tell someone and stop it all. But, she couldn't bear the thought of losing Kate as a friend, and knew that would happen if she told anyone. Rachel finally turned around and headed up the hill toward her house.

Kate waited half an hour before the carriage appeared. Her Irish temper was beginning to flare, as she was thinking of 'teaching the fellow a lesson' and leaving, when the carriage pulled up in front of her. The door opened and Sean Foley stepped out.

"Oh, me beautiful Kate. How divine ye look, me lovely Irish princess."

"And what kept your Irish princess standing on the corner for this length of time, sir? I was about to take myself over to Rachel's."

"I'm so sorry, me darlin' young lady. I had some important business to tend to, and it took longer than I expected. Please forgive me, my sweet lassie." Sean patted the pocketbook full of money in his pocket, delighted that his luck had held out at the poker table. "Don't ye worry, darlin', we'll be having the time of our lives tonight."

Charmingly, he took her hand and kissed it gently. Then slowly, he raised his smiling eyes to meet hers. Her heart was thumping loudly, as she looked into his handsome face, and he led her into the carriage. He gently untied the top of her cape, and slipped it off of her shoulders, revealing her beautiful bosom encased in blue velvet.

"Ye are truly lovely!"

He kissed her neck. Passion welled up within her at his touch, and when he pressed his lips on hers, she felt as if her heart would burst forth from her chest. She knew she should push him away, but she also wanted him to keep kissing her.

Sean finally pushed himself away and said huskily, "Oh Katie, me girl, now is not the time for this. I must take ye to one of me favorite places. I'm taking ye to the hottest new saloon south of Market Street. It's kind of bawdy and a little loud, and not a place I'm sure yer used to, but ye said ye wanted to see the 'real people of San Francisco'."

"Oh yes, I want to see it all. I would probably never see it, if it weren't for you."

"I know. I'm not sure I'm proud of that. Yer father wouldn't like it very much, and neither would me little niece, Mary Sweeney."

"They'll never know, Sean. Besides, I agreed to come."

"I hope not, because if Mary found out she could ruin things fer me here. Let's forget about her and have a good time."

"Yes, lets!" Kate opened her bag and pulled out a short blue velvet matching cape, and a small clutch bag, which held tiny pearl earrings and her rouge. She put them both on as Sean watched, admiring her every move.

'Rich and beautiful,' he thought. 'It's too bad she is so young. If she were a little older, I might run off and marry the lass. Then her father would have to accept me.'

"Here we are!" The carriage stopped in front of the seedy looking place.

"Don't worry! It's not as bad as it looks. It's on the second floor."

As they climbed the stairs, loud raucous laughter and fiddle music could be heard from the landing. Kate was excited and afraid at the same time. She took a deep breath to calm her fears, before they entered the room. There were men dressed in all types of attire, and a few brightly dressed women, in the smoke filled room. The foggy haze made her cough as she entered. Sean led her to a small booth off the main room. It had red velvet curtains pulled back with tassels, which could be undone if one wanted more privacy. The booth was round and could easily seat eight, but he slid in next to her.

"It's less smoky here. I reserved this room just for us, so we could have a little privacy."

The waiter arrived, as Sean helped her take off her little cape.

"I like it because we can see everything from here, and yet we don't have to get involved. But, we can get involved with each other without anyone else bothering us."

Kate blushed at his words, as the waiter leered at her.

"What can I get for you tonight, sir?"

"Bring me a bottle of your best champagne, George."

"Right away, Mr. Foley."

"He seems to know you well, Sean." Kate said, after the waiter left.

"Yes... Well, I have been here a few times."

The waiter came back quickly and ceremoniously popped the cork on the champagne. He poured a little bit for Sean to taste, then filled both of their glasses. He left the bottle in a crystal ice bucket and departed. Sean picked up the glasses and handed her one.

"Let me offer a toast, to the loveliest lass in all of San Francisco!"

They touched their glasses together and drank. The bubbles tickled, as they flowed down Kate's throat, and she felt like giggling after she finished the second glass. She rarely had champagne, only sips at home on special occasions. The more she drank the more relaxed she felt, and the more romantic she felt about Sean.

The music became more upbeat and the lights went down, as scantily clad ladies began dancing on the stage in the front of the room. Kate began to really enjoy herself, as she watched the girls kick their legs higher and higher while singing a bawdy tune. By the time the show was over, Kate was feeling wonderful. When Sean began kissing her neck, she began to feel hot all over. Sean reached over, untied the tassel on the curtain and closed it. He gently kissed her eyelids, her ears, the tip of her nose, and finished with a long sensuous kiss on her lips. His hands slowly moved down to her luscious breasts. She wanted to stop him, but it felt so good that she couldn't bring herself to. Kate had never felt such an uncontrollable feeling before.

Sean's voice became husky. "Let's go to the carriage, me darlin'."

"Oh Sean, I don't want to stop kissing you."

"I know, my sweet. Let's go to the carriage where we can have more privacy."

"Sean, Sean, I think I love thee." She was feeling very giddy now, and a little dizzy, but she trusted him completely.

"Oh, me girl, ye know I love thee too. Ye are me wild Irish rose."

He put her cape around her shoulders, took her by the arm and quickly escorted her outside, down the stairs, and into the carriage where the driver was waiting for them.

Pulling the cape off of her shoulders, he began kissing her neck and moved quickly to her breasts. The fresh air seemed to sober her a little and she was suddenly a little afraid. She knew it was time to stop, and she tried to tell him.

"Sean, please don't!"

He covered her mouth with his and began kissing her passionately at first and then violently. Fear overtook her, as she tried to push him away, but his strong arms forced her backwards onto the carriage seat.

"Stop, please stop!" She gasped, pulling her lips from his, but he put one hand over her mouth.

"Hush, Kate. Hush!" He was breathing fast.

She struggled, to get him off of her, but he was much too strong. With his other hand, he pulled her skirt up and began fondling her. She tried to scream, but he covered her mouth so forcefully that she could hardly breathe, much less speak. "No, NO!"

He held her so tight, she couldn't move. She felt horrific pain, as he forced himself upon her and repeatedly pounded his body into hers until his body convulsed, and he lay spent on top of her. By then, the tears were streaming down her face. She was angry and in tears, as she pushed him off of her.

"YOU FILTHY PIG! HOW COULD YOU?" She sobbed hysterically.

He put his hand over her mouth again, "Now lassie, that wasn't so bad, was it? I'm sorry, I just lost control of meself. I found yer lovely body irresistible. Don't worry, darlin', now yer a real lady. But, don't ye be telling anyone about this, me girl. Both of our reputations are at stake here, ye know."

She wanted to beat on him and scream, and scream, but all she could do was sob. 'My life is ruined.' Her mind raced with horrible thoughts. Her father would kill him if he knew, but she couldn't tell him. 'It's my fault! I should never have gone with him. How could I have been such a fool?' She just wanted to get away from him and didn't know what to do.

"I don't ever want to see you again, Sean Foley! I trusted you!" She finally gasped, between sobs. "Just take me to Rachel's house."

"Now Katie, me girl, don't tell me ye didn't enjoy it? Ye were asking for it. Ye were kissing me back with all yer heart."

"Don't say anymore, please! Just take me to Rachel's! And let me out around the corner, so I can go in the back way." Sean was straightening his clothes and his hair, as he got out of the carriage to tell the driver where to go.

She didn't speak to him all the way back to Rachel's. Wiping her eyes with the handkerchief, she put on the old blue cape and tried to make herself presentable, so she could enter the house without anyone realizing what was wrong. When they pulled up around the corner, she got out and slammed the door on the carriage.

"Kate, Kate! Now don't ye be doing anything stupid, like tellin' anybody!"

"Sean Foley, I don't ever want to hear from you or see your face again!"

She ran around the corner to the back entrance of the Goldstein house. Rachel had seen her coming, from her bedroom window, and was at the door waiting for her. She looked shocked when she saw Kate's appearance, but put her finger to her lips and quietly led her down the hall and up the staircase. Luckily, no one heard them. Kate immediately went to Rachel's bed and lay down, sobbing uncontrollably. Rachel tried to comfort her to no avail.

Finally, Kate spoke. "Rachel, you were so right and I was so wrong!" She couldn't stop crying, and finally sobbed herself to sleep, leaving Rachel to wonder what terrible thing had happened to break her dear friend's heart.

Chapter Eighteen

"Secrets"

June, 1877

"Is there something you girls want to talk about?"

Mary came home early the next morning from Margaret's house. It was a cold, foggy morning, but she enjoyed the brisk walk back to the Goldstein's. She fixed breakfast for Hannah, but let Rachel sleep later than usual. The girls finally came downstairs around eleven. When she saw Kate's face, Mary was shocked, as she'd never seen Kate look bad before. Her lovely eyes were swollen and red, her dimples hid behind a sad frown. The dress Kate was wearing was an old one of Rachel's that Mary had put in the basket to go to the poor. Rachel wasn't smiling, but she didn't look upset like Kate did.

"Kate Murphy, whatever is wrong? Ye don't look a bit yerself today, me girl. Are ye feeling poorly?" Mary never was one to mince words, but the girls were ready for her questions.

"Yes Mary, I think I caught a touch of something, as I really am not feeling too well this morning. Maybe it was something I ate yesterday."

"I hope that's all it is. Rachel are ye feeling poorly too?"

"No, Mary, I'm okay. I've just been tending to Kate most of the night. I'm fine, really."

"If yer not better by tomorrow, ye should see a doctor. I heard there were a few cases of Yellow Fever showing up in California. I don't want to scare ye, jest want ye to watch it."

"Thank you for your concern, Mary. I'm sure I'll be all right." Kate spoke slowly, trying her best to smile, though her heart was breaking. She managed to hold back the flood of tears that wanted to spill from her eyes. The pain in her chest was real, as she felt it with every breath she took.

"Is there something ye girls want to talk about?" Mary tried to look each girl in the eye, but they both looked away, trying to avoid her gaze. For a moment, Mary thought Rachel was going to speak, but Kate glared at Rachel. When she finally spoke, it was to deny any problems.

"There's nothing to talk about, Mary. Kate's just not feeling well."

"Ye know ye can tell me anything. Don't ye, girls?"

"If there were anything wrong, we would tell you." Rachel answered, a little too quickly.

"Sit down, lassies. I just squeezed some fresh orange juice and made another batch of biscuits. I figured ye girls would be mighty hungry when ye got up."

Mary retrieved freshly churned butter, homemade raspberry jam, biscuits, and orange juice from the kitchen. As she watched the girls eat, she knew there was something seriously wrong with Kate. The girl wasn't sick, she was unhappy about something. Swollen red eyes meant she had been crying. Mary didn't like it at all, but she didn't know what to do about it. Rachel was her charge, but Kate wasn't. Whatever it was, Rachel had promised Kate she wouldn't tell, and she couldn't force her to break her word, no matter how much she wanted to help Kate. Rachel was hungry, and began eating as if famished, but Kate only nibbled on a biscuit and sipped from her glass, as she stared into space with wet, red-rimmed eyes.

"Margaret said Johanna was coming over to see ye today, Rachel. I told her I didn't think ye had any plans. By the way, yer mum was upset that ye just left us a note yesterday. She wondered why ye didn't come to our rooms before ye left."

Rachel's face turned red as she began stammering, "I...I...I'm sorry, Mary. I...I thought it would be nice to...let you both sleep a little longer than usual. I did tell you, when I saw you outside."

"Yes, but if I hadn't left at that time, ye wouldn't have. Please don't do that again, Rachel. Yer mother told me that she wanted to have lunch with ye yesterday, to talk about the plans for yer birthday. She was very disappointed."

A knock on the front door saved Rachel from responding. Johanna entered the house as cheerful as always. Mary realized immediately that whatever was bothering Kate had not been shared with Mary's little sister.

"Kate? Whatever is the matter? Ye look terrible!"

Tears started flowing at her friend's words. Kate wiped her eyes on her napkin and left the room, leaving Rachel to explain.

"Kate has been feeling real poorly all night, Johanna. It might be contagious, so maybe we should cancel our plans for today. I wouldn't want you to catch whatever it is. I've already been exposed. I'll come over tomorrow, if I'm not down with it too."

Rachel tactfully got out of telling Johanna anything. She excused herself, and followed Kate up the stairs, leaving the two sisters alone in the dining room. They both sat quietly, each wondering what was really wrong with Kate Murphy.

Later that afternoon, Mary made another trip to the post office. She usually went to pick up Mrs. Goldstein's mail, a couple of times a week, but lately she'd been going daily, as she was always looking for a letter from John. She was surprised to find one, tucked in between Mrs. Goldstein's letters and periodicals. After delivering her employer's mail to her in the library, she took the letter to her room, so she could lay down on her bed and open it. When she looked at the postmark, she realized that this one was posted shortly after the previous letter.

My dearest Mary,

Words cannot say how much I miss your sweet smile. I think of you every day, and wish we were already married, but I know I must be patient. I don't want to endanger your life by bringing you here at this time. The war with the Nez Perce has finally started.

I am sorry to tell you that blood has been shed. After the Counsel at Lapwai, Chief Joseph got his tribe ready to leave the "land of the winding waters." When the band got to the Snake River, rafts made of buffalo-hide took the women, children, and their possessions across the river to Idaho. The people made it, with no problems, but while they were driving the stock across, a sudden storm came up and the roiling water swept many of the ponies and cattle to their death. Joseph left braves to guard the rest of the animals, who were told to wait until the river calmed before taking them across. When they finally attempted the crossing, several white men attacked them and drove their stock away. The angry Nez Perce then joined White Bird's camp, at Rocky Canyon, where the tribes held a counsel. The Indians took turns telling their grievances against the white men. The two main chiefs argued their different opinions. Tulhuthulsut stirred the young braves up, while Joseph tried to calm them down. One brave related how his father was killed in an unprovoked quarrel over land by a white settler. He was angry that the man was not punished for his crime. Tulhuthulsut threatened to take revenge on the whites, and he finally left the Counsel. Joseph was not aware that several young braves left camp, and stole liquor, which got them more fired up. Three of White Bird's young braves went after the white settler who fled to the Florence mines, disguised as a Chinaman. When the Indians couldn't find him, they killed an English sailor who had always treated the Indians badly. I think it was one of Bane's men. The next day they killed three other men, and wounded another, all of whom had treated them poorly. They took the white men's guns, horses, and ammunition. These reckless young braves started the war between the Nez Perce and the white man. I was told all of this by Arthur Chapman, who is known to be a good friend of Chief Joseph. The chief tried everything to keep his people from going to war, but Chief White Bird does not want to move from his land.

Many of the Nez Perce warned their white friends to leave, and most white settlers have fled with their wives and children to the protection of the settlements. Work on the railroad has ceased again, for the time being. Everyone is worried that trouble will spread to the Weiser and Paiute Indians.

Please pray, Mary, that whatever happens is over quickly, and that few people will be hurt on either side. Do not worry about me as I am known to be a friend of the Nez Perce, and should not be harmed if they attack. They are good people who just want to live on the land of their ancestors. I am very sad and worry about what will happen to these simple people.

To change the subject to something more pleasant, you asked me to tell you about my family in your last letter. I am happy to tell you about them, as you will someday (soon I hope) be related to them. I am, of course, named after my father, John Stephen Troy. My mother's name is Anna Bailey Troy. I have two brothers, Maurice and Mike. My sister's names are Bridget, Ellen, Kate, Fannie, Lizzie, and Nora. My older siblings all want to join me in America soon. I hope that some of them will be at our wedding. At the present time, all but Mike and I live at the Peafield Farm, which is located just outside Glenbeg in County Cork. It seems to be fate that you and I lived so close to each other, in our native land, and yet we did not meet until our journey to America.

When I left Ireland the last time, my mother asked when she would see me again. You must be so happy to have your family close to you. Perhaps I will be that fortunate in the future, although my parents are very much attached to their homeland.

I will write again soon, my sweet one, but I must end this letter now, so it can go out with the next rider from this settlement. Please take care of yourself and write soon. I miss you sorely, and love you dearly. Pray for all of us. I do not know when I will be able to post another letter, but I will as soon as possible.

Yours forever,

John Stephen Troy

Mary folded the letter carefully, and she added it to the others that were tied with a blue gingham ribbon. Then she stored them in the back of the bottom drawer of her large dresser. She took her rosary out and knelt down by the bed, to pray for the man she loved, and for the people he cared so deeply about.

The two girls stayed in Rachel's room all day. Kate left shortly before dinner. Rachel walked with her to meet the cable car. Her eyes were still swollen, but her hair was combed and she was nicely dressed in another one of Rachel's gowns. Mary wondered what happened to her clothes. Two days later, she found out when she found the beautiful blue velvet gown stuffed behind Rachel's bed. 'Why would Kate, who usually took such good care of her beautiful things, treat this lovely gown so shabbily?' There were stains on the dress and it smelled musty. When she held the lovely fabric close to her face, she almost choked from the smell of smoke and liquor that emanated from it. Mary's concern grew, as she suddenly had a feeling that Kate's problems had to do with a man.

Chapter Nineteen

"The Land of the Winding Waters"

Eastern Oregon ~ June & July, 1877

"That is something men have questioned since the beginning of time."

John and Ah Kim left for the long trek to Fort Lapwai, after hearing the warnings from the cavalry. They suggested that all settlers, in the Northeast Oregon and Idaho territories, go to the fort for their own safety. The soldiers who were traveling to the fort from Portland were asked to warn everyone that the Nez Perce were ready for war.

When John stopped at the Baker City Post Office to mail his letter to Mary, he ran into his friend, Noah Johnson. Noah and his large family were loaded into two wagons, while three of his boys were herding a few cattle close behind. The man told John that they were on their way to Utah, they were leaving their ranch by the Salmon River in Idaho, and they most likely would not return. As a Mormon family, they were not only afraid of the coming Indian war, but they had decided Utah might be a better place for the family, since many people of their faith already lived there. John and Noah had worked on the railroad together. Noah said that they had left a lot of supplies at the ranch, as they had stockpiled more than enough for the next year, and they could only take as much as they could fit in the two covered wagons with them.

"If you wish to stay at our ranch, you are welcome to all the supplies that are there. I will be giving the deed to the ranch to a friend of mine, who lives in Utah, but he won't be coming up here until after the Indian rebellion is over, and most of the supplies will spoil by then."

"Thank ye, Noah. That is very generous of you. I'm on my way to pick up a friend, and we will be heading to Fort Lapwai, to see what is happening with the war. We might take ye up on that offer, if it is too crowded there. Have a safe trip, and good luck to ye and yer family."

It was a long journey to Fort Lapwai from Baker City, for John and Ah Kim. If they traveled straight through the country, it was over 115 miles across rough terrain, and it would take longer if they took the main trails. They decided on the main roads, thinking that if they traveled at a good speed that they could make about ten miles an hour. Not wanting to wear out the horses, they took a few breaks, and arrived late in the afternoon of the second day. They wanted to get the latest news about the war, and find out if it was safe enough to go on to the Johnson Ranch to spend the winter. The ranch was thirty miles south of the fort.

They only stayed at the Fort for a week. There were several reasons for leaving that safer place. First of all, there were too many settlers already taking refuge there. Secondly, John didn't like the treatment that Ah Kim received by most of the soldiers and white people staying there. And, John didn't want to fight the Nez Perce, as he knew that the white men had started all the trouble. If the Indians attacked him, he would defend himself, but he would not join the civilian volunteers to fight against the people he admired.

The day that Bane and his band showed up to join the volunteers, was the day John and Ah Kim decided that Fort Lapwai wasn't big enough for all of them. His loud and bawdy group of men came in riding fast, shooting their rifles and pistols into the air. A small band of Indians followed them at a distance, but stopped about a half mile before the fort and watched the white men. Soldiers opened the big log doors of the fort to let the riders in. When John saw who it was, he almost wished the Indians would have caught them.

John was sitting on the stoop outside the stable, smoking the cigarette he had just rolled, and Ah Kim was grooming the horses just inside the small wooden structure. Jack Bane's loud gruff laugh brought a warning of danger to Ah Kim, who stepped outside to confirm the owner of the dreaded voice. John looked at his face, with its deformed nose, and he was not happy to see the troublemaking ex-seaman. Bane recognized Ah Kim almost immediately. While his men talked to the soldiers about their run in with the Indians, Bane headed for the stable and Ah Kim. He rode up fast, dismounted, and gruffly handed the reins of his sweating, snorting stallion to the Chinaman.

"Fancy meeting you here, slant eyes!" Take care of my horse, if you want to keep that pig tail on your head, and that head on top of your shoulders."

The big man's cold eyes gleamed with joy, as he taunted the little man. Ah Kim simply bowed politely, and took the reins of the man's horse. But, as he turned around, Bane swiftly raised his foot, kicking the smaller man with his heavy boot. The blow landed on Ah Kim's right hip, knocking him sharply to the ground, as the huge horse reared up and almost trampled him. John got there just in time to grab the reins, and calm the horse down, while Bane laughed.

"I heard you two were around this area. I've been wondering when I would run into you. Whatever happened to that Irish wench you saved from me clutches?"

John felt sick at the thought of what this evil man would like to do to his beloved Mary.

"Last I heard, she went back to her family in Ireland."

"Now, why would a lass who is brave enough to disguise herself as a boy, and live with a bunch of sailors on a ship crossing the ocean, turn tail and run back to the land she was running from? I don't believe it! If ye know where she is, ye better keep her out of my sight. Every time I look in a mirror and see what the little hellion did to me nose, me blood boils. I told her once what I'd do if she told on me, and she did it anyway. Nobody rats on Jack Bane, nobody! Man, girl or Chinese... When I say I'm going to do something, sooner or later I do it!" He hissed the threat angrily at both of them. Ah Kim started to get up, and Jack Bane kicked him again.

John jumped in, grabbing Bane's leg with the hand that wasn't holding the reins, and pulled Bane to the ground. The horse began to buck again. As he was about to land on Bane, John pulled him back. Bane was irate when he got up, but before he could do anything John handed him the reins.

"Take care of yer own horse!"

Hearing the commotion, a sergeant and two soldiers came to see what was going on. Bane just stood there, glaring with hatred at John.

John and Ah Kim were going to leave the next morning, but they decided to wait, when Bane and his group rode out the next morning with the cavalry and other volunteers, for what turned out to be the first big battle between the Nez Perce and the Cavalry. When the surviving troops came limping back the next day, they heard several versions of the "Battle at White Bird Canyon". They thought Bane was just as dangerous as the Indians, so the two men saddled their horses and decided it was time to leave.

A few braves were on the hill overlooking the road as they passed by. John held his hands up with his palms out, to show he meant no harm, and they were allowed to pass. The Indians seemed to know that the Chinese people were treated poorly too. They usually let them pass, unless they endangered the Indians in some way.

"Mister John, we could go to my small abode on the outskirts of Baker City. I think we would be safe there. I respectfully invite you to share my home. You are welcome to stay as long as you wish."

"Ah Kim, I would be happy to take ye up on your offer, but that is a long way from here. I think we would both be safe at Noah Johnson's abandoned ranch, which is not far from here. I heard the soldiers say that the recent battle took place close to there, as one of the soldiers mentioned the ranch itself. After the beating the white men took, I'm sure they're not going to meet them in White Bird Canyon again. One of the soldiers said that this battle was the second worst defeat that the United States had suffered against any Indians so far. The Custer Massacre last year was the only one where the cavalry suffered more losses. If you remember, Ah Kim, there were few troops who survived that one. We needed to leave the fort though, as Bane will surely continue to harass us. I do not want to fight the Nez Perce people. I do not blame them for being angry with the white man, and yet I cannot stand by while me own people are killed. I do not know why people have to treat each other poorly, just because their skin is a different color."

"That is something men have questioned since the beginning of time, Mister John. I cannot understand the violence and hatred that abides in our world."

When they reached the Johnson Ranch, they could see that some fighting had actually taken place on the ranch, as had been reported. The soldiers said that the skirmish had ended there. The fence was down in some places. Arrows and bullets were strewn across the grounds. It was obvious that some blood had been shed there.

The officers had sent for more troops when they returned, and they were told that many more cavalry were on their way. Troops from Alaska that were on their way to California were said to be rerouted, and on their way to Idaho. Listening to the soldier's tales of the battle had given them a sense of what had taken place. At the urging of the townspeople, General Howard had sent Captain Perry to attack the Indians. A large number of Indians had been reportedly heading toward White Bird Canyon. The Nez Perce moved the tribe's thirty lodges to a camp at Cottonwood Creek. The chiefs then decided they needed the protection that the woods would provide, so they moved the village to a hill east of the Salmon River. Perry led the cavalry, with Officers Trimble, Parnell and Theller, and some of the treaty Nez Perce Indian scouts. An ex-confederate major, George Shearer, led eleven civilian volunteers, including Bane and his group.

When the white men came down into the canyon, Chief Joseph sent a committee with white flags to negotiate peace. According to reports, Chapman, who was an interpreter for Perry, fired at the truce party. John's first thought was that Bane and his men were probably a part of that. Jonas Hayes, who was a friend of the Indians, and was married to one of the Nez Perce, wanted to talk to the Indians, but when Chapman fired... all hell broke loose. The Indians returned fire and the battle ensued.

When the cavalry entered the canyon, the warriors divided into two groups, one led by Joseph, and the other by his brother, Alokut. Only fifty of the braves had guns. The rest had bows and arrows. The cavalry wound its way for four miles down into the canyon, first one by one, later in columns of four. Theller and eight men rode 100 yards ahead of the others. Perry sent nine of the civilians to hold the knoll on the left.

The Indians charged the civilians and wounded two of them. The other seven volunteers broke and fled immediately, leaving the knoll to the Indians who opened fire on Perry's troops. This was said to be the turning point of the battle.

When it was over, the Indians had three wounded braves. But, thirty-three soldiers, including Lieutenant Theller, had been killed. This was one third of Company F and H. After the battle at Cottonwood Creek, the Nez Perce moved a few miles down the river. They crossed at Horseshoe Bend and held a strong position in the mountains on the other side.

John and Ah Kim knew that the Indians had moved up river, and that the ranch had been abandoned before the skirmish took place. They decided that it would be a good place to stay, until the fighting was over. John had written another letter to Mary, relating the sequence of events, and mailed it from the fort before they left.

Chapter Twenty

"Good Samaritans"

Eastern Oregon ~ Summer, 1877

"Who keeps his tongue keeps his friend."

The two men rode slowly up the trail to the large log cabin. They wanted to make sure that no one else had decided to take up residency at the Johnson Ranch. Everything seemed quiet, so they stopped and picked up the arrows, feathers, army buttons, and other small items that were left after the battle that had been fought there. An apple orchard rimmed the front edge of the ranch. The main house had a large porch, with several pots that contained a variety of plants that were almost dead, to the left of the front door. A sturdy wooden swing made from hemp hung from the over-hanging roof, to the right of the door. The eaves came out about two feet and gave the swing some shade from the hot sun in the late afternoon.

All of the possessions that John and Ah Kim brought with them were in their saddlebags, or rolled up in blankets on the back of their horses. They hoped that the supplies had not been raided by soldiers, or Indians, and they entered the house slowly, to make sure no one was waiting in ambush for them. There was no way to know how long the war would last, or how long they would be staying at the cabin. The house seemed to be untouched so they sighed in relief.

"Thanks for coming along on this journey, Ah Kim. I think we will be safer here than at the fort. As long as we have the Johnson's supplies, we should be okay for a while." He laughed as he told Ah

Kim of Mary's words in one of the letters he had picked up at the post office; "Mary's proverbial sayings always seem to fit the occasion. Her last line was *'the Lord does always seem to provide!'"*

Ah Kim smiled, "Miss Mary always knows the right thing to say."

"If I hadn't run into Noah Johnson, I don't know how else we would survive, until this Indian thing is finished. Without the railroad work, supplies would have been pretty meager. I hope this is over quickly, because I haven't saved much for the fall and winter seasons to come. Let's check the cellar and see if it really is stocked full of supplies."

"Why did this man not take his supplies with him when he left?"

"He took only what they could load in the wagons. He has a large family; including two wives and ten children. They worked this land for ten years, and he also worked for the railroad when he could. The women canned, smoked, jellied, and stored up everything they'd need in an emergency. As they left in a hurry, they didn't have enough wagons to take it all. Noah said the other settlers were givin' them trouble, because he had two wives. A group of settlers, led by the local minister, talked a travelin' judge into orderin' the sheriff to arrest Mr. Johnson. They are Mormons, ye know. They believe a man should have as many wives as he can take good care of."

"Does the government have the right to tell a man to go against his religion?"

"I don't know, but the law does say a man can have only one wife. What was most surprising to me was what Noah told me about the Indian skirmish that took place in the Oregon Cascade Mountains, during 1858 and 1859. Noah was a young boy, but his father told him the story. It seems the Mormons of Utah backed several Indian tribes, against the white settlers, and tried to get the Nez Perce to join them in exterminating all white people in the area. As the Nez Perce were the most powerful tribe, they needed them to accomplish the feat. When the tribe turned them down, they gave up, but the Mormons had promised the tribes that they would supply them with arms, ammunition, and civilian troops. When the soldiers put down the hostiles, they reportedly found muskets and balls that contained the Mormon brand. It sounds like the Mormons have been fighting with the settlers for a while. Anyway, Noah said that a group of men had threatened to burn them out several months ago, if they didn't leave, and when the Indian war seemed to be eminent, the family decided it was time to go. Most likely, it was the same group of troublemakers who started the Indian War. We are very lucky that I ran into Noah."

"Mr. Johnson has been very generous."

"Let's see how generous he has been."

They were amazed at the amount of food that was put up in the cellar. There was a cold room where plenty of jerky and bacon were hanging as well as a half a side of beef. Jars of fruit, vegetables, and jams filled three shelves. Fresh picked beans, potatoes, strawberries, and other picked fruit and vegetables were in baskets on the floor. There was only one empty shelf, and space for several more baskets on the floor. Three kegs held flour, salt and sugar, a small amount of freshly churned butter, and there was a large basket full of eggs. The room was deep in the ground and was much colder than other parts of the house. It was like finding a gold mine. They had seen a chicken coop, behind the farmhouse, and chickens running wild on the way there, so they assumed some of their chickens had gotten away from the Johnsons as they left. They would round them up shortly.

"The Mormon people certainly know how to prepare for a long hard winter!" John was pleasantly surprised, as there was enough food to feed many people for months. As it turned out, that was exactly what they needed.

A few days after their arrival, Ah Kim saw four Nez Perce braves in full war paint, riding across the meadow, and ran to find John, who was chopping wood in the back of the house.

"John Troy, the Indians are coming!"

John started to drop the axe, but then thought he might need it, so he walked to the front of the house with it in his hand. Ah Kim set two rifles upright behind the tree, as he joined him. The two men stood on either side of the tree, within reach of the rifles.

"Do not worry, Ah Kim, they are a gentle people at heart. Let us hope these are not some hostiles who have been drinking fire water"

"I will certainly let you speak for us, John Troy."

As the four Indians got closer, the war paint looked more frightening. John raised his arm in a friendly greeting.

"Good morning, may I offer ye a refreshing drink of water or some coffee?" He hoped that they spoke English, as many of the Nez Perce did.

The tall brave, who seemed to be the leader, spoke. "Where is the man who lives here?"

"The man and his family left this land, and went south, to live in a place where they are more welcome. I am John Troy, friend to the Nez Perce. Chief Joseph and his brother, Alokut, know me name. Ye and yer friends are welcome here, as long as ye come in peace."

"Who is this man? Where does he come from?"

"This man is me friend, Ah Kim. His native land is across the sea, a great distance from here. He is a good man and also yer friend. Ye are welcome to have supper with us, if ye are hungry."

"You have not yet heard of the battles that have taken place close to here?"

"We have seen troops close by, and a few braves, but we have only heard of the battle at White Bird Canyon, and that the Nez Perce bravely won that battle. Ah Kim and I do not wish to take sides in this war. We believe this land belongs first to the Nez Perce. We are thankful that ye have kindly let the white man live on your land. We are not in agreement with the cavalry, and want no part in killing our friends on either side."

"I am Yellow Wolf. I have come to ask for help of the white man, who is known to be a friend of the Nez Perce people. Let me relate the events of the last few days. Many of the white soldiers have taken refuge at the Norton Ranch, which is also called the Cottonwood House. The soldiers waited there for supplies and extra ammunition to arrive. The ranch is not far from here. The Nez Perce braves have won many small battles. Our people moved to the mouth of Cottonwood Creek, where it meets the South Fork of the Clearwater River, east of the Bitterroot Mountains. This is a favorite spot of the Nez Perce, where the hunting and fishing is good, and our people eat well. The battle that followed our move was long and hard. Our men fought bravely and well, but after two days of fighting at Clearwater, the soldiers with their 'Gatling guns' and long rifles finally turned the war in their favor. Our warriors climbed high up above Cottonwood Creek, past the river, when it became necessary. We had to leave behind 80 of our tepees, and much of our supplies; including jerked beef, flour, cooking utensils, buffalo robes, clothing, and blankets. Some of our weaker people, including Chief Joseph's wife and new daughter, were left behind in the rush to leave the camp. The women were all supposed to have left, but the weaker could not keep up.

"The Nez Perce have fought off the soldiers for the time being, but they will return. Our chiefs have decided to take our people north. Yesterday, forty Nez Perce, members of Red Heart's Band, were captured and taken prisoner. These people, twenty-three warriors, seventeen women and children, were not part of the warring tribes. They were reservation Indians. They were returning from hunting for buffalo in Montana. Our Chiefs at counsel, after many disagreements, have decided to lead the people to freedom in Canada, but they are concerned for the women and elders, who are not able to travel as fast at this time.

"We heard that this ranch was deserted, and that there were many supplies here, so we were going to bring the weaker members of our tribe here to stay, until we could quietly return to take them with us when the soldiers have gone. A mile from here I met two of our scouts, who told me that they had seen John Troy heading toward the ranch. They believed that you are a friend to the Nez Perce, and that you are now living here. I am hoping that is true, as I wish to ask for your help for the weaker members of our tribe."

While he spoke, John looked at the braves and could see they had been in battle. The war paint had been put on over mud, dirt and blood. One of the braves had a wound on his leg, as a cloth was wrapped tightly around his thigh and blood was beginning to seep through.

"Yer leg is hurt. Come inside, and I will bandage your wound. The man who lived here left bandages and medicines, and his women grew healing herbs."

"I also have medicinal herbs that will help your leg heal." Ah Kim spoke for the first time.

"Bring yer elders, women and children here. We will take care of them until yer war is over. I will protect them with me life." John replied.

"I will speak to the counsel. If they are in agreement, I will bring some of our sickest, oldest, and youngest to you for safekeeping, only those we feel will not survive the journey. You will be known forever, as a friend to the Nez Perce, and honored by our people."

"Yer people will be safe here. If the white man finds out that they are here, our lives will be in danger too. I will not abandon those who need me help." John assured him.

"If we are not here by the time the sun leaves the sky, you will know that we are not coming. I will leave a brave on the edge of your land, to make sure the soldiers do not come."

"We will prepare food for yer people, me friend." John replied.

Yellow Wolf turned his horse, and the four braves raced quickly across the meadow and entered the dense timber on the edge of the forest.

"John Troy, this is dangerous for you if the white man finds out. They will have no care for me, but they will be angry with you for helping the Indians."

"Jesus would help them, and I was taught to try to be like him."

"You admire this Jesus very much, don't you, John?"

"Yes, Ah Kim, I do. Someday, I will tell ye all about him. He was a man above all men. If man would try to be like him, then all men would treat each other well."

"I would like to hear about him, but we have much work to do now. I will prepare some soup, and rice, a large pot of beans, coffee and tea. I must pick the last of the vegetables in the garden, before I begin."

John picked up the rifles, took them in the house and hung them above the fireplace. Then he went down to the cellar to retrieve blankets, bandages, medicines, and whatever else he could find that they might need. They both worked until sunset, to make sure the many rooms were ready for guests. The smell of the cooking vegetables, in Ah Kim's soup, made the dusty house smell wonderful. John put blankets on all the beds in the house. The large Mormon family had left lots of bedding that would help them house several Nez Perce. There were five large rooms beside the large main room and cooking area. Two beds were in the main room. John and Ah Kim would take those. A large rectangular table, with long benches, sat in front of the fireplace, and a wood stove was in the corner behind the table. Two handmade rocking chairs sat on each side of the fireplace. There was a small table in between the beds, with an oil lamp on it. A second oil lamp sat in the middle of the square table

John wondered what Noah Johnson would have thought of him taking care of the Indians in his house, or even having Ah Kim stay there. He sat on the porch swing, waiting for the Indians to arrive. The sun was beginning to set in the summer sky, when he saw the group of Indians.

They emerged from the trees, just as dusk began to settle on the land. There were three young women walking in front of the horses. Two carried babies on cradle boards, and the third was pregnant. Three small children walked among them. Four older women walked with two elderly braves who led ponies. The three braves that accompanied Yellow Wolf earlier in the day pulled three wounded braves on stretchers behind their ponies. Two of the other ponies carried large packs with buffalo robes and other belongings. Yellow Wolf escorted the group across the fields. John went to the door and told Ah Kim that they were coming. When they got closer, he opened the gate and welcomed them all inside.

Ah Kim set the large soup tureen in the middle of the table, and was ladling soup into bowls and setting them around the table. They could smell the coffee brewing and see the steam rising from the tea kettle. The little Chinese man put cups on the table and set the tea and coffee pots by the soup tureen. He put plates in a stack and large bowls of rice on both ends. Then he added biscuits and a bean pot. Ah Kim had become a good cook out of necessity. He wanted to eat well and had asked Mary for some of her simple recipes, on the train, during their long trip across the country. The biscuits she made were even better than the sticky buns he was used to.

John realized that the three braves were badly wounded and that one of them would be lucky to survive the night. Yellow Wolf and his braves carried the men to the first room, which held three beds. Ah Kim brought in three bowls of soup, and the older women bowed in thanks. They took the bowls from him and fed it to their wounded friends. When they returned the bowls, one still had most of the soup in it. The badly wounded man hadn't eaten much. Ah Kim had watched for a moment when one of the younger women held the barely conscious man's head, while the older one fed small portions of the soup into his mouth. The rest of the women and children sat on the benches and ate the food Ah Kim had put on the table. Ah Kim motioned to Yellow Wolf and the rest of the braves, old and young, to sit and eat too. The Indians had brought many eating utensils with them, so they didn't have to take turns eating.

The older men sat at the table, the younger ones took their food outside. Everyone ate silently.

When they finished, one of the younger women took over the cleaning of the dishes.

After they ate, Yellow Wolf spoke for the first time. "Chief Joseph and Chief White Bird send you many thanks and warm greetings. They will send word, as soon as they can, and will return for their people as soon as it is safe. They wish you to know that your kindness will be repaid someday."

"Tell the chiefs, they owe me nothing. I am ashamed of the treatment yer people have received from the white man. I will do everything I can to take care of yer people, until ye return. I am honored by yer faith and trust in me."

As the braves said goodbye, John realized that many of them were related. One of the older women appeared to be Yellow Wolf's mother, as he witnessed a tender goodbye between the two. The youngest of the four braves, the one with the bandaged leg, was Yellow Wolf's younger brother. One of the other braves was leaving his pregnant wife and two children with John and Ah Kim. The little family shared some caring looks that John had rarely seen between white people. He and the fourth brave appeared to be brothers, as even with war paint adorning their faces, they resembled each other. One of the young mothers, with the other small child, stayed close to the brave who was hurt the worst. The third woman, with the smallest baby, was very lovely and held herself like a princess. Yellow Wolf introduced her as Chief Joseph's wife, Toma Alwawinmi (Spring of Year, or Spring-time). She had given birth to the baby girl, just before the battle at White Bird Canyon. Her baby was very small and quiet. Another older woman took care of the other wounded braves and the pregnant woman. After Yellow Wolf and his braves said their goodbyes, they left the ranch by the light of the moon.

When the house was quiet for the night, John worried about all the people he had taken in. 'How long would they be here? What if the soldiers came? Could he protect these people from them? Would they take them away?' He thought about Mary, and her blessings and proverbs. She would surely have an appropriate one to say right now. He would write her a letter tomorrow, because he knew she would worry, but he wondered when he would be able to send it.

Chapter Twenty-One

"Kate's Dilemma"

San Francisco ~ August, 1877

"The truth comes out when the spirit goes in."

Mary hadn't received a letter from John for several weeks, and she was worried. The San Francisco Examiner said that the soldiers were fighting the Nez Perce in Northeastern Oregon and Idaho, and she knew John was right in the middle of it. She spent every night praying for John and Ah Kim and their safety.

One morning, when she went downstairs to prepare breakfast, she found Rachel waiting for her in the kitchen.

"Mary, we need to talk to you."

"We?"

"Kate is in my room. Can you come now, Mary, please?"

Mary heard the urgency in her voice. They hurried up the stairs together. Rachel shut the door quietly behind them as they entered the room. Kate sat on the bed leaning over a bowl. As tears ran down her cheeks, Kate retched and gagged and finally brought up whatever she had eaten the day before. She was sweating and very pale. Her hair was damp and limp, and there were large circles under her lovely green eyes. Mary was shocked at how bad she looked.

"Me darlin', Kate, whatever is the matter? What can I do?"

The young girl fell into her arms, weeping uncontrollably. Mary held her and rocked her as she cried.

"There now, please don't cry. Tell me what's wrong. I can't help ye, until ye tell me. It can't be that bad, can it?"

Kate sobbed for a few more minutes and finally seemed to get control of her emotions.

Rachel sat in a chair across from them, looking at her friend sadly.

"It's the fault of your Uncle Sean, Mary." Kate exclaimed.

Suddenly very alert, Mary responded quickly, "Sean? What does he have to do with this?"

"He had his way with her! That's what!" Rachel blurted out, and Kate started to weep again.

"He did what? I swear I'll kill the bastard! I told him to stay away from ye girls. I warned him the first day I saw him. I should have known the lecher would set his sights on ye." Mary got up, and started pacing back and forth across the room. "It's me fault. I should have told everyone when he first arrived."

"Told them what, Mary?" Rachel asked.

"He was one of the reasons I left Ireland. He has a problem with the drink. Like they say, *'The truth comes out when the spirits go in.'* And, when he's drinking, he can't control himself where young ladies are concerned. A few nights before I left, he accosted me in me own home, with me parents in the next room. I bit him hard on the shoulder, and me brother, Jerry, came in and wanted to pummel him to pieces. I should have told on him then, but I didn't want to hurt me Mum and Da, and I was sure he'd lie his way out of it. Wait till I get me hands on him!"

"No, Mary. Please let him be. I am so ashamed. It was my fault too. I told him I wanted to see the Barbary Coast, and I lied to my parents to see him. It's my fault! I dressed up all pretty. I tempted him, Mary. The devil must have been in me, and now I am carrying his child!" She wailed woefully, threw herself on the bed, and continued to sob.

Mary sat next to her and gently rubbed her back. "Are ye sure yer with child, Kate? Perhaps ye have got another type of ailment causing yer sickness."

"I'm sure, Mary. I've not had my monthly twice now, and I've been sick for weeks."

Mary unbuttoned the top of her dress and saw the prominent veins in her chest, as well as her larger than normal breasts that were overflowing her bustier. There was no doubt about it. Kate was going to have a child.

"Have yer parents noticed? Have they heard ye being sick?"

"No, no! I can't tell them, Mary. It will kill them. They have so many hopes for me. I am such a disappointment. Rachel told me not to go. Why didn't I listen?"

"Why didn't I tell Mary?" Rachel jumped in.

"Listen lassies, ye can't cry over spilt milk. We have just got to figure out what to do next. Katie darlin', do ye love him? Do ye want to marry him? He is the father of yer child."

"No, Mary, I hate him! I was crazy about him, until he forced himself upon me. I told him no, but he was too strong."

"Ye mean to say he raped you?"

"Yes, Mary, I guess you could say that."

Mary began pacing again. She was angry now. Her Irish temper was boiling, and she wanted to scream.

"If we tell the police everyone will know, yer reputation will be ruined, yer parents and me parents' lives will be destroyed. Perhaps, Ah Kim's friends in the Tong should take care of him."

"No, Mary! No police, no Tong! Remember, no matter what, he is me baby's father."

"Katie, I don't know what else to tell ye. I think we must tell yer parents. I heard of a place back home in Ireland. It's run by the nuns. They take in girls that are in a family way, and they help them place their babes with good Irish families after they're born."

"Can't I just go there without telling mom and pop?"

"What would ye tell them, Kate? Don't ye think it's best to bare your soul?"

"No, Mary, I don't. Pop has a mighty bad temper. I don't want him killing Sean and going to jail. I have enough on my conscience now. Besides, I am too ashamed. Can't I just run off like you did, then write and tell them I'm visiting abroad?"

"Why don't ye talk to them about taking a trip abroad? Tell them ye want to travel this year, before ye enroll in college. Me sister Margaret has a friend who might help us. She is a wealthy woman who travels everywhere, and she is very understanding and trustworthy. Perhaps yer parents would let ye travel with her for a year. Ye could write letters ahead of time, and she could mail them from wherever she is. I'm sure she would agree to escort ye to the home in Ireland. She is planning to leave within the month. I think she plans on being gone for six or eight months. Ye could come back with her when she returns."

"Oh Mary, that would be wonderful. Do you really think she would do it?"

"I'll ask her, Kate, but I really don't like lying to yer parents. I don't feel right about it."

"Mary, you are sworn to secrecy. Like you always tell us, *'Who keeps his tongue keeps his friend.'* You cannot tell anyone without my permission. If you take me to see her, I will do the talking. Please, please Mary? I knew we could count on you"

"I jest hope I'm doing the right thing, but I will be saying something to Sean, Kate. I won't be able to relax until I give that devil a piece of me mind. I'm really sorry, Kate, that this has happened to ye."

"It is not your fault, Mary, it is mine. Thank you for your help. When can we visit this woman?"

"We will go over to her house after lunch. Straighten up yer face and clothes, come down for lunch, then we will go."

"I'm afraid I will be sick again if I eat."

"I will fix ye some broth. Hurry now, girls. I'm going to prepare the food. Take a deep breath, Kate. This will be a very painful year for ye, but with the grace of God, ye will get through it. Some good tough praying would help right now, Kate. Ye are in my prayers."

"Thank you, Mary"

Mary kissed her on the head, held her hands for a moment, then turned and left the room. She said another rosary while she prepared the meal, praying for Kate and for the babe in her womb. After the meal was done, they went to see Mrs. McCleary. Mary didn't know her well, but she had heard what a wonderful woman she was, and that she was never one to share a secret. Her home was a ten-minute walk from the Goldstein mansion. Mrs. McCleary answered the door herself and invited them in immediately.

"Good day, how nice to have visitors! Please come in, ladies."

"Hello, Mrs. McCleary. We're sorry to bother ye without an invitation, but we have a problem that needs tending to immediately."

"I'll be happy to help ye, if I can. Please come into the parlor. I just made a pot of tea."

She went to the beautiful buffet, took down three more cups and saucers, and set them by the silver tea set on the table. Then she carefully poured each of them a cup. There was already a plate of biscuits in the middle of the table. Mrs. McCleary laid white lace napkins in front of each of them, and then she sat down to enjoy her own cup of tea.

"Now, what can I do to help ye lovely lasses on this fine summer day?"

Mary started to speak, but Kate interrupted her.

"No, Mary, this is my problem. I should be the one to confess me sins."

"Now, me dear, we all have sins. No one here will be casting the first stone. Just blurt it all out. I'll be listening."

Kate took a deep breath and told her story, as simply as she could. When she finished talking, tears were flowing freely down her face. The older woman came over and put her arms around Kate, and she held her till she was done weeping. Mary and Rachel dabbed at their eyes too.

"What is it that ye think I can do to help ye, me dear?" The old woman asked kindly.

"Mary said you were going abroad soon. I hoped, maybe I could travel with you and stay in Ireland, until the birthing of my baby. I'll be giving the child to some good Irish folks and returning without my parents knowing anything about it."

"Are ye sure ye shouldn't be telling your mum and pop about this?"

"No, ma'am, I know my father. With his terrible temper, he would surely disown me. If you could just talk to him for me, and ask him if I could go with you, I think he would agree. You know, tell him that traveling with you for a few months would further my education. Then mail some postcards for me from the places you visit."

"Are ye sure I can't talk ye out of this, me dear?"

"I really think this is the only way, ma'am. I would be forever grateful."

"I would be happy to help ye. I will go talk to ye parents tomorrow. I leave one week from tomorrow. Can ye be ready by then?"

"Thank you, thank you, Mrs. McCleary, you have saved my life." Kate's face held a faint glimmer of hope. She smiled for the first time in weeks. "I'd better get home and start making plans."

"Now give me your address, and I'll be over tomorrow around 1:00 p.m. Be prepared to help me convince your father and mother that this trip is important to ye."

"Don't worry, ma'am. I'll be ready."

That evening, Mary sat down and wrote a long letter to John. There was so much she wanted to tell him and couldn't. Instead, she asked him what was happening in Eastern Oregon. She didn't know when he would get her letter, or what was happening there, but she hoped and prayed he was okay, and that she would hear from him soon. As usual, she ended the evening with a rosary, praying for

Kate, for the unborn babe, for John and Ah Kim, the Nez Perce Indians, and finally she prayed for Sean's soul.

Chapter Twenty-Two

"Living with the Nez Perce"

Eastern Oregon ~ August, 1877

"Well, well, what do we have here? I see a couple of stray squaws and a papoose."

Living with the Nez Perce gave John and Ah Kim more reasons to respect the gentle people. The tribe members who were living at the ranch were polite, kind, and respectful.

Those who were able, always did their share of the work. After a couple of weeks, John went to Mount Idaho to see if the white settlers had gone home, to find out what news he could about the Nez Perce and their trip over the Lolo Trail, and he also wanted to mail a letter to Mary.

Before that day, the gentle people quietly stayed inside the ranch house. John came to wish he had not gone to town, with what transpired while he was gone. Two of the women, Little Moccasin and Quiet Prairie, had gone to the creek at the edge of the forest, to wash what they needed for the babies and to bathe. Little Moccasin had given birth the week before, and she left her newborn with the other women at the cabin. They took Quiet Prairie's oldest child as a look out, but she saw some squirrels and began watching them play. The noise of the squirrels and the birds kept her attention, and she didn't see the two white men riding slowly across the meadow. The men saw the child playing on the hill above the creek, and since they heard that the Nez Perce tribes were on their way north, they decided to find out how she came to be there. They were hunting for game, to feed themselves and the gang of men they hung out with. The men were camped a few miles south of the Johnson ranch. By the time the child saw them, it was too late, as the men were a few feet away. The largest man grabbed her quickly, holding his hand over her mouth. Little Moccasin and Quiet Prairie were dressing when they heard her muffled cries. They looked up as the men came down the hill holding rifles, and the taller man was carrying the squirming child under his arm.

"Well, well, what do we have here? I see a couple of stray squaws and a papoose. I thought yer people were headed north. What are you doing here?" The shorter man grabbed the closest woman and wouldn't let her go. Quiet Prairie struggled, and he hit her with the butt of his rifle, knocking her to the ground.

The little girl quit struggling when the man threatened to hit her too. He tied her wrists to the unconscious woman on the ground. Then the two men decided to have some fun with Little Moccasin.

"Don't worry about putting them clothes on, missy. You ain't going to need them for a while."

The two men laughed as they pulled down their trousers. When she started to run, the large man dove for her legs, tripping her, and slamming her down on the hard ground. The tiny maiden scratched, hit and thrashed, but he held her wrists to the ground, laughing at her inability to move.

"Just what I like... a wild Indian squaw."

"Hurry up. I want my turn."

John saw the saddled horses grazing in the meadow, when he came from town. As he rode across the meadow, he heard the woman's scream. Pulling his rifle out of its scabbard, he jumped off his horse. He got to the top of the hill, just as the big man climbed on top of the Indian maiden.

"Get off of her, or ye'll be dead shortly!" John yelled.

The other man turned around quickly, and aimed his rifle at John. John pulled the trigger at the same time. He ducked and the bullet whizzed past his head, as the man with the rifle fell to the ground. John aimed at the other man who now stood there, in his long johns, looking angry and scared.

"I know you. You're John Troy. Bane will be happy to know what you're up to. We should have known you'd be a friend of the Red Man and a traitor." The man laughed eerily, trying to pretend that he wasn't afraid.

"Yeah, and yer one of those turncoats, who ran at Cottonwood Creek and got a lot of men killed, aren't ye?"

"Now that you've killed a white man to save an Injun' squaw, I'm sure you'll be wanted everywhere."

Quiet Prairie came up behind him with the knife she had hidden in her clothes. With rage in her eyes, she viciously rammed it into the large man's back. A look of surprise crossed his face as she shoved him, and he fell into the creek and quit moving. John was trying to decide what to do next, as Quiet Prairie freed Little Moccasin and the child. The two women quickly took over. They pulled the men's trousers up, and with John's help, put them over their saddles. After they cleaned up the blood, they led the horses toward the woods.

"Where are ye going?" John asked.

"We will bury these white men where they will never be found, then we will let the horses go free."

"Can I help?"

"No, John Troy. You saved us again, and now you are in danger with us. Go home. We will return shortly."

John took the child, went to the ranch, and told Ah Kim what happened.

"We must be careful, John. If these were Bane's men, he must be close. He will kill us all, if he finds out."

"Ye are right, Ah Kim. We cannot let him see the Indians if he comes here."

They were all on alert, for the next few days, and the Indians stayed in the house as much as possible. Two days later, Bane and the rest of his marauders showed up. John told Ah Kim to stay inside, as he went out the front door with his gun in hand. Ah Kim gave rifles to all of the Indians and set them at the windows, in case they needed their help.

"Well, well, my old friend, John Troy." Bane said, with his evil laugh.

"What do ye want, Bane?"

"I'm looking for two of my men. Their horses came back without them, the day before yesterday. Did they pass through here?"

"I haven't seen anyone. Now, if ye don't mind, I've got work to do. So, please, take yer men and leave me land."

"Yer land? I thought this was the Johnson ranch."

"It was. Johnson asked me to take care of it, before he left."

"So yer by yerself, are ya?" Bane pulled his rifle out of its sheath, and Ah Kim walked out the door with his rifle aimed at Bane.

"Ah, ye've got the Chinaman for protection." He laughed again.

Just then, rifles popped out of every window and crack of the log house.

"Many of my cousins, the Tong, are visiting too, Mr. Bane."

Bane slowly let the rifle slide back into its case.

"Ye win this time, Irishman. But, ye better be on yer guard, cuz there will be a time when I'll find ye alone."

"I'll be waiting for that day, Bane. Now, get off this land and don't come back!"

Bane turned his horse, and he led the five men down the road.

"Thank ye, Ah Kim. That was very clever."

"I am happy that I could be of service, John Troy."

"I was thinking of trying to get the title to this land from Noah Johnson, but now that Bane knows about it, I don't think that is such a good idea."

"I heard that there was a good bit of acreage still available for homesteading about eighteen miles east of Baker City, Mister John. It has two creeks running through the property and lots of good grazing land. One of my cousins looked at it and thought it would be good for raising crops. He wanted it, but because of the way the Chinese are treated here, he decided not to pursue it. It might be perfect for you and Miss Mary."

"I will look into that, when we are able to return to the area. Thank ye, Ah Kim."

Ah Kim bowed, and John slapped him on the back, as the two men entered the cabin.

Chapter Twenty-Three

"Mary Confronts Sean"

San Francisco ~ September, 1877

"Ye ought to be strung up by yer neck, fer what ye've done!"

Kate's parents reluctantly let her go with Mrs. McCleary. After much talking and begging from Kate, the women convinced them that a trip abroad would benefit her education. The older woman told Kate she could send her brochures and books relating to where she traveled, so that Kate would learn about those places, and be able to speak of them when she returned.

Mary, Rachel, and Johanna waved to Kate at the pier as the boat left port, and two of them were praying for their dear friend to get through her ordeal safely. Both Kate and Mrs. McCleary wrote often. Mary quickly burned the envelopes, with Kate's real address in Ireland, as soon as she received them, as did Rachel. They didn't want Hannah Goldstein to see where those letters really came from

Mary didn't talk to Sean until after Kate left. Then she decided he needed to be taught a lesson. She had received a letter from Ah Kim with the new address of his cousin, Li, who had owned the laundry they had gone to, upon their arrival in San Francisco. Ah Kim said that she should contact him, if she had any problems she couldn't take care of on her own. He added that his cousin was a member of the "secret society" in that city. When Mary told Li about Sean's offenses, she found him eager to help.

Sean was playing cards in a saloon on the waterfront when they found him. As Li knew many people in that area, he was able to convince the man at the door to let him go inside. Mary waited outside, trying to pretend she was not afraid, but she was. She was very afraid. 'What if Bane, or one of his friends, was still in San Francisco? If so, this is surely where they would be,' she thought. Most of the men who entered the saloon were very rough looking. The women, who passed through the door, wore bright red rouge on their cheeks, low cut dresses and had very red lips. She was relieved when Li returned with Sean, who looked more afraid than she did.

"Mary, what are ye doing here?"

"Hello, Sean. Come with us!" Mary demanded.

Sean looked at the Chinaman and said, "Okay, Mary, what's the matter? Is Mum sick?"

"Just come along, Sean. We will talk when we get there."

Mary led the way, Sean followed, and Li was right behind him. Li lived in Chinatown, only ten blocks from the waterfront. However, they weren't going to Li's, they were going a block further. Li had already told Mary where they were taking him and what they had planned. When she got to the building, she stopped and looked at Li for assurance that they were at the right place. Li nodded and pushed Sean to the door roughly. He knocked what sounded like a code on the door. After a curtain was pulled back from the window on the door, to check their identity, the door opened. After Li said something in Chinese, the man bowed and invited them to enter. The man led them down the stairs to the basement. A tantalizing aroma came from a corner of the dark room and filled the room with smoke. When her sight improved, she saw that there were several cots around the main room, with curtains between them. Two curtains were drawn, and smoke came from beneath them. Mary was getting nervous. The man led them through the main room and down the hall. He opened a door and motioned for them to enter, then he closed the door behind them. The dimly lit room held a cot, a table, and two chairs.

"Sit down!" Mary ordered Sean, who by this time wasn't able to speak above a whisper.

"Okay, Mary." He said breathlessly.

"Sean, I told ye when ye got here not to touch any of the girls, didn't I?"

"I didn't Mary. What are ye talkin' about? Please, yer scaring me. What are we doing here? This is an opium den. The Tong run this place."

"I know, Sean. I'm sure ye know Li is not only a member of the secret society, but he is also a friend of mine. They wanted to take care of this matter by themselves, but I talked them out of it. This is yer lucky day, Sean, because they have decided to let ye live. There is only one reason for that Sean, and that is because of me dear mother. Do ye understand me, Sean? Only fer me dear mother, not fer ye."

Sean's face was so pale he looked as if he might faint.

"Mary, I swear to ye..."

"Sean, don't be adding lies to yer sins. Yer so full of the devil now that ye'll be burnin' to a crisp down there. I am hoping that ye'll change yer life with this last chance, and do some good for the world with the rest of yer time here."

He just sat there looking scared and sick, waiting for her to tell him what he had done.

"Kate Murphy is pregnant with yer child, ye slimy bastard!"

Sean's mouth fell open, both from the news and from hearing Mary use that word.

"Pregnant?"

"Yes, Sean, and the way I hear it, she was raped! Don't say a word, Sean, until I'm done! I've never in me life been so ashamed of me kin. Why didn't ye stay in Ireland or go to some other place? Why did ye have to come here? Kate is a beautiful girl, who had a bright future, and ye have ruined her life. Ye ought to be strung up by the neck, fer what ye've done!"

Sean started getting his senses back. "Mary, Mary, please let me speak. I'm so sorry. I felt so bad, after it happened. I had too much to drink. I quit drinkin' after that, Mary. I've rarely touched the stuff, since then. I'm sorry! She was just so beautiful, so desirable, I couldn't control meself. But Mary, I love the girl! I'll marry her. I'll marry her right now... tonight!"

"She doesn't want to marry ye, Sean. After what ye've done, she hates ye, Sean! She can't stand the sight of ye!"

"Oh, but I'll change her mind. I'll make her love me. I'll make it up to her, Mary, I promise! I'll be a wonderful husband to her and a good father to the baby. Please, Mary, forgive me!"

"Sorry, Sean, it's too late. Kate is on her way to Ireland to bear the child and give it up for adoption."

"Oh no! Oh no!" Sean seemed genuinely upset. Mary was surprised, as she thought he would be happy that she was gone.

"Where has she gone, Mary? I'll go after her. I'll convince her to marry me."

"It's too late, Sean!"

"Jest give me a chance!"

"She left two weeks ago and I don't know the address. I will let ye know when she writes to me, if she wants to hear from ye. In the meantime, ye better show me a responsible, non-drinkin' man, or get out of town! If I hear anything else about ye, I'll let the Tong have their way with ye. Do ye understand me, Sean Foley?"

"Yes, Mary. Please let me know as soon as ye hear. I want to go after her. I'll be saving me money for the trip."

When they left the opium den, Sean headed up the hill instead of back to the waterfront. Li thanked the man at the house, paid him, and walked Mary to the Goldstein's big home. She tried to give him what he had paid the man, but he would not take it.

"I do this for my cousin, Ah Kim."

"Thank ye, Li. Thank ye very much."

He bowed to her and she bowed back. Then she went up the stairs to the beautiful mansion she lived in, hung up her coat, and climbed the staircase to her room. After she changed into her nightgown, she splashed water on her face from the pitcher on the dresser, and she sat down to brush her beautiful, long hair. When she finished, she moved the kerosene lamp over to the desk and sat down to write a letter to John.

Chapter Twenty-Four

"The War is over"

San Francisco ~ November, 1877 - January, 1878

"Chief Joseph would not leave the rest of his tribe, who could not flee fast enough."

Mary received several letters from John, before she received one telling her that the battle was over. The Nez Perce had almost made it to Canada. There had been one last skirmish a few miles below the border where Chief Joseph had finally surrendered to General Howard. She was relieved to learn that the war between the United States government and the Nez Perce was over, but she was sorry to learn that the Native Americans had lost the fight for their land. It was heartbreaking to hear that many of their people had been killed. Many of the soldiers and volunteers had died too. It reminded her so much of her own country's battles for independence. John was still caring for several of the tribe, including Chief Joseph's youngest wife and five month old daughter. He wondered when and if Yellow Wolf would return to retrieve his friends and family. The most severely wounded warrior that had been left in his care died shortly after the Indians had arrived. Those who were able had taken him somewhere in the forest to bury him. When she wrote back to John, she asked him to be careful, and stay safe, as she knew that if he was discovered with the Nez Perce he would be in trouble with the other settlers. Mary was beginning to wonder if the United States would really ever become *"the land of the free"*. She didn't understand how the country could have a civil war to free blacks from slavery, then follow it with wars to take away the Native American's freedom and land. Whenever she posed that question to men, she was told to "hush!" Mary thought it was time that women got to vote. In her next letter to John, she stated her opinions about those things. She was surprised with his response in his return letter.

November, 1877

My dearest Mary,

You are right, me girl. It is a contradiction! The way I heard it, the Civil War was really fought over land, and not slaves at all. The people in power just seem to do what is best for them, not what is best for the people. I do think we need a change in many policies. Giving women a say in how the country is run, is something that I hope will happen in the near future.

Several braves showed up quietly yesterday to take my guests with them. I had grown quite fond of all the people that stayed here. Two of the younger women were quite brave, and one saved my life. I will tell you that story someday soon. I am worried about Chief Joseph's little daughter, as she does not seem to be a very strong baby.

Yellow Wolf told me many details of the tribe's sad fight for freedom over the Lolo Trail. They fought many battles and skirmishes with the soldiers and civilian volunteers. The Battle of White Bird Canyon was one of only three that it is said they won. Yellow Wolf said their journey was over 1800 miles, and Chief Joseph thought they were home free when they camped in the Bear

Paw Mountains, which is only a couple of miles below the Canadian border. They did not know there were two battalions of soldiers waiting to attack them. The last battle was at Cow Island. Several chiefs were killed in that last two day battle, which was fought during a blizzard.

Yellow Wolf said that it was Chief Looking Glass who insisted they Camp there, instead of going on to Canada. Chief Tuhulhutsut, Chief Alokut (Chief Joseph's younger brother), Hush-Hush-Cute, Pile of Clouds, and Poker Joe (Lean Elk) were all killed on the first day of that battle. Chief Looking Glass was killed on the last day. Some of the Nez Perce did escape to Canada, including Chief Joseph's 12-year old daughter, Sarah, and his older wife. They are said to be with Chief White Bird in exile there. Many also went to Chief Sitting Bull's Sioux camp for protection. However, Chief Joseph would not leave the rest of his tribe, including many who were wounded, as well as the women, children, and elderly, who could not flee fast enough.

Yellow Wolf said that Chief Joseph would not have surrendered if General Miles had not told him that the Nez Perce would be able to return to Lapwai. He repeated Joseph's words; "I believed him, or I never would have surrendered. He could not have made other terms with me at that time. I would have held him in check until my friends came to my assistance, and then neither of the generals, nor their soldiers, would have left Bear Paw Mountain alive."

When the last battle was over, the cavalry had suffered at least twenty percent casualties. Twenty-five Nez Perce were killed, and forty of the eighty-seven people who surrendered were wounded. That is not counting 184 women and 147 children. 800 Nez Perce left Idaho and only 418 returned.

Yellow Wolf is taking my friends to Chief Joseph. The tribe is presently camped on the Yellowstone River, where they are supposed to be able to remain until spring. Yellow Wolf is concerned that they might be moved elsewhere, so he needed to get the rest of the people up there, before that happens.

Although, it is a relief not to have to worry about the Indians being discovered anymore, I was very sad to see them go, and so was Ah Kim. We are both very fond of them. They are a kind, hardworking people. I was impressed by their treatment of each other. They certainly are no more savage than you or I. I talked often with one of the older men, as he liked to practice his English, and found him to be a very wise man. I learned a lot during our conversations.

Anyway, the war IS over and work resumes on the railroad next week. Ah Kim and I are leaving for Oregon tomorrow, so you can again write to me in care of the Baker City Post Office. We should be able to get a lot of track laid before the snow comes. The sooner I go back to work, the sooner we can get married. I hope you are still planning on becoming my wife. I miss you so much.

There are 2,000 good acres that I have heard about, eighteen miles east of Baker City. The railroad will run right through the middle of those acres. I hope to be able to homestead some of that land, and to purchase the rest someday. I am going to stay in a small shanty by the tracks while we finish the job. The railroad foreman said I could stay there at no cost. That way I can start saving money. I have again been appointed crew boss, and Ah Kim has recruited several of his cousins to be on my crew. Perhaps your Uncle Sean should come up here and go to work. He's a big strong man and we could use him.

I must go now, as we are low on kerosene, and the light is dim. Pray for me, dear Mary, and say a few of your blessings for all of us, especially the Nez Perce nation.

Your husband to be,

John S. Troy

There was only one part of John's letter that concerned her, and that was the part about wanting Sean to come work on the railroad. Mary didn't know how to tell John that she didn't want Sean to come up there, without him wanting to know why. She couldn't tell him about Kate, and she wasn't ready to tell him about the incident in Ireland either. Mary decided to just not tell Sean about the job. It was a big relief to know that she could now quit worrying about the Nez Perce War. Her only worry now was the dynamiting they did while working on the railroad.

And then there was Kate. A letter arrived from her in late December. Mary could tell from the letter that Kate was very depressed, and that she hated the place where she was staying.

"The babies stay with their mothers until the adoptive parents arrive to tear the child from its mother's breast." Kate wrote that she did not want to see the child after its birth, for fear she would want to keep it. She planned on leaving as soon as she could after the baby was born. Mrs. McCleary promised to return to be with her when the child was born, and they planned to leave as soon as Kate was fit to travel. Kate expected the child to arrive in mid-February, and she promised that she would write to Mary before she left.

"I am planning to travel with Mrs. McCleary to Paris, where we will stay until at least May. After that, I have no plans. And No, I don't want Sean to know where I am. I never want to see him again as long as I live!" Her words about Sean were adamant.

Sean arrived at her door the day after Mary received the letter from Kate.

"Did ye hear from her yet?"

"Yes I did, Sean, and she doesn't want to see ye at all. I'm sorry."

"Mary, ye've got to give me her address. I love her! I want to marry her! Don't ye see how important this is? I must stop her from giving our babe away."

"Sean, I truly wish that had been her answer. I cannot go against her wishes."

"Mary, please? I've changed. I've saved some money. I want to make it on my own. I don't want any help from her father. I'm going to go over there and look for her. I have booked passage on a ship leaving in two weeks. Please give me her address before I leave."

"Sean, I do hope ye have changed, but I still cannot give ye her address, unless she tells me to. I'm sorry. Do ye want a cup of tea before ye leave?"

"Yes, thank ye, Mary. That would be nice." He sat on the sofa with his head in his hands and his eyes closed. Mary went to the kitchen to fix the tea. Sean felt someone touching his arm, and he opened his eyes to find Rachel standing there.

She put her finger to her lips. "Shhh!" Then she placed a small folded piece of paper in his hand and quietly left the room. He opened it quickly before Mary returned. Kate Murphy and an address in Dublin were printed on the paper. Mary entered the room just as Sean slipped the paper into his shirt pocket. Sean put his head back between his hands and said a prayer of thanks.

The ship that was to take Sean to Ireland was delayed in leaving because of a storm at sea. It didn't sail until mid-January. Rachel told Mary after he left that she had given him Kate's address.

"I know ye shouldn't have, but I'm truly glad ye did. I wanted to give it to him meself, but knew I couldn't."

"She can just be mad at me. I hope he gets there in time to stop her from letting the baby be adopted."

"So do I, but how will she explain to her parents? What a mess! I think I'll be praying on this one real hard for the next few weeks. Ye best be praying too, little one."

"Yes, Mary, I've been doing a lot of praying. Have you heard from John Troy lately?"

"Yes, Rachel. I just received a letter from him, and he sent me a late Christmas present."

"He did? What did he send you?"

"I haven't opened it yet. It's been a busy day."

"Why don't you open it now? I can't wait to see what he sent you."

Mary laughed. "Okay, Rachel, come to my room and I'll retrieve the package."

"I would have opened it immediately. How can you wait?"

"It wasn't easy."

Mary pulled the package out from under her bed. She took off the string that held the worn paper, covering its hidden treasures, then she removed the paper. Shining blue silk peeked boldly from amid the shabby wrapper. It was the most beautiful cloth Mary had ever laid her eyes on. It was a deep blue, the color of the ocean, and there were at least four yards of it. Mary could make a lovely gown from this fabric. She held it to her face and enjoyed the soft cool texture of the material.

"Ah Kim must have had a hand in this. This must be the famous Chinese silk. It's lovely." A box fell from inside the cloth as she unfolded the fabric. It was hand carved in an Oriental design. Inside was an exquisite hand carved wooden rosary. Its fragile beauty brought tears to her eyes.

"This had to be made just for me."

"Oh Mary, John really loves you. Those are beautiful."

There was a small piece of paper at the bottom of the box.

To my dearest Mary,

I wish I could have spent Christmas with you. I so missed you on that holy day. I know this will arrive late, but I had it made for you and I just received it. Forgive me, and I hope you like it!

Your betrothed,

John S. Troy

Mary would cherish the box and the rosary forever. She would take the rosary to church with her on Sunday to have Father Pat bless it. Later that night, after she said her first rosary on the tiny beads, she went to put it in the box and dropped it. As she bent to pick it up, she knocked the box off the table with her elbow.

"Oh no, I broke it." Mary's heart sank as she picked up the box, but upon a closer look, she realized the box wasn't broken. There was a secret compartment with a tiny latch on the bottom of the box. The latch had not been fastened tight, and the extra slat had slipped out. Mary immediately thought this would be the perfect place to hide Ah Kim's envelope, which she worried was not safe in her quilt, as she could hear the paper crinkle when she moved the quilt. She checked the latch on the box carefully, removed the envelope from the quilt and folded it to a third of its normal size, before placing it between the two slats on the bottom of the box. It fit perfectly! Then she put her rosaries, the old and the new, and the note from John inside the box. Looking closely at the hand carved ornate design on the box that she first thought was Chinese writing she saw that it was her name carved in fancy script. She knew Ah Kim had designed this exquisite piece just for her, and it would always remind her of her trip across the country with Ah Kim and Ming at her side. It all seemed so long ago now.

Mary walked over to the desk, and she took out her newly purchased writing paper and bottle of ink. Picking up her favorite quill pin, she dipped it in the inkwell and began to write.

Chapter Twenty-Five

"Sean Searches for Kate"

Dublin, Ireland ~ February, 1878

"If only you'd have arrived a few days earlier."

Sean Foley didn't reach the house in Dublin until mid-February. The furious winter seas stormed all the way across the Atlantic, and Sean was deathly ill throughout the trip. He had to take an extra day to recuperate after his arrival. Sean's stomach finally settled down, and he rented a rig at the stable next to the Inn where he was staying. It took him forty-five minutes to find the address that was on the paper that Rachel gave him. Sean stopped the buggy in front of the large old house at the end of Glengarry Road. The dark and gloomy place was on a hill, and he had to climb three flights of wooden stairs to get to the front door. Shivers ran up Sean's spine as he climbed. It took a long time for someone to answer the door. While he waited, he thought about his beautiful Kate, delivering his baby in this horrible place, and a terrible shame overcame him. He suddenly realized what Kate had to endure because of his unforgivable sin. His heart ached at the thought of her giving up their poor babe. He had ruined two lives, the lives of the two people he now knew he loved the most. Sean swore to himself that he would make it up to her no matter how long it took. Finally, the huge door opened slowly, and a stern looking nun greeted him.

"What can I do for ye, sir?" She was not unkind, just very formal.

"Top of the morning to ye, Sister." Sean took off his hat. "I'm sorry to bother ye this early in the day, but I need to find me fiancé, Kate Murphy."

"There is no one here by that name, and if there were, I'd not be allowed to tell ye without her permission."

"Of course, she would not be here under her real name. She is a beautiful red headed American girl. Is there anyone here like that?"

"Only one red headed American girl was here, but she had no fiancé. The lassie had been taken advantage of by a certain ill-reputed Irish gentleman, who now lives in America."

"Surely that gentleman is me, dear Sister. I beg fer yer forgiveness, just as I intend to beg forgiveness from the lovely Kate. I came to marry her and give her and the babe a home."

The nun looked at him sadly and shook her head. "Dear boy, if only ye had arrived a few days earlier. Come into the parlor for a cup of tea, and I will explain." She led him into a room off of the long hallway, and she returned a few minutes later with a tray. After pouring him a cup of tea, she poured her own and sat on the chair facing the sofa.

"I'm afraid ye are a wee bit too late. Miss Smith, as we knew her, gave birth to her child almost a month earlier than it was due. Although the baby was small, he was very healthy. Miss Smith was very distraught after the birth, and when her friend from America arrived shortly afterward, she insisted on leaving with her. We didn't want her to leave so soon after giving birth, but she is a strong-minded lass. The new baby was adopted a few days later. They are a good family, whose own child died at birth. The new mother desperately needed a child to suckle and love."

Sean suddenly began to weep uncontrollably. He had failed again. The nun came over and put her arm around Sean, trying to comfort him.

"It is meant to be, sir. The babe will have a happy home."

"Did I understand ye right, that the babe was a boy?"

She hesitated, wondering whether she should divulge that information.

"Yes, it was a baby boy, with a beautiful face and his mother's red hair and big blue eyes. He was a happy, healthy baby. That is all I can tell ye."

"Can ye tell me what they named him?"

"No, sir, I have told ye too much already."

"Can ye at least tell me the name of the lady she left with? Perhaps I can catch them before they leave Dublin."

"Let me check with Sister Anna. She spoke with that lady and might know her name. I will be right back." As soon as she left the room, Sean shuffled through the stack of files on the left of the desk. The second one said K. Smith. Swiftly, he swept open the file and perused its contents. On top were the adoption papers. They were signed; Kathryn Smith alias K. Murphy. The adoptive parents; Eliot and Eileen Briscoe, and the child's name was Robert Sean Briscoe. Birth date; 10th day of February, 1878. Sean photographed the page in his memory, closed the file, and put it back in its place just before the nun returned.

"I'm sorry, Mr. Foley. Sister Anna is getting quite old and forgetful. She thought her name was McCleary or McRory, and she thought their ship was sailing yesterday. I'm afraid that is all the information I can give ye, sir."

"Thank ye, Sister." He shook her hand and left the building, looking much sadder than when he arrived. The harsh winter wind came up suddenly, and whipped around his back, as he went down the steep staircases. When he looked up, the rain began to pelt his face.

"I will find them, God. I promise, I will find them! WE WILL be a family someday. I know I'm not deserving of them, but I swear I will spend me life making it up to them, if you just please, help me find them!"

Sean climbed in the buggy, picked up the whip, and he snapped it over the horse's head. Lightning flashed, hitting a tree right in front of him, and thunder cracked so loudly that it frightened the horse. The lively mare started to bolt, then began running for home, as the rain poured from the heavens. Sean was too upset to be scared. He just held the buggy reins, lightly, and let the horse take him back to the Inn.

Chapter Twenty-Six

"Kate & Sean"

San Francisco ~ February - June, 1878

"Those who bring sunshine to the lives of others cannot keep it from themselves."

Kate went to the Goldstein mansion the day after she arrived back in the states. Mary wasn't expecting her for another month, so she was surprised to find Kate standing there when she opened the front door. Kate threw her arms around Mary as if her life depended on it. The warmth of Mary's comforting arms released a flood of tears from Kate. Mary led her friend into the parlor and held her for several minutes, until Kate began to calm down.

"I'm sorry, Mary. That was not a very pleasant hello."

"Don't ye be worrying yer pretty little head about that. A girl needs to get her emotions out. I'm sure yer heart has been feeling very heavy lately. I'm praying that ye will heal soon."

"Are you alone, Mary?"

"I am, Katie. Rachel and her mum went shopping. Come in, and I will make ye a cup of tea."

Mary helped Kate take off her cape, and she laid it over the sofa. Kate sat down while Mary went into the kitchen to get the tea. Her eyes were closed when Mary returned.

"Okay, Katie, if ye need to talk, I'm ready fer listening. Whatever ye say, will go no further than this room. Did Sean find ye?"

"Sean? No! I don't ever want to see him."

"Did ye know he was looking for ye? His ship left toward the end of January, and no one has heard from him since."

"Maybe his ship went down at sea. That would be a blessing."

"Kate! Ye don't mean that. What he did was unforgivable, and he deserves to be punished, but he appears to be repenting and trying to make up for his wrongdoing. He went to Ireland to find ye and beg ye to marry him."

"Well, I'm glad he didn't find me, because I don't want to see him, ever. It was awful, Mary!" Kate's eyes filled with tears again. "To suffer all that pain, to hold that beautiful baby in my arms only once. I love that child with my whole heart, and to have to give him to another woman, to suckle and raise as her own baby, was so awful." The pain on her face unmasked the pain in her heart. "To hand over my own flesh and blood, knowing that I will never see that darling child again..."

Kate began to sob again, and Mary went to her. As if Kate were her own child, Mary held her head to her breast and rocked her. Mary's heart broke for the young Irish mother, as she could easily imagine herself in Kate's place. She thought it must be 'just about as terrible as losing a babe in childbirth.' Finally, Kate broke the silence.

"I'm going to leave again with Mrs. McCleary. I have to get away. My mother and father will become suspicious if I cry all of the time. I find it hard to smile for even a minute. We are going to India for six months, perhaps longer. We will be doing some missionary work. After that, I don't know. Mrs. McCleary wants to pay me to be her traveling companion. She says that she feels safer when I'm with her, than when she's alone, and we enjoy each other's company. I think that spending my time helping others is just what I need right now. It will help me clear my mind of my own problems."

"That should be good for ye, Kate. Just remember: *'Those who bring sunshine to the lives of others cannot keep it from themselves.'* What did yer mum and pop say about ye not going to college?"

"Thank you, Mary, I always find your little sayings helpful. Daddy is, of course, very disappointed that I decided not to go to college, but I can't even think of studying, and I may never feel like it again. I told him I would think about it when I return."

"Rachel will want to see ye before ye leave."

"I'll come by tomorrow and take Rachel to lunch. Will you come too, Mary?"

"Maybe ye two should go alone. What about Johanna?"

"She doesn't know, does she?"

"No, she doesn't."

"I plan to see her on Friday. The three of us can get together for lunch another time before I leave. If you see Johanna, please tell her

I'll be coming to have lunch with her on Friday." Kate stood up to go.

"I'm sorry about everything, Kate. I have always said, 'things are meant to be.' I don't know why this should happen to a girl as wonderful as ye are, but maybe someday God's plans will be revealed. I know it's hard to see those plans in the present situation, but ye must try to have faith."

"Yes, Mary, it is hard to understand. I often feel angry with God about this, and yet I know it was my own fault. This must be my punishment for my sins."

"Just keep praying, Katie. Don't lose yer faith."

"I'm trying not to." Mary put Kate's cape around her shoulders, kissed her on the cheek, and watched her walk down the long staircase to the street.

~ ~ ~

Sean stayed in Ireland for several months trying to track down his son. When he finally arrived back in San Francisco, Kate and her companion had sailed for India the week before. Sean was very disappointed to find that he'd missed her again. Shortly after he returned, he went to see Mary.

He wanted her forgiveness and her help. Mary wasn't surprised to see him. Remorse was written all over his face. His face looked almost as sad as Kate's. The anger that had raged through her when she had taken him to the opium den was replaced with sympathy.

She could see that God was punishing him for his sin, as Sean couldn't have looked more miserable. Mary held out her arms, and Sean walked in and clung to his niece's small frame.

It was the first time she had let him touch her, since that night in Macroom. Mary felt his sadness as she led him to the parlor. He sat down on the sofa where Kate had sat only a few weeks ago. She brought him some hot biscuits, butter, and raspberry jam. Then she put the water on for tea and prepared the teapot with cups on a tray. Some biscuits were already gone from the plate when she returned. When she took a good look at him, she realized how thin he was. He obviously hadn't been eating well.

"Were ye seasick this time, Sean?"

"Yes, almost every day. The weather was terrible. Yer biscuits have revived me energy a bit, I think. Thank ye, Mary, and thank ye for even letting me in. I don't deserve yer forgiveness. I am the lowest of the low. I cannot forgive meself. I love the girl, Mary. Kate is everything to me. And I, who love her beyond anything, have ruined her life because of me own selfish lowlife character. I am so ashamed. If I could just take it all back..."

As he spoke, he got down on his knees, held both her small hands in his large ones, and looked sadly into her eyes. "What can I do to get her back? Oh Mary, help me. I looked all over Ireland for that child!"

"Did ye now? Did ye have any luck?"

"Yes, I did. Even though I was too late to find Kate, I was able to find the babe and his new family. I arrived the day after Kate left.

The babe had already been adopted, but I looked at Kate's file when the nun left the room, and I found their names and the boy's. I went to a fella who does that kind of work, and I asked him to find me son for me. He was sympathetic to me cause, and he only charged me half of what he normally would. They weren't hard to find. I then had to question meself, as to me motives, and I asked God what I should do. I watched them from a distance for several days. The child is beautiful. He has dark red hair, like Kate's, and the most angelic face I've ever seen. Finally, I approached the man in the park on his daily walk, and I asked if I could speak to him for a few minutes. We sat on the wooden bench, while I poured out my heart. I told him all of it, and amazingly, he was very sympathetic. I assured him, I would never steal the child, but that I would like to be able to see him from time to time, if they would be kind enough to allow it. He said he would have to talk to his wife about future trips I take to Ireland, but he said he would bring the boy to the park the next day, for me to see him before I left. He knew the child was so young that he didn't have to worry about him remembering me.

"When I got that child in me arms, I was sorely tempted to run as fast as me legs would carry me. I truly wanted to run away with him, but there was no way out of Ireland without getting caught. Serving a term in the Dublin jail wouldn't do anyone any good. I have never felt such love for a human being, as I felt for that small face that day. He has Kate's hair, eyes and dimples, but the rest of his face is mine. I predict a ruggedly handsome young man someday.

"His name is Robert Sean Briscoe. They call him Bobby. Eliot Briscoe has my name and address, and he promised to send me a letter with some photographs from time to time. If I just keep in contact, maybe someday we'll all be able to see him. Perhaps I can bring him over to visit me, and he could meet his mother. He doesn't have to know who we are. We could be an aunt and uncle, if Mr. and Mrs. Briscoe approve. Anyway, that is me one goal in life, well that, and getting Kate to marry me. Please, Mary, ye've got to do everything ye can to help me. I'll show ye that I've changed. I quit gamblin' and drinkin', and I'm going to get meself a job and save some money. When Kate comes back, I'll ask her to marry me."

"I really hope ye mean that, Sean. Ye owe it to Kate. She is very upset at the loss of her babe. Her melancholy is almost a sickness. She has lost weight and doesn't seem well. She has gone to India to do some missionary work. I am hoping it will give her a reason to live and get her mind off of the babe. At least ye found the child. I would say that the luck of the Irish helped ye there. The Lord works in strange ways."

"Yes, perhaps this is just part of me punishment. Poor Kate! What a wretch I am. Please, can I have her address, so I can write to her?"

"I will give it to ye as soon as I hear from her. Do ye want to stay for supper, Sean?"

"No, thank ye, Mary. Mum and Da are expecting me to come over for supper. Jerry and Jim are going to be there. They might know of a job. Thanks, Mary, for listening and making me feel better."

"Sure and ye better be keeping up this good attitude. I'm praying for ye and Kate, and fer the wee babe. Be strong, Sean, and remember this: *'How does one mention time? No, not in days, months or years... it is measured by the most precious of all things, love. Without which all beings and things whether brave or beautiful would perish. "'*

Chapter Twenty-Seven

"Rachel's Wedding"

San Francisco ~ 1878-1883

"I promise to always take good care of her, to make a good home for her and our children, and to be a faithful and dutiful husband."

Sean got a job in the Oakland shipyards with Jim and Jerry. Each letter Mary received from Kate sounded a little more cheerful, than the last one. Although she wrote twice a month, it took a month to receive them. She wrote about the hundreds of orphaned children in India, and how sad it was to see them, but also how rewarding it was to be able to help them, even if it was just by feeding the babies, or reading stories to the older children. Rachel and Johanna received letters from her too, and they always showed them to Mary. Time seemed to go slowly, but four years later, Mary's friends and family all seemed to be doing well. Rachel was very busy being courted by several suitors, and Johanna had one young fellow who called on her often. Jim had met a lovely girl, and he and Molly Sullivan were planning a small wedding a few years from now. Jerry was still looking for his true love. Jeremiah and Margaret Sweeney's little beach shop was doing well despite their health problems. There was another baby due at Catherine's house, and Margaret was helping her with the boys, still hoping for one of her own. Hannah Goldstein seemed content, but she was getting much less able to get around as she aged. Mary was now doing many of the things with Rachel that Hannah liked doing, but the older woman just wasn't able to keep up with her daughter anymore.

Letters from John arrived at least once a week, and she received a letter from Ah Kim about once a month. John and Ah Kim had been working hard on the railroad in Oregon, and Mary was beginning to wonder whether they would ever finish the job. The Chinaman was also doing some mining with his relatives, but they were keeping that a secret, except from John and Mary, whom Ah Kim trusted completely. The months seemed to crawl by, while John saved his money and planned for his future with Mary. Mary spent the little free time that she had making tablecloths, napkins, sheets, and pillowcases. She purchased dishes, cooking utensils, and anything else she thought she would need, for her future with John.

Finally, Mary received a letter from John saying that the work on the railroad was finished.

Mary, my betrothed,

The rail line is finally through to Baker City. Don't you think it's time we get married? Why don't I purchase a ticket, and you can come up here, so we can get married. I miss you so much. I think it's time we tied the knot. Please write to me as soon as possible. I will buy the ticket, as soon as you tell me.

Your husband to be,

John S. Troy

The night before the letter arrived from John, was the night Rachel announced her own engagement. Levi King was a handsome young man who had been pursuing Rachel for months. Mary and Hannah were both very fond of him. Mary had served a lamb dinner in the kosher Jewish custom, as Hannah had taught her to do when she first arrived in their home. Hannah insisted she sit down and eat with them. After she had served the dessert and cleared away the dishes, Levi had asked her to join them for their tea. He then asked Hannah for Rachel's hand in marriage.

"Mrs. Goldstein, I assume you know that I am in love with your daughter. Rachel is the sweetest, most wonderful girl I have ever met. I would like your permission to marry her. I promise to always take good care of her, to make a good home for her, as well as our children, and to be a faithful and dutiful husband."

Hannah sat there for a moment, while her thoughts became words. Tears of happiness formed in her eyes. "Is this your wish too, Rachel?"

"Oh yes, Mummy, I love Levi very much, and I want nothing more than to marry him."

"Mary, your valued opinion means a lot to me. How do you feel about this?"

"Everything I have seen or heard about Levi has been good. He seems to be a fine, upstanding young man with a good future. If they love each other and ye approve, Hannah, I am certainly in agreement with ye. I love Rachel, as if she were me own sister, and want only her happiness."

"Yes, that is my opinion too. I believe her father would have approved of you, Levi."

"Thank you, Mrs. Goldstein, and Miss Sweeney. I am honored that you both approve. I have purchased a plot of land downtown, and I plan to build a new home for Rachel. We can live in an apartment, while we build the house. I was just promoted to vice-president at the bank, so we will do well financially."

"When are you planning to get married?"

"Mother, we know it's short notice, but we were hoping to get married in September, and to honeymoon in Europe in October, before it gets too late in the year to travel."

"Usually a wedding is planned a full year in advance, children."

"We were hoping to have a small wedding that could be planned in three months. What do you think, Mary? Can we do it? You're so good at everything. We can work on nothing else from now until then."

"Well, I suppose it can be done, if we throw ourselves into it. Is it okay with ye, ma'am?"

"I hate to lose my daughter so fast. I was hoping to have a year to say good-bye."

"Mrs. Goldstein, it is not goodbye." Levi assured his mother-in-law to be. "We will be living close, and I have already commissioned for extra living quarters to be built, so that you can come and live with us when you are ready."

"Mary, would you bring the brandy and four glasses into the library, so we can discuss this further? Leave the kitchen until morning, my dear. This is a celebration."

The next morning, Rachel helped Mary clean the kitchen before they went to the dressmakers, to see about a wedding dress for Rachel. They stopped at the post office and Mary opened her letter from John, while the seamstress was taking Rachel's measurements.

"Rachel, Rachel! John has just proposed to me!"

"That is wonderful! Do tell me what he says!"

"He wants to send me a train ticket, for me to join him in eastern Oregon."

"Oh, no! You have to have a wedding like mine, or at least get married here, so I can be there on your happiest moment. Isn't that wonderful? We are both getting married! Don't worry about Mother. We will just insist that she move in with us right away. What are you going to tell him?"

"I am going to write him back and tell him that if he wants me to marry him, he'll have to do the proper thing and come down here to marry me. I would like to be married on Saint Valentine's Day at Saint Mary's Cathedral. That would be four months after yer wedding. Ye should be back from yer honeymoon by then, and ye'll be able to help me with the planning of me own."

"Mother is going to be very unhappy at the prospect of losing you too, Mary, but our new home should be finished about that time, and I will let her help pick out the furnishings, for her little suite."

"We must be gentle in how we tell yer mum. I'll be missing ye both sorely. It has been lovely watching ye grow into a beautiful woman and living with ye and yer dear kind mother."

"Oh Mary, you have been like a sister to me. I don't know how I will make it without you."

"We still have several months together, and we will always keep in touch."

"Your lovely hair and eyes will be set off by a simple satin gown."

"I will be making me own gown, and yes, satin would be lovely."

The next few months were busy, full of excitement, planning, and parties. Rachel had three wedding parties. An engagement party was put on by Levi's family. Johanna and Mary hosted a surprise tea for Rachel at Margaret's house in late August, where her friends and bridesmaids showered her with lovely gifts. The third party was a luncheon put on by Hannah and Mary, for all the women friends and relatives on both sides to get acquainted. It was held two weeks before the wedding. All three parties were written up in the society page of the San Francisco Examiner.

Kate arrived in San Francisco two weeks before the wedding. She had been traveling around Europe and Asia with Mrs. McCleary, and she sent her measurements to Rachel right after her friend had asked her to be her maid of honor. She only needed one final fitting after she arrived. Johanna was one of the six bridesmaids. Mary declined the honor, saying she felt that she should be with Hannah throughout the ceremony. Catherine's oldest boy was the ring bearer, and Rachel's cousin's five-year old daughter was the flower girl.

Rachel's dress was made of ivory satin and taffeta, and it was trimmed with delicate lace and tiny seed pearls. It had a full skirt with four layers of taffeta ruffles and was trimmed with lace and pearls. A high neckline on the fitted satin bodice was trimmed with matching pearls, and the puffy satin sleeves ended in a vee of tiny pearls on the back of her hands. The veil flowed out from a lovely pearl encrusted tiara. Tiny pearl earrings danced in her ear lobes. Her lovely hair was swept up under the pearl tiara, with long gentle curls tumbling from within the crown and down the back of her head. She was truly a vision of loveliness.

Kate's pale pink satin gown fit her perfectly, and the wide brimmed straw hat made a nice frame to her lovely face. The bridesmaids wore similar dresses and hats, but they wore a brighter pink and were trimmed with a paler pink ribbon that matched the maid of honor's gown. Their flowers were pale pink, white carnations and roses with a brighter pink cluster in the center. The maid of honor's bouquet was done in the opposite colors.

The bride's bouquet had tiny white roses surrounded with white and pink baby's breath that gathered around three fragrant gardenias in the center. The gardenias were to be removed and used as a bridal corsage after the ceremony. Huge matching floral bouquets were placed carefully throughout the synagogue and later transferred to the reception hall. The groom, his best man, and ushers looked elegant in gray tuxedos with dark blue waist bands and pink roses in their lapels. And, of course, they all wore round Jewish skullcaps. Hannah Goldstein wore a lovely dress of navy blue and pink with a navy satin jacket that had a tiny pink lace flower trim. Mary wore a simple navy and pink floral patterned dress with a matching ribbon pulling back her long curls.

The ceremony was perfect, except when Levi had trouble untying Rachel's wedding ring from the ring bearer's pillow. There were a couple of giggles from the groom's side of the synagogue that only made the wedding more memorable. Levi smiled as his nervous fingers finally untied the knot and it slipped from the pillow. He caught the ring before it fell to the floor. The happy couple grinned, as Levi slipped the ring on Rachel's finger. Rachel beamed as she nodded to everyone on her way out of the church with her arm entwined with her new husband's.

Standing in the back row of the synagogue, was one uninvited guest. Sean wanted to see Kate so badly that he borrowed a Jewish friend's cap, and he snuck in on the groom's side. He couldn't take his eyes off of her, as she floated down the aisle in a vision of pink. Her beauty delighted him and made him sad at the same time. The sin he had committed against her loomed before his eyes. He berated himself. How could he behave so beastly? If she hated him forever he couldn't blame her. Surely he didn't deserve her, but they did have a child together, and he felt that somehow that bonded them together. Hoping that she would speak to him for a minute if he approached her, he slipped out the back door as everyone cheered the newly married couple, and he waited by the door to the reception hall for her to come that way.

When the crowd from the church arrived at the hall, Sean stood to the side of the door waiting nervously for Kate to arrive. The happy couple came first followed by a cheerful, giggling wedding party. Kate saw him, just as she arrived.

Sean stepped forward and said, "Miss Murphy, could I speak to ye for a minute before ye go inside, please?"

She hesitated, but not wanting to make a scene, she decided it would be better to talk to him and get rid of him, before her parents arrived and questioned her actions. They stepped away from the door, so no one could hear.

"I told you, I never wanted to see you again."

"I know, Kate, and I'm sorry, but I had to talk to ye for a minute. Did ye get me letters? I never received an answer."

"Yes, I got them, and they went directly into the fire."

"So ye never read them?"

"There is nothing you can say that I want to hear. Now, I must go inside."

"Wait please, Kate. Let me say one more thing, and I will leave ye alone. I promise."

"Hurry up, I must go inside."

"Kate, words cannot tell ye how sorry I am. I know I am the lowliest scum of the world, and ye have every right to hate me. I promise to spend the rest of me life makin' it up to ye. I have found our son."

Kate started to listen. "Yes, and what have you done?"

"Nothing! But I have seen him and held him. He is a beautiful child, who looks like you. He is happy in his home, and I don't want to hurt him, but I am hoping that someday he will be allowed to visit. The parents are very wonderful people, and they love him very much too. Katie, if we keep in touch, even if he knows us as an aunt and uncle, it is better than never seeing him at all. Please let us stay in touch, if only to converse about little Bobby."

"Bobby..." Her eyes filled with tears. "Must you bring me more pain? Leave the poor child alone. Don't you know, you will only hurt him? I must go in. Do not contact me again." She turned around, wiped her eyes, and walked into the reception.

Sean sat on the steps of the church, listening to the festivities for hours. He sat in the shadows, so no one could see him, and he listened to the conversations of those who came outside for a breath of fresh air. When it was over, and everyone had gone home, Sean walked slowly down to the waterfront and sat there for hours. It was a warm, clear night in San Francisco, one of the most beautiful times of the year in the city, but for Sean, it was a very lonely night.

Chapter Twenty-Eight

"Mary's Wedding"

San Francisco ~ February, 1884

"May the luck of the Irish possess you, may the devil fly off with your worries, and may God bless you forever and ever."

John arrived in San Francisco by ship. The train took him on the new rails from Baker City to The Dalles, Oregon, a new thriving city on the Columbia River. There he boarded a sternwheeler that took him down the river to the Port of Astoria and the mouth of the Pacific Ocean. The much larger steamship he boarded there, took him down the coast to San Francisco. Mary and John Troy would take the same route on their way back. It was the trip to the train station in Oregon that remained on John's mind throughout his journey to retrieve his beloved. Ah Kim had driven John to the train station in the used buggy that John had just purchased. He spoke from his heart on their way to the station.

"I sincerely wish I could be present when you and Miss Mary say your wedding vows. I know that you both would welcome me, but my presence might not be welcomed by others. I believe I can be of more service here. I will make sure that your cottage is ready to welcome your new bride upon your return, John Troy."

Ah Kim would return, to pick up the happy wedding couple, with the buggy that he planned to repaint while his friend was gone. It was a cold damp morning in early February, when the two friends traveled quietly on the path from John's small cabin. The horse's prancing hooves were the only noise, as they hit the wet mud that paved the trail. They were only a couple of miles outside of Baker City, when they heard horses running behind them. Ah Kim pulled on the reins, stopping the horses, so the riders could pass them. One of the horses reared up, as the riders got close. He understood the horses fear when John saw Bane's face. Bane and his gang of cutthroats brought dread with them wherever they went. The four horsemen stopped in front of the buggy.

"Well, well! If it ain't John Troy and his slant-eyed pal! Funny we should meet up again."

"It is certainly not me pleasure, Bane. What do ye want?"

"I heard congratulations are in order. Rumor has it that your bride to be is, none other than the lovely, 'Miss Mary Sweeney', who likes to dress up in disguise and maim faces with her teeth. Is that true?"

"Bane, ye leave Mary alone. What happened between ye two was a long time ago. Let it be. She was but a young girl then."

"That young girl left me scarred for life. See this nose? No good lookin' woman will look at me now."

"Maybe ye should have left her alone."

"Then this little yellow bastard comes along to help her out." Bane's eyes were filled with hate. "I'm not done with any of you! I swear that I'll be paying you all back for crossing Jack Bane. I'll be watching you, and when you least expect me, I'll be there. I promise you, you'll all get yours, if it's the last thing I do."

He pulled up on the reins, and the horse reared up splattering mud everywhere. Then he turned the horse and galloped away, with the other men closely following him down the trail.

John stood up to check his clothes for mud, and he only found a couple of spots, which he was able to brush off. As Ah Kim drove the buggy down the hill toward town, the two men didn't speak. Words weren't necessary, as they both knew what the other was thinking. Concern for Mary had replaced their cheerfulness. When they reached the edge of town, Ah Kim broke the silence.

"John Troy, I have a bad feeling about Mister Bane. His presence brings evil. We must be careful, or I fear he will kill us if he finds us alone. Mary probably did not tell you that Bane is responsible for my father's murder. I believe he is also the one who caused your uncle's early death. If he knew that I am my father's son, he would surely have more reason to bring about my demise. As you have already purchased your return tickets from San Francisco, he could easily find out when that is, and he may have plans to ambush you and your bride."

"Ye are right, Ah Kim. The hairs stand up on the back of me neck, whenever he is around. If he knew what happened to those two men at the Johnson place, I'm sure I would already be dead."

"Yes, you are surely right. I will tell everyone that you are coming back a week after you are due to return. Perhaps he will not be expecting you until after you have arrived."

"Let's hope that works, Ah Kim. Ye have been a good friend to both Mary and me, for these many years. Yer friendship is very much appreciated."

"I will be at your wedding in spirit, as you both have always been my true friends."

"I cannot wait to see Mary, as I am sure she has grown into a lovely woman since I last saw her at age nineteen. I'm a lucky man, to have such a sweet Irish rose. Anyone could have swept her off her feet and away from me."

"Yes John, you are a lucky man. Tell her for me that I greatly look forward to the pleasure of her company again."

"I will tell her, Ah Kim. Ye can leave me here. I do not want ye to be in any danger, because of yer friendship with me." John took his bag and climbed down from the buggy. "Be careful, Ah Kim. I will see ye soon." He bowed to Ah Kim, and he began his walk into town, to the railroad station.

"You be careful too, John Troy, and have a safe trip." Ah Kim pulled on the reins, and he turned the buggy back toward Pleasant Valley.

The train ride to The Dalles took almost six hours, as the train made many stops. John spent the night in a rented room, and he rose before dawn to board the sternwheeler. The Columbia River was rough, but it was nothing compared to the Pacific Ocean and the trip from Astoria to San Francisco. The ocean in winter was as rough as the weather. When it rained, which it did most of the way, the waves grew in size, and the wind howled and rocked the ship. The swells were huge and many people were seasick. The sound of people retching came from everywhere. John stayed on the top deck most of the trip, even though it was rolling badly. He knew there was less chance for sickness with the fresh air, but the ship seemed to roll more up there. He hoped the weather was better on their return trip.

When the ship finally docked, John went directly to Margaret and Robert Sweeney's home. They had invited him to stay there until the wedding day. His brother and best man, Mike Troy, would stay there too. Amazingly, John arrived on the day he was expected. Margaret was pleased to see him.

"John Troy, yer looking more handsome than ever. Me sister made a good choice for a husband. Come in, come in."

"Thank ye, Margaret. I'm glad I have yer approval. Where is that fine husband of yers?"

"He's at his office, John. He'll be home around six, and he's looking forward to seeing ye, and so is me dear sister."

"I can't wait to see her, but I thought I'd better clean up after the trip. Wouldn't want her to see her betrothed looking like a dusty old cowboy, now would we?"

"Well John, if that's what ye are, then she'll see ye that way soon enough, won't she?"

"Yes, but I don't want her to change her mind about marrying me."

"Yer room is at the top of the stairs. I'll be fixing ye a cup of tea, while ye clean up!"

Margaret made John a plate of food, while he washed up and changed into a clean shirt.

He thanked her, ate quickly, and left for Mary's. It was around four in the afternoon, when he knocked on her door.

When she opened the door, John couldn't believe how lovely she looked. Mary literally took his breath away, when he saw what a beautiful woman she had become. She wore a light blue cotton dress with a bodice that showed off her tiny slim figure. Her curly auburn hair tumbled over her shoulders, her green eyes sparkled, and her impish grin was even more endearing than he remembered. He put his arms around her and held her close, never wanting to let her go.

"Mary, me love, I have missed ye so."

"John, me darlin', no more than I have missed ye!"

She thought he looked wonderful too. His mustache had grown and so had his hair. His large dark eyes were more irresistible than she remembered. It felt so good to have his warm arms around her that she didn't want him to ever let go. Pulling him inside the house, she took off his heavy jacket, and dragged him into the parlor where they cuddled, talked and giggled, for what seemed like hours. Rachel and Levi brought Hannah home about five thirty. Hannah had sold her home, and she planned to move in with the couple shortly after Mary's wedding. They were happy to see John and discussed the wedding plans at length.

The next two weeks were filled with last minute planning, shopping, decorating and partying. Three of John's sisters came to town for the wedding, as well as his brother. All of Mary's family was there, as well as Hannah Goldstein, and the Murphy family. Mary, Rachel, Kate, Margaret, Catherine, and Johanna spent the last week making sure everything was ready.

Following tradition, John's sisters and brother hosted a dinner the night before the wedding. Margaret offered the use of her home for the festivities. Mike brought a keg of beer and a case of champagne. His sisters prepared sliced sausages, sliced tomatoes, pickles, crackers, and cheese. The siblings catered a sit down dinner, of roast beef, mashed potatoes, and gravy, for later in the evening. Fresh fruit and several different salads completed the meal. Everything was ready when Mary and John arrived.

"We all wanted to spend some time with you two, since it will surely be a long while before we are able to get together again, seeing how you two are moving so very far away." Jerry gave his treasured sister a big hug.

"This is wonderful, thank ye all. Mary and I are delighted to spend this evening with the people we love." John added, "I want to make the first toast to me beautiful bride, Mary; *'Wishing you always, walls for the wind, a roof for the rain, and tea beside the fire. Laughter to cheer you, and those you love near you, and all that your heart might desire'.*"

"John, the day we are married, I will have all me heart desires. Me blessing for ye is: *'May the luck of the Irish possess you, may the devil fly off with your worries, and may God bless you forever and ever'.*"

John and Mary touched their beloved Irish crystal together, entwined their arms and sipped their champagne, both giggling like school children. When their glasses were empty, John leaned over and gave her a sweet affectionate kiss. Everyone cheered, and then they all took turns spouting their favorite toasts and blessings to the couple.

When they were all finished, John raised his glass one more time. "I have waited a long time, to make this lovely lass me wife, and I just want to thank ye all, for all ye have done for us, and fer letting me take me little lady so far away. I want ye to all promise to come and see us soon, because me darlin' Mary will be very lonesome for all of ye. Mary and I want to bid ye all, 'Cead Mile Failte,' for those of ye who don't speak the Gaelic language, 'One hundred thousand welcomes!'"

"Slainte!"

"Cheers!"

Sean Foley arrived late, just before dinner. Mary hadn't even missed him. When she saw him, she realized how uncomfortable this must be for Kate. After greeting everyone, he asked Mary to dance. As they glided around the floor, he apologized.

"I am sorry to be late, Mary, but under the circumstances, I felt it best to only come for a short time. I did not want to cause any more pain for Kate, but if I had not attended the party the rest of the family would have been angry at me."

"I understand, Sean, and thank ye for considering her feelings."

"I'm happy for ye, Mary. There is no one more deserving of happiness, than ye and John. I hope ye have forgiven me for my past indiscretions."

"I forgive ye, Sean, jest as long as ye never hurt another, like ye did Kate."

"I swear to ye, Mary, I'll spend the rest of me life making it up to her, for what I did."

"I'll be holding ye to that, Sean."

"If ye ever see me do wrong again, I'll expect ye to turn me over to the authorities, and I'll be taken me just dues."

The hired fiddler stopped playing, and Margaret called everyone to the table to eat. When Mary saw that Sean and Kate had been seated next to each other, she quietly switched Sean and Mike Troy's names and took her seat at the table. Kate had noticed the names earlier, and she was relieved when she saw she was no longer sitting by Sean. The evening ended early, so that everyone would be well rested for the high noon ceremony at Saint Mary's Cathedral. Levi took Rachel and Hannah home, and John took Mary to the Goldstein's later, so he could spend a little bit longer with her.

"Goodnight, me lovely lass! Tomorrow ye'll be me bride."

"And ye'll be me husband."

"I cannot wait for tomorrow."

"Neither can I."

He kissed her passionately, and she blushed the color of her auburn hair. Then she glowingly walked up the stairs, to her last night in the Goldstein mansion.

Mary woke well before daylight, and she lay on the soft feather mattress, enjoying her last moments in the bed she had slept in for many years. She was both sad and happy, as she couldn't wait to start her new life with John in the beautiful Oregon valley, but she would miss her family, Hannah, and Rachel terribly. Tears came to her eyes, as she thought of the dear older woman she had grown to love so much. Her own parents weren't very young either. 'Would she see them again?' Sadness overcame her, for a few moments, and she let the tears flow. Then she heard commotion in the kitchen and footsteps on the stairs. A light rap on the door was followed by Rachel's voice:

"Mary, are you awake? It's your wedding day. Get up, sleepy head, we are heating water for your bath. Mary, can I come in?"

Mary smiled at the sound of her voice, and she wiped the tears off with her blanket. "Of course, Rachel, come in." As she entered the room, Mary patted the bed, and Rachel laid down beside her to talk, as they had for the last few years. "I was just enjoying this wonderful room, for a few more minutes. By the way, what are ye doing here so early in the morning?"

"I asked Levi to bring me over early, so I could spend your last day with you."

"I'm so glad. I'm going to miss ye so much!"

"No more than I'm going to miss you!"

"Promise to write me often?"

"I promise, and you'd better write back."

"I will."

Just then, Margaret came to the door.

"Come on, little sister, yer bath water is hot."

"What are ye doing here so early?" Mary asked her sister.

"Levi and Rachel picked up us Sweeney women on their way over. Robert and Levi went back to help John get ready. Now come on, let's get ready for this wedding."

Rachel stood up and handed Mary her robe off the end of the bed. Mary pulled the covers back and climbed out of bed. She put her robe on, reached over and gave Rachel one last warm embrace. Then Margaret and Rachel each took one of her arms and led her to the upstairs bathroom, where the big tub had been filled by Johanna with hot water and bubbles. She languished in the deliciously warm water. The bath relaxed her. Rachel and Johanna took a pitcher of water and poured it over her hair, as she lay there with her head back and her eyes closed. She squealed in shock, and they laughed as they poured expensive shampoo on her hair and began lathering.

"This is wonderful. I feel like a queen."

"When ye get to Oregon ye'll be lucky to have a stove to heat yer water on, or soap to wash yer hair with." Johanna laughingly teased her older sister.

"Thanks a lot, little sister. That made me heart soar."

Rachel said she was going to fix Mary a big breakfast, but Mary said she couldn't eat because she was going to have communion at her wedding, and that way she would eat heartily at her reception. Kate arrived, and the girls giggled and talked, keeping Mary in good spirits, as they dressed her and themselves. Kate and Johanna fixed

Mary's hair, piling the auburn curls on top of her head and pinning the simple veil into her hair, with an elegant antique pearl comb that Hannah had loaned her. The pearl comb was the something borrowed and something old. The something blue was the garter Mary wore on her left leg over her fine silk stockings. Margaret gave her the something new, when she bought her the stockings a few days earlier. Teasing Mary in a sisterly manner, she told her, "It is probably the last pair ye'll own for a long time." Mary put a penny in one of her white satin slippers and a dab of perfume behind her ears. Johanna produced some light pink lip color, which she also rubbed into Mary's cheeks, giving her a lovely pink glow. Mary's mother and Catherine walked in, just as Johanna put the final touches on her lips.

"Mary, ye are so lovely, ye take me breath away!" Margaret Sweeney kissed her daughter on both cheeks.

"Thank ye Mum. I'm going to miss ye so much."

"I'll be missing ye terribly, me little girl. At least this time, I'll be knowin' where ye are and who yer with. Ye better be writing to yer poor mother."

"Don't ye be worrying Mum, ye'll be getting lots of letters from me."

There was a sharp rap on the front door just then. It was the man who came to take her luggage down to load it on the ship. The old chest was already by the front door. It held her trousseau and all the treasures, she had stored for this day. Also in the chest was a beautiful pair of oil lamps that Hannah had given her. Margaret and Rachel were going to send the gifts the couple received today, by ship sometime next week. Shortly after the man left with Mary's luggage, the drivers arrived to take the women to the church in their rented fancy black rigs.

The older Margaret Sweeney and Hannah Goldstein went in the first rig with Rachel, Johanna, and Kate. Mary rode in the second rig with her two older sisters.

Margaret, Catherine, and Johanna wore gowns of light blue satin. Margaret had sewn them all. The two older sister's dresses had rounded necklines and long tapered sleeves. Satin bands of darker blue accentuated their waists, and their full skirts billowed out and stopped at their ankles. They wore blue slippers on their feet, white pearls around their necks, and blue ribbons in their hair. Johanna's gown was of the same material, but had a high neckline and a fuller skirt. Her ribbon was tied around her long hair with the bow on the top of her head. They all looked lovely. Johanna's long hair flowed down her back, and Margaret and Catherine's hair were braided and pinned neatly around their head.

Mary's white satin gown was simple, but elegant, enhancing her slim figure with its smooth shiny fabric. Similar to Rachel's gown, Mary's had beautiful long sleeves, which puffed out at the top and ended at a vee at the top of her fingers. The high-necked bodice ended at her tiny waist. The skirt hung loosely to her hips and began widening at her knees, where it flowed longer in the back into a short train that added to the elegance of the simple gown.

Nervousness overcame her, as she watched her sisters walk down the aisle of Saint Mary's Cathedral. Finally, her turn came. Mary took a deep breath and clung tightly to her father's arm as she began the walk. 'This is where those crossroads have led me. This is me destiny.' Mary thought, as she strolled slowly down the aisle.

John, his brother, Mike, and Father Pat waited for them at the altar. Her groom looked handsome in his dark blue suit and lacy white shirt. His brown eyes sparkled, and a grin spread upon his face, as he gazed at his lovely bride. 'How could I have been so lucky to have earned the love of this beautiful woman?' He asked himself. He thought she was even lovelier than the first time he saw her on that ship, so long ago. John had never known anyone like Mary. He even loved her hot Irish temper, he thought she had a lot of spunk.

When they reached the altar, Jeremiah Sweeney took his daughter's left hand, kissed it gently, and placed her hand gently on top of John's, as the priest asked; "Who gives this woman to this man?"

"Her mother and I!" Jeremiah said, with tears in his eyes. He quietly took his seat next to his wife. Margaret Foley Sweeney's tears flowed freely, just as they had when her other children had married.

The wedding was a high mass, and the service took over an hour. At the end of the ceremony, Father Pat pronounced them man and wife, and he told John that he could kiss his bride. John gently lifted the veil from her face, gazed smiling into her eyes, before he placed the sweetest kiss on her pink lips. His gentleness took her breath away and happiness enveloped her. The happy couple beamed at each other, as the priest introduced them to their guests as "Mr. and Mrs. John Troy". The newlyweds happily walked together down the aisle.

It was a wonderful Irish reception, held at the pub down the street from the church. Jeremiah had engaged the restaurant for his daughter's reception. He knew the proprietor well, and he had gotten it for a reasonable price. Kate and Rachel took care of all the particulars for him. The guests were served corned beef and cabbage, with their choice of beer or wine. It was an informal affair, and one of the most memorable receptions, for all who attended. Jerry played the fiddle and Johanna danced. Later, Mike Troy sang some Irish tunes and they all danced. Irish blessings were toasted to the bride and groom, throughout the afternoon.

There was only a moment when Mary thought things might go wrong. Kate was drinking a lot of beer, and Mary knew she wasn't used to its effects. When she started openly flirting, and dancing, with a guest at the reception, Mary saw the look on Sean's face. He had been sitting quietly most of the day, drinking ginger ale, and keeping an eye on Kate. When he saw Kate start to leave with the man, he jumped up to intervene, unaware that Kate had asked the man to escort her outside, because she felt dizzy and needed a breath of fresh air.

"What are yer intentions for taking this respectable young lady outside, sir?" Sean took the man by the arm.

Before the man could answer, Kate jumped in angrily. "What business is it of yours, Mr. Foley, as to who escorts me where? I asked this gentleman to escort me outside, and I'll be thanking you to keep your hands and your questions to yourself."

"I'm sorry, Miss Murphy. I've never seen this man before, and I wanted to make sure ye were safe."

"That's quite all right, I understand." The man began to introduce himself, but Kate stopped him.

"No, it's not all right. It is none of his business!" Kate said loudly.

"Excuse me. I apologize to both of ye for interrupting." Sean's face was red with embarrassment.

Kate didn't answer him, but took the man by the arm and headed for the door. Sean headed directly for the bar to get a drink. Mary excused herself from John and went over to Sean.

"How about dancing with me before I leave, Sean Foley?" She took him by the hand. Sean looked sheepish, canceled the drink order, and went to dance with Mary.

"I'm sorry, Mary. I didn't intend to cause a scene at yer wedding."

"That's okay, Sean. Just don't go back to the drink."

"Ye are right, Mary. I've been thinking about something, and I wanted your opinion. What do ye think about me coming up to Oregon and starting a new life for meself? Maybe if I show Kate that I've changed, and that I have something to offer her, maybe she'll forgive me and marry me someday."

"Ye do need to put yer life in order. Maybe it'll work, and maybe it won't, but it'd be good to be working at something."

The tune ended, and John came over to get his bride. At three o'clock, John told her that it was time to go to the ship. They went outside and found their rig decorated with flowers, ribbons, and old shoes that had been tied to the back. They kissed everybody one final time, climbed in the rig, and Mike Troy drove them to the pier. Several rigs followed them, and their loved ones shouted and waved as they went up the gangplank to the ship. Mary almost tripped on the train of her dress. She had to fold the extra material over her arm, as she walked up the plank. She had taken off the veil earlier, and she wanted to go change her clothes, but she didn't want to miss waving to her family as the ship left port. It was breezy and cold, so John put his jacket around Mary. Shivering uncontrollably, she stayed on the deck, waving, until her family was nothing but little dots in the distance.

Everything would have been perfect, except for one thing. John hadn't told Mary about Bane's threat, or even that he was in Oregon. He didn't want to ruin the wedding for her, but he knew he would have to tell her something about it before they reached their new home. The question was when, and what should he tell her? It would have to wait until they were almost there. When they reached their small cabin, John picked her up and carried her inside, to spend their first time alone together as man and wife.

Part III

Chapter Twenty-Nine

"The Honeymoon"

Eastern Oregon ~ February, 1884

"Here's to a wonderful life and a wonderful night."

Mary couldn't ever remember being so sick. The long trip across the Atlantic had never been this rough, but it was mid-February, and the winter winds were still howling on the Pacific Ocean in 1884. The voyage had begun in beautiful weather. Their wedding day was blessed with sunshine, a rarity for the bay area on Valentine's Day. The morning fog had cleared away around eleven, leaving blue cloudless skies overhead, and a 67 degree temperature outside, which is a warm day for winter in San Francisco.

The newlyweds enjoyed each other's company for hours in their small cabin. A bottle of champagne on ice, and a basket filled with sausage, bread, cheese, and fruit was waiting in their room when they arrived. The accompanying note read:

Here's to a wonderful life and a wonderful night! Best wishes from your best man and best brother!

Mike Troy

Mary giggled when she read the card. John was just as nervous as his bride, but when he took Mary in his arms and felt her warm sensuous body, everything came naturally. The climactic evening was worth waiting for. They were surprised at the strong passion that developed, and by the end of their wedding day, they loved each other more than either of them had thought possible. After drinking the champagne, and feasting on the goodies in the basket, they happily fell asleep in each other's arms. It was early the next morning when the storm at sea began to roll the ship back and forth. Mary's stomach turned upside down in that twilight moment between wake and sleep. The champagne bucket was the closest receptacle, and Mary barely got there. John was by her side in seconds. At first, she assumed it was the champagne, then she realized how violently the ship was moving back and forth, and she knew she was seasick.

"Get dressed, darlin'. We'll go top ship. The fresh air up there should make ye feel better."

As the ship continued to rock back and forth, Mary felt a need for the bucket again. Running her fingers through her hair, she put on her cape and followed John, holding the champagne bucket under her arm. The upper deck held fresh air, but the large swells made it a dangerous place to stay. A large wave could easily sweep someone out to sea. They sat inside with a multitude of seasick passengers. After an hour, she decided their small cabin would be better than listening to the retching of others, which only seemed to make her feel worse. Mary lay on the bed in the tiny cabin, while John gently brushed her face with a damp cloth, as he tried to ease his own rolling stomach. They were both miserable until after they reached the Port of Astoria and the mouth of the Columbia River. After they changed ships and sat aboard the sternwheeler, the ride was much smoother. Although it rained much of the way, and the waters were choppy, it was nothing compared to the rolling ocean.

John and Mary spent the day cuddling on the top deck under a blanket, enjoying the beautiful countryside until dusk. Suddenly, they were both famished, so they finished eating what was left in the basket from Mike and started on the tea and sandwiches from the basket Margaret handed them as they boarded the ship. When they arrived in The Dalles late that evening, John rented a room in the hotel. They would take the train early the next morning to Baker City, where Ah Kim would meet them and take them to their section home close to the railroad in Pleasant Valley, a few miles east of Baker City.

After being on the ships for several days, they still felt the movement of the water beneath them, even though they were now on land. Mary tried to lie quietly on the bed to get rid of the movement, but she still felt a little dizzy. John seemed to be weaving back and forth too. It must have been the effects of that storm, or the Pacific was a rougher ocean, she thought, because she had not been dizzy like that after their voyage across the Atlantic.

"I'm going to get some tea to settle us down, so we can get some sleep." John kissed her on the cheek and went to the dining room to get a pot of tea and two cups. While he waited at a table for the girl to bring him the tray, he had the feeling he was being watched. He turned around to see two men sitting at a nearby table brazenly staring at him. They looked familiar, but he wasn't sure where he had seen them before. 'Were they Bane's men?' He thought so, but he couldn't be sure. 'What did they want? Were they following him?

How long had they been following them?' A chill went up his spine when one of the men crossed his leg, set his large brimmed hat forward on his head and laughed loudly, still staring straight at John. The two men looked like a couple of cowboys right off the range. They were dirty and dusty, and still wore their guns and spurs.

The girl brought him the tray with the teapot, two cups with saucers, cream, sugar, and a plate of cookies. John thanked her and took the tray upstairs, trying to ignore the cowboys. As he left the room he heard one of them say, "Going back to his little bride." Then he muttered something John couldn't hear.

'They are Bane's men and they're following us.' John was dismayed, as he knew that it was time to tell Mary about her enemy. After entering their room, John loaded his guns and hung them where he could reach them, then he locked the door.

"What's wrong, John?" Mary asked from the bed, where she was trying to sit up without feeling dizzy.

"Nothing, Mary. I just don't like the looks of a couple of cowboys I saw downstairs."

"Ye could put that chair in front of the door too."

"That wouldn't hurt none." He slid the back of the chair under the doorknob. "Are ye feeling better, me darlin' Mary?"

"Yes, John, I am. How about yerself?"

"I'm feeling fine." He put the tray on the table by the bed, and they both munched on a few cookies and drank a little sweet tea.

"Would ye mind if I joined ye under the covers?"

"Please do." She blushed a lovely shade of pink. "I'd be happy to have ye join me."

John sat on the side of the bed, slid his breeches to the floor, and climbed in bed with Mary.

"I am so happy to be yer wife." Mary said boldly as she put her arms around him.

John held her close, although the two cowboys were still on his mind. He would tell her about them in the morning, as there was no reason to worry her tonight. Gently kissing his bride, he made love to her for the first time on land.

'So this is me destiny,' she thought. 'How could I ever be happier? John is so wonderful. Thank ye, Lord, for granting me all yer blessings.'

They woke before it was light out, still lying happily in each other's arms. John rose first and began to repack their things. Mary climbed out of bed a few minutes later, smiling happily. She hummed an Irish tune as she dressed, washed her face, fixed her hair, and put on her bonnet.

"Do ye want me to bring yer breakfast up here?" John asked.

"I thought we were going to eat together in the dining room before the train arrives."

"Of course, I just thought maybe ye still weren't feeling well?"

"Now John, me darlin', did I act like I wasn't feeling well last night?"

"No, Mary, ye certainly didn't."

He opened the door, escorted her downstairs, and led her into the dining room, where John chose the table to the right of the door. He sat where he could see all entrances. John ordered them both plates of eggs, pancakes and ham, with two cups of coffee. They were famished from the long trip and were eating hungrily, when the two men entered the dining room. The cowboys sauntered in as if they owned the place. John's last bite stuck to the roof of his mouth, which had suddenly become very dry.

"What is the matter, John? I don't like the look on yer face"

"I'm okay, Mary, but the two fellas that just walked in are bad news."

The two men walked up to their table and stared at Mary. John stood up. "Is there something I can help ye gentlemen with?"

"We just wanted to meet yer bride. We heard you was marrying that wild Irish girl that likes to bite off noses."

Mary's mouth fell open as fear entered her heart.

"I don't know who ye fellas are, or what ye want, but I'd appreciate it if ye would let me wife and I eat in peace. We have a train to catch."

"We'll be catching that train too, Mr. Troy. Enjoy your meal, Mrs. Troy." The two men bowed ceremoniously, then laughed, hit each other on the back, and sat down at another table.

Neither John nor Mary ate another bite. They finished their coffee and retrieved their luggage from their room. John paid a couple of boys to carry them down the street to the station. Holding hands, they silently walked to the train station. Their luggage sat by the bench on the platform. After John purchased their tickets, they sat on the bench to wait for the train.

Mary finally spoke. "John, what is going on here? Why didn't ye tell me Bane was around?"

"I'm sorry, Mary, but I didn't want to upset ye any sooner than I had to. I thought he was finally gone from Oregon, until the day I left. I hadn't heard about him since before the end of the Indian war, so I was hoping he'd either left the county or got killed in the action. He showed up when Ah Kim took me to the train station. I should have told ye, but I guess I was afraid ye wouldn't have married me."

"Of course I would have married ye, but ye should have told me, so I wouldn't have looked so surprised"

"Ye were so happy! I didn't want to spoil it."

"I'm still happy, John. I'm happy because I have ye. It doesn't matter where I am, as long as I have ye."

"I'm happy too, Mary. Don't ye be worrying about Bane. I'll be taking good care of me lovely little bride."

"I know ye will, John. I know ye will."

The train whistle echoed through the town as it came around the bend, announcing its arrival, and the two men walked out of the hotel. John and Mary put their luggage on the bench across from them on the train so the men couldn't sit there, but the cowboys sat across the aisle from them anyway, so they could taunt them mercilessly. John could feel the tenseness in Mary when he put his arm around her, and he was feeling the same. Finally, he went over and sat across from them.

"What do ye want? Why are ye following us?"

"We're following you because Bane pays us to follow you. He wants to know what you are doing all the time. He says you and your wife have caused him much pain throughout his life, and he wants to make sure to cause you that same pain."

"Bane brought everything that happened on himself. We have no problem with Bane. That's in the past. Just leave us alone and we'll stay out of yer way."

"I don't think Bane is as forgiving as you are. Besides, Bane thinks your little bride may still have something that belongs to him."

"Mary has nothing that belongs to Bane! If she did, we'd get rid of the vile thing. Don't cause us any problems, ye hear?"

"Yes sir, Mr. Troy. We'll just sit here and not bother you, okay?"

He laughed as John returned to his seat, put his arm around Mary, and rested her head on his shoulder. He couldn't wait for the trip to be over. Mary felt that old fear gripping her tightly. She wondered if she would ever be entirely rid of that feeling, or of Bane.

Mary was elated when she was able to get off of the train and away from the smell of the cowboys. She sat on the bench by the tracks, taking deep breaths of the fresh air, enjoying the view of the little Oregon town, and the sunshine that was giving them some momentary rays. John watched the men as he unloaded their bags. Ah Kim would wait until the crowd had dispersed at the station before he arrived, so John took his time collecting and stacking their things on the wooden walkway where he was sure Ah Kim would bring the buggy. The two men picked up their boarded horses at the stables and went into the saloon, leaving their horses tied up to the hitching post out in front. It was close to dusk when Ah Kim drove up. He bowed to Mary and returned her emotional hug.

"Mrs. Mary Troy, I am so happy for you. Welcome to your new homeland. I am sorry if you had to wait long, but I felt it best not to come at the busy time."

"Ah Kim, I am so happy to see ye. I did not mind waiting. I will be living here for a long time. I think I can wait a few more minutes to see me new home."

"I am sorry you will not see the land until morning. It is beautiful."

"I saw much of the country on the train, and I will have plenty of time to see the land, Ah Kim."

"We must hurry, as I see two men standing by the door of the saloon. They seem to be watching us."

"I'm sure they are Bane's men. They were waiting for us at the hotel in The Dalles, and they were on the train."

Mary climbed into the front of the buggy while the two men loaded the trunks. Ah Kim took the reins, and he drove the newlyweds the eighteen miles to the little cabin in Pleasant Valley. John carried Mary across the threshold of their first home and hoped she would not be disappointed with the tiny little cabin.

She was thrilled with the simple two room shanty, and she thanked Ah Kim for making sure it was in good condition for her arrival. The second room held a feather bed and wooden table with a lamp. The main room contained the wood stove, a fireplace, a sink, a table with two wooden benches, and two roughly hewn rocking chairs that sat by the fire. An old white tablecloth covered the table. A kerosene lamp and a hand woven Chinese wedding basket were sitting on top of it. Mary pumped water from the sink into the teapot she found on the stove. Ah Kim added wood from the pile by the stove, to stoke the fire, which was already burning low.

The two men brought in the trunks, unhitched the horses, and put the horses and the buggy in the shed that stood about 100 yards from the cabin's door. When Ah Kim came back into the house, he pulled a small bag out of his pocket.

"I want to give you a wedding gift. This is for your future." He rolled a large gold nugget out of the sack onto the table. "Your friendship is most important to me, and I want to give you this to help you get started in your new life together. My wish for you both is much happiness and many healthy children."

"Ah Kim, this is too valuable. The basket on the table is more than enough."

"The basket is sent from Ming and Quan, with much love and good wishes. Do not worry. There are many nuggets where that came from. My cousins and I have been secretly mining the claim and selling the gold in Sumpter. We are saving our money and sending most of it to our families back in China, so that we do not draw attention to our good fortune. Bane knows nothing so far, but he is on our trail. I am sure that he has found out by now that the map he took from you is a fake, and he knows there is a real mine. Someday, he will find it, and I believe he will do anything to get control of the mine, including kill for it. He already has it in for all three of us, so we must be very careful and stay out of his way. I am not telling either of you where the mine is for your safety."

"I do not want to know where it is, but I am very worried about ye."

"Do not worry. Take this nugget and keep it, until you can purchase a large portion of land. This should pay for many acres. Do not let Bane find this nugget, nor the envelope you hold for me."

"It is in a safe place, Ah Kim. I will put the nugget with it. Thank ye, Ah Kim, I will be very careful." She bowed to Ah Kim and then gently hugged him and kissed him on the cheek. "Sit down, Ah Kim, and be the first to have a cup of tea with Mr. and Mrs. John Troy, in their beloved home."

John came in from outside and took off his jacket. Then he grinned and teased Mary. "Is that all that me pretty bride knows how to cook? All I get is tea?"

"It'll take me a few minutes to whip up some of me famous biscuits, or if ye want more substance, it'll be taking me a bit longer, Mr. Troy."

"Some of those biscuits would be jest right to hold me over till morning, Mrs. Troy. We will take Ah Kim home in the morning when we go into town for some supplies."

Mary got the jam and butter out of the basket that Margaret had sent with her, and she put it on the table. When the stove was hot enough, she made her biscuits and dropped them on the baking sheet that she retrieved from one of the trunks. A short time later, they were enjoying the fluffy biscuits slathered in butter and jam.

"Mrs. Mary, tomorrow we will all go together to town, but please do not ever go into town alone. There are many tough cowboys who frequent the saloons in town, which makes it not a safe place for women to be alone."

"I know Bane is here, Ah Kim, and I promise I will not go there alone. But, if he wants to kill me he could probably have an easy time of it."

The conversation upset John. "Ah Kim, ye may put yer bedroll on the floor here in front of the stove. Ye will be warm and safe there."

"Sleep well, good friend, we will say goodnight." Mary dusted off her apron, hung it up, and went to the bedroom.

John and Ah Kim checked on everything outside, and they made sure the latches were solid on the shed and the cabin. John said goodnight and went to the bedroom, while Ah Kim warmed himself by the stove.

Mary snuggled up in John's arms. "I'm so happy to be here."

"I'm so happy yer finally here. I've been so cold at night. I just never could get warm. Most nights I leave the door open so I can get the warmth from the stove, but I don't want to do that tonight. This is our first night in our home together."

"I didn't know ye were such a talkative man. Maybe ye should stop talking and kiss me?"

John laughed and obliged her with a passionate kiss. They made love as quietly as they could, and then they fell asleep feeling warm and cozy in each other's arms.

Chapter Thirty

"The Wild West"

Pleasant Valley, Oregon ~ 1884

"Mary could hardly breathe when she saw his cruel eyes and the ugly scarred nose."

Mary woke up with a chill. She couldn't remember ever being so cold. The temperature had dropped during the night, and she was surprised when she realized that her teeth were chattering. John got out of bed and put on his long johns, heavy work pants, a warm sweater, and boots.

"Stay under the covers for a few minutes, Mary. Yer not used to these cold winters yet. I'll stoke up the wood stove, and it'll be warm real soon. There's an extra set of long johns in me bag, ye should put them on. They'll be a bit large for ye, but they'll keep ye warm."

"Okay, John." She was shivering as she finally stuck her head out from under the covers, got the long johns, and put them on under the covers. When she got out of bed she realized she had them on backwards. After she turned them around, she put her warmest long dress on over the wool underwear, wrapped her shawl around her, and laced up her black high top shoes. John had built a fire in the fireplace too, so she sat in the rocking chair and warmed her hands by the fire for a few minutes.

Ah Kim came in from feeding the horses, and snow blew in the door with him. She glanced out the little window and was thrilled to see a layer of snow covering the ground.

"It's so lovely it takes me breath away."

"Isn't it? I know ye are going to love it up here, Mary, just like I do."

"Oh yes, I surely am."

John put his arms around her, and they both gazed out of the window at the winter wonderland. A doe and her fawn were walking gracefully across the meadow below the cabin.

"What shall I fix ye fer breakfast, husband?"

"Some of those marvelous biscuits would fill me stomach. Our supplies are low, but there's plenty of flour. We'll go into town after we eat."

"Biscuits and tea it is then. Is that okay with ye, Ah Kim?"

"Oh yes, Mrs. Mary. Your biscuits are by far the best I have ever enjoyed."

"The recipe comes from Ireland, and me great-grandmother Foley, but I guess now ye could say they have become American biscuits."

"Most of the best things in America, including the people, have all come from other countries."

"Yer right, Ah Kim, it is too bad that most people that enjoy this land don't realize that."

"The men who fought for this country created laws that state that all men are created equal, and yet many of its people do not treat everyone that way."

"Did ye notice that it only mentions men in that constitution? Women have no rights either, Ah Kim."

"Yes, but that is so in many countries."

John had been quiet until then. "It is true what ye say, but this country is still young. Let us hope that it will grow better with age."

Mary prepared the biscuits and tea, while John and Ah Kim got the buckboard ready. When they came in, stomping the snow off their boots, Mary became concerned about traveling in the cold weather.

"John, me shoes will fall apart in the snow, and this is the only wool dress I own."

"I guess I'll just have to carry ye into the store, because I'm sure there are things we need that I might not get if ye are not there. Besides, I want ye to see the town and I don't want to leave ye here by yerself."

"Do ye think it might snow some more and we won't get back?"

"It's not that far into town. Even if a blizzard came upon us, we should make it home okay. If there is a storm, we will need those provisions to see us through. The sky looks pretty ominous so we better get a move on. I have plenty of money for food supplies, and we can purchase some boots and yardage fer ye on me account. Ye need warmer clothes here this time of year."

They sat down quickly, ate the biscuits, and drank the hot tea. Mary put on her bonnet, wrapped the heavy shawl around her, and grabbed her quilt to cover up with in the wagon. John put some small pieces of wood in the stove to keep the cabin warm while they were gone. Ah Kim had brought in three more buckets of water from the well in case the pump in the sink froze up, so Mary would have water for her cooking and washing needs. True to his word, John picked up his tiny wife and carried her to the wooden buckboard.

The snow started to fall again, and John got the horses moving at a much faster pace. After they dropped Ah Kim off at his cousin's small shanty, they drove to Main Street and the general store. There was a bustle of activity, as everyone could tell a storm was on the way and they were stocking up on supplies. While they rode into town, Mary had written down a list of supplies they would need on the small sheet of paper she had brought with her. John took the list to the proprietor at the General Store, while Mary went to find some new boots and some yardage. She was looking at fabric in the front of the shop where she could see the colors better, when Bane walked in the door. Mary could hardly breathe when she saw his cruel eyes and ugly scarred nose. All she wanted to do was to run to John for protection, but she knew the worst thing she could do was show fear, so she tried to hide her terror.

"Well, well, if it isn't the new little bride, Mary Troy! You've certainly grown up, since you pretended to be a boy."

"Now that ye know that I am a woman, why not leave me alone? It appears to me that yer interest is in young boys, not girls anyway."

Bane's cruel eyes suddenly filled with fire. She could feel the heat of his anger as he started to speak. John suddenly jumped between them.

"Bane, leave me wife alone. Whatever happened between the two of ye is over. It's in the past. Let's all start fresh. We will forget what ye did, just leave us alone."

"But I won't forget. I have to look in a mirror, Troy. That's why it'll never be over for me. You better take care of yer wife, and keep her out of me sight. You better take care of her good." His piercing eyes seem to burn through to her soul. Then he turned and stomped out the door, leaving the wood floor shaking. Mary was shaking too.

"C'mon Mary, get what ye need, and let's get out of here. The snow is coming down much harder now. I'm going to put these supplies in the wagon. Mr. Foster will put what ye want on our account, and I'll settle up next time I come to town. Hurry now, Mrs. Troy." He looked her in the eyes and smiled, then patted her gently on the shoulders, picked up some of the supplies and went outside.

Mary took a deep breath, quickly picked up a bolt of blue wool and a pair of boots. She asked Mr. Foster to put them on John's account, signed the receipt, and went out to the wagon. John had just finished loading the large bags of sugar and flour. Mary climbed in the front, put the shawl around her head and shoulders, and covered up with the blanket. When John finished loading the supplies he got in and she covered him up too. He pulled his hat firmly down and picked up the reins. Snow began to fall as John drove the wagon as hard and as fast as he could toward their small cabin. The railroad was letting him stay there for nothing, as he was still working as a crew boss for the line they were putting through to Huntington. When he wasn't working there, he was searching for property that they could farm when the railroad work was finished. John had his eye on the acreage that Ah Kim had told him about, just outside of Pleasant Valley, and he hoped to be able to homestead some of it. With the gold nugget Ah Kim had given them, he might be able to purchase a few more acres than he had planned.

The snow was coming down so heavily now that they could barely see six feet in front of them. It was blowing in drifts, and the fear of getting stuck in the snow became a reality. Just as they came over the hill in sight of the cabin, the right wheel stuck tight in a deep rut filled with snow. As they were only about a half mile from the cabin, John got out and helped Mary down.

"We've got to get to the house as fast as we can. Carry what ye can. I'll come back and get the rest of it and the horses."

They started walking in the thick snow. Mary had donned the new boots on the way back. The three or four inches had grown to seven or eight, and there were three or four foot drifts in spots. Mary fell down twice and was shivering violently by the time she made it to the cabin door. Quickly, she put the supplies on the table and stoked the still glowing embers in the old stove, with several pieces of wood that the men had piled high before they left. John came in pulling the flour and sugar sacks, then hurried back out to get the last of the supplies. Mary could only see the horses now from the window, but not the wagon. She couldn't keep the shuttered window open long, as the wind was shifting and blowing it inside. The snow was covering everything. When he came in with the last of the supplies, she had the shawl back around her and was sitting in the rocker by the fire.

"I'm going with ye to help with the horses."

"No, yer not, Mary. No need for two of us to get lost out there. Keep both the fire and the stove goin'. I'll bring in more wood when I finish with the horses. I will be able to see the smoke. Dry yer feet before ye get frostbite. I'm dressed for the weather. Don't worry! I'm not going to leave me pretty little wife now that I finally have her. I'll be right back, Mary, I promise."

She put more wood in the fireplace and stoked it to make a bigger fire. Knowing her husband would be hungry, she set about fixing her first supper in the cabin, while silently praying that John would find his way back safely in the worsening storm. The horses whinnied as he led them to the barn, then she couldn't hear anything except for the howling of the wind. Mary began worrying about what she should do if he didn't come in soon, when the door finally opened and the fierce wind blew him inside the door.

"John, I was so worried about ye."

He looked surprised. "Don't ye be worrying none about me, Mary, me girl. I guess yer just not used to life in the 'wild west' yet. I had to make sure the shed is warm enough for the horses, and that they had enough hay and water to last for a few days, in case we get snowed in. It's jest part of life in Oregon."

"I guess I'll be learning about life here soon enough, especially with Bane hanging around."

"I don't think we'll have to worry about him tonight, anyway."

"I guess we'll just have to spend our first night alone, in our first home, as Mr. and Mrs. John Troy."

"Well yes, this might be quite enjoyable."

Mary giggled. "The stew is ready, and I'm thinking that we might need the energy this food will give us."

John laughed. "Ye are a rare woman, Mrs. Troy. I don't think most women enjoy the love making as much as ye do. This will surely be a memorable blizzard."

Mary's face turned scarlet. "Now, John, don't ye be teasing me. No one ever told me that love making would be so enjoyable. I was told it was a woman's duty to please her husband. Maybe I just got me a real special husband, who makes me feel real nice."

"Whatever the reason is, me dear, ye are me wild Irish rose and I love ye just the way ye are." He put his arms around her and kissed her gently and sweetly.

Mary put the pot of stew on the table and ladled them both generous portions. Then she put the biscuits on the table and filled their cups with coffee. When they finished eating, Mary cleared the dishes, while John put more wood on the fire and brought the soft feather mattress to the main room in front of the cozy hearth. It was too cold to sleep in the back room. They piled three quilts on the mattress and filled the kerosene lamp on the table. Mary put on her long nightgown and fixed them both a cup of hot tea, to warm them up. They climbed into the soft down and each other's arms. They watched the hot crackling flames, licking the logs, and listened to the howling wind and heavy snow beating on the cabin outside, happy in each other's arms.

"Mary, I feel like I have put yer life in danger by bringing ye here without telling ye about Bane."

"I'm not a wee babe, ye know, John. I wish ye had told me, and yet I'm glad ye didn't. I would have worried, but I would have married ye anyway. So, I guess I was better off not knowing. I'm just happy to be here. What ye didn't tell me was how cold it is up here."

"Yeah, it's a wee bit colder than our beloved Ireland."

"That it is." Mary pulled John down to kiss her, and they enjoyed each other for the first time in their little cabin without having to worry that they would be overheard. As the wind whipped the snow around the cabin and piled it in high drifts, Mary and John reveled in each other's company.

The storm lasted for three days straight. On the fourth day, the wind died down and the snow stopped falling. By then, John and Mary were the best of friends and expert lovers. They went outside on the fourth day and played in the huge drifts, throwing snowballs at each other. They built a snowman, and they spent that day enjoying the beauty of the snow in the gorgeous Oregon valley. The snow would melt soon and the hard work of living off the land would resume, but for a few days they had only each other.

It took a couple of weeks before all of the snow melted and the land returned to its winter gray. Mary had just settled into a good daily routine, when one morning she woke feeling very nauseous. She made it just outside the cabin door, before last night's dinner came up and splattered to the right of the door. After several days of the same sickness every morning, Mary realized what her symptoms meant. John was thrilled when she told him that around the end of November he was going to be a father.

"Our first wee babe, already? I can't believe it, Mary! Ye have made me every dream come true!"

Mary sent the good news to her family with her weekly letter to her mother. She followed it up with letters to her sisters, Rachel, and Kate Murphy. John received a letter from Sean Foley, shortly before Kate's letter arrived. Sean knew there was still work to be finished on the railroad, so he asked if they would mind if he came to the Baker valley to start a new life, like his niece and her husband had done. Mary thought it was a good idea until she heard from Kate. Sean was already on his way to Oregon, when Mary received the letter from Kate.

Dearest friend Mary,

I was so happy to get your letter with the exciting news. I am so envious of your happiness, and wonder if I will ever be fortunate enough to find my own. Will you need help when the baby arrives? Or before? Mrs. McCleary is no longer able to travel. She had a stroke a few weeks back. It was not a bad stroke, but it disabled her enough so that she is not able to travel anymore. She has her faithful housekeeper and has no need of me. I am bored and unhappy. I do not like any of the suitors that have been knocking on my door. They bore me with talk of business and themselves. I do not see any future for me here. Could you use my help, if I came to be with you when your time comes? I do not want to be of trouble to you and John, but hope I might visit you for a few weeks, to help out during that trying time. I thought perhaps I could start a new life in Oregon, and that you would enjoy having an old friend close by.

Please do not feel obliged to invite me. If you have made other plans I will certainly understand. My father will, of course, pay for my passage up there, and he'll finance me for several months thereafter. Please write soon, and let me know if you need me. Late summer or early fall would probably be the best time for traveling. It will take me a month or so, to obtain the proper clothing and toiletries that I might need.

I wait anxiously for your reply, and if the answer is yes, perhaps you could include some suggestions for what I need to bring with me.

With love from your dear friend,

Kate Murphy

Mary was thrilled when she received Kate's letter, as she had worried about being alone during the birth of the baby, and it would be so nice to have her friend there. Sean's coming up there to work was her only worry. Mary knew not telling Kate that Sean would be there also was not right, so she wrote back immediately.

My dearest Kate,

I was so happy to receive your letter. You are most welcome to come up here. I would love your company and assistance, with the babe's birth, and for as long as you want to stay. It would please me greatly to have my dear friend here. You will love Oregon as much as I do, and it could be a new start for you. However, I must tell you what transpired shortly before I received your letter. Sean Foley is on his way up here to work on the railroad with John. If I had known you were coming, I would have told John to tell him not to come. He will not be staying with us, but from time to time you will have to see him, as John knows nothing of the previous circumstances. I am so looking forward to your coming, and I pray you do not change your mind.

As far as suggestions as to what you will need, warm clothes and boots are essential in the winter months as snow and ice are on the ground for several weeks in the winter. Although I have not endured the summer here yet, I am told that it gets quite warm. You will need creams and lotions for dry weather. If I think of anything else that you need, I will tell you in my next letter

I am looking forward to seeing you. It has been so long since I have enjoyed your company. You are most welcome at any time.

With love from your dear friend,

Mrs. Mary Troy

Mary stayed at home most of the time so she did not see Bane often. Only twice during her pregnancy did she run into him when she and John went into Baker City. Once he came out of the saloon with two of his gang and glared at her as she rode in the buckboard down the street. The second time his gang was leaving town as she and John arrived. The gang tried to block the road, but John just kept going so they had to move. Bane's face relayed his hatred as they passed.

Ah Kim kept them informed of Bane's activities, as his many cousins kept a close watch on him when Ah Kim left on his trips to the secret mine. Bane and his gang put fear in the hearts of many of the Baker County residents, especially the Chinese and Indians. Sheriff Barkley was intimidated by Bane, and in his fear, he let him rule the small town that Mary only went to when it was necessary.

Although life was tough in the growing area, Mary and John settled comfortably into their small cabin. Working as a crew boss on the railroad line to Huntington brought John home a good wage, and they were saving to buy land so they could build a larger home. John wanted to be a rancher, and Mary wanted to be his partner in running that ranch. Life was hard, but they worked well together, and their first year together wasn't as rough as they both expected.

Mary and John had only one major disagreement, which was after Sean arrived and went to work with John. Her uncle seemed to be trying hard to live a good life, but one night when Mary was in her sixth month, John came home quite late. The pair had stopped at a saloon "to quench their thirst" after work. Mary had dinner waiting and was pacing the floor when John arrived, smelling of whiskey. The smell of liquor made Mary so angry that she lost her temper.

She ranted and raved at John while he sat in the chair smiling at her, with his red eyes, and reached for her every time she came near him.

"John Troy, how could ye do that? Good man that ye are. Where have ye been? Sitting in the saloon getting pie eyed, it looks like to me. Don't ye know that yer wife is home worrying about the likes of ye, and with yer dinner ready too?"

"Ah, Mary, me girl, now don't be angry with me. I jest stopped for a meetin' with the ranchers in the saloon, and I had a jigger or two with yer uncle afterward. That's all."

"That's all, John? That's all ye say? Sean, eh? I should have known. Me uncle ain't nothing but a drunkard. I knew he should never have come up to this land. He'll jest be causing me heartaches."

"Now Mary, me darlin', it weren't nothin'! We had important plans to make, woman, and we had a couple of swigs, whilst we were talkin'. That's all."

"It seems to me, ye had lots more than a couple of swigs, John Troy. I'm telling ye right now, husband, ye best not be makin' this a regular thing, cuz yer goin' to be sleeping elsewhere if ye do!"

"Mary, Mary, I haven't seen yer fiery side before."

"If ye keep doin' this, ye'll be seeing a lot more of me fiery side!"

Mary dished up the hard brown wrinkled potatoes and carrots, and overcooked meat, then slammed the tin plate down in front of her husband. She poured him a cup of strong coffee and sat it down sharply in front of him, almost spilling it. Then she sat down in the rocking chair in front of the fire, and rocked hard and fast, with an angry look on her face, while John quietly ate his dinner.

Mary gave Sean a stout lecture when he came by the cabin a few days later. "Sean, I'll only be telling ye this once. Don't be taking me John into the saloon to be gettin' drunk ever again."

"Mary, our lips were dry as the desert. We only had a couple of swigs. We jest got to talkin' about manly things and stayed a wee bit longer than we planned."

"Don't ye know, Sean, I'll be blaming ye, if ye lead me husband astray."

"Mary, I promise, I'm not drinkin' anymore. Two swigs is me limit, and I rarely do that. Don't worry. John is a fine man, and he loves ye very much. Ye are the last person I want on me bad side, as I know that temper of yours."

"Sean, I want ye to promise me, ye'll leave Kate alone when she arrives. She's here to help with the babe, and she wants nothin' to do with ye."

"I'll leave her alone, Mary. I'll jest be happy to be able to see her every now and then."

"Ye jest stay away from her, Sean."

"I hear ye, Mary. I hear ye!"

Chapter Thirty-One

"New Arrivals"

Eastern Oregon ~ 1884-1885

"Mary ran into the cabin, put the baby on the floor, and took the rifle from behind the door. She heard the shotgun explode as she went out the door."

John picked up Kate at the train station in mid-September. Mary wasn't feeling much like traveling, as it was a bumpy ride into town and painful at this stage in her pregnancy.

"I want to have a nice hot meal for Kate when she arrives." She smiled at him, as he started driving the buckboard down the dusty road.

After John left for the train station, Mary started frying the freshly killed and plucked chicken that John had brought her. When it was a crispy golden brown, she covered the pan and let it simmer on the hot stove. The aroma of the frying bird permeated the cabin with an appetizing aroma. Then she peeled the potatoes, she had picked from her garden, and put them in a pan of water. The home grown green beans were just beginning to boil, when she heard the sound of the wagon bouncing up the path to the cabin door.

"I can't tell ye how happy I am to see ye!" Mary laughed with glee when she greeted Kate, as John helped her down from the wagon. The excited women's voices made John smile, as he unloaded Kate's things and put them in the corner. He was delighted to see Mary so happy, so he left the two women alone and went out to feed the horses. When he returned, they had the late afternoon meal on the table, and they all sat down to enjoy it. Neither woman stopped talking until bedtime, as they filled each other in on the happenings since their last letters.

John kept himself busy making the corner of the main room a little more private for Kate. He made a frame for a bed, by using some boards he had left over from building the chicken coop. Mary had sewn a mattress and stuffed it with chicken feathers, and John put it on top of the narrow frame. A rope that John nailed to the roof at two foot intervals surrounded the area, holding the long muslin curtains that Mary had sewn to give Kate some privacy.

After the women cleaned the kitchen, Mary set a pitcher and bowl upon the small chest of drawers that stood next to her bed. Mary didn't tell Kate that Sean had built the dresser, as he had asked her to keep it "their secret." Kate put her things away, while Mary sat in the rocking chair sewing some baby clothes. John had gone outside to latch everything down for the night.

"Mary, you look wonderful."

"How can ye say that? I look like a fat cow, and I waddle like a duck."

"Mary, I'm so jealous. I wish I looked just like you right now."

"Oh, Katie, I'm sorry. This must be quite painful for ye."

"I'll get over it. I just had to get out of San Francisco. I was going nowhere there. Thank you for letting me come here."

"Thank ye for coming, Kate. I'm delighted yer here."

John came in from outside with another stack of wood for the fire. It was still warm during the day, but the nights were chilly, and a fire kept the little house warm.

"Now Mary, I came to help, and I don't want you working so hard, like you did tonight preparing that wonderful meal. You're not supposed to be waiting on me."

"Ye can take over tomorrow, Kate. The dinner was my way to thank ye for coming."

"Ye are looking a bit tired tonight, Mary." Her husband was concerned about her.

"I'm feeling pretty tired, John. This babe is getting bigger, and it seems to be a lot heavier to carry around this last week."

"And all the canning and preserving ye've been doing has worn ye out."

"Kate's here now to help me. I'll enjoy the work with her here."

Kate spent the next few days learning Mary's routine. Mary grew all of their vegetables, and they had fresh eggs and chickens from their own growing brood. The rooster woke them early every morning. The couple were saving most of the money from his railroad job, as they planned on homesteading some land in the spring. With the baby coming, they needed a bigger house, and John was planning on building it with Sean's help.

In just a few weeks, Kate learned how to work the ranch and felt good about what she found herself capable of accomplishing. Having been raised by servants, Kate barely knew how to take care of herself when she arrived. She soon realized why Mary was so tired, as she worked from dawn until dusk and didn't seem to be eating enough. Kate insisted that she slow down, and she took over most of her jobs. After she began eating at least three meals a day, Mary's energy level improved. John and Sean brought home a deer and a bear. Mary taught Kate how to dress and smoke the meat, and they stored it in the small smoke house. The two men often went fishing on the Powder River, on the weekends, and brought home a variety of fresh fish for frying. Kate and Mary picked wild berries that grew everywhere, and they made jellies and jams for the winter. Mary made her own bread, and they had fresh milk from the cow daily. The two women made butter, and they sold or traded the excess milk, butter and eggs, to their neighbors. Over the next few months, they canned beans, carrots, and tomatoes, and they made pickles from the cucumbers.

Mary was big with her child by the time they got everything stored away for winter, and it was mid-November when she lost all of her energy. It was November 28th when she first felt some pain in her lower back. The women prepared a wonderful meal, to celebrate the end of their harvesting and canning. John had invited Sean, as he had killed the deer they were eating for dinner. When the dishes were clean and put away, Mary began feeling pretty bad.

"Mary, I think it's time for you to go lie down and stay down. By the looks of your belly, it could be anytime." Kate saw Mary looking pained, as she sat in the rocking chair by the fire.

"Yer working too hard, Mary." John looked concerned. "Please get yerself to bed and take a rest. The new priest is coming here to say mass Sunday morning, and I'm sure many of our neighbors will be over as well, so I don't want ye overdoing it."

"All right, John. I am feeling a bit tuckered out. I hope the babe doesn't come during mass on Sunday."

"That would be a predicament, wouldn't it?" Sean commented. Kate glared at him. It was hard to endure having dinner with him, but having a discussion with him was out of the question. Kate just got up and started doing the dishes, instead of saying something that would alert John to a problem. Mary's low back pain continued to worsen that night, and it continued for the next day and a half. It was Saturday afternoon, when she started moaning in agony. John went into town to find the doctor, or the mid-wife, to deliver the baby. Kate held Mary's hand, rinsed her forehead with a damp cloth and prayed with her, in between the sharp pains. John came back without the doctor, who had gone to Union to deliver another baby. He left a message for him, and then he tried to get the midwife, but she had gone to Cove to visit her niece.

Mary's pains became increasingly more intense and longer, on the last day of November. Kate was concerned, as she had never delivered a baby. It wasn't that she didn't know what to do, as she had seen her own child born, but her baby had not taken so long to arrive. It was late in the evening, and there was no time between the pains. The doctor had still not arrived, and Mary felt as if she was being ripped apart. She knew that the baby was finally coming. Kate had water boiling and clean towels ready. She could see the baby's head crowning, as the doctor entered the room.

"Thank God!" Kate muttered. He washed his hands and went straight to work. Kate held Mary's hand and cooled Mary's head, as she panted her way through the difficult birth.

"Oh Mary, your baby is beautiful!" Kate said, when the baby's head was out. It was a few minutes later, when the rest of the tiny bundle arrived.

"It's a girl!" The doctor announced, as he cut the cord and put the squalling infant into the clean blankets that Kate held. Mary tried to smile as the last pain of after birth shuddered through her. Kate laid the baby next to Mary's face, and her exhausted eyes filled with tears of joy.

"Isn't she lovely?" Kate loved the child immediately, as if she were her own. Looking at the baby made her long for the little boy she left in Ireland. Her joy for Mary's happiness was mixed with the pain of her own loss, leaving her with a confusion of emotions.

When the priest and her neighbors arrived the next day, Mary was sitting in the rocking chair, with her baby sound asleep in her arms and her grandmother's quilt tucked around them both. Kate had picked some late blooming wildflowers and put them in a bottle on the table, with the lovely lace tablecloth that Mary had brought with her from San Francisco. The priest would use the table for an altar. After Father Henley said mass and gave communion, John got up to speak.

"As ye can see, we have been blessed with a beautiful new daughter. We have asked Father Henley to baptize our daughter this afternoon. I would like to invite ye all to join us, for this special occasion and for a small supper afterwards."

Everyone was delighted. John had risen early and killed three chickens for dinner. Kate prepared the meal, and Sean had procured a couple bottles of wine from the saloon in town the day before. The neighbors consisted of three young couples, one of whom was also expecting a child. The two other couples had small children of their own. All of the men worked on the Huntington Railroad with John, and they lived in small houses provided by the railroad.

The settlers had brought their own chairs in their wagons for the mass, so the men sat and visited, while Kate and the women prepared the meal. When supper was almost ready, the priest put on his baptism vestment, which he carried in a black valise, and he stood in the middle of the room.

"Who will be this child's godparents?"

"Me friend, Kate Murphy, will be her godmother." Mary answered.

"Sean Foley, Mary's uncle and me good friend, will be her godfather." John added.

Kate and Sean both looked surprised, but accepted graciously because of their love for John and Mary and their new daughter.

"What will this child's name be?" The priest asked before beginning the ceremony.

"As is Irish custom, the firstborn daughter will be named after me mother, Anna Cecile. She was born late last night, on the 30th day of November."

Mary handed the child to Kate, who then stood by Sean holding the child in front of the priest. John stood by Mary's chair, holding her hand, and they both beamed happily as tiny cries came from their daughter, when the priest poured water over her little forehead, baptizing her a Roman Catholic. There were tears in Kate's eyes, as she wondered what it would have been like to watch her own child baptized.

It was a joyous day, but Mary was glad when it was over and the guests left, as she was exhausted. Mary nursed her little girl until she fell asleep. Then Kate took the sleeping child and laid her in the wooden cradle that Mary's father had made by hand and sent with Kate to Oregon. The next morning, while Kate held and cuddled her new goddaughter, Mary wrote letters to all of their family and friends, informing them of the blessed event. Within the next six weeks, they received lovely baby gifts in response. Most were tiny hand-made dresses, knitted sweaters, hats, booties, and quilts. Mary's parents sent the baby a tiny rosary. Kate's parents sent a silver cup, with "Anna" engraved on it, and a silver baby spoon. Mary was delighted. She was blessed with a sweet tempered little girl. The baby cried when hungry, or when her diaper was wet, but smiled and slept the rest of the time.

Kate stayed through the fierce winter that followed, and she became very attached to Anna. She loved her as if she were her own child, and the thought of leaving brought pain to her heart. It was a warm day in May, when their peaceful existence was rudely interrupted. Mary was hanging clothes on the line in her yard, while five-month old Anna sat happily in an apple crate next to her mother's basket of wet clothes. John had gone to town to pick up some supplies, while Kate was in the hen house feeding the chickens and collecting eggs. Mary was preoccupied, as she talked happily to the cooing, giggling baby while she worked, and she didn't hear the horses until they stopped behind her. When she saw Bane glaring down at her, she screeched and reached for Anna. Bane swung down from his horse and pulled Mary close to him, before she could get the child into her arms.

"I told you I'd get to you someday, didn't I? I'll bet your cowardly husband would be mad if he found me having my way with you, wouldn't he? You want your baby safe, don't you?"

"Leave me baby alone, ye monster!" She beat on him as she tried to get free.

"I'll get even with you, any way I can, for the damage to my face." He held both of her hands behind her back, and he started trying to kiss her. Bane's two companions laughed, as she squirmed and wiggled, when the baby began to cry.

"Leave her alone!" Kate stood by the side of the shed with a shotgun aimed at them. She had heard the horses.

Bane held only Mary's arm now.

"I said, LET HER GO!" Kate was angry.

Bane roughly released her. Mary quickly picked up the apple crate, baby and all, and ran toward Kate.

"Take the baby in the house, Mary, and get the other rifle."

Mary ran into the cabin, put the baby on the floor, and took the rifle from behind the door. She heard the shotgun explode as she went back out the door. Blood ebbed from the wound on the chest of one of the men, who was lying next to her clothes basket. Mary aimed the rifle at Bane and went to Kate's side.

"You murdering bitch! Billy didn't do nothin' to you! You'll hang for this!" Bane was seething.

"He was coming at me. You know he was!" Kate was shaking, but she kept the gun on the other two men.

"It's your word against mine."

"And mine!" Mary said, cocking her rifle. A cloud of dust was visible in the distance, as John and Sean rode toward the cabin.

"I'll gladly blow yer head off, Bane, if ye take one more step." Mary felt stronger, knowing John was almost there. "The world would be a better place without the likes of ye, now wouldn't it."

Kate went to see if the man was alive.

"He's dead."

"What happened here, Mary?" John asked, as he rode up.

"These men came and Bane attacked me! Kate came to me rescue. She shot this man when he came at her."

"Now, Mary Troy, isn't it true that you were in the house when this murdering woman shot Billy? She shot him for no reason, Troy. They'll hang her for it."

"No they won't, Bane. Everyone in town knows ye and yer gang. No one will believe ye."

"You're wrong there, Troy! You know the sheriff is a friend of mine. He owes me a favor."

"Keep your hands up, Bane! We're taking ye all into town."

John and Sean held their guns on the two men, who were riding in front of them, all the way to the sheriff's office in town. They put "Billy" in the back of the buckboard. Mary drove it into town following the men, with Anna in Kate's arms next to her. They went straight to the jailhouse and related the events to the sheriff. After hearing all four sides of the story, the sheriff finally spoke.

"I have to put Miss Murphy in jail under the circumstances, until the judge comes to town to hold a trial. That's the law."

"She was just tryin' to protect me and me baby!" Mary protested.

"What did he do, Mrs. Troy? You look fine to me. What about you, Miss Murphy? Did Billy harm you? Why did you shoot him?"

"He was coming at me to take the gun away!"

"Can't say that I blame him, I wouldn't want you pointing a gun at me either."

"Sheriff, Bane's been threatening me life for a long time! He came there today to do me harm."

"Maybe he did, but I'm not a judge, and that's who you have to tell your story to."

"When is the judge coming?"

"He's due here week after next, if I remember rightly."

"Sheriff, let her come home with us until the trial. We will make sure she gets here on time. She's not a danger to anyone."

"My nephew, Billy, is dead! This woman needs to be locked up." Bane was still ranting.

"I'm sorry, I will have to lock her up until the judge arrives and makes his decision." It was obvious that the sheriff was afraid to cross Bane.

Both women began crying, and so did the baby, but their pleading with the sheriff didn't do any good. Gruffly taking Kate by the arm, he pushed her in the cell and locked the door.

"Sheriff, this is wrong. Ye can't do this. Please send for the judge right away. Ye can't leave her in here like this!" John protested.

"I'll send a telegram to the judge in the morning. Sorry, that's the best I can do. You can talk to her for a few minutes before you leave."

"Kate, don't worry, we'll get ye out of here as soon as possible." John assured her.

"Here's me quilt to keep you warm, Kate. I'll bring ye some food now, and be back in the morning with some clothes and baskets of food from the house. I'm so sorry. Ye were just tryin' to help me."

"I'm glad I did it." Kate said, with hate in her eyes. "You should have seen the look on that man's face as he came at me. It was pure evil! I will never let a man take advantage of me again."

Sean looked sick. "Kate, we'll get ye out of here, I promise!"

Kate just glared at him. Anna held her arms out to Kate, who cried as she kissed her goodbye through the bars of the small cell.

The next day, Mary and Sean arrived early with fresh fruit, vegetables, fried chicken, biscuits, pickles, and tea. Mary brought Kate a carpetbag with a fresh change of clothes and Kate's bible and rosary. The deputy told them that the sheriff had sent for the judge, and that he had responded that he would arrive in three days.

"I'll be here every day, Kate, don't ye worry." Mary and Anna were both crying as they left. Sean drove Mary and Anna back to the cabin in the buckboard, because John had stayed there to tend to the animals.

"I can't believe this is happening to Kate," he said. "After what I put her through, now she has to endure this. I'm going to go back and stay in town, to make sure nothing happens to her while she's in that vile place."

"That would be a good idea. I don't trust Bane or the sheriff. It's Saturday, and people get pretty wild in town on Saturday nights."

Sean left Mary at the cabin and went back to keep an eye on the jail. He planned to spend most of the weekend on the wood bench across the street from the jail, watching who went in and came out of the jail. The deputy locked the jail after he brought Kate dinner, then he went across the street to the saloon. Sean dozed off after the sun went down, and he woke to see the door closing on the jail, but too late to see who had entered.

Kate had finally gone to sleep on the hard cot, when she heard the front door of the building open. The lights were out, but it was dusk and she could see a silhouette enter the room. When she heard the key drop on the sheriff's desk, she thought it was him, until she heard the ring of jail keys being removed from the peg on the wall. She started to panic when she saw the big man, fumbling with the lock on her cell. The sheriff wasn't a big man, and neither was the deputy. Hoping his eyes hadn't adjusted to the dark yet, she quietly slid off the mattress and crawled along the floor, where she hoped he wouldn't see her. She felt sick, when she heard the jail door close behind him. All she heard was his breathing, and she knew it was Bane. She could barely make out his shape as he headed towards the cot. She lunged for the door, hoping to find the key that she knew he must have left in the lock. He came up behind her.

"There's my little whore! You couldn't wait for me to come, could you? You should be working in the brothel; a little slut like you." He pushed her against the bars and started kissing her. "Let me have what I came here for, and I'll tell the sheriff to set you free."

"Get off of me, you slimy bastard!" She pushed him as hard as she could, but he just laughed. He ripped her dress, exposing her breast, and grabbed at her flesh.

"I can make it worse for you. My man and I will testify that you shot Billy for no reason. Two against one and you'll hang. After you satisfy me, I'll see that the charges are dropped."

He held her pinned in the corner of the cell. He pulled her dress up, ripped her pantaloons off and was pulling his trousers down, when she heard the cell door open. The pressure of his arms was released as he was pulled off of her, and she heard the crack of knuckles hitting bone. She knelt down in the corner, sobbing, while the two men fought. Then someone lit the kerosene lantern, and Kate saw a battered faced Sean holding it and Bane lying on the floor unconscious.

"Are ye okay, Kate? Did he hurt ye?"

"He was just trying to do what you did, Sean Foley." She couldn't stop weeping.

"Oh, Katie, I'm so sorry. Come on, I'm getting ye out of here. I'll not be leavin' ye here with the likes of him."

Sean wrote a letter to the sheriff explaining why Bane was in the jail cell, instead of Kate, and left it on the desk.

If you want Kate for court Tuesday, come and get her. I will be testifying that you gave Bane keys to the jail and allowed him to take advantage of your prisoner. If you decide to drop the charges against her, then do not come for her on Tuesday.

Sean Foley

Sean took Kate back to the cabin and left her with Mary. Nothing was ever said about the killing again. No one came to get her on

Tuesday, and the sheriff never mentioned it. John heard in town that the sheriff had told the Judge that new evidence had caused him to realize that she shot him in self-defense. But, Kate was not the same after that. It was as if the incident brought back the pain she had spent years trying to forget.

She became so melancholy that not even little Anna could bring a smile to her face. An unhappy frown was always on her face. She moped around, had trouble sleeping at night, didn't want to get up in the morning, and seemed to have no energy. Kate spent a lot of time just staring off into space. One day, she went into town and never came back. John and Mary were worried to death.

Sean had been staying in the shed since the incident, and he went into town late that night to look for her. He found her in the saloon, drinking and laughing with some cowboy.

"Kate, what are ye doing?"

"What I was meant for, Sean. You knew it when you first met me, isn't that why you treated me that way? Everyone knows it. They just look at me and see a sign that says, 'use me,' so I might as well 'use me' to my own benefit."

"Kate, stop this right now. A lady like ye doesn't belong in a place like this."

"Oh, yes I do. Tell Mary, I'm sorry and that I love her, but I think I've found my place. Go away, Sean, and leave me be, or I'll shoot you too. I have a reason to, don't I?"

Sean berated himself as he rode back to the cabin, to tell John and Mary. He knew it was his fault. 'How could he have hurt the one he loved so much? What could he do to get her out of this? He must find a way to save her. He must do something to help her.'

Chapter Thirty-Two

"Kate's Predicament"

Eastern Oregon ~ 1886-1889

"What's the matter, Kate?" "I have some terrible news, Mary!"

Mary went to see Kate at the saloon, and she begged and pleaded with her to come home. She took Anna with her and put her on Kate's lap, when they sat down at a table.

"Kate, ye wouldn't want yer mum and pop to know where yer living and what yer doing, would ye? It would break their hearts."

"Mary, they'll have to find out sometime what kind of daughter they have."

"I won't have ye talkin' that way about yerself. Yer a good girl, Kate Murphy, and ye didn't do anything wrong. God jest made ye too pretty, and some men just can't control their urges with a lovely girl like ye. What happened with Sean wasn't yer fault."

"Yes it was, Mary. I disobeyed my parents and snuck out to meet him, then drank with him. What did I expect him to do?"

"Katie, Katie, no matter what ye did, Sean had no right to touch ye. It's me fault! If I had told me parents what happened with Sean back in Ireland, maybe he would never have come to America. And that skunk, Bane, should burn in hell. Does he come in here?"

"Not lately. I hear he's spending his time givin' the Chinese miners a bad time."

"Oh no! I hope he leaves Ah Kim alone."

"I'm sorry, Mary, but I was so depressed seeing you with little Anna that I thought of killing myself. I just had to get away from everything. This is where I need to be right now."

"Anna misses ye, Katie. Look how happy she is on yer lap. Yer her godmother, and as such, ye promised to make sure she is raised true to her Catholic faith. Ye cannot teach her good things and live here."

"You're right, Mary, as soon as I have earned enough, I plan to open a ladies clothing store."

"Why not ask yer father for the money to do that?"

"My father would not approve."

"Would he approve of what yer doing now?"

"He would probably disown me if he knew about the baby, so it makes no difference."

"Katie, dear, please don't be so down on yerself. Yer parents love ye so very much. I do not think they would disown ye."

"It doesn't matter, nothing matters anymore."

Mary looked down, took a deep breath and blurted out. "Kate, I am going to have another baby. Would ye at least consider helping me again before the babe is born?"

"Oh Mary, another baby, how wonderful for you and John. God has blessed you both in many ways. Of course, I will come and stay with you the last month or two."

"Yer welcome to come now, if ye change your mind. John and I worry about ye here by yerself." Mary felt sick thinking about Kate living at the saloon. Worrying about Kate was all Mary seemed to do these days.

"By myself? Sean comes in all the time. He sits on that chair at that corner table, and he leers at me for an hour or two. He knows better than to talk to me. I just can't forgive him, Mary. My life is ruined because of what happened that night. I know he's sorry, and he constantly tries to make it up to me, but whenever I look at him, I see the wee babe I left in Ireland." Huge tears welled up in her eyes as she spoke.

"I know, Kate, it must be very hard. Ye know he would marry ye in a minute if ye would have him."

"Mary, when I look at him, hate fills my heart. Living here keeps my mind off the baby. I'm too busy to think about my loss, which is what I need right now. Don't worry, Mary, I'm not bedding any of these cowboys, but I get good tips just for talking and drinking with them. I'm good at listening to their problems and tall tales. It seems the more I smile at them, and bat my eyelashes, the more they tip me, but I can't stand the thought of any of them touching me. I'll give a little kiss once in a while, for a better tip, but that's it. So quit worrying, Mary, the bartender watches out for me too."

"I'm glad for that at least, Kate. What about Bane? He's already hurt ye once, girl. What if he comes in and starts bothering ye?"

"I don't go anywhere by myself, and my friends here will take care of me. Thanks, Mary, I appreciate your caring, but quit worrying. I couldn't love you any more if you were my sister. Please go now, you shouldn't be seen in a place like this." Kate stood up and kissed Anna on the forehead and handed her back to her mother.

"Ye shouldn't be seen in a place like this either, me girl." Mary stood up, hugged Kate, and started for the door. Her eyes were wet with tears that she didn't want Kate to see. Mary saw a man come up to Kate as she was leaving. She turned to wave at Kate and saw her flash that beautiful smile at him. Mary watched for a minute as the man spoke to her, and a flirtatious aura transformed her face into a girl she didn't recognize. The sudden change in Kate's demeanor surprised Mary, as the anger she had shown only seconds before had disappeared. Mary left before Kate realized she was watching her. A feeling of hopelessness and guilt overtook Mary as she climbed in the wagon next to John, who had loaded the supplies they needed in the wagon while she went to the saloon. He didn't like Mary going in there all by herself, but she had insisted that she needed to talk to Kate alone.

Mary didn't know how to help her friend. She didn't know what she could say or do, to talk her into coming back. Her prayers didn't seem to be working, and she wondered if God had forsaken her. The nausea was much worse with this pregnancy, and she was not eating right because of it. Her sleep was constantly interrupted with thoughts of Kate at the saloon, and from the guilt caused by protecting Sean.

Things were bad enough, when a letter arrived from her sister, Margaret. The shock was almost too much for Mary. A severe strain of influenza had hit the bay area, which her mother and father had both caught, and died from, within two weeks of each other. When her mother died, her father seemed to lose all reason to fight for his own life, and according to the letter, he just quit taking nourishment. Margaret said that many elderly had succumbed to the virus. Several of her relatives had contracted the flu too, but everyone else had survived. Mary was too ill to travel, so she missed her parents' funeral and grieved deeply for both of them.

As the months went by, she found herself becoming sullen and losing her temper with John and Anna over minor occurrences. She seemed to be angry and miserable all of the time, and all she wanted to do was sleep. John confided in Sean that he was very worried about Mary, so Sean decided he must tell Kate.

When Sean approached her at the saloon she glared at him. Kate had made it quite clear that he was not to talk to her at all. Anger spread across her face as she realized he intended to talk to her, and she abruptly turned away.

Sean grabbed her arm. "Miss Murphy, could I talk to ye for a few minutes? It's important."

"You can talk to her if you buy her a drink," the bartender interrupted.

Sean laid some money on the counter. "Bring the lady a drink."

"How about yourself?"

"Coffee would be fine, if you have some."

Sean led the angry Kate to a table, and he waited until the bartender delivered the drinks, before he spoke to her. "Kate, John is very worried about Mary. She is very melancholy and not acting like herself at all. He says she is eating very little and that she cries all of the time. Little Anna is crying all the time too. Can ye do something? They need ye, Kate. Mary needs ye right now. For their sake, can ye forget me evilness and come back to the house?"

"You better not be lying to me, Sean Foley."

"I swear it on me dead mother's grave, Kate. Come see for yerself. If ye don't want to stay, I'll bring ye back in the morn."

"All right, Sean, but you better be telling it like it is. I'll meet you outside at ten o'clock. I'll have to sneak out the back door or Jake would never let me go. I'll leave him a note, grab my things, and meet you at the back door. And, don't you be looking at me or talking to me, Sean Foley, unless it's about Mary or her family."

"Whatever ye say, Katie, I'll be there."

"Don't be calling me Katie or Kate. It's Miss Murphy to you." Every time she looked at him, she saw her baby's face and felt pain in her chest.

"Yes, Ma'am! I'll be waiting outside the back door at ten."

Sean rose and bowed to her, never touching his coffee. He went outside to wait in the buckboard at the end of the road. If he stayed in the saloon, he was afraid he might order a drink.

Kate was shocked when she saw Mary. At six months pregnant she was barely showing because she was so thin. Her skin was sallow, and she seemed to have aged five years in the last few months. Kate felt sick with shame when she saw her friend.

"Oh Mary, I'm so sorry! What have I done? How could I abandon you when you needed me the most? I am so ashamed. You are the one who has always been there for me, and I wasn't here for you when you needed me."

"No, Katie, please don't blame yerself. I just got very homesick I guess. When I heard about me mom and da dying, and I couldn't be there, it was just too much."

"It's my fault. I came up here to help you out, and then I abandoned you."

"No, it's me fault. That thing with Bane and Billy never would have happened, if it weren't fer me. I'm so sorry, Katie."

"So that's it, is it? You are blaming yourself? Don't you dare do that, Mary Sweeney Troy, what happened has happened. It's over, and there isn't anything we can do about it.

"Let's just learn from it and get on with our lives. Seeing you like this just shows me how selfish I am. I'm so sorry! I'll stay as long as you want me to. I'm taking over now. You go lay down, and I'll fix you some broth and tea."

John took Kate's bags to her little makeshift room that still awaited her. He was relieved to see her, and he thanked Sean several times for bringing her back. John invited Sean to stay, but Sean told him that he'd sleep in the barn and said "goodnight."

Mary's despondency disappeared immediately, and Anna returned to her happy self within a few days. Mary gained weight and the color returned to her face. Kate put her mind on helping the Troys, and life improved greatly in the little cabin. Jeremiah Joseph Troy was born on April 1st. The sweet smell of lilacs filled the cabin on the day he arrived, as the purple blossoms on the bush outside the window had opened the day before. Anna was sixteen months old when her brother was born, and the adorable blond was curious. She was at an age where she had to be watched every minute.

When the baby boy was two months old, Kate started making plans to open a ladies' shop in Baker City. She found two expert seamstresses among the ladies who lived there, and one among Ah Kim's cousins. Kate had been designing her own dresses for years. She ordered several bolts of fabric from San Francisco and asked each seamstress to make one of Kate's designs. The owner of the general store agreed to let her display the dresses in his shop. Then she made some cards with her name on them for the owner to give to ladies when they asked about her dresses. She used the calligraphy she had learned in school, to print each card with her name on it.

Kate Murphy
Personal Dress Designs
for every day or special occasions

Her dresses and cards brought the general store business, as women would buy his fabrics and bring them to Kate to have their dresses made. She made a deal with him to order fabric for her at lower prices. When she had enough ladies buying her dresses, she rented the building next door, which was also owned by the general store owner. As it had living quarters upstairs, she was able to move from the Troy cabin, and eventually put her three seamstresses to work. John and Sean built her shelves to display the cloth, and they made some racks to hang her dresses on. Kate ordered some dressmaker mannequins from the Sears & Roebuck catalog, and she displayed her dresses in the window.

Kate still hated Sean, but she admired John so much that she tolerated Sean when he was with him. The arrangement with the store owner worked out well for both of them. As promised, she ordered most of the fabrics through him, and he sent the ladies to her, and sometimes he sent the gentlemen, who wanted to buy their wives something special. Kate sometimes sold the material with a pattern, or her dressmakers would make the dress. Sometimes she would design a special one for a lady. Since there was no other shop like it in town, she became quite successful in a short time. Later, she added accessories like scarves, shawls, hats, and shoes.

Kate usually had her girls watch the shop on weekends, when she went to help Mary and John get settled in their new ranch. John and Mary homesteaded 240 acres about a mile from the small town of Pleasant Valley not long after Jeremiah was born. They purchased another sixty, with the money they got from the sale of the gold nugget and other monies they had saved. The cabin was just too small for the growing family.

They could get 120 acres for each child they had, so they added another 240 adjoining acres, bringing their land to 540 acres. John hoped to add more acreage to his farm as the years went on. The two men worked every weekend for several weeks building Mary's dream house. They hired Ah Kim and several of his cousins to help, when they weren't working the mine. He had his eye on another thousand acres which adjoined his ranch, but he was told that someone already owned it, although no one lived on the land, or seemed to know who the owner was.

The railroad was finished, so John began working his ranch. He hired Sean as his foreman. The two men worked long hours on the land and with the small herd of cattle they owned. There were two creeks that ran through the land, and a wonderful fresh spring. They used the creeks to make an irrigation system to keep his apple and pear orchards wet in the hot summer months. They built the well house over the spring, and piped the water to the ranch house, which they built only a few feet away. The well provided Mary with all the water she needed to run her home.

When John tried to find out who owned the thousand acres he wanted, he found out that Bane was trying to get that land too. No one recognized the name on the recorded deed, but everyone agreed that if Bane found out who the owner was, he would do anything to acquire that land. The townspeople tried to figure out why he wanted the land, as they didn't think he wanted to farm it. It was rumored there was gold on the land, as Bane had been trying to make his fortune ever since arriving in the area.

Mary knew that Bane was still looking for Ah Kim's mine, and she was afraid of what he would do to the owners if he found it. Ah Kim and Mary had never talked about the map, or the mine, since

Bane's men had stolen her bible on the train. She hoped that wasn't where Ah Kim's gold mine was, and that it was just a rumor. John and Mary only wanted the land for their orchards and to graze their cattle. They loved the land, and wanted to leave it to their children and grandchildren. Their fervent wish was that Anna and Jeremiah's children, and grandchildren, would someday inherit and love the land as much as they did.

John started buying cattle, two head at a time. With a little work on breeding his stock, the herd was growing. A small crew of Chinese workers helped him fence in part of the land, as well as planting and harvesting the fruit trees in his orchard. John treated the Chinese people fairly, and paid them well. As a result, they worked hard for him. The ranch was beginning to prosper, and things were looking up for the little family until, as Mary would put it, "the roof fell in!"

Mary was three months pregnant with her third child, Anna was four, and Jeremiah was two, the day she heard the news. Kate rode up fast on horseback, which wasn't like her at all. She usually drove her little rig. Concerned, Mary went to meet her.

"What's the matter, Kate?"

"I have some terrible news, Mary. Please come in and sit, so I can tell you."

"OH, NO! Is John Okay?"

"I'm sure John is fine, Mary. It's not John. Come in the house and sit down please, Mary." Kate helped Mary in the house, and sat her down in the rocker by the fire. Anna and Jeremiah were playing in the corner with some hand carved Chinese dolls that Ah Kim had given them. Kate looked at the dolls and began crying.

"What is it, Kate? What is the matter?" Mary started to tremble, knowing if it made Kate cry, the news must be bad.

"Mary, I'm so sorry. I came as soon as I heard the news. Ah Kim has been murdered."

Mary gasped. "Oh Lord, no!"

A flood of tears poured down her cheeks. "Me dear friend! Oh no! What happened?"

"All I know is that seven miners were found murdered, and their gold stolen. I heard it before the bodies were brought to town in two wagons. I recognized Ah Kim and one of his cousins."

John came in just then. "What's up, Kate? I saw you riding in very fast."

"Oh, John, it's the most terrible news." Mary sobbed. "Ah Kim has been murdered."

"Oh, no!" John felt as if he'd been punched in the stomach. "What happened?"

"Seven miners were murdered, and he was one of them. I thought I'd better come and tell you, because I knew what a good friend he was."

"Mary, I'm going into town to see what I can find out. Kate, can ye stay with Mary until I return?"

"Of course, I closed the store. I'll stay until morning."

"Thank ye, Kate. I'll be back as soon as I can, Mary. I'll find out what happened, I promise."

John met Sean racing toward the ranch on horseback. He could tell by the look on John's face that he had already heard the news. Sean reigned in his mare and rode with John back to Baker City. It was dusk when they reached the main street. They dismounted in front of the sheriff's office, just as the sheriff was leaving the building.

"Sheriff, wait up. I'd like to talk to ye."

"What about, John?"

"About the Chinese miners you brought in today."

"You mean them dead yellow eyes?"

John jumped off his horse and got into the sheriff's face. "Them 'yellow eyes' put through that train track that brings most of our supplies here, Sheriff, and from what I've seen, most are better humans then ye ever thought of being."

"Now watch what you're saying, John Troy."

"No, Sheriff, ye watch what ye are saying! Ah Kim was a dear friend of mine, and a finer man ye will find nowhere, so don't ye be bad mouthing him, or any of his cousins. Just tell me what happened."

"Calm down, John. Come inside." He went back in and sat behind his desk. John and Sean stood, waiting for his answer.

"Some other Chinamen brought them in. They said they found them in the mine. Their throats had been slit, and there was blood everywhere. They swear that two bags full of gold nuggets are missing too."

"Where is this mine, Sheriff? I want to go take a look."

"The Chinamen are taking me there tomorrow. If you want to go along, I'm sure the Chinamen trust you and will allow it. They mentioned your wife, and said that Ah Kim told them to go to her if anything happened to him. Do you know anything about it?"

"No, I don't." Suddenly, John remembered that Mary had something important that belonged to Ah Kim. A wave of fear overcame him as he realized her life might be in danger again. If it was Bane who did this, he knew she was at risk.

"Oh, dear God! Mary! Let's go, Sean." He turned and rushed from the building, hopped on his horse, and took off for the ranch with Sean close behind him. The sheriff followed them outside and called out to them, but they just kept riding.

"Come to the ranch in the morning," John hollered into the wind over his shoulder. "We'll go there together." John knew the killer had to be Bane.

They saw riders off in the distance, dust still not settled from where they had left in a hurry. Mary and Kate were crying hysterically when they entered the cabin. Kate was lying on the floor holding her face. Sean went to her. Blood was pouring from a deep gash on her right cheek, and her eye was turning black. Mary was holding Jeremiah and they were both sobbing. "Where's Anna?" John shouted.

"They took her. They took me little girl." Mary's face was a flood of tears, and she could barely speak. "They just burst in the door without warning. Bane kept telling me to give him what Ah Kim left with me. I told him I didn't know what he was talking about. I knew he'd kill us all as soon as I gave it to him, and I promised Ah Kim. Only four came inside. One held each of us. They stole me Anna! Bane put her under his arm, and Kate tried to get her. Bane hit her in the face with his fist twice, and left her bleeding on the floor. One of the other men had Jeremiah. I thought they were going to take him too, but he kept squirming, and screaming, and the man set him down hard on the floor. It all happened so fast. I think they knew ye were coming, so they left. Bane hollered his demands from the door."

John started to go after them.

"Wait, John! I know where they went." She tried to get control of herself, so she could save her precious daughter. "And I know what they want." Taking a deep breath she went to the mantle over the fireplace. The beautiful box that John had given her so long ago sat there. Mary took out the rosary, slid out the secret compartment, and pulled out the envelope Ah Kim had given her for safe keeping.

"Ah Kim asked me to give this to a lawyer, and his cousin, if anything happened to him. I think this is what they were looking for. Bane said to bring the deed, and meet him on top of Lookout Mountain at sunup tomorrow, or he would kill me little Anna." She started crying again. "He said he'd kill her if I brought anyone with me besides Kate and Jeremiah. Me poor little baby!" She sobbed and sobbed as John comforted her and Jeremiah.

"Don't worry, Mary, we will get her."

"What if he harms her in the meantime?"

"He won't. If he does, he's a dead man, and I'll be the one to kill him. Open the envelope, Mary, we must know exactly what he's after if we're to save us all. I have a feeling he has plans for ye on top of Lookout Mountain."

Sean was holding a wet rag on Kate's face, to stop the bleeding, and she was weakly leaning against him. Mary carefully opened the envelope and pulled out its contents. There was a long hand written will, which had been witnessed by an attorney and Quan. Inside the will was a deed to the one thousand acres of land that John wanted to buy. It was in Ah Kim's father's American name. An attached document explained the alias, and another denoted that Ah Kim's name had been added to the deed. On the bottom Ah Kim had deeded it over to John Troy and Mary Sweeney in case of his death. Mary and John were in shock. Then they read the will. It was in legal terms, most of which they didn't understand, but they knew what it said. Ah Kim had secretly owned the land all along. He and his cousins were mining on the property. Ah Kim wanted his cousins to continue to work the mine for the next ten years, while John and Mary were to receive ten percent of the profits. After that, the mine would belong to John and Mary. The will stated that he trusted only John and Mary to carry out his plans, and to make sure his cousins received their shares. He was sure that by that time, they would all be wealthy and have built a good life for themselves. Ah Kim wanted a Chinese burial, and to eventually have his remains shipped back to their homeland, so he could be buried there.

They sat there without speaking for a time, their minds working overtime.

"How do we save Anna, and follow Ah Kim's wishes?" John voiced out loud.

"I have an idea." Sean got up abruptly. "I'm going into town to speak to some of Ah Kim's cousins."

"Bane said he'd kill her if we told anyone!" Mary pleaded.

"Don't worry, Mary, I will be cautious. I know who to speak to. I think they can help us. I will be back before nightfall with a workable plan, I hope."

"Hurry, Sean, and be careful." Kate said. For the first time, her heart softened toward the man that she had hated for so long.

Chapter Thirty-Three

"Lookout Mountain"

Eastern Oregon ~ 1889

"Tears were streaming down her tiny face from eyes filled with fear."

It was close to midnight when Sean returned with four Chinamen. They came through the woods behind the house in case they were being watched. The group stayed up all night working out a plan. It was still dark when Mary, Kate, and Jeremiah boarded the wagon. John kissed Mary gently and told her to try to stay calm. Sean held Kate's hand as he confided in her.

"Kate, there is something important I want ye to do on Monday. There is a package coming on the afternoon train, and ye must promise me to pick it up, just in case I am not able to pick it up meself. I promise to make sure that nothing happens to ye today, but please be careful. Bane and his men will do anything to get that land. Before we go, please tell me ye forgive me for all the pain I've caused ye over these last few years. I'd take it all back if I could. I am so sorry, Katie! Please forgive me for me sins."

"Sean, I do forgive you. Let's just put it in the past. Be careful."

They went into the barn to board the wagon. He kissed her on the cheek that wasn't swollen, wrapped her shawl around her, and helped her up to the bench. Two of the smallest Chinese men climbed into two coffin-like compartments the men had stayed up all night building and attaching underneath the wagon. They had to ride flat on their stomachs in the narrow cubicles. They each had a flask of water, and as members of the Tong, they had their long knives. Mary drove the wagon toward Lookout Mountain. Kate sat on the hard bench next to her, holding Jeremiah. The other men went back into the barn, and they pulled out the other wagon that was hidden there. John and Sean climbed into the two large empty barrels in the back of the wagon, taking with them flasks of water and loaded guns. The other two Chinese got into the front of the wagon, and after waiting fifteen minutes, drove it toward Lookout Mountain.

Mary was so nervous that her hands were shaking as she held the reins, but drove the horses as fast as she could. She was praying the rosary in her mind and worrying about her "little Anna." Kate was holding Jeremiah and singing to him softly. His little eyes were tired, and he soon drifted off to sleep with the movement of the wagon and Kate's soft singing. In an envelope inside the bodice of her dress Mary held a deed. The man who called himself Hong had copied the deed perfectly, only leaving John and Mary's names on it, and signed the wrong name where the deed was supposed to be certified. He had written on the old parchment paper that Hannah had given Mary long ago. It wasn't the same paper as the original deed, but she hoped Bane and his men would be fooled by it. Her heart was beating so fast that she could barely breathe. The fear that welled up inside her was far worse than any she had felt before. Not knowing whether her child was alive or dead, or what her little girl had gone through since her kidnapping, was the worst part for Mary. 'Anna must be even more afraid than we are,' she thought. Tears flowed freely down her cheeks. Even though the temperature was in the low forties, Mary's shivering was not from the cold.

Kate rocked the little boy quietly, as the wagon took them to meet their fate. The right side of her face was swollen and throbbing with pain. Contrary to Mary's reaction, Kate's pain and worry for her goddaughter just made her angrier as the rough road brought them closer to their destination. Although Lookout Mountain wasn't as tall a mountain as many in the area, they could see why Bane had chosen it as their meeting place, and how it had earned its name. There was no way anyone could sneak up on the mountain. From its plateau you could see everywhere. Trees surrounded the base of the mountain, but around the trees were open areas where anyone approaching could be seen.

Mary tried to control the trembling, but it continued as she reached the trees. She prayed silently that they would all survive the events she knew were ahead of them. Kate tried to control her anger as she held the tiny child protectively against her bosom. Bane had told them to bring the boy. He had threatened to kill Anna if they arrived without the little boy. They assumed he meant to kill them all, and that John and Sean would be Bane's next victims. Their plan had to work!

"Kate, just take care that nothing happens to Jeremiah, I will look out for Anna."

"Don't worry, Mary, I will not let anything happen to this little guy."

Two men on horseback stepped out of the trees. The big one with the full beard and large black hat spoke first.

"You better be alone." His booming voice woke Jeremiah, who started crying at the sight of the men who took his sister. Pointing his rifle at Mary he said, "Shut that kid up and follow me."

Kate rocked and sang to Jeremiah, covering his head with the blanket so he couldn't see.

The bearded man led them up the path, while the other man followed, after making sure no one was following them. The narrow rocky trail circled the mountain as it climbed. Mary feared the horses would slip, and that they would all fall to their death. It was barely big enough for the wagon. It seemed forever before they reached the top. Jeremiah continued to whimper under the blanket, even though Kate kept rocking him, and Mary continued to pray silently. When they finally reached the top, the man led them to where Bane and another man were standing in front of a small tree and clump of bushes. Mary didn't see Anna and she started to panic. Bane stood up as she approached.

"Where's me daughter?" Mary demanded as she got out of the wagon, her fear was turning to anger. Kate stayed where she was, rocking the little boy.

"Where's the deed? You'll get your daughter when I get the deed."

"Ye won't get yer deed till I get me daughter."

Bane laughed his wicked laugh. "I can take it from you, after I kill you."

Mary walked to the edge of the cliff while she spoke, as if looking for her daughter.

Her adrenaline took over as she pulled the envelope out of her bodice.

"Shoot me and I'll destroy yer deed on me way down the mountain."

Bane laughed again. "There, there, Mary, control that Irish temper, or you'll be killing your little girl."

"If ye hurt any of us, me husband will track ye down and kill ye."

"Don't worry, Mary, I'll make sure I take care of your yellow-bellied husband next. Two of me men are on their way to your ranch right now. I'd like to have your land too."

Mary's stomach hurt, and the new babe was stirring considerably.

"Jest give me back me little girl, and I'll give ye the deed. Then ye can leave us all alone. Ye'll have yer gold mine and yer land. We won't tell anyone. Can't ye just do the right and decent thing for once in yer life?"

"Ah, Mary, you are a spunky tart. Too bad you'll be dead soon."

Just then the man who had followed the wagon spoke. "Bane, there's another wagon coming."

"Who did you bring with you?" Bane said angrily.

"No one, we came alone."

Bane pulled out an eyeglass and looked toward the wagon. "Oh, it's just some 'yellow eyes' probably headed for that mine. Donaldson go head them off. They probably plan on loading gold in those barrels."

The two men climbed back on their horses and rode down the path to the bottom of the mountain.

"Where's me daughter?"

Bane motioned to the fourth man to get the girl. The man went into the brush and came out with Anna. Her hands were tied with rope, and a scarf was around her mouth. Tears were streaming down her tiny face from eyes filled with fear.

"Dear God! Untie her, Bane, if ye want this deed. How could ye do that to a child? Ye are the devil himself!"

Bane laughed loudly, and so did his stocky friend. He signaled for the other man to untie her. Anna pulled the scarf out of her mouth as soon as her hands were free, and she ran into her mother's arms sobbing loudly.

"You, the murdering bitch in the wagon, get down and go stand by Mary there."

Kate slowly climbed down from the wagon, carrying the whimpering child. Just then, shots rang out from the bottom of the mountain. Anna screamed and clutched her mother's legs.

"Two more 'yellow eyes' bite the dust." Bane's devilish laugh echoed throughout the valley. Mary held the deed over the cliff as she pushed her little girl behind her.

"Give me the deed, Mary."

"Why, so ye can shoot us all too?"

"Now, Mary, you know I wouldn't really hurt you."

"Put the gun down, Bane."

"Don't get excited, Mary, just give me the deed. If you drop that deed you will all be dead very soon."

"Seems to me we'll be dead anyway."

"Don't you trust me, Mary, me girl?"

"Not for a second!"

As Bane moved toward them slowly, Mary and Kate stood close together, shielding the children from the two men closing in on them. They stood just inches from the cliff. The two hidden Tong suddenly appeared from nowhere with long knives in their hands. At the same time, John and Sean came up the path from the road on foot. The Tong let out a blood curdling scream as they flew through the air toward the surprised criminals. Bane turned and fired his gun. He got off four shots before the four men got there. One of the Tong fell to the ground, the other killed Bane's companion with one swoosh of his long blade. As Bane fired, Sean jumped in front of the women and children and took the bullet in his stomach. He slowly fell to the ground. John landed with full force on Bane, but the big man held his ground and hit John with the butt of his pistol, knocking him down and stunning him for a second. Bane aimed at John, and Mary screamed:

"Here goes yer deed, Bane!"

Holding it over the cliff she ripped it in half, taking his attention away from John, who had regained his wits and lunged at Bane's legs bringing him to the ground. John's anger took over, and he started beating Bane mercilessly. They struggled for the gun that finally fell from Bane's hand. Mary scrambled on her knees to the gun. Bane rolled over and pulled out a knife. He raised the knife in one hand as he pummeled John with his other fist. Then Mary fired the gun.

Bane's mouth opened in surprise, as he realized the blood bubbling from his chest was his own. A piercing scream came from his mouth as he fell backwards down the rugged mountain, hitting every pointed rock on his way to the depths of hell.

Mary dropped the gun, grabbed Anna, and ran to John's side. Kate sat Jeremiah on the ground as she tended to Sean's wound. The other two Chinese arrived with Bane's two men tied over their saddles. They went to their fallen companion's side. John's face and hands were bruised and bloody, but he was okay. He picked up his daughter who was crying hysterically.

"It's okay, me little darling. It's all over now and we are all okay. Those bad men will never hurt anyone again. Did they hurt ye?"

Anna continued to sob, "No, Papa, I don't think they hurt me. I was just so scared."

Putting her head on her father's shoulder, she continued to whimper.

"John, I just killed a man."

"Ye saved all of our lives, Mary. Don't ye dare be feeling badly about ridding the world of that bastard. God be praised for your quick wits. He was going to kill us all, me girl." It was then that John saw that Sean was not moving.

"No! Sean! Is he okay?" The Troys surrounded Sean and Kate, and Mary picked up her thumb sucking little boy, who sat in a daze beside Kate. Sean was bleeding profusely from a stomach wound, and although he was breathing heavily, he was unconscious. Kate was ripping her petticoat in pieces, using it to stop the seeping blood from the wound. She pressed tightly for several minutes while John wrapped a longer narrow strip around his chest and tied it tightly. The men lifted Sean into the back of the wagon, and they put the slain Chinaman in the wagon with him. Kate rode with them in the back of the wagon. Mary, John, and the two children rode in the front, while the other three men drove the other wagon. They retrieved Bane, when they got to the bottom of the mountain, and put him with his deceased companion in the back of the other wagon, then tied the two captive men's horses to the back.

There were horses coming toward them as they neared Baker City. John stopped and reloaded his gun, expecting the two men that were sent to kill him. When the dust cleared, he realized it was the sheriff. Not knowing whether he could trust the sheriff, John still held his gun.

"John Troy, I'm glad to see you're not hurt. I came to warn you that Bane was out to get you. Bane shot one of his men last night in an argument and left him for dead alongside the road. Ted Larkin found the man still alive this morning and brought him to town. He told us Bane was coming to kill you all. What do you have in the back of the wagon?"

"Bane's dead, Sheriff. He kidnapped me little Anna last night, so he could take the deed to the thousand acres that sit next to me land. He and his men killed those Chinamen in the mine. He found out that Ah Kim owned the land, and that he had given Mary the deed. We need to hurry into town, Sheriff. Bane shot Sean Foley and he's bad off. We must get him to the doctor soon."

"I'll follow you and you can give me the details when we get to town."

Pushing the horses as fast as they could go, it still took over an hour to get to town from the mountain. Kate kept ripping off more of her petticoat trying to stop the constant seepage from his wound. When they got to the doctor's house, John and the Chinamen carried Sean inside to the back where he had his office. Sean was still unconscious and moaning when they arrived. The doctor removed the bullet and dressed his wound, while Kate and the doctor's wife assisted. John and Mary took the children and went to the jail to talk to the sheriff. The Tong took their slain cousin to Baker City's Chinatown to prepare him for burial.

"I'm sorry if I've caused your family any problems in the past," the sheriff began. "I know that Bane made things rough for you these past couple of years."

"Never mind, Sheriff, it's in the past." John was too upset to listen to the sheriff's blubbering. He just wanted to get his family home. "Do ye know what happened at the mine?"

"Yes, I do. One of the Chinamen escaped when Bane and his men showed up. The man hid deep in the mine, and he didn't find his way here until this morning. He seemed dazed when he walked into town. It took him a while to tell the story as he was very upset. One of his cousins had to translate for us, as he doesn't speak much English."

"Did he see everything?"

"Yes, he's lucky he's alive! Ah Kim and the others suffered greatly at the hands of Bane and his men. I don't know if your wife wants to hear this."

"Mary, do ye want to take the children and wait for me in the wagon?"

"No, John, I want to hear what happened to Ah Kim. Besides, Anna is asleep from exhaustion, and Jeremiah doesn't understand what we are talking about." Both children clung to their mother, one on each knee, as she rocked them gently back and forth.

"It seems the miners were hard at work when Bane and five men showed up with guns. He recognized Ah Kim, and seemed to know that he was the leader of the group. The man said Bane tortured him trying to find out who had a claim on the mine, and who owned the land. Bane ranted that the mine belonged to him, that three Chinamen had given it to him a long time ago. Ah Kim told him the mine belonged to him and his family, and that he would never give it to him. Bane asked him how he got possession of it, and Ah Kim boldly said his uncle had deeded the land to him after Bane had killed his father many years ago. He laughed at Ah Kim's words and started whipping him continually with his horsewhip. No matter how Bane tortured him, Ah Kim wouldn't give in, and sign the quit claim deed that Bane had prepared, so he started on his cousins. The cousins kept telling Ah Kim in Chinese not to tell Bane, even though they were being tortured."

The sheriff took a deep breath and sighed before he spoke again. "Those men were much braver than I would have been. Ah Kim must have known they were going to kill them all anyway. Bane cut out one of the men's tongues out before he killed him. He tied one of the men to four stakes, lit a kerosene soaked torch, and burned him, while the others watched. One of the Chinamen got free from the cowboy who was holding him, and grabbed Bane's rifle. He mercifully shot the burning man to stop his screaming. Bane's man shot the Chinaman before he could kill Bane. The other prisoners fought bravely to get away, but they had no weapons. Ah Kim's hands were tied. Bane's men killed two of them in the struggle. Then they lit a fire and were going to kill the last man by burning him alive. Ah Kim couldn't stand it any longer and finally conceded and said, 'Will you kill us quickly if I tell you where the deed is?' Bane said he would. Ah Kim said 'Will you promise not to hurt the one who has the deed?' Bane swore on his mother's grave and untied them both. Ah Kim told them he had left the deed entrusted to Mary, but that she didn't know she had it. The Chinaman said Bane laughed as he spoke his last words to Ah Kim. 'Sorry, Yellow Eyes, I lied!'"

The sheriff took another deep breath, before he told them the last of the story. "He slit both of their throats and left them to die. The hiding Chinaman was so scared and said he couldn't move for the longest time. He hid deep in the mine and never heard his relatives arrive to find the bodies. Now you tell me what happened today."

Mary dried her eyes, and then told him about Anna's kidnapping and the drive to Lookout Mountain to rescue her daughter. John related Sean's plan, and his ride into town to get the Tong to help. The sheriff seemed surprised when John bragged that Mary had been the hero, the one who had shot Bane and saved them all.

"What about the men who were coming to kill John, Sheriff? Where are they?"

"There are four men in the cell behind me. They are the last of Bane's gang. Two of them are the two men you just brought in, and the other two were just arrested at your ranch. After the Chinamen showed up, I took some men and went to your ranch. The two I arrested were skulking around outside when I arrived. I recognized them from the Chinaman's description. I sent two of my men back to town to lock them up, and I took the other two with me to look for you. They told me that Bane went to Lookout Mountain, and that's where I was headed when I ran into you. Thank you, Mrs. Troy, for saving me a heck of a lot of trouble. I'm just sorry about your friends."

"Sheriff, last I heard, ye were calling them 'yellow eyes.'"

The sheriff looked sheepish. "I want to apologize for that. I was wrong. What I heard about their bravery today changed my mind about these people. Guess a man can't be right all the time."

"Glad to hear that, Sheriff."

Just then Kate came in.

"How's Sean?" Mary asked.

"He's not doing well, Mary. He's still unconscious. I'm going to stay by his side all night. Why don't you all go home? The children need to be in their own beds."

"Ye are right, Kate. Mary's exhausted too. I'll come back first thing in the morning."

"I'm coming back with ye, John. Sean is me uncle."

"All right, Mary, if ye are feeling up to it."

The ride home seemed to take forever. Though they were worried about Sean they were exhausted. After they ate a simple meal, they put the children in bed with them, and they all fell sound asleep.

Chapter Thirty-Four

"Saving Sean"

Eastern Oregon ~ 1889

"Always remember to forget the things that made you sad, but never forget to remember the things that made you glad. Always remember to forget the friends who proved untrue, but don't forget to remember those that stuck by you."

A confusion of emotions ran through Mary, as she woke up with the images from her dreams running through her mind; Sean struggling to survive, Bane burning in hell, Ah Kim's torturous death, Anna fleeing Bane, and Mary shooting him. Those events seemed to be etched in her brain, and they continually flashed through her tortured sleep. The child inside her was moving, so she was relieved that the new baby seemed to have survived the ordeal. She lay there, quietly thanking the Lord for keeping her family safe, praying for Sean, and for the souls of Ah Kim and his cousins, who had suffered such torment before their deaths. She also prayed to free her soul from the misery of the hatred she felt for Bane and his band of marauders. Then she added one more: 'Lord, have mercy for her enemies' souls, even though she knew in her heart where they had gone.'

In spite of the nightmares, Mary felt a huge weight lift from her. For the first time since her arrival in Oregon, the fear of Bane was gone. She had always felt like the lamb in the flock waiting for the wolf to attack. Most of that fear had been with her since she'd left the ship in Boston. Now she was just worried about Sean. Rising quickly, she got dressed and went to check on the children who were already up with John. He had already started the fire, so the house was warm. He was outside feeding the livestock. She was delighted to hear the children's laughter as she went into their room and found them playing happily. They seemed to have conveniently forgotten the events of the last two days.

Mary walked around her new home, really enjoying it for the first time. Maybe they would now have some normalcy in their lives. The little cabin that they had finally left had been far too small for their growing family. There were still many things that needed to be finished on their new home. It would eventually have five bedrooms, but they already had a real bathroom. Then she remembered Sean, and she felt guilty even thinking of the house, with his life hanging on by a thread. He had helped John build their home, and had changed his life, becoming a fine human being and showing great remorse for his past sins.

Mary took the children with her to gather eggs from the chicken coup and ham from the smoke house. It was a beautiful day with a blue sky and sunshine. They were all singing happily when they returned to the house. Mary changed the children's clothes and got them ready to go into town. Then she fried some eggs and bacon and made biscuits and coffee. The smell of the bacon frying brought John in with a pail of fresh milk. Anna set the homemade jelly along with freshly churned butter on the table, and the small family sat down to eat.

John decided to say; *"Always remember to forget the things that made you sad, but never forget to remember the things that made you glad. Always remember to forget the friends who proved untrue, but don't forget to remember those that have stuck by you."*

Mary added; *"Often has the likely failed and the unlikely succeeded. Thanks be to God this time!"*

"Amen, Amen! I'm hoping ye'll be getting back to yer little Irish sayings, Mary. I haven't heard ye spouting any of late."

"I guess I haven't, have I? I didn't know ye were that fond of me blessings, John."

"Aye, that I am, Mary. I'm very fond of everything ye do and say." He stood up and kissed her on the cheek. The children giggled and Mary blushed.

"We'd better be getting into town to see how Sean is doing."

"Yes, give me a minute to put the dishes in a pan to soak, John. I'll wait till I return to wash them. Anna, get your shawl and bonnet, and help Jeremiah get his sweater on, please."

"Yes, Mummy."

It was still early when the Troy wagon arrived in town. Their ranch was eighteen miles East of Baker City in Pleasant Valley. John brought Ah Kim's will and the deed with them. He wanted to talk to Ah Kim's relatives and the town lawyer, before he filed the documents properly. They didn't want any more problems over the land. They went directly to the doctor's house, where he took care of his patients in the two back rooms. Kate was putting a damp cloth on Sean's head when they entered, and his eyes were still closed.

"How is he, Kate?"

"Not good, Mary. Even though the doctor took the bullet out, it's a stomach wound, and he's lost a lot of blood. He has a concussion too. I guess he got that when he hit the ground. That's why he's been in and out of consciousness. I think he's just sleeping now, because he woke up earlier and was talking to me, but the doctor said it doesn't look good."

Sean moaned and slowly opened his eyes.

"Hello, Sean. How are you feeling?"

"Hello Katie." He was so weak that his voice was barely audible.

"Don't talk, Sean. Save your strength for when you're better. John and Mary are here too."

"I must talk now, Katie. I don't think I'll be getting much better."

"Now, don't you be saying that, Sean Foley. You've just got a lot of recovering to do."

"No, Kate, I don't think so." The pain was evident in his voice. "Kate, please tell me that ye forgive me for what I've done to ye."

"I forgive you, Sean, I forgive you."

Tears filled Sean's eyes. "I can't tell ye how happy that makes me, Katie. I love ye with all my heart. I'm so sorry for not doing right by ye. I'm hoping I can make it up to ye before I die."

"Forget it, Sean, there's no need. You risked your life to save us all yesterday. That certainly makes up for everything."

"Katie, what time is it?"

"It's morning, Sean."

"Don't forget to meet the train, Kate." Then he moaned heavily. Kate poured the medicine into the spoon and fed it to Sean. The doctor told her to give him some whenever the pain got bad. He had gone to deliver a baby. Mary and John sat with Kate while she tended to Sean. His breathing got very shallow, and Kate had tears in her eyes. About an hour later they heard the train whistle.

"I'll stay with Sean, Kate. Ye go get the package for Sean. John, why don't ye go with her, and make sure she gets something to eat, because I don't believe she's eaten much since she's been here."

"The doctor's wife made me eat last night, but I haven't eaten since then. I guess I just haven't been very hungry."

"Come on, Kate."

John took Kate by the arm and led her out the door. Anna and Jeremiah sat on the floor playing with their Chinese puzzles, while Mary tended to Sean. The train was already there when Kate and John arrived, so they went inside the station and up to the counter.

"I'm supposed to pick up a package for Sean Foley!" The man behind the counter was stacking some boxes in the back room.

"I don't see anything for Sean," he said after looking through the stack.

"Well, maybe he was wrong about when it was due to arrive." She said and turned to go. As she started to walk out the door, she saw a young boy of about ten sitting on the bench with a small carpetbag in his lap. There was something very familiar about him. He looked scared and alone, and he had an envelope in his hands. Kate saw Sean's name on the envelope. Then realization hit her like a bolt of lightning. The shock of "who" the boy was, almost knocked her over. It took her a second to get her composure. She had no idea what the boy knew about her. Taking a deep breath, she walked over to him and sat down.

"Are you here to meet Sean Foley?"

"Yes, ma'am." He spoke with a thick Irish brogue.

Kate's eyes filled with tears. His hair was dark red and curly like her own and his eyes were the same green, yet he looked like Sean. He was the most beautiful boy she had ever seen. She suddenly found something deep within her that had been missing since she left Ireland ten years ago. Her heart felt whole again.

"My name is Kate. Sean sent me here to meet you."

"Are you me mother?" The boy spoke quietly.

The tears started flowing freely down her face. "I am." She choked back the tears as she took him in her arms and rocked him back and forth. John looked shocked as he sat next to them without speaking a word. After Kate got control of herself she spoke again. "Are you hungry? You must be."

"I'm starved, Mum."

"Of course you are, and so am I. Let's go to the hotel and get something to eat."

"This letter is fer ye, I guess." He said taking her hand.

When they sat in the hotel dining room, Kate opened the letter.

Dear Mr. Foley,

Thank you for taking in the boy. I thought it best under the circumstances to tell him the facts of his birth. His adoptive parents taking sick like they did, was very hard for him. I was afraid if he stayed here he might come down with the consumption too. It is damp and cold in the orphanage, and America must be a better place for a young boy to grow up. Since you said the boy's mother was there also, I thought it best to tell him of his parentage. I assume you two are married now, or are getting married, or you wouldn't want to raise the boy. He's a good boy, and has been raised well. Enjoy him and take good care of him. I have grown quite fond of him in the six months that he lived here.

Fondly,

Sister Mary Catherine

Kate handed the letter to John, after she read it, and began talking to her son. John was still in shock as Mary had told him nothing of her friend's secret.

"Where's me Da?" the boy asked.

"Bobby, I'm sorry to tell you that your Da is not in the best shape right now. I will take you to see him, but I must warn you, he's been shot."

"Shot?"

John spoke for the first time. "Your Da is a real hero, me boy. He jumped in front of a bullet to save yer mother, me wife and children. If it weren't for his swift movements, I am sure a couple of them wouldn't be on this earth right now. Ye should be very proud to have such a brave father."

"Who shot him?"

"The man who shot him is dead, and so is the rest of his gang. They were very bad men and they hurt a lot of people. After ye finish your meal, we'll go see your Da. If anything would make him feel better, it would be seeing ye."

They quickly finished eating and went back to the doctor's house.

Mary was sitting in a chair by the bed feeding Sean some broth when they entered the room. He was very weak, but he sat up a little and smiled when Kate and the boy entered the room.

"Sean, this is Bobby, your son. Sister Mary Catherine told him we were his parents." Kate beamed with pride. Mary almost fell off of her chair. John went to her side with a smile on his face.

"Are ye goin' to be all right, Da?" The boy asked.

"I don't know, me boy. I'm hurt pretty bad. But, if I don't make it, ye just remember, seeing ye here has made me the happiest man in this whole world. We have been sorely missing ye for all these years, me boy."

"Mr. Troy said ye were a real hero!"

"If there's any hero here, it's ye, Bobby. Coming all the way from Ireland all by yerself, and going through the last ten years without yer real mum and pop. Believe me, ye are the real hero."

"Aw, it weren't so bad," he said, looking real proud.

"Are ye and mum married?" He asked suddenly.

"You got here just in time, Bobby." Kate said softly. "I heard Father Mulroney is in town. Your father and I are going to be married tomorrow, right here in this room. John, would you go see if you can firm up those plans?"

Sean's eyes began filling with tears again, and a weak smile came to his face. Mary still sat in the chair, speechless. Anna brought her little brother over to meet their second cousin, and John grinned broadly as he went out the door to look up the priest.

Father Mulroney arrived at quarter till twelve for the ceremony the next morning. Sean was too weak to be moved. Mary, John, and the children arrived in their best clothes. Kate donned the best gown from her shop, and she had her seamstresses sew some new clothes for Bobby.

John had informed the priest of the urgency of their request, and he agreed to marry them without the normal six weeks waiting period, because of the special circumstances. Mary and the children picked some wildflowers for Kate's bouquet, and John bought a gold ring from one of Ah Kim's cousins. The priest heard both Kate and Sean's confessions privately, before he started saying the private wedding mass. Since they were both Catholics, he agreed to have a full church ceremony in the small room. The dresser in the corner served as his altar. Kate's eyes were wet throughout the ceremony. Sean held his bride's hand, and he smiled at her in between the sharp pains. He was so weak that he couldn't lift his head from the down pillow. Bobby stood on the other side of the bed, with his hand proudly on his father's shoulder. When Kate said, "I do," Sean brought her tiny hand to his lips and kissed it. He held her hand there until he slipped the gold ring on her finger. They both took the Holy Eucharist and sipped the wine at the end of the ceremony, uniting them fully in the sacrament of Holy Matrimony. When the service was over, Kate bent down and gently kissed Sean on the lips. The kiss transformed his face; a calm, peaceful serenity replaced the pain.

Mary took Bobby home with her every night that week, while Kate spent the nights in the chair next to Sean's bed. Bobby came back every day, and spent his time getting to know his parents. Father Mulroney came every day to give them communion. The doctor told Kate five days after their wedding that Sean was dying.

"There's nothing I can do, Mrs. Foley. He's lost too much blood. I think he's bleeding internally. A stomach wound is a painful thing, and it usually becomes infected no matter what I try. I'm very sorry."

Kate went to her shop and cried bitterly in the back room. Then she dried her eyes and went back to Sean, smiling as best she could. The hardest part was telling Bobby. He cried and clung to her for an hour, while Mary and John stayed with Sean. That night, John took his children back to the ranch, and Kate, Mary, and Bobby stayed with Sean. Sean was so weak that he could barely open his eyes. Kate sat by the bed and held his hand in hers.

"Kate?"

"Yes, Sean."

"I love ye, Kate. I love ye, Bobby."

"I love you, Sean."

"I love ye too, Da."

"I am sorry I can't stay with ye, but God has other plans for me. He is calling me home."

"Please don't go, Da." They were all crying now. Father Mulroney had given Sean the last rites, and he now stood by the end of the bed praying quietly.

"Please forgive me. Take care of each other. I've got to go." Sean closed his eyes and a peaceful smile overtook his face as his life slipped away.

The three of them clung to each other for a long time. Mary spent the night with Kate and Bobby at Kate's small house in town. Three days later, Sean was buried on John and Mary's land under the big elm tree, where he loved to sit and contemplate the beauty of the land. They held a wake at John and Mary's new home, which Sean had helped build. They all took turns toasting their fallen husband, father, uncle, and friend.

Late that night, Kate and Bobby said their goodbyes as they climbed into Kate's rig. They went back to the little house they now shared in town, where they started their new life together, as Sean would have wanted.

Chapter Thirty-Five

"Anna Troy"

Eastern Oregon ~ 1889-1906

"Now Mary, seems to me, I remember a girl much younger then Anna who set out on her own adventures, without even her parents' permission."

Sean's death had a profound effect on Kate and Bobby. Bobby only met his father and spent a week getting to know him before he lost him. After Sister Mary Catherine had told him about his parents, he had spent a lot of time fantasizing about a wonderful life with a father and mother who loved him. Losing his father so soon was difficult, especially since he had just lost the mother and father who raised him. Kate wished she had forgiven Sean earlier and given him the opportunity to show her his good side. She felt as if she'd wasted too many years on bitterness and anger. Now that she had her son, she knew she must erase all of the pain of the last ten years and devote herself to making a good life for him. Kate worked in her shop during the day and Bobby helped her in the afternoons and on weekends.

The boy went to school during the week. When he first met the other children, they teased him about his heavy Irish brogue, and his work at a ladies' shop. However, the boy had already experienced so much in his short life that he only laughed with them, and soon he became the boy at school who was most admired. The loss of his new found father, and his adoptive parents, showed him how important it was to make the best of every situation. His talent for laughing when things were toughest endeared him to everyone, especially his cousins. The Irish brogue faded as time went on and soon was barely noticeable. The Troy children became his best friends and loyal companions. Bobby often spent weekends at the Troy ranch. Kate worked hard at her business and became quite successful. Miraculously, Baker City residents soon forgot that she once worked at the saloon, and she became a respected member of the community. Kate saved her money in the local bank and became good friends with the people who worked there. She wrote to her parents, shortly after Sean died, and brazenly told them the truth about Bobby and Sean. Then she asked for their love and forgiveness. When the return letter arrived, Kate was afraid to open it. Sobs of relief and happiness came flooding through when she read her parents' reinforcement of their love and concern for her.

"It is hard for me to believe that they have accepted these circumstances so readily." Kate told Mary. "I must assume it's because I'm now a widow instead of an unwed mother."

Mr. Branson, from the bank, began asking her to have dinner with him about two years after Sean died, but Kate refused his requests, not wanting to disrupt the life that was now going well. When Bobby was fourteen, Kate finally accepted his offer and went to a Church social with him.

Will Branson was a rich man, who owned much of the property in town, including the bank. Ten years older than Kate, his first wife died in childbirth a year after their marriage. Their child had only lived for ten days. Heartbroken, Will hadn't looked at another woman until Kate had come into the bank to open an account. He spent ten years drowning his sorrows in hard work, and it had paid off. When he met Kate, he came alive again for the first time since his wife's death. He was crazy about her, and he pursued her persistently until she finally accepted his offer. They were married a year later, and Bobby couldn't have been happier.

Mary and John loved their new home. They followed Ah Kim's will exactly, letting his cousins work the mine for years. Their family grew fast. Margaret was born the 27th of November, 1889, and Francis followed less than two years later, on November 23rd, 1891. Elizabeth arrived two years later on December 2nd, 1893. The four girls' birthdays were within ten days of each other, as Anna's birthday was November 30th. As was the custom, Margaret was named after Mary's mother, since Anna had been named for John's mother. Fan and Zee, as Frances and Elizabeth were fondly called, were named after two of John's favorite sisters, who still lived in Ireland. Mary delivered two stillborn babies, both born too soon, before their last child, John Stephen Troy Jr., was born on May 17th, 1896. He was named after his father and grandfather. Both of the boys were born in the spring, as Jeremiah's birthday was April 1st.

They were a happy and busy family. The children helped with the chores while growing up, and attended the Troy school, which was built on part of their two thousand acres. John hired many of the Chinese people from town to pick the apples and pears at harvest time. They all loved John and Mary because they were so kind to them, at a time when many in Baker City still treated the Chinese people poorly. The Catholic priest said Sunday mass at their home almost every Sunday, and many of their neighbors attended. The women would bring food, and they would have a potluck supper every week after church. Mary spent an hour every day teaching her children their catechism. The Troy children grew into fine, healthy, moral adults, who treated others the way they had been treated, and were admired and respected by all who knew them.

John and Mary stood up for the Chinese people, and for the Nez Perce Indians, whenever the subjects were brought up. Only a small group of the tribe had returned to Lapwai. Joseph and the remaining 150 were sent to a reservation at Nespelem, Washington. In 1900 Joseph returned for a couple of days to the land that he loved at Wallowa Lake. He visited the tombstone where the older Chief Joseph was buried. Many people, including John and Mary, had written to congress asking that Joseph and his tribe be able to return to their land, and an Indian Inspector, James McLoughlin, was sent with the Chief to investigate the possibility, but nothing ever came of it. That was the last time the Chief saw his homeland. John and Mary both wept when they read in "The Blue Mountain Gazette" that Chief Joseph had died of a broken heart. The reservation doctor said that he fell over and died as he sat by his campfire, for no other apparent reason, on September 21st, 1904. On his tombstone, at Nespelem, was written "Thunder rolling in the Mountains" - the Indian's English translation of Joseph, and "He led his people in the Nez Perce War of 1877".

The kidnapping seemed to have no lasting effects on Anna. She was quiet for a few months afterward, but then she seemed to come out of it. Her little brother never mentioned the incident, and appeared to be just fine, so John and Mary assumed he was too young to remember, and they never spoke about it again. The two oldest Troy children grew into happy healthy adults.

After Anna finished school, she decided she wanted to be a teacher. She got the books the teachers used, and studied them every spare moment. After taking the teacher's exam, Anna taught as a substitute teacher at some of the outlying schools in the County for a couple of years. One day in mid-summer of 1906, Anna saw an advertisement in the "Blue Mountain Gazette" for a full time teacher over in Union County at the Hempe School. The location of the school was near the small town of Union on the Hempe ranch. The ad said "fair pay, with room and board." Anna wrote and applied for the job. She got a nice letter back asking her to come for an interview. Mary was concerned about her oldest daughter moving so far away, but John's response was to tease his wife.

"Now Mary, seems to me, I remember a girl much younger then Anna, who set out on her own adventures without even her parents' permission!"

Mary scowled at John for a second, and then she laughed. "Yer right, John, I guess me little girl is old enough to follow her own destiny. Anna, I hope yer crossroad signs are easier to figure out than mine were."

"Oh, Mama, whatever are you talking about? I am just going to see about a school teaching position. I have not been offered the position yet."

Mary and John gave each other a knowing smile as their daughter brushed them off, after they gave her their permission to go. Anna had become quite a beauty. Her long hair had a dark auburn tint to it, and her eyes were dark brown like her father's. She had a delightful dimple in the middle of her chin, and her usually serious face lit up when she smiled. Not quite the adventuress that her mother was, it took a lot for her to take off on her own. John accompanied her to town to rent a rig for the drive to Union. She was very nervous and seemed to want her dad to talk her out of going. John rented the rig for her and gave her some last minute instructions, before sending her on her way. He didn't let her know how worried he was when he slapped the mare's rear flank to get her going, but a concerned frown stayed on his face as he watched his daughter drive the buggy down the road.

Anna had only enough clothes for an overnight stay, as she planned to return the next day. The position didn't start for another three weeks, if she were hired. It seemed to take forever to get to the small town. She worried several times that she had missed her turn, or passed it while thinking of something else, but finally she saw the road sign which pointed right to the small town of Union. 'The Hempe ranch must be close,' she thought. She felt quite relieved until she turned the corner and heard the rattle of a loose wheel just before it broke, which effectively crippled the rig. The horse almost tipped the rig over before Anna got her under control. Her parents had spent a lot of time teaching her how to handle horses, and she was thankful for that now.

Suddenly, she realized what a spot she was in. 'What if no one comes this way before tomorrow?' It was very warm, and it was getting hotter as the temperature rose in the late afternoon. Her long dress was warm and the sweat was rolling off of her forehead. The horse was hot too. She was thankful her mother had made her take a jug of water and some sandwiches with her. It was too hot sitting in the wagon, so she unhitched the mare and took her and the food and water by the big willow tree that was on the corner so they would have some shade. She didn't want to leave the rig there, so she decided to wait a while, before she rode the horse down the road in search of help. Anna said a prayer that help would come soon. It was much cooler under the willow tree than sitting in the Eastern

Oregon sun. She ate a sandwich and an apple, and laid down in the shade. The heat of the day made her drowsy and she soon fell sound asleep.

The sound of a horse's hooves woke her. Opening her eyes, she sat up just as the rider approached. She rubbed her eyes as she stood up and waved at him. The sun was bright, so she shielded her eyes as she walked to the road where her rig sat. He dismounted when he reached her. For a moment, she was absolutely stunned by his good looks. She had never seen any man so good-looking, and she couldn't seem to speak. When the young man flashed a warm friendly smile, his blue eyes twinkled, and Anna suddenly felt weak in the knees.

"I see you have broken a wheel on your buggy, Ma'am. If you please, I would be happy to fix it for you. Let me introduce myself, my name is George Hempe. I live just down the road a ways."

"Oh, you are my good fortune! I was coming to meet Frank Hempe, to see about the teacher position at the Hempe School. My name is Anna Troy"

"Frank is my father. If you would like to ride with me on the back of my horse, I will take you to the ranch. I can come back and fix your buggy and bring it back to you when I'm finished. Then you won't have to sit in this hot sun any longer."

"Thank you, that would be much appreciated." Anna's heart was beating so fast that she could hardly speak. No man had ever made her feel this way before. It scared and thrilled her at the same time.

"Let me tie your mare to a branch of the tree until I get back." He walked over to the tree and made sure the horse was secure before he came back to help her get on his horse.

"Here, you sit in the saddle, and I'll ride behind you, if that's okay with you?"

"That's fine."

He helped her climb into the saddle, even though she was a very experienced rider. When she put her foot in the stirrup, he put his hands around her waist, and boosted her up.

She swung her leg over the horse, smoothed her long skirt so her petticoats wouldn't show, and sat down gently in the saddle. Grabbing the saddle horn, he easily swung himself up behind her. Putting his arms around her, he grabbed the reins and gently nudged the horse with his heels, and it trotted down the road. The hot wind blew her hair into the young man's face, and he could smell the sweet scent of her homemade lilac soap from her freshly washed tresses. His breath smelled sweet as it drifted by her face, and her mother's words echoed in her ears.

'Was he her destiny? Would she read the signs, or would she see the signs?' As she rode tucked within the young man's warm arms, she knew a new chapter of her life was just beginning and she had a sudden yearning to know her destiny.

Mary Sweeney

History versus Fiction

John & Mary Troy

There are many true facts in "The Emancipation of Mary Sweeney" and there is also much fiction. Mary Sweeney and John Troy are my great-grandparents, and they were born in Ireland and did come to America. The names of their families mentioned in the story are true, except for Sean Foley, whose heritage and story is complete fiction. I'm sure there are many Sean Foleys in this world, but I have not found them in my ancestry. Kate Murphy and her family are complete fiction, as well as Ah Kim, Jack Bane and friends.

Mary Sweeney did work for a Jewish family in San Francisco when she lived there, and the woman she worked for gave her a Hurricane Lamp when she left there to go to Eastern Oregon with her new husband, John Troy. Although they were both born in Ireland in the places mentioned in the book, they did not meet until they were in San Francisco at Mary's sister's home. Margaret Sweeney did marry a man with the same last name.

Mary actually came to America with her whole family when she was about eleven years old, and John Troy came with his brother, Mike, many years later. The couple were married in San Francisco at Saint Mary's Cathedral, and then traveled to Eastern Oregon to begin their life together. The record of their marriage was destroyed in the San Francisco Earthquake and Fire. Saint Mary's Cathedral survived the earthquake but was gutted by the inferno the following day. According to a tape recording made by one of John and Mary's children late in her life, John Troy did travel to Oregon with the Cavalry to help put down the Indian rebellion, but the fracas was already over when he arrived. She also said that John wrote to Mary asking her to come to Oregon to marry him, and she wrote back that if he wanted to marry her he would have to come down and get her and "do it proper like." John and Mary were very religious, and the priest came to their home often to say mass with many of their neighbors in attendance. Their granddaughter, Sister Helen Hempe, told me that their children were taught their catechism daily.

John Troy did work on the railroad in Eastern Oregon and ran crews of Chinese putting that railroad through. He was known as a friend to the Chinese. John and Mary homesteaded two thousand acres in Eastern Oregon, which is located in Pleasant Valley, eighteen miles east of Baker City. There is a spring that is next to the century old ranch house and apple orchards on the land. There are two creeks that run through the property. My great-aunts, Fan and Zee, never married, and they ran the ranch for many years, both living until they were in their late eighties and nineties. John Troy died at about 84 and Mary Troy lived to be 96. Although I was ten years old when she died, and I did meet her, she did not give me her diary, as that story is fiction. Through my grandmother, Anna Troy Hempe, and my father, Bert Hempe, I own one thirtieth of that property. My second cousin, Lindia Troy Williams, and her husband, live in the old house and work the ranch at this time. The house and ranch have been deemed a Century Home and Ranch by the state. The railroad does run through the land, as does Interstate 84 and old Highway 30. The Troys left their land in a trust to the family.

There was a massacre of several Chinese on the Snake River and a China Town still exists in Baker City. The Chinese were treated poorly in the area at that time, and much of those historical facts are hard to find as the area is ashamed of that mistreatment. I was told of those facts by my Aunt, Sister Helen Hempe, before she passed away in 2003. The Nez Perce history in the story is true, according to the facts I found in the book listed in my bibliography.

My grandmother, Anna Troy, met her future Husband, George Hempe, when she went to the Hempe ranch in Union, Oregon, to apply for a job at the Hempe School. Her rig broke down on the way and George Hempe came to her rescue. They both passed away within one month of each other in 1958, within two months after their fiftieth wedding anniversary.

About the Author

Dani Larsen

"The Emancipation of Mary Sweeney" is Dani Larsen's first novel. She started writing it in the 90's after delving into her ancestry and spending time with an aunt, who told her wonderful stories about her great-grandmother, Mary Sweeney. Dani was living in California at the time and was attending the College of Alameda. Fictional History became a favorite genre for her, while she was tutoring for her Creative Writing Professor.

Betty Roberts, the first female Oregon Supreme Court Judge, had been one of Dani's high school teachers. When she spoke with her at her 25th class reunion, in her Oregon home town, Betty encouraged her to go back to school. After raising five children, with a ten year old daughter still at home, she worked hard at getting her Associates Degree in English at College of Alameda, where she tutored for Professor Jon Ford in his Creative Writing and English classes. She minored in History, and her 4 point GPA earned her the title of Class Valedictorian. She was thrilled when UC Berkeley called to accept her application and offered her a scholarship in the English Department, from where she earned her Bachelor's Degree in English Literature.

This historical fiction novel about her great-grandmother began while she was attending classes, raising her daughter, and her three year old granddaughter, who had been dropped off on her doorstep during her last year at Berkeley. She continued working part-time throughout, and went back to her sales career after graduation.

Dani wrote a story for a national Magazine that was published in 1997 and won 2nd place in a creative writing contest about the Millennium in "The Olympian" Newspaper in 1999. She worked as a freelance journalist for several years, publishing seventy plus human interest articles for the Sandy Post and the Clackamas County Gazette in Western Oregon. These were all published under the name Dani Bailey.

A High School boyfriend, who had recently lost his long time wife, contacted her in late 2006. A year later, they were married and bought a home in a retirement community, in Arizona. They spent a lot of time traveling and researching for her book. Finally, feeling her novel was perfected with the added research, she decided it was time to publish.

Dani has raised six children (including her granddaughter). She has eleven grandchildren and one great-grandchild. Her husband has two grown daughters and five grandchildren. Writing, traveling, ball room dancing, swimming, and golf are her loves, but she has another book in the works.

BIBLIOGRAPHY

Howard, Addison Helen, "Saga of Chief Joseph", University of Nebraska Press, A Bison Book printed in 1978. Original Copyright, The Caxton Printers, LTD. Caldwell, Idaho 1941 & 1965.